"I THINK WE'RE DONE TALKING BUSINESS."

Her lips pressed together, giving them an alluring pout. He had to find out what they felt like.

Then he was touching her again, this time grazing her lower lip with the pad of his finger, and discovering it was as velvety as he'd expected. What the hell was up with him? He couldn't remember ever having such little control over his impulses. But Amy didn't seem to mind his lack of control. Her eyes closed and her tongue darted out to flick his skin. She moaned like women did when tasting a first bite of chocolate. It was a sound of pure pleasure that sent Kellan's integrity flying out the window.

"Amy?"

"Hmm?"

He dipped his face toward hers until a scant inch separated them. "I think we're done talking business."

Her eyes opened a little and she offered him a dreamy smile. "What do you propose we do, cowboy?"

Boots, his hat—this lady had it bad for cowboys. No problem. He could work with that. Shaking his head with amusement, he let out a gruff chuckle and set her coffee mug on the counter. "Darlin', we can do whatever you want."

BOOK YOUR PLACE ON OUR WEBSITE
AND MAKE THE
READING CONNECTION!

We've created a customized website just for our very special readers, where you can get the inside scoop on everything that's going on with Zebra, Pinnacle and Kensington books.

When you come online, you'll have the exciting opportunity to:

• View covers of upcoming books

• Read sample chapters

• Learn about our future publishing schedule
  (listed by publication month and author)

• Find out when your favorite authors will be visiting
  a city near you

• Search for and order backlist books from our
  online catalog

• Check out author bios and background information

• Send e-mail to your favorite authors

• Meet the Kensington staff online

• Join us in weekly chats with authors, readers and
  other guests

• Get writing guidelines

• AND MUCH MORE!

**Visit our website at
http://www.kensingtonbooks.com**

THE
TROUBLE
WITH
COWBOYS

Catcher Creek

MELISSA
CUTLER

ZEBRA BOOKS
KENSINGTON PUBLISHING CORP.
http://www.kensingtonbooks.com

ZEBRA BOOKS are published by

Kensington Publishing Corp.
119 West 40th Street
New York, NY 10018

All Kensington titles, imprints, and distributed lines are available at special quantity discounts for bulk purchases for sales promotion, premiums, fund-raising, educational, or institutional use.

Special book excerpts or customized printings can also be created to fit specific needs. For details, write or phone the office of the Kensington Special Sales Manager: Attn. Special Sales Department. Kensington Publishing Corp., 119 West 40th Street, New York, NY 10018. Phone: 1-800-221-2647.

Zebra and the Z logo Reg. U.S. Pat. & TM Off.

ISBN-13: 978-1-4201-3004-1
ISBN-10: 1-4201-3004-8

First Printing: October 2012

10 9 8 7 6 5 4 3 2 1

Printed in the United States of America

To my husband and mom.

*Thank you for giving me
the encouragement,
time,
and space
to spread my wings and fly.*

ACKNOWLEDGMENTS

This book owes its success to so many people. Cori, your friendship and writing know-how has made all the difference to my success. My endless thanks also goes to the wonderful people in my romance writer community who read my work and offered me advice: Janet, Georgie, Mary, Judy, and Samantha H. This book also owes its success to the people who supported my dream: my family and my husband's family. Thank you for listening to me ramble about imaginary people and places all these years. Finally, my deepest gratitude goes to the people who dared to take a chance on an unproven writer: my agent, Jessica Alvarez, and my editor, Megan Records. Thank you for changing my life.

Chapter 1

Chefs the world over loved to riff about ingredients as inspiration, about tender leaves of fresh-picked basil or fall's first crop of apples sparking the creation of whole menus in their minds. For many chefs, food spoke to them like muses, guiding forces of creativity. Not Amy. She felt the life in each pot, the potential in every pan. In the way the light reflected off stainless steel and the hiss of a gas stovetop. And no matter which kitchen she cooked in, from Los Angeles to Paris, she carried with her the most invaluable inspiration of all—her knives.

Specifically, her nine-inch MAC SPK-95 Classic chef knife. Standing at the counter in the kitchen she grew up in, she withdrew it from its canvas bag and moved it over her arm, relishing the perfectly balanced weight of the blended steel tool.

"Hello, baby," she crooned.

Airport regulations had required her to stow the MAC in her checked bag yesterday for the flight to New Mexico, a rule she followed grudgingly, and this morning was their first reunion. Being that this was her first time back in Catcher Creek since the *Ultimate Chef Showdown* debacle and with an afternoon lawyer meeting on the horizon, she needed this moment more than ever. She needed to dice.

With practiced ceremony, she sharpened the knife with a pass along a honing rod. The zing of metal sliding over metal sent chill bumps crawling over her skin. A second pass over the rod, and this time, the vibrating zing of steel tightened her nipples. She smiled, a secret, wicked smile, as her stress evaporated. She adjusted her grip on the hilt of the honing rod, set the base of the knife against its shaft, and pulled.

Zing.

Who cared that for her thirty seconds of fame as a reality TV star she was the laughingstock of the nation? She didn't have to face the vicious gossip of Catcher Creek's locals anytime soon if she didn't want to. She was no coward, but today was going to be hard enough without their judgment.

Zing. Damn, she loved the feel of friction sliding up her arm.

Who cared about the pressure she'd piled on herself in returning home—the suffocating stress of her sisters counting on her to save them all from disaster? She wouldn't crack. Unlike her mother, Amy didn't have that luxury. Which was why, for a few quiet minutes, she needed to lose herself in knife work, in the mindless task of dicing perfect cubes of celery.

Zing.

She flicked the tip of the blade with her finger and licked her lips. Lethally sharp, just the way she liked it. The MAC was ready for action. As was Amy. She placed the knife on the cutting board and moved to the refrigerator. She had no idea the sort of produce her sisters kept on hand, but certainly they'd stocked celery, knowing how important dicing vegetables was to regulating her stress levels.

She opened the refrigerator door and gasped. Except for a bottle of ketchup and a gallon of milk, every shelf and both crispers were empty. She slammed the door and raced to the pantry. Empty. Not even a potato. She glanced sideways at her MAC, which sat impotently, waiting for her. And just like that, her usual anxiety returned with a vengeance.

The Quick Stand was roasting inside. Whoever set the thermostat either had a poor understanding of electronic devices or the misfortune of being born cold-blooded. Sure New Mexico was experiencing a cold snap, but nothing justified heat this sweltering. The refrigerator display cases whirred nonstop, and Amy debated the merits of staging a citizen's arrest of the leathery-skinned farmer at the coffeepot who'd forgotten to apply deodorant. Then again, that would mean stepping out of the line she'd already invested ten minutes of her time waiting in.

She glanced around. Busy place for a Saturday, probably because it was the only store open before ten o'clock for twenty miles—a fact she'd learned the hard way. With each padlocked door and darkened store she'd driven by, the more viciously the day's stress seized up in her belly.

When her turn arrived, she took a deep breath and stepped to the checkout counter. A niggle started in her throat, like a first tickling of hysteria. She swallowed it back. *Please, please, please have celery.*

Charlene Delgado, who'd been the cashier for as long as Amy remembered, smiled in surprise. "Well, if it isn't the famous actress home from Hollywood. I watched you on that television show. A shame, what happened with that cowboy contestant. He played you bad, for sure, but your tantrum"—she whistled—"that was one for the ages."

Amy ground her molars together and painted a pleasant

smile on her lips. She'd wondered which Catcher Creek resident would be the first to bring up *Ultimate Chef Showdown* and Cowboy Cook Brock McKenna. In town less than twenty-four hours, she hadn't been kept waiting long. And how fitting that Charlene, the leader of the local gossip brigade, delivered the initial blow.

Charlene was spot-on about Amy being shamed, even if she got the details wrong, but she wasn't about to point out that the show filmed in New York City, nor that Amy was a chef, not an actress. If she'd been anything of a decent actress, that tantrum would've never happened. She pushed her smile as wide as her lips would stretch. "Thank you for watching the show. The support of my Catcher Creek neighbors has been such a blessing." If one counted deafening silence as support.

"What can I do for you, dear?" Charlene asked.

"Does the Quick Stand carry celery? I couldn't find any and I really, seriously, need some this morning." Like a turning of the screw, thinking about her futile celery search across the county twisted her belly into a tighter, more painful knot.

"Celery? You cooking some sort of gourmet breakfast, like that time on *Chef Showdown* where you had to make a dessert using vegetables? Wait . . . you're pregnant, aren't you? You have a craving for celery."

"No . . . *NO!* Nothing like that. It's just—"

A woman in line conspicuously cleared her throat. Amy froze. And so it began, the whispers and stares she'd faced all her life in this small community, the disdain she faced for being a Sorentino. Her cheeks heated, but she didn't dare turn. Let them all look. Let them whisper to each other behind their hands, *Like mother, like daughter*. Amy had gone up against worse bullies and survived. Not always with dignity, she amended, thinking about *Ultimate Chef Showdown,* but she'd survived nonetheless.

"It's just that I'm a chef, and I need celery," she finished, forcing her smile wider.

"I wish I could help you, but we don't carry celery."

"How about onions? I could make do with onions."

Charlene shook her head. "We don't carry any produce here."

"Nothing?"

Charlene trudged to a refrigerated bin and removed a Styrofoam snowman from the top. She fished something out, waddled to the checkout stand, and slapped a three-ounce bag of baby carrots on the counter.

Cringing, Amy poked at the bag. "Fine. Give me everything you've got."

The woman in line cleared her throat again, followed by a muttered "Those Sorentinos. . . ."

This time, Amy whipped around. "Is there something you want to say about my family?"

The woman's eyes widened in shock and, Amy liked to think, a healthy dose of fear. *Yeah, that's right, lady. Don't mess with a Sorentino. I might go all crazy on your ass.*

A man stepped forward, his expression placating. "Now, ladies. Let's stay calm. No need to get riled up on this fine morning."

Amy cursed under her breath. A cowboy. Just perfect. She was already primed with need from her knife-sharpening session, pent up with nervous tension that needed releasing. She'd tried to take the safe route to stress relief by sticking to celery, but it looked like the universe had different ideas, throwing a cowboy into her path.

Dark brown hair curled beneath his dust-coated cowboy hat and his long legs ended in scuffed, aged boots that settled a familiar, heavy ache between her thighs. True, she was the only woman she knew who got hot and bothered every time "Desperado " played on the radio, but there was something about boots, snug jeans, and a worn-in Stetson that flipped a switch in her. And this particular cowboy— *oh, Doctor*. She pictured him tossing bales of hay into a truck bed, his burly biceps bunching, his broad, strong back flexing, his brow sweating from the effort.

Snapping her gaze away, she mentally shook herself. The last thing she needed in her life was another cowboy, especially after Brock McKenna, even if this one clocked in at an eleven on the hotness scale.

She looked at him again with fresh eyes, this time registering his patronizing grin. Amy hated to be patronized. Brock had done that on *Ultimate Chef Showdown* and it was as grating to her nerves now as it had been then. The longer she thought about it, the more she wanted to smack the arrogant smirk off this new cowboy's sexy, stubbled jaw with her bag of baby carrots, then stuff it down his throat. How dare he barge in on her stressful day with his tight jeans and T-shirt that showed off the muscles beneath like he was God's gift to women? Snatching the bag from the counter, she gave a little practice swing with her three ounces of whoop-ass.

No. She wouldn't cause a scene. Her tattered reputation couldn't handle another public freak-out. Her gaze drifted over the crowd of people in the market. From those in line to the people doctoring up their morning coffee, all eyes in the place were trained on her.

Too late. She'd already caused a scene. The heat of her cheeks spread over her neck. She'd been seconds away from bludgeoning a man with a bag of carrots. Unbelievable. She should never be allowed out of the kitchen again. She counted down from ten before speaking in her calmest, most rational voice. "I'm not riled up. I'm buying carrots." She dangled the bag in front of her face. "See?"

Lifting his hat from his head, the cowboy's grin broadened. He ran a hand over his mop of hair as he moseyed her way, his boots clomping along the linoleum. She couldn't tear her gaze from him. The way he moved got her visualizing him swinging onto a horse, taking the reins, issuing a command. The prick of heat on her skin grew unbearable. She had to get away from him before she embarrassed herself even further.

"Perhaps we could step out of line to talk in private and let these good folks get on with their morning." His voice was a low, lazy drawl that turned her legs rubbery. She allowed him to take her arm and lead her to a rack of magazines in the corner, mostly because she wanted to feel those large, work-worn hands on her skin.

Get a grip, Amy. Remember rule number one.

She twisted her arm away. "What do you want?"

"Just trying to keep the peace, Miss Sorentino—Amy. You looked like you were ready to go postal on Linda Klauss. I had to do something."

She shook her hair back and lifted her chin. "Let's stick with Miss Sorentino. And who are you?"

"Kellan Reed, your neighbor."

Damn. Her morning just went from bad to worse. "*You're* Kellan Reed, owner of Slipping Rock Ranch?"

"At your service."

With the way he was looking her over, she bet he was. "I'm opening a restaurant here. You're on my list to call."

"Is that so?"

"I have a business proposition for you." She felt dirty saying the words, like from them he might divine that she was imagining how he'd look astride a horse. Shirtless.

Lordy. Maybe she could hand this particular negotiation off to Jenna.

"I look forward to discussing it with you, so long as you leave your bags of carrots in the car." Amy balked and he held up his hands. "I've got some time now. Why don't you follow me to my ranch and we'll talk about what it is you want from me? Business-wise, of course."

She chewed her bottom lip, considering. After Brock McKenna in all his cowboy glory played her for a fool on *Ultimate Chef Showdown,* she'd added a new number one rule to live her life by—resist temptation by steering clear of cowboys. Unfortunately, she was opening a restaurant that would feature locally grown food, and her success depended on securing contracts with the best ranches and farms in the region. Kellan Reed's cattle ranch sat at the top of that exclusive list because of its reputation for producing the most coveted, high-quality beef in the southwest. Not to mention the most expensive.

So if Kellan Reed offered her an invitation to talk business at his ranch, she had no choice but to take him up on it. The way she saw it, she had the drive from the Quick Stand to his property to strategize a way to convince him to sell Slipping Rock beef to her at an under-market rate. That was going to be a problem because, even now, she was having trouble stringing together a single intelligible sentence with him looking at her with those deep brown eyes—and they weren't even alone yet.

She would have to be strong. No going inside his house, no needless small talk. They could negotiate outside, where she had quick access to a getaway vehicle should she sense her self-control crumbling. After securing the beef contract, she'd thank him and be on her way like a reasonable, responsible adult. No problem.

She afforded him a terse nod. "It's a deal."

"Excellent." His dark eyes twinkled with lusty purpose—or maybe that was only a product of Amy's overactive imagination. "Char, would you put these on my tab?" He waved a candy bar and a bag of pretzels in her direction.

"Breakfast of champions?" Amy asked.

"More like lunch, I've been up so long. But if you want to call me a champion, I'm not going to argue." He winked.

Amy sucked in an unsteady breath, then tried to hide it with an indignant huff as she squeezed her thighs together. "Let's get on with it," she said, her voice coming out far huskier than she intended.

"By all means, after you, ma'am."

"I know where Slipping Rock Ranch is. I'll meet you there."

"Fine with me." He replaced the hat on his head and tipped the brim low over his eyes. "And, honey, I know you're having a tough morning, but watch your speed on my property. Wouldn't want you to spook the horses." With another wave at Charlene, he left.

"Cowboys, ugh," she muttered. Still, her eyes tracked the swish of his tight jeans out the door and into the driver's seat of a run-down truck across the lot. Her rule book might forbid her from getting too close to cowboys, but it didn't say a thing about looking.

Kellan hadn't meant to boldly flirt with a member of the notorious Sorentino family at the Quick Stand. All he'd wanted was for the pretty girl at the counter to move along and stop disturbing the peace. He had a low tolerance for people airing their messy lives in public and the Sorentino family had the worst reputation in town for staging scenes wherever they went. He'd spoken up in an effort to run damage control for Charlene before a catfight erupted in the middle of her morning rush, but the minute he got up close and personal with Amy Sorentino, he changed his tune.

He'd heard plenty of talk about Amy. Nothing flattering.

Nothing that hinted at her beauty or vivacity. Nothing that captured Kellan's interest the way the actual woman had with a toss of her hair and a few terse words. Not to mention that heart-shaped ass and the fire in her eyes as she gave him the once-over. She rubbed him the right way straight out of the gate.

Not that he was looking for a relationship with a woman with a screwed-up family and a penchant for public commotions. Once upon a time, he'd belonged to a dysfunctional family. He knew better than to let history repeat itself.

When she pulled up in front of his house, driving too fast like he knew she would be, he was waiting for her on the porch. From that angle, he was treated to a perfect view of her legs stretching from the car to the ground one at a time. She froze at the base of the porch stairs and fiddled with her car keys.

He hooked his thumb toward his front door. "Come on in. We can discuss your business proposition over coffee."

She took a step back and mumbled something that sounded like "rule number one."

"I didn't catch that. What did you say?"

"I said it's a beautiful day. Let's talk outside."

He kicked away from the wall, intrigued. Maybe he read her body language wrong at the Quick Stand. "Okay. How about you have a seat on the porch? I'll bring out the coffee."

Her mouth screwed up as she eyed the porch suspiciously. "Fine. I can handle that. No problem."

She perched on the edge of a wicker chair, wringing her hands. Maybe she'd heard talk about his no-nonsense business ethic and was nervous about entering into a negotiation with him. "One more thing," he found himself saying without giving it much forethought, "I grow celery.

I give most of it away, but there's three bunches in my fridge right now. You're welcome to it if you want."

"That would be . . . Thank you." Her hands stopped fidgeting, which he took as a positive sign.

"Okay. Good. I'll get the celery and coffee and be right back."

Bracing his side against the door frame, he tugged a work boot off and there was no mistaking her long hiss of an exhale. Interesting. When he started in on the second boot, he watched from the corner of his eye as her fingers smoothed over her skirt and locked on her bare knee.

Note to self—the lady's got a thing for boots.

"Rule number one," she said in a bare whisper.

"What? Something about a rule?"

"Huh? Me? I didn't say anything." She jumped to her feet, color staining her cheeks.

Kellan stifled the urge to brush his thumb over her pink-laced freckles. In the spirit of discovering what else turned the skittish Miss Sorentino on, he lifted his work hat from its peg by the door and dropped it on his head.

Amy's eyes turned dark. She bit her bottom lip.

That look alone was worth feeling like an idiot by putting on a hat to go indoors. Working hard to keep a triumphant smile off his face, Kellan swaggered into the kitchen, leaving the door open behind him. He busied himself at the coffeemaker until a long shadow materialized on the tile floor. Amy had moved into the doorway.

He glanced at her. "You want onions too?"

"Celery should be enough to get me by."

Her throaty voice was turning him all kinds of hard. He felt her eyes on his ass and gave her a real good look as he bent into the open refrigerator, pretending to search for the celery that lay in plain sight on the bottom shelf.

"You want all three bunches?"

"Yes, I'll take it all."

The room went darker. The door clicked shut. *Well, well, well* . . . He rose, celery in hand. Maybe his instincts were right after all.

"Oh, that's a relief." Amy's voice was shrill, excited.

Kellan turned to see her peering into his living room. "A relief?"

"You're married. I mean . . . that's wonderful. I didn't know because you're not wearing a ring."

He set the celery on the counter. "Why would you think I'm married?"

"The Christmas tree, the decorations. Cinnamon-scented candles. Your wife did an amazing job. The house looks great."

He sauntered toward her, tugging on the brim of his hat as he went, and enjoyed the stain of color spreading over her delectable skin. "Amy, I'm not married."

"Girlfriend?" she squeaked.

He shook his head and leveled his most enticing gaze at her.

"You live with your mom?"

She sounded so hopeful, Kellan almost laughed. She was so darn nervous, yet obviously aroused, that all he could think about was how badly he wanted to kiss her. Totally inappropriate, of course. She was there to discuss Slipping Rock Ranch business, probably hoping to negotiate a price discount for her restaurant, and he had enough integrity not to mix business with pleasure. No way did he want her to mistakenly feel like doing business with him obligated her to get physical. But getting physical with Amy Sorentino was the only thing his mind and body could focus on at the moment, and instinct told him she was equally conflicted.

Lucky for him, once they wrapped up their negotiations for a beef contract, there was nothing in the law books preventing two consenting adults from enjoying each other naked.

But even with all that integrity and self-control, he couldn't stem the urge to press a fingertip to the crease between her eyebrows. She looked up at it and her eyes crossed, which only made him want to kiss her worse. He dropped his finger and averted his gaze. "I love Christmas, that's all. I love the lights and the songs. I love the way it smells, and the way it feels to sit in front of a cozy fire with a big old tree taking up space in the corner. No one lives here but me and Max."

"Max?"

He met her whiskey brown eyes again, hoping his didn't reflect his fraying willpower. "My dog."

The flush of her skin spread to her neck, and he wondered if she tasted as delectable as she looked. Her lips, ripe and ready, parted enough for him to see a hint of her rosy tongue. She was everything he loved about women, all soft curves and sweet smells. He slid his hand up her forearm to cup her elbow and she leaned into his grip. Her body was so damned responsive it was killing him.

"We need to talk business," she whispered.

He swabbed a hand over his mouth and stumbled back. *Whoa, boy.* "Yes, we do. I'll get the coffee."

Instead of taking a seat at the kitchen table like he expected, she trailed him to the coffeepot. "My sisters and I are transforming our farm into a vacation spot for families, including a restaurant."

"Like a dude ranch?"

"Sort of. We're not going to call it that."

He handed her a mug of coffee. "What are you going to call it?"

"Sorentino Farm will now be Heritage Farm." She touched the mug to her lips and blew across the surface of the coffee as though to cool it.

He busied himself with cream and sugar in an effort to get his mind out of the gutter. "And your restaurant?"

"The Local Dish. Because I'm going to highlight locally grown ingredients."

The Local Dish. Cool name. "Which is why you'd like Slipping Rock to supply the beef."

Her lips pressed together, giving them an alluring pout. He had to find out what they felt like. "You've got the best reputation in New Mexico, but I can't afford the price on your Web site. I . . ."

Then he was touching her again, this time grazing her lower lip with the pad of his finger, and discovering it was as velvety as he'd expected. What the hell was up with him? He couldn't remember ever having such little control over his impulses. But Amy didn't seem to mind his lack of control. Her eyes closed and her tongue darted out to flick his skin. She moaned like women did when tasting a first bite of chocolate. It was a sound of pure pleasure that sent Kellan's integrity flying out the window.

"Amy?"

"Hmm?"

He dipped his face toward hers until a scant inch separated them. "I think we're done talking business."

Her eyes opened a little and she offered him a dreamy smile. "What do you propose we do, cowboy?"

Boots, his hat—this lady had it bad for cowboys. No problem. He could work with that. Shaking his head with amusement, he let out a gruff chuckle and set her coffee mug on the counter. "Darlin', we can do whatever you want."

Amy raised a brow, then slung an arm around Kellan's neck and locked her open mouth to his. Stepping back and pulling him with her, she slammed into the wall. His hat toppled off. With any luck, he'd get the hint that she didn't want it slow and easy. Nothing short of high-octane fireworks was going to diffuse her anxiety today.

She wasn't sure what made her take this plunge. Maybe it was the charming incongruity of a room that smelled of testosterone, leather, and a recent fire in the hearth, but looked like Martha Stewart had stopped by to decorate for the holidays that tipped Amy over the edge of reason. Or maybe it was simpler math—one eyeful of Kellan's perfect, hard ass in those cowboy jeans plus one horny, stressed-out, sex-deprived woman equaled instantaneous combustion. All she knew was that she suddenly didn't give a damn about rules or celery—what she really needed this morning was a down and dirty cowboy quickie.

It had been months since she'd last felt a man's hands and mouth on her skin. Ten months, to be exact. That manipulative bastard Brock McKenna had been her last—and he hadn't even been all that good in the sack. With him, she'd had to do a lot of closed-eyed visualizations of fantasy cowboys riding bucking broncs or wielding lassos to bring herself off. Somehow, she didn't think she'd have that problem with the cowboy presently dragging his tongue along her neck.

He hitched her knee around his hip and pressed into her. She ground her body into his and relished the vibrations of his groan against her tongue. *That's right, cowboy. It's been a while for me, but I haven't forgotten how it's done. . . .*

Next thing she knew, he'd scooped her into his arms and was hustling up the stairs, into a bedroom. He set her on the bed and unzipped her boot. She shimmied to the edge of the mattress and lent him a hand, flinging her shirt and bra onto the floor. The faster they got to the good stuff, the better. After all, she had places to go and things to do . . . and she didn't want to give herself any time to consider why this tryst may not be the best plan she'd ever come up with.

It took Kellan some effort to figure out how to remove Amy's boots. They weren't practical work boots, like he was used to, but a pair of those strap-happy high-heel types women seemed to dig. He might've considered leaving them on, as hot as they made her legs look, but the heels looked like dangerous weapons he didn't want anywhere near his naked self. When he finally looked up after tugging the second boot off, his gaze lingered on her perfect, full breasts before roving to the black silky fabric shimmering between her thighs. He swallowed hard and smoothed his hands up her thighs, bunching her skirt until it collected at her waist.

"Amy, your panties are coming off now."

She set her feet on his chest. "Cowboy, you better get busy before I remember why I shouldn't be doing this."

All right then.

He tossed the panties aside and touched the smooth, wet folds that told him she was as turned on as he was. He eased a couple fingers inside her and swirled his thumb over her clit.

Her reaction was a thing of beauty. She threw herself into the experience with the same reckless fire she seemed to do everything else with. Whimpering, she fisted the quilt, pulling it taut as he settled into a slow, steady rhythm.

"Better than celery?" he teased.

She grinned and pulled away from his touch, rising to her knees on the bed. "It's time for your clothes to come off, cowboy." She reached for his jeans and, with impressive one-handed skill, undid the buttons.

She shoved his jeans and boxers to his knees and wrapped her hand around his cock, then her lips. Oh, man, did it feel dynamite. He rolled his eyes to the ceiling, tangled his hands in her hair, and concentrated on the friction of her wet, hot mouth against his shaft. He stopped her while he still had enough reserves to fuck her brains out the way he wanted to. Gently but firmly, he pushed her onto the bed and stripped her skirt off, then grabbed a condom from his nightstand drawer, rolling it on while she watched.

She slid her toes up his leg. "I want to ride you."

He'd planned on being the one doing the riding, but he was a smart enough man to give a lady what she wanted. He stretched onto the bed and pulled her up to straddle him.

He drove her onto his cock with a slow upward thrust. Her head dropped forward and she braced her hands on his chest, her hair falling in sheets around her face. Her skin, damp with perspiration and flush with desire, glowed in the morning light streaming through the window. She was so pretty, he forgot about everything except giving her pleasure. Then she rotated her hips in a slow grind and took him straight to the edge of control. He clamped his teeth together and fought against his body's demands.

"Touch me." Her voice was low, thick.

His hand trembling with his wavering control, he burrowed a finger against her clit. She gasped her approval as she moved, her hips rocking them both straight to the finish line.

Kellan held himself inside her until the last pulses of his orgasm faded away, then, panting and sated, he eased her to his side and tucked her into the crook of his arm. Just as he was congratulating himself on being the man to help Amy Sorentino relax, she shot from the bed like someone had stuck her with a cattle prod.

"Rule number one," she shrieked.

They were back to that, were they? Kellan propped a pillow behind his head and regarded her with lazy interest as she hopped around, trying to stick her feet though her panties. "What's rule number one?"

She shot him a withering glare, like he was guilty of some heinous crime against humanity. "Rule number one is to stay away from cowboys."

Her admission was so unexpected, he couldn't help but chuckle. "That rule doesn't seem to be working for you. What's rule number two?"

She pulled her skirt on. "Go to church every Sunday."

"Seems like your priorities are messed up if the cowboy rule trumps church."

The lacy black bra went on next and he bid a silent farewell to her fantastic rack.

"True, but there's a much greater likelihood of me making it to church, with or without the rule book, than me staying away from—" She lifted her sweater over her head and sniffed her arm. "Ugh. I smell like sex. I can't face my sisters like this, not to mention the lawyer. I have to take a shower." She wrestled her clothes back off and stomped in the direction of his bathroom.

No doubt about it, Amy Sorentino was adorable. And sexy as hell. He swung his legs over the side of the bed, slipped his jeans over his hips, and headed for the hall linen closet. Grabbing the towel on top, he let himself in through the closed bathroom door.

"Brought you a towel, but something tells me you're not going to let me wash your hair."

"Back off, cowboy. I had a moment of weakness, but I have myself under control again."

"I hate to burst your bubble, but I consider myself more of a rancher than a cowboy."

"I can't hear you," she hollered, ducking her head under the water. He chuckled again and left her to scrub the sex off her body in peace. He, for one, wanted the smell of her to linger on his skin all day long.

Ten minutes later, when she sprinted into the kitchen, he had her celery ready to go in a plastic grocery bag. She peeked inside, sighing. "I'll take those onions, too, if you can be fast about it."

He must have been feeling merciful, or at least extremely satisfied, because he didn't even consider teasing her. "You got it." He walked to the pantry and rummaged through a bin. "What's rule number three?"

"Apologize when I know I should."

Good rule. One he wished he were better at. He dropped three fat, golden onions in her bag. "Does that happen a lot?"

She hustled out the door, speed-walking so fast she was almost running. "More than I like, that's for sure."

Kellan's time with Amy was coming to a close. He jogged ahead and planted himself in front of her car door. "May I at least get your phone number?"

She went still. "What?"

"We still have business to discuss."

She smacked her forehead and seemed to wilt a little. "Oh my gosh. I forgot about the beef contract. This is why I need rules." She wrung the handles of the bag. "Just so you know, I didn't sleep with you so you'd give me some sort of deal on beef. I'm not . . . I mean—" Regret dropped like a rock in his gut. Why couldn't he have kept his hands to himself until they'd solidified a contract to avoid all this awkward misunderstanding? Apparently, Amy wasn't the only one who needed rules.

"I know, Amy. It's okay. I needed a little stress relief too. No big deal. We'll work out a business arrangement just fine."

Her spine steeled again, her shoulders squared. "Good. I'll have my sister Jenna call you about the contract."

He knew Jenna Sorentino as a neighbor, and could easily work out a supplier contract with her, but no way was he about to let Amy weasel her way out of meeting with him again that easily. "I don't want to talk to Jenna. How about you come over one night this week and I'll fix you dinner."

Whoa, boy. That came out sounding more like a date than he intended. Last thing he wanted was to give her the wrong impression. A little harmless sex was one thing, but he wasn't in the market for a relationship and probably needed to make sure Amy was clear on that point as well. He was confident they could come to a mutually beneficial understanding. Such as neighbors did who occasionally got together for a little stress relief when the mood struck.

"No way in hell is that going to happen." She shouldered him out of the way. He could've held his ground, but wasn't in the practice of overpowering women. "What part of rule number one do you find so hard to grasp?"

"For the record, I wholeheartedly object to rule number one."

If she heard him, she gave no indication as she jumped behind the wheel, slammed the door, and barreled forward. At the edge of the driveway, the car skidded to a halt. After a considerable pause, she reversed it, her window opening. Rolling her eyes, she shook her head. "I apologize. That was rude."

It was hard work, not smiling. Actually, looking at the earnest expression on Amy's face, Kellan wanted to rip her door open and kiss her senseless. He didn't think that would go over too well. Instead, he leaned in through the open window and managed to keep a straight face. "Apology accepted."

"I'll have Jenna call you about the contract."

"You do that." He'd just have to politely explain to Jenna that he'd only deal directly with Amy. Over dinner.

She rolled her tongue along the inside of her lip. "Thank you for the celery . . . and the other thing."

"You're welcome." And because he knew it would rile her, he planted a big kiss on her pursed lips, praying she didn't raise the window and choke him. Lucky for him, she merely squeaked in protest. "Bye, Amy. I'll see you soon."

"Cowboys, ugh," she muttered as her window rolled up. Then she shot out of his driveway like his house was on fire.

Chapter 2

Amy pushed through the squeaky front door of her house and stopped in the foyer, inhaling deeply. The space smelled of Christmas and daily living, of the bacon and Gruyère omelets she'd prepared for her sisters and nephew that morning, of evergreen and the dust of heirloom holiday decorations that had long since passed their prime. It smelled of home.

Jenna, five years Amy's junior, had done an amazing job sprucing the house up for their new business. The front room had been rearranged to accommodate a welcome desk for the inn's guests, and a large, ornately decorated Christmas tree commanded attention near the front window. A smattering of family photos remained on the bookshelves, but now, instead of rows of photo albums and their father's favorite books, the shelves housed tomes of New Mexico photographs and guidebooks of the state's points of interest.

Although the sisters would soon be sharing the house with strangers, the rooms guarded the secrets of its history. The couch she, Jenna, and their older sister Rachel hid behind during hide-and-seek. The spindly-legged side table Amy once knocked over in her hurry to answer the door when her date, Bucky Schultz, a junior rodeo champ, pulled into their driveway in his father's truck. The gash in the hardwood floor from the time Rachel, after receiving a pony as a tenth birthday gift, dragged her new saddle across the floor because she couldn't stand the idea of parting with it overnight.

The floor creaked under her boots as she deposited her purse in the coat closet, a hollow sound that reminded Amy she was alone. Being that it was eleven o'clock in the morning, Rachel would be tending to the endless demands of the farm's maintenance. Jenna, probably the same, only with her son, Tommy, in tow.

This was a new experience for Amy, being alone in her family's house during the day. Until she graduated high school, she worked seven days a week with Rachel, their father, and various hired hands to keep their alfalfa business afloat. Before Tommy, Jenna had never lifted a finger to help, and their mom was usually preoccupied, dosing herself with prescription downers or hiding from the world in her darkened bedroom.

Increasingly often, Dad had been preoccupied too, off on some lark of a moneymaking scheme, and the responsibilities of the farm had shifted onto Rachel's and Amy's shoulders. Then Amy, bursting with the need to escape the crushing pressure of the farm, fled New Mexico for a culinary academy in New York, leaving a twenty-one-year-old Rachel alone with the burden.

With the clack of her boots echoing in the stillness, she strode through the den-slash-dining room. Jenna had removed the dividing wall and refurbished the space as the restaurant's dining hall, with long communal tables locally crafted from weathered barn doors. She skirted the tables and pushed through the door into the kitchen. Her domain. Always had been, even in the years before Tommy's birth, when Amy rarely made it home for a visit.

Resenting the inevitable clashes with Rachel and unwilling to witness her mother's mood swings or her father's money spending, Amy couldn't even bring herself to show up for Christmas, often volunteering to spearhead holiday brunch at the restaurants she worked at so people with children and close-knit families could be together.

Tommy, Jenna's son, had changed Amy's priorities. The little blond-haired baby breathed new energy into everyone's lives. On holidays and Tommy's birthdays, Amy learned to endure Rachel and her parents for the sake of harmony, though a lot of teeth gnashing and silent counting had been involved. And now, with both her parents gone in their own ways, she felt blessed to have had that time with them. Still, regret clawed at her. So much time lost, so many things she'd do differently. But she was home for keeps now, stronger this time, less selfish. Ready to fight for her family's survival.

She unloaded the celery and onions from the bag, then picked up her knife. She pet the blunt end of the blade with her fingertips, then angled it so the light from the window above the sink glinted off it, creating a rainbow of color and light against the far wall. "Ready?" she whispered, smiling, as she wrapped her fingers around the hilt. Light shimmered on it in response.

Squaring her hips to the counter, she separated the ribs of celery, took a cleansing breath, and began to dice.

The rhythmic *snap-snap-snap* of the blade on the board soothed her as much as the steady, repetitive motion. Her shoulders relaxed, the world with all its stresses fell away, and soon the cutting board was covered with mounds of tiny, perfect, green cubes. Beautiful.

Halfway through the second bunch of celery, though, something terrible happened. Amy's mind locked implacably on Kellan Reed. The celery got her thinking of how grateful she was to have acquired it, which led to the memory of Kellan at the Quick Stand, with his patronizing smile and lazy drawl. From there, it was a mere skip of the mind to the feel of his lips on hers, the dark look of need in his eyes when they reached his bedroom, and the hard plane of his chest against her palms when she rode him.

A small, stinging pain sizzled up her arm. She sucked a breath in through her teeth and watched a drop of blood trickle over her knuckle from the side of her finger. She'd nicked herself.

"Cowboys," she cursed, turning to the sink to run the cut under water.

Once again, she'd allowed herself to be distracted by sexy boots and the next thing she knew, she'd been hurt. One could postulate that, after being humiliated by a two-faced cowboy on *Ultimate Chef Showdown,* Amy would've learned her lesson. Guess she wasn't that smart. In fact, the way she'd courted trouble by catapulting herself into Kellan's bed, she was getting stupider by the day. With her family home on the line, the last thing Amy needed in her life was more cowboy trouble. Especially with a potential business associate.

"What's wrong?" Rachel stood in the threshold, her cheeks red and filmed with perspiration, her shirt crumpled and her brown hair flat, probably due to one of the utilitarian sun hats she wore while working.

With her finger under the stream of water, Amy shrugged. "No biggie. I cut myself."

"You okay?"

"Yes. Happens all the time."

"Then why do you look so upset?"

Because I let another damned cowboy get under my skin. "I'm mad at myself for getting distracted is all."

The explanation must have worked for Rachel. Or maybe, after their heated conversation the previous night, she was walking on eggshells the same way Amy was. She nodded and pushed off the door frame. "First-aid kit's in the right drawer of the bathroom. You need my help patching that finger?"

"No. Thanks anyway."

"Then I'm going to shower so we can get to the lawyer meeting on time."

"Where's Jenna?" Amy called after her.

"Dropping Tommy off at the sitter." Rachel's voice sounded from the stairwell. "She'll meet us out front at noon."

With the weekend chore list at the farm as long as the weekday one, Amy hadn't had much face time with her sisters—not counting their failed attempt at a calm discussion about their mom's care the night before—so she welcomed the three-hour drive to Albuquerque as a chance to make peace and reconnect with them before they needed to show a united front to the lawyer.

Her gaze drifted to the stack of paperwork on the table, proof of their mother's complete and irreversible mental collapse. A whole pile of evidence, from letters by her doctors to bank statements, proving Bethany Sorentino had permanently lost the capacity to care for herself. Though this latest legal development had been coming on for nearly a year, Amy still felt the heavy drag of sadness every time she thought about what happened to her mom.

She wrapped her injured finger in a paper towel and grabbed a bowl for the diced celery. Out back, the four sows squealed at her approach and jutted their heads through the slats of their pen, clamoring for the unexpected treat.

She tipped the celery into the trough. "Here you go, ladies. *Bon appétit.*" They jostled for position, grunting enthusiastically as they chowed down. "And you might as well know up front, you're going to be dining on a lot of celery from now on. You can bank on it."

* * *

At noon, Amy climbed into the backseat of Jenna's car. Rachel, as bossy as she'd always been, took the wheel. Jenna rode shotgun.

Amy patted the empty car seat next to her. "Who's watching Tommy?"

"Charlene Delgado," Jenna answered. "She works the early shift at the Quick Stand on Saturday, so she was available. She badgered me about hiring her grand-daughter instead because she's in college and needs the money, but Tommy's at a tricky age and I trust Charlene to handle him. She's the best babysitter in Catcher Creek."

Rachel glanced at Amy through the rearview mirror. "You remember Charlene? She used to babysit us too."

"We were reacquainted this morning."

Jenna snickered. "Charlene told me about your great celery search."

"I'm sure she did. If I'd known it would be so hard to find, I would have stockpiled it in Albuquerque after I flew in."

Jenna twisted, raising a brow in Amy's direction. "Good thing Kellan Reed was there to rescue you."

Amy sank deeper into the seat. "Yup."

"Charlene said he offered to give you his . . . business."

Leave it to Jenna to add up the facts faster than a Mensa applicant. "Yup."

Jenna straightened forward, but Amy saw the bunch of her cheek that meant she was grinning like a madwoman. "I bet he gave it to you and then some."

A remark like that could only be answered with physical violence. Amy leaned forward and yanked Jenna's pony-tail. She yelped and held her hair off to the side, out of Amy's reach, giggling under her breath.

Thank goodness Rachel didn't have an ear for nuance.

Jenna's teasing implication sailed right over her head. Desperate for a subject change, Amy smoothed the binder of legal documents and medical evaluations on her lap. "What we're doing today, it's so surreal. I feel like we're conceding defeat by admitting that Mom'll never get better."

"I don't like it any more than you do, but if we want our farm to be around to see Tommy grow up, this is our only choice," Rachel said.

"You're right, I know. With Amarex Petroleum breathing down our necks, we've put this off for too long already. How much is this lawyer costing us?"

"One-fifty an hour," Jenna said.

"We're paying a lawyer $150.00 an hour to help us legally take on a potential lawsuit and thousands of dollars of Mom's debt?"

"One-fifty is a bargain. You should've heard some of the quotes I got. And besides, it's Dad's debt we're taking over. Mom had nothing to do with it."

"That's the truth," Amy muttered.

The car went quiet. After a while, Amy cracked her window and stuck her fingers into the crisp air, humming in appreciation of the view of the high desert flatlands carpeted with deep green shrubs and cacti, and the red-sand tops of the distant mesas spotted with a thin dusting of snow. And she adored gawking at the tourist shops, motels, and eateries looking to capitalize on the nostalgic appeal of Old Route 66. The neon signs and kitschy themes filled her with a bubbling sense of optimism and sparked her imagination with stories of the people behind each quaint business.

"Amy?" It was Rachel, sounding serious, which could only mean one thing. Damn it all, she had some nerve kicking up the embers again. "I know we got into it last night and our tempers got the best of us, but I want to make sure you—"

"—like I told you, I'm here for the long haul. I understand becoming Mom's legal guardian means I can't leave again and I'm fine with that. More than fine, actually. Besides, it's pointless to debate it. We signed papers to start the restaurant and secured loans months ago. We set a grand opening date and alerted the media. The wheels are in motion. There's no turning back for any of us."

"We ought to change the farm's name to Hail Mary," Rachel grumbled.

Jenna propped her elbow on the seat. "I can't believe you two are cutting me out of this conversation again."

"We're not having this conversation again. That's my point," Amy said.

Rachel let out an exasperated sigh. "We're not cutting you out of anything, Jenna. We've gone over this dozens of times. You have Tommy to worry about, so you can't drop everything at a moment's notice and race to Albuquerque every time Mom has a health scare. But Amy can, because she has a flexible schedule. And it makes sense for me to take over Mom's estate."

"How does that make sense?" Jenna asked. "I'm better at finances than you and you hate desk work."

Rachel wrung her hands on the steering wheel. "True, but I already run the farm."

"And I've been handling the ledgers since Dad died. Let me tell you, they're a disaster. Maybe if *someone* had taken over the business side of the farm sooner, we wouldn't be in this mess."

"You better watch what you're implying, Jen. Dad wouldn't let me near the ledgers and you know it. He went nuts when I asked to see them."

"What about the Amarex letter we received that threatened a lawsuit?" Jenna asked. "We need to hire an oil rights lawyer and weigh our options before they railroad us straight into bankruptcy. Since you want to run the estate, I'm assuming you've already looked into hiring an oil attorney?"

"Not yet, but—"

Jenna *tsk*ed. "Figures."

"Are you volunteering to take care of that?" Rachel's tone was thick with condescension.

"Yes, I am," Jenna said. "You think you're the only one qualified to make decisions around here?"

Amy put her arms up in a gesture of surrender. "All right, all right, we need to take a few deep breaths and stop snapping at each other. Today's meeting is going to be hard enough without us mad at each other. If we're going to make this new business work, the three of us need to support each other."

"I'm all for that if Rachel is," Jenna said.

Rachel cracked her knuckles and shook out her hands. "Yeah, you're right."

After a few moments of tense silence, Jenna shot Amy a sly grin. "Does that mean we can talk about Kellan Reed some more?"

"Nice try."

"He's known around these parts for supplying that sort of service, you know."

"Are you talking about his cattle?" Rachel asked. "Because Slipping Rock Ranch puts out some of the highest quality beef in the state."

Jenna poked her tongue against the inside of her cheek, as though to keep from laughing. "Hear that, Amy? Best piece of meat in New Mexico."

Amy had a scathing retort on the tip of her tongue, then cringed as a disgusting possibility occurred to her. "Have you"—she glanced at Rachel, who drove on, oblivious—"have you sampled the product?"

Jenna chuckled. "Don't worry, sis. Not my type."

Rachel pulled a face in surprise. "What are you talking about? You love beef. We ate steaks for dinner last night."

Amy blinked at Rachel and considered slapping the side of her head to see if it was as dense as it seemed.

"Oh, yeah. What was I thinking?" Jenna said, tussling Rachel's hair.

Rachel snorted. "Sometimes, I have no idea."

The black road disappeared behind them and the minutes dragged into hours. Amy's words to Rachel echoed in her mind and pressed heavily on her heart. *There's no turning back.* She'd given up her career, sold her condo, and handed her life savings over to Rachel and Jenna as start-up money. Tough choices, sure, but not the root of her anxiety.

This new business was Amy's brainchild, and the consequences if she failed would be devastating. She had a sick mother, two sisters, and a four-year-old nephew counting on her. She had a farm on the line that had been in the family for fifty years. The pressure was enormous, more than enough to make her fold under its weight. Exactly like she had on *Ultimate Chef Showdown.* Exactly like her mother had after their father died.

That was the problem with a precedent. Despite all her years of stress management and self-imposed rules, Amy could see the writing on the wall from miles away. Only difference about this time was that, if she sailed off the deep end, it wouldn't be a national spectacle like *Chef Showdown.* It would be something far, far worse. She would have become her mother.

The peal of the phone sent Kellan shooting straight out of bed from a dead sleep. He'd been dreaming of Amy Sorentino, probably because his pillow smelled like her shampoo. The clock read one-thirty in the morning. His heart thumping like crazy, he stared out the window at a layer of ice blanketing the barn's rooftop before lifting the phone out of the receiver on the fourth ring, not bothering to check the caller ID. He was pretty sure who it'd be.

"Yeah?"

"Good morning, Kellan."

At the sound of the voice on the line, scratchy with the irreparable damage of a two-pack-a-day habit, his stomach dropped. He'd been right. "Morton. What are you doing waking me up in the middle of the night? We've talked about that."

"Our company's encountered a bit of a delicate situation 'round about your parts. Thought I'd give you a heads-up on it."

"It's not *our* company. I want nothing to do with it."

Morton chuckled. Asshole. "Be that as it may, one of my associates is waiting on your porch to deliver a file to you."

Kellan squeezed his eyes closed. "At my house, right now? You son of a bitch."

"Now, that's no way to talk to family."

"You're about as far from being my family as a man can get, Morton. You made that choice years ago."

"There you go whining about the past again. And here I thought we'd made amends."

Kellan opened his nightstand drawer and withdrew his Colt .45. Typical Morton, calling in the middle of the night and giving one of his so-called couriers leave to trespass on Kellan's property instead of mailing him the information. That was how his uncle operated, manipulating situations and people as a means to control. He seemed to regard Kellan as a rival, probably because Kellan had pegged his game early on and refused to be

bullied, and the two had been locked in a clash of wills
going on fourteen years now.

Holding the phone with his shoulder, he loaded rounds
into the gun's magazine. "Why involve me in one of your
delicate situations? You know I won't play along."

"Your name came up at a meeting. The board of direc-
tors hopes you'll be willing to convince a Quay County
family to sell us their failing farm without involving the
courts. I told them you wouldn't be up for the job, even
though it would be a win for both parties."

Bullshit. If Amarex was involved, then Kellan had no
doubt the family in question would get a raw deal. "And if
this family refuses to sell?"

"Our lawyers are ready to sue for breach of contract,
should we be forced to act on such an unsavory choice."

Kellan shook his head. "I'm hanging up, Morton. Gotta
shoo a pest off my property." Holding the Colt near the
phone, he snapped the magazine in place so Morton got an
earful of the metallic clank. "Don't call me again."

"Can't guarantee that. And son, play nice with my boy
downstairs. We wouldn't want the heir of an oil empire
acting like a short-fused, simple-minded cowboy around
the help, would we?"

Morton sure did know which buttons to push. Being a
rancher was the only career Kellan wanted in his life.
When he'd hitchhiked to his uncle's Texas ranch after high
school graduation, he'd certainly never expected Amarex
Petroleum, Bruce Morton's manipulations, or the slew of
battles he'd had to fight over the years.

Without turning on a light or bothering to slip pants
over his boxers, he plodded downstairs and flipped on the
porch light. Through the peephole, he saw a scrawny kid
probably no older than Kellan had been when he ran shady,
middle-of-the-night errands for Morton.

He didn't see a weapon on the kid, but that didn't mean

it wasn't somewhere on his person. Kellan held his gun aloft and swung the door wide. The kid started and jumped back, clutching a manila envelope to his chest. The December night air was frigid, hitting Kellan's bare chest and legs like a million needles.

"I'm . . . I'm here on behalf of Mr. Morton," he stammered.

Kellan felt for the guy, he did, but it wouldn't do either of them any good to offer up a mug of hot chocolate and testimony about how he could change his life like Kellan had, before Morton sank his clutches in too deep. Best he could do for the kid was scare him witless. Maybe then he'd rethink his career choice. He snatched the envelope out of the kid's hands and leveled the .45 at his chest.

"Get off my property before I shoot you."

Gulping, the kid fled the porch and leapt into an old beater of a truck. As soon as he was out of range of a stray bullet, Kellan squeezed a round off into the sky to hammer home his point. Dust flew behind the little truck as it barreled into the distance, its headlights disappearing behind a hill.

Hugging himself against the cold, Kellan stared at the sprawling acres of ranchland he'd poured his blood and sweat into for fourteen years. Despite Bruce Morton's needling attempts to throw him off balance, Kellan knew who he was, deep in his bones. Not some crooked oil tycoon like his uncle, not criminals like his parents.

Everything he loved about his life—his beef business, his honorary family, his standing in the community—he'd created from scratch, from the dregs of a childhood better off forgotten. The rest was background noise, annoying distractions trying to tug him away from the life he deserved.

After locking the front door, he tossed the folder on top of the refrigerator and let out a long, slow breath. One of his Quay County neighbors needed help, which was just the sort of situation Morton relished. He loved to watch Kellan squirm, loved to jerk his chain, and watch him scramble for footing. And he knew the most effective way to do so was to keep Kellan apprised of his unethical business dealings in New Mexico.

For Kellan, this amounted to a *damned if you do, damned if you don't* way of life. Either he sat on his hands and watched Amarex browbeat his Quay County neighbors and friends, or he risked his uncle's wrath to aid regular folks while walking the tightrope of anonymity, all the while hoping Morton didn't publicly reveal Kellan's ties to the company screwing over the community who'd accepted him with open arms.

With his morning alarm set to ring in two hours, it was time for Kellan to hightail it to bed. Tomorrow night, he'd study the folder. If the situation warranted action, he'd slip the card of his friend Matt, an oil rights attorney, to the family anonymously. Matt was good at helping folks out of messy situations. Better than Kellan anyway. He didn't have the patience or desire to deal with other people's complicated family dramas. God only knew, he had enough of his own.

He trudged upstairs and fell into bed, tucking the pistol beneath his pillow. Any other morning, he'd reset the alarm, giving himself an extra hour. But today, he wanted to make the eleven o'clock service at First Methodist Church. Never a religious sort, he'd be there to ruffle the feathers of a certain curly-haired brunette with a penchant for celery.

With a smile of sweet anticipation, he burrowed deeper into the pillow to catch a whiff of Amy's shampoo.

Chapter 3

Kellan was working hard not to appear as uncomfortable as he felt.

Not that church made him nervous like it did some folks, but because—between his leather bolo tie and the starched collar of the black, embroidered Western-style shirt he picked up in town yesterday—his clothing was conspiring to strangle him to death. To top it off, his seldom-worn dress boots pinched his toes. Discomfort was a small price to pay, however, if his strategy paid off. And he had a gut-level hunch it would. Big time.

The first person to notice Kellan when he walked into the packed sanctuary was Chris Binderman, the nicest guy he'd ever met. This morning, Chris looked every inch the family man, with his infant son, Rowen, strapped to his chest in one of those cozy-looking baby slings. With an amused grin on his face, he maneuvered through the gathering parishioners to reach Kellan. The two men shook hands and lightly thumped shoulders, being careful not to squash the baby.

"Look who the cat dragged in. This is a nice surprise."

Kellan brushed a few fingers over Rowen's soft, wispy-haired head. "What can I say? I was moved to attend."

"Is that so? Well, no matter the reason, I'm glad you're here. That being said, I'm assuming you're aware this opens you up to a lifetime of nagging by my wife about coming to church every Sunday, now that she sees it's possible."

"I can live with that." He felt a tug on his shirt and looked to see Chris's daughter, decked out in a poufy pink dress and hair ribbons, smiling at him.

"Hi, Uncle Kellan."

"Daisy dear, you sure look pretty today. But bigger than when I saw you a few days ago." Squatting, he dropped his cowboy hat on his goddaughter's head and gave her a tight hug. "My hat almost fits you. Did you grow again?"

"I think so."

"Could you do your uncle Kellan a favor and take a break from that for a little while? Five years old is big enough."

The little girl scratched her chin, considering. "I'll have to work on that."

Kellan took his hat in hand and tugged one of her blond pigtails. "Please see that you do." He stood to find Chris's wife, Lisa, pointing at his outfit, her face screwed up like she was fixing to laugh.

"What?" he asked her.

"Is that the belt buckle you got at our Christmas party? The white elephant gift?"

Kellan pecked her cheek, then ran a hand over the cool metal ridges of the buckle. "'Bout time I tried it on. Do you like it?"

She smushed her lips together and shot him an *Are you crazy?* look. Good thing she wasn't the one he wanted to impress.

"What's so bad about it?"

She yanked one of the leather straps of his bolo tie.

"With this tie, the hat, the buckle, and the boots, you look like a cowboy on Halloween."

"I see a dozen other men in this room dressed the same exact way." He'd been worried about drawing the wrong kind of attention to himself by looking foolish until he took inventory of the other men in attendance and discovered ten bolo ties, twelve belt buckles, and so many boots that he lost count.

"True, but on you it's all wrong. This getup isn't who you are."

"It is today." And if it got him laid again, it would be worth the discomfort and the ribbing by his friends.

Someone slapped him hard on the back. He twisted to see Vaughn.

Kellan bumped knuckles with his best friend. "What's up, Vaughn?"

"I was across the room when I saw you mosey in, that little bitty belt buckle shining like it was real gold."

Kellan rolled his shoulders in a show of mock-indignity. "You all are getting a lot of mileage out of this. Glad I could bring so much joy to your morning. Is this buckle actually small? I think it looks fine."

Vaughn let loose with a belly laugh. "You know the saying, you can tell a lot about a man's goods by the size of his buckle? Well, don't you worry that pretty-boy head of yours about people getting the wrong impression. There are enough rumors around town to the contrary where you're concerned."

"Vaughn Cooper," Lisa hissed. "We're at church. You're the sheriff."

"So?"

"So act like it."

"I came to morning worship, didn't I? And since I'm here doing my pillar-of-the-community thing, I might as well perpetuate a law-enforcement stereotype and retire to the courtyard for a doughnut. Daisy, you care to join me?"

Daisy regarded him with soulful eyes. "I have to wait until after church, Uncle Vaughn. And only if I mind my P's and Q's. Right, Mommy?"

Lisa gave her a thumbs-up. "That's right."

Vaughn knelt, his hands on his knees, and winked at her. "Well, sweetie, the trick with P's and Q's is to keep them on a short leash. That's what your mama's always telling me."

He stood and slugged Kellan in the shoulder. "Are we watching the game at your house this afternoon?"

"Yep. You bring the beer, I've got the steaks."

"And I've got three new cheeses for you to taste test," Lisa said.

"Sounds like a party," Vaughn said. "I'd better see about that doughnut before Pastor Schueller calls us to order."

With a wink, he wandered off, shaking hands and greeting parishioners as he went. The guy might act like he didn't have a care in the world, but Vaughn was the best sheriff Quay County had ever elected and one of the most decent men Kellan was lucky enough to call a friend.

"Okay, Daisy," Lisa said. "Let's use the restroom before the service starts." She took Daisy's hand and off they went.

Kellan scanned the crowd for the pretty face that had been dancing through his mind all weekend. The reason for his attendance and joke-worthy accessories.

Chris sidled up next to him, leaning in conspiratorially. "I know who you're looking for."

"Who's that?"

"The middle Sorentino sister. Amy."

Kellan scowled despite his efforts to mask his irritation. He'd never been the subject of salacious gossip, and the idea didn't sit well with him. Now that he thought about it, what the hell was he doing chasing a chick who, along with her family, would win the award for *Most Whispered About*? "They ought to rename this town Gossip Creek. How many sources tipped you off?"

Chris counted on his fingers. "Nancy Tobarro sent a picture to Lisa's cell phone of you two talking, then Jillian Dixon and Kate Parrish stopped by the dairy to pick up cheese for their Bunco party and filled me in about Amy holding up the checkout line at the Quick Stand, and how you stepped in to smooth things over."

The Catcher Creek information pipeline was as robust as ever. "Nothing's going on between me and Amy Sorentino."

Chris motioned with his head toward the front of the sanctuary. "Then you don't care that she just walked in."

Kellan knew he shouldn't look. He should walk to his truck and ditch the buckle and the tie. If he ignored Amy for the duration of the service, he'd go a long way toward squelching the rumors about their involvement and keeping his reputation intact. But he couldn't help himself. Curiosity got the better of him and he turned.

Sure enough, she stood by the side entrance near the first pew, her coat and a Bible in hand. She wore a long, dark green dress that hugged her curves in exactly the right way and another pair of impractical, high-heel leather boots that were sexy as all get-out. It was easy to picture her standing in nothing but her skin and those boots, with her dark, curly hair kissing the tops of her shoulders and her full, pink lips beckoning him. An image like that almost made the inevitable gossip worth it.

Her gaze shifted briefly in his direction and he didn't miss the way her cheeks pinked. Or the way her eyes darted to the nearest door like she might bolt should he take a step nearer. The flush of pink spread to her neck, then her chest. Kellan couldn't take his eyes off her.

Charlene Delgado and her granddaughter, Sloane, cornered her before she had a chance to run. Maybe she was grateful for the distraction from Kellan because she seemed to throw herself into the conversation a little too enthusiastically, smiling and nodding with exaggerated pep. She should exercise more caution, though, because Kellan knew from experience that Charlene could twist a conversation around like no one else in Catcher Creek. One minute you'd be discussing the weather, all casual like, and the next you'd find yourself agreeing to repaint the fellowship hall or call bingo every Wednesday for a month. Anyone in the know dove for cover when Charlene came around.

"Chris?"

"Hmm?"

"That is a beautiful woman."

"Yes, she is. Too bad you're not interested in her." Rowen stirred, stretching one tiny hand upward. Chris slipped his finger into Rowen's palm. Rowen gripped it tight and brought it to his mouth to gum.

"I'm not. I swear." Even Kellan couldn't believe such a half-hearted denial.

Amy's gaze slipped in his direction before darting away once more. Her skin flushed a deeper shade of pink. Oh, man, he wanted to drag his lips over that soft, sweet skin until her body melted against him.

"Kellan, the Sorentino family and my family go way back in this town. If you're not sure what you want from her, then you should find someone else to scratch your itch. She's not the kind you mess with."

That threw Kellan for a loop. "Why not?"

"Delicate constitution like her mother is what people say."

Kellan huffed in protest. "What a bunch of B.S. Amy Sorentino does not have a delicate constitution. She's a firecracker through and through."

"Obviously there's nothing going on between you two. Right."

"Nope." He studied her from across the room, riveted by those juicy curves and big, brown eyes, and knew he'd told Chris one hell of a colossal lie.

"Hypothetically," Chris said, "if something were happening between you and Amy Sorentino, what would your plan be today?"

He straightened his tie and ran a hand over his head, knowing full well the attempt would be futile with his unruly hair. "I'd ask her to my place for dinner. Hypothetically."

"Couldn't you do that over the phone and save all this cowboy costume drama?"

"Absolutely no drama." His tone was a bit too earnest, but Chris needed to be clear on that point. "I did ask her, but she wasn't amenable to the idea."

"And today's going to be different?"

He gripped the hat he'd been spinning on his finger and hooked a thumb behind his belt buckle. "Yes. Because today I have a plan."

The minute Amy's eyes found Kellan Reed across the room talking to Chris Binderman, she took stock of every exit door in the sanctuary, calculating her distance from each. Her panic flared when she saw the Stetson hat he was twirling on his finger and the shiny gold belt buckle on his jeans. She didn't stand a chance of maintaining her composure if he came to talk to her while dressed in full cowboy attire. One *Howdy, ma'am* and she'd probably pull him into an empty classroom, rip her panties off, and beg him to plow her like a field.

Thank goodness for Charlene Delgado's intervention. Amy pounced on the conversation, though she was too distracted to listen to the older woman's nattering. Something about her granddaughter, Sloane, whom she'd brought with her that morning—a shy, nubile junior college student with long black hair tucked in a severe ponytail and a dress that looked better suited for an Amish bride—needing a job.

Next thing Amy knew, she and Sloane were shaking hands. Charlene looked satisfied. That couldn't be good. Of course, asking for a recap would definitely make her seem stupid and rule number five on her list was *Don't say anything stupid*. She'd said some real whoppers on *Ultimate Chef Showdown*. Cringe-inducing statements captured on film that were quoted on entertainment Web sites and replayed on the show's highlight reels. No longer. She'd made a vow when she'd woken for church that from now on, come hell or high water, she was following her rules. No exceptions.

"Great meeting you, Sloane," she said instead.

"See you tomorrow, Amy," Sloane said with a wave as Charlene hustled her to a pew on the opposite side of the room.

Amy waved back. "Okay." Ugh. Hopefully she hadn't agreed to cochair a church yard sale or something. She glanced across the sanctuary to find Kellan's eyes on her.

God was testing her resolve. Clearly he'd heard her renewed vow about following her rules and decided to find out if she meant it this time.

Kellan started her way. If she made a break for the nearest door now, a hundred people would bear witness to her cowardice. Not the impression she wanted to make her first week back in town, especially after her celery theatrics at the Quick Stand. With all the cool and calm she could muster, she dropped into a pew and opened her Bible.

His shadow loomed over her from the aisle. "Good morning, Amy."

"Kellan," she said without looking up.

He sidestepped into the row, like he planned to sit next to her. She jumped out of her skin a little at the idea, recovering soon enough to spread her sweater and purse across the bench. "Sorry, these seats are taken."

He stopped, leaning against the back of the pew. "You're here with Jenna and her son, I'm assuming?"

"How did you know?" Looking at him up close, he was even hotter than she recalled, with a crisp button-down shirt and a clean-shaven face that highlighted his strong jaw. It looked like he'd tried to tame his wavy brown hair with gel and a comb, but judging by the bits and pieces falling all over his head, he'd had little success. Which was fine with her. She preferred them with a hint of wild.

Horrified to have let such a thought slip into her head, she cleared her throat and did a mental head smack.

"I see them whenever I attend. Rachel here today too?" He licked his lower lip, his gaze wandering with blatant appreciation over her dress.

It was all she could do not to raise the hem a few inches to give him a better view. She drew a flustered breath. "No. She says she sees God clearer on the open range."

Kellan rocked on his heels, grinning. "I'm likely to agree with her."

"Then why are you here?"

He looked at her, quiet like, his eyes dark.

Oh.

He started toward her again. Amy scrambled across the polished wooden bench until Kellan's hand clamped onto the back of the pew, halting her progress. Resting a knee on the bench, he ducked his head toward her ear, smelling good enough to devour.

"You're blocking my light and I've got to read this Bible," she blurted frantically. Damn it. Rule number five down the toilet. Unbelievable.

He grazed her temple with his nose and little shivers

crawled through her limbs. "I'll move out of your light in a second. After I give you fair warning."

"Warning about what?"

"You should know I'm going to sit a few rows behind you. And I'm going to have my eyes on you the whole time." A heavy sensation started between her thighs. She bit her lower lip, fighting the urge to offer her mouth to him right there in the middle of church. "And after the service, I'm going to ask you to dinner. You think about how you're going to answer."

He straightened and she didn't miss the strategically placed cowboy hat covering his midsection. Filthy mind she'd been cursed with, her first thought was to knock the hat away so she could get a good look at what he was hiding behind it. She blew a strand of hair off her cheek, annoyed at herself. Thank goodness she was at church, because she needed some godly housekeeping to scour the dirtiness from her thoughts.

At least she managed to stop herself from craning her neck to watch him walk away. Score a point for her pride with that brief moment of self-control.

A few minutes later, Jenna and Tommy returned from the restroom. Jenna settled Tommy next to her and produced a bag of toy cars from her purse, dropping them on his lap. Then she poked Amy on the shoulder. "He's here. Sitting four rows back."

"Who?" Playing innocent never worked for her, but she had to try.

Jenna raised a brow suggestively. "Your cowboy."

"He's not *mine*. In fact, I'm assigning him to you."

"I told you, he's not my type."

"No! Not like that. You said you wanted more responsibility at the farm. So I told Kellan you'd be contacting him this week to negotiate a beef supply contract."

Jenna's shoulders shook with a silent chuckle. "Oh,

sweetie, since you're in Catcher Creek to stay, you're going to have to stop tormenting yourself. Quay County is ranch country, densest population of cowboys this side of the Texas border."

"Why do you think I hightailed it out of town when I was eighteen?" Actually, that had nothing to do with her decision to leave, but she needed to persuade Jenna any way she could.

"The way I see it, you can either surrender to your cowboy fetish or swear them off cold turkey."

Amy rolled her eyes heavenward. "I swear them off cold turkey every day. Doesn't do me a lick of good."

The organist opened the service with a quiet song. The minister, a tall, lanky middle-aged man Amy didn't recognize, stepped front and center. Everyone got to the business of praying and singing hymns, a ritual as comfortable and familiar as it was uplifting.

Usually. Except today, she felt Kellan's eyes between her shoulder blades. She felt his gaze on her neck when she bowed in prayer. And when she stood to sing, her skin tingled with heat, imagining him watching her ass. She smoothed a hand along the fabric near her hip to double-check that her dress hadn't bunched, then scolded herself for letting a cowboy's incendiary declaration get the better of her.

Fanning herself with the program, she worked hard to concentrate on the pastor's words instead of strategizing about the fastest way to remove a belt buckle.

"With Christmas around the corner, we're taking the opportunity this month to reflect on the choices Jesus made in his life, the lessons we can learn from his decisions, and how those lessons matter in our modern lives. Every week of family worship in December, we are asking ourselves a simple question—What Would Jesus Do?

"There's a lot of pressure on folks around Christmastime. Everywhere we turn, it seems, we're pressured to do things we know aren't in our best interest. For some of us, we're tempted by material goods, to buy our family members gifts we can't afford, to spend, spend, spend. Others may be tempted to cheat on a diet with that extra piece of fudge at a holiday party or drink one cocktail too many. All these temptations turn our focus away from the true meaning of Christmas. And so, today, the question I want you all to ask yourselves is, What would Jesus do . . . about temptation?"

With a snicker, Jenna elbowed her in the ribs. Amy sunk lower in the pew and fanned herself more vigorously.

Inspired by the pastor's teachings, by the time his sermon was over, she'd practiced her polite refusal to Kellan's dinner offer. Her life was complicated enough without adding a cowboy to the mix. She'd never met a single one worth her time or trust. The pastor said the trick to rejecting temptation was being prepared for it, to know it was coming, and have a ready response.

To prove Kellan's powers of seduction were no match for her willpower, she resisted the urge to turn and locate him until the closing prayer of the service. When the congregation bowed their heads, she glanced over her shoulder to where Kellan sat. Staring at her.

Not really staring, but smoldering. She could've handled it better if he'd smiled or done something cheesy like winked at her. But his expression was fiery and unblinking, his eyes shadowed her with wicked intent, as though he were picturing himself stripping her dress off and running his fingers over her bared flesh. Or maybe she only wished he was thinking about doing that half as much as she was.

She jerked her face forward again, a hand on her chest, and let her breath out long and slow. So much for Plan A. The moment the pastor stopped talking, she'd sprint out the nearest side door and call her sister from the supermarket down the road to pick her up. After all, Pastor Schueller said the only surefire way to resist temptation was to run in the opposite direction.

Too bad for her that when the pastor released them, Tommy took her hand. "I want a doughnut, Auntie. You promised if I was good, you'd get me one with sprinkles. Wasn't I good?"

Since Amy's arrival in Catcher Creek, Tommy had clung to her like she might vanish into thin air should his attention waver from her. She turned, prepared to send Kellan packing with a searing glare, but he was nowhere to be seen. Relieved, she squeezed Tommy's hand. "You were a perfect angel. Let's get you a doughnut."

She ushered Tommy through the double doors to the courtyard and saw Kellan talking with a girl a year or so older than Tommy. He bent over the refreshment table, giving Amy a full view of the same perfect ass that got her in trouble the morning before. She tried to shift her gears into reverse, but Tommy urged her on.

"I want the pink one, right there, Uncle Kellan," the little girl said.

"Then that's the one you shall have. And lucky you, because it looks like this is the last one with sprinkles."

"Oh, no, Daisy," Tommy wailed, stomping to the table and throwing his arms up. "That was for me."

The little girl looked at the doughnut in her hand, then at Tommy. "We could share."

"What a great idea, Daisy. That's a nice thing to do." Kellan patted the top of her head, then split the doughnut for the two kids.

Amy's nipples hardened. Good grief. Who in their right mind got so turned on by a man breaking a doughnut in half that she wanted to grab him by the tie and kiss him senseless? *That's right—Amy Sorentino, the easiest lay in Quay County.*

Once he got the kids settled, Kellan straightened to his full height and regarded Amy from beneath the low brim of his Stetson. Amy grabbed a glazed old-fashioned and shoved it in her mouth before she smashed her own record time for rule breaking.

"Did you enjoy the service, Amy?"

"Yup," she said with her mouth full.

"I did, too, except for one point. It's my opinion that the tricky part about temptation, what Pastor Schueller was remiss in mentioning, is recognizing the difference between good temptation and bad." He raised a hand and she angled her face toward his approaching fingers, anticipating his touch. Instead, he flicked at her cheek. "Errant sprinkle."

"Thanks." She swallowed and licked at the corners of her lips. "I disagree. I think most people know bad when they see it." And thank you, Kellan, for bringing her mind around to the sermon. With the pastor's words in her head, she was confident she'd be able to keep her desires in check. In fact, she was ready to meet her temptation head-on. "Are you going to ask me to dinner now?"

His eyes shifted, taking in the noisy courtyard full of parishioners. "Not yet."

She opened her mouth, ready to give the obstinate man her answer anyway.

"Aunt Amy? I need a napkin." She smiled at Tommy, whose face had gone pink with frosting and sprinkles. "You need more than a napkin, buddy. I'll take you to the restroom and wash you up." Without looking in Kellan's direction, she grabbed Tommy's hand and hustled off.

Jenna ran into them in the vestibule.

"Here, take Tommy. You can pick me up at the supermarket when you're done."

"What?" Jenna called after her.

"I have groceries to buy. See you there."

She tore across the sanctuary, ducked through the door behind the organ, and skidded into a dusty side room with an exit she remembered from Tommy's baptism four years earlier. Bursting out onto a narrow breezeway between the sanctuary and the administrative offices, she chanced a look over her shoulder as she jogged. The coast was clear. She was running like a yellow-bellied coward, but at least there weren't witnesses.

Kellan's imposing form materialized at the end of the breezeway, blocking her progress. He folded his arms over his chest and propped his shoulder against the wall.

Amy yelped and lurched to a halt. "You scared me."

"Sorry about that."

She took in his casual stance. "You don't look sorry."

"I'm ready to ask you out."

"Oh." She tried to calm her racing heart, breathing deeply. Impossible. "Go ahead."

"Amy, may I make you dinner at my house on Friday?"

She was ready with her answer. "No. Not a good idea. Sorry."

"Why?"

"Rule number one. I put it in place for a reason."

"Rule number one," he muttered, swaggering closer, his thumbs hitched on his belt buckle. Not that she was looking there. He stopped close enough to touch her. She took another step back and bumped into the wall. "Amy, may I have dinner with you?"

"No." The word was little more than a note on the wind.

She flattened her palms against the cool stucco wall as her eyes trailed a vein in his neck from where it began at his shirt collar to where it ended at the locks of hair peeking from beneath his Stetson. Something shifted inside her, something carnal and potent. She waited for him to touch her, arching her back, thrusting her breasts up, desperate to feel his hands on her body. What he did, though, was far more dangerous.

With a blazing expression in his eyes, he unbuttoned his cuffs and rolled his sleeves to his elbows. "All this fancy stuff . . . I don't think it's for me," he murmured.

The tie was off next, stuffed into a pocket. Maybe he heard her ragged intake of air because his gaze shifted to her lips as he unfastened his belt and dropped it to the ground. The metal buckle clanged on the cement. He loosened the top three buttons of his shirt, then tipped the brim of his hat lower over his brow.

Oh, damn . . .

She rocked to her toes and lassoed his neck with her arm. His hat tumbled off as she brought her lips to his. His hands wound into her hair. Crushing her to the wall, he devoured her. Thoroughly and without mercy, pinning her in place with his lower body as his lips and tongue caressed her. She snaked an arm around his side and grabbed his rock-hard ass.

With a labored grunt, he wrenched his lips from hers and propped his arm against the wall behind her, panting. She opened her eyes, expecting triumph in his expression, but all she saw was a raw heat that matched her own.

"I'll pick you up Friday at six."

Scooping his belt and hat from the ground, he walked away, listing a bit. She felt a stab of vanity for inducing that drunk walk. Then she asked herself what Jesus would do about temptation and sobered up in a hurry. Jesus would not give in to baser instincts because some cowboy was an amazing kisser and looked great in a pair of jeans.

Squaring her shoulders, she marched in the direction of the supermarket. Hopefully, when Jenna picked her up, she wouldn't ask why her lips were swollen.

Chapter 4

Vaughn poked at the plate on his lap with a knife. "Lisa, why is there greenery on this cheese? I don't have to eat it, do I? You know how I feel about greenery."

Lisa took the plate from him and untied the string holding the leaf in place. "It's something new we're trying at the dairy, wrapping goat cheese in grape leaves to age it. You're my testers."

Kellan poured salsa into a bowl, tucked a bag of chips under his arm, and strolled to the living room, taking stock of the perfect picture before him—the Christmas tree that had taken him over an hour to select from the tree lot in Clovis, the fire crackling in the fireplace, and everyone he loved crowded onto his overstuffed sofa, save for Daisy and Max, who were out front playing fetch.

He handed a beer to Chris, who was snuggled deep into the sofa cushions with a sleeping Rowen on his shoulder. "I don't see how you've survived this long with your eating habits, Vaughn."

Lisa set the plate of unwrapped cheese on the table and reached into her bag for a second wedge of cheese. "Yes, well, he'd better shape up because someday he's going to have a wife who insists he eat his veggies."

"If I ever find a woman lucky enough to snag me as a husband, she sure as hell's not going to force-feed me greenery. I am not livestock. Pigheaded yes, built like a stallion, absolutely, but there's a difference."

Lisa handed him a cheese-topped cracker. "Try it."

Vaughn complied, stuffing the entire cracker into his mouth at an angle. He hummed in appreciation and flashed a thumbs-up to Lisa, then reached for a second cracker. "You think city folks have any idea how gourmet we country hicks can be? I'm sitting here eating some of the best cheese ever produced, about to have a steak dinner grilled for me by one of the top beef purveyors in the nation."

Chris snorted. "And what do you add to the party, Cooper?"

"Entertainment," Lisa and Kellan said at the same time.

Kellan chuckled and settled on the sofa to watch the last few minutes of the quarter before he got busy grilling steaks at half-time. Having the gang over on Sunday afternoon was his favorite time of the week. He loved every minute of it—talking football with Chris, Lisa setting up a plate of cheeses from Binderman Dairy, and Vaughn doing his fake-machismo act. He loved Daisy's squeals of delight filtering in through the window and Rowen's occasional yawn or hungry cry.

He never experienced that growing up, not even when his mom and dad had the same day off work. They were too world-weary to do much more than lie around and smoke weed. Holding a family dinner, much less entertaining friends, had been out of the question. Even his brief stint in a foster home, as loving as his foster parents had been, hadn't satisfied his craving for family, for *warmth*. It was an absence that registered in his bones more like a loss, one he'd been working to make up for the better part of his life.

Vaughn rapped Kellan on the knee with his knuckles. "Heard you invited Amy Sorentino here yesterday."

Lisa looked up, an incredulous grin playing on her lips. "I saw you two talking at the doughnut table this morning. Her sister, Jenna, told me you gave her a bag of celery. Really?"

There was going to be no getting around this conversation, Kellan could tell. He could deny an attraction to Amy until his face turned blue, but his closest friends wouldn't buy a word of it. "Onions too."

Vaughn tipped the neck of his beer in Kellan's direction. "I'm betting he bagged more than her groceries."

There was a collective groan from the room.

"You're not going to let this drop, are you?"

"Nope," all three of his friends chimed in.

"If that's the way you're going to be, then I suppose it's my obligation to set the record straight." Kellan leaned his elbows on his knees, cleared his throat, and waited for their undivided attention. "I do not appreciate the implication that Amy Sorentino is anything less than a lady. At all times. That you would besmirch the Sorentino family name with such a flagrant rumor is insulting—"

"Did you say *besmirch*?" Vaughn cut in.

"Yes, I did say 'besmirch.' Weren't you all in church this morning? Is this any way for good Christians to think? Shame on you all and your filthy minds."

Lisa let out a low whistle. "You dog."

Vaughn burst out laughing, "I don't know how you do it, man. You're my hero."

Daisy and Max came bounding into the room. Vaughn snagged her hand. "Daisy, when I grow up, I want to be just like your uncle Kellan."

She gave him a bright smile. "Me too. Then I could ride Pickle all the time."

Kellan raised his hand for attention. "I don't want this

spread around, but today after church, I asked Amy to dinner."

"Against my advice," Chris added.

Kellan held his hand up. "Let the record show I asked her out against Chris's advice. Happy now?"

"Not really. Did she agree this time?"

"Not at first. She declined my offer twice. But I finally brought her around to my way of thinking."

Lisa patted Kellan's knee. "I wouldn't take her refusal too personally. Those Sorentino sisters have a lot on their plates, with their mom's poor health and their money troubles."

"Money troubles?" That caught Kellan's attention. "I haven't heard mention of her finances, only of the restaurant Amy's opening at their farm."

Chris shifted Rowen to his other arm and sat up straighter. "She and Lisa have an appointment this week at the dairy. She wants to contract with Binderman Dairy, which I think is great."

"True, and I'm happy to do business with the Sorentinos," Lisa said, "but word is the restaurant and inn they're opening are a last-ditch effort to save their farm from foreclosure. My cousin Isabel, who works for the bank in Albuquerque, said Amy, Rachel, and Jenna were in a few months ago applying for loans and meeting with a foreclosure agent. I bet their mom's care is bleeding their bank accounts something terrible."

Dread rippled through Kellan. Sorentino Farm was on the verge of foreclosure? A terrible possibility took shape in his mind as he thought of the manila folder hidden above his refrigerator. If Amy and her sisters were the subjects of an Amarex lawsuit, a personal relationship with her would not only be unethical, but against Kellan's moral code. And if she discovered his link to the company fighting to squeeze her family out of their home . . .

Oh, man, he couldn't even think about how she'd react. He choked down a swig of beer, fighting the urge to rip open the file and assuage his rising anxiety.

"What about royalties from oil leasing rights?" Chris asked. "Amarex contracts keep most of the ranches and farms around here afloat. Including ours."

Chris's question put his mind at ease. No way could Amy and her sisters be the victims of his uncle's latest bullying attempt. The very reason they were in financial trouble rendered the possibility of Amarex's interest in purchasing the land unthinkable.

He shook his head and relaxed back into the sofa cushion. "The Sorentino land is as dry as mine. Both are Quay County anomalies. No crude oil underground to be had. And you can bet your bottom dollar Amarex has explored every inch of both our properties in search of a source." Probably, he should've tried to sound less joyous about that. "I read the reports on Amarex's contract negotiations with Gerald Sorentino years ago because the guy was too cheap to spring for a lawyer to look out for his interests—exactly the sort of stupid choice Amarex salivates over. Exploration crews scoured his land and came up empty. No oil, no lease money."

Lisa sighed. "What horrible luck that family's had. It's a shame Amy didn't fare better on *Ultimate Chef Showdown*. The winner took home three hundred grand. Did you watch it, Kellan?"

"Nah. You know me; I don't have much use for television. But I remember hearing a lot of chatter that the competition didn't go well for her."

Vaughn winced. "That's putting it mildly. A word of advice? Don't bring up the show during your date. It wasn't Amy's most flattering moment. But here's what people don't know—her dad, Gerald, died a matter of days before *Chef Showdown* began filming. And the episode she lost her marbles on was after her mom's collapse. She never allowed anyone on the show to mention it—didn't want people's sympathy vote—but those are the facts."

Chris shook his head. "Man, that's rough."

"How do you know all that?" Lisa asked.

Vaughn peeled the label on his bottle, looking uncomfortable. "I spent a lot of time at Sorentino Farm during the investigation into Gerald's car crash, then Bethany's breakdown. In my job, you learn people's secrets. Most of them aren't of the positive variety."

Kellan's jaw clamped shut and refused to budge. Impotent frustration coursed through him, thinking about what Amy and her family had gone through. She deserved so much better than the hand she'd been dealt.

"I see the wheels turning in your head, Kellan," Chris said. "What gives?"

"I'm working hard to keep myself from driving to her house with my checkbook and taking charge."

Vaughn scoffed. "If you tried, I'd probably get called out to arrest you."

"That's why I'm still here."

"Well, I think it's a good thing you're having dinner with Amy," Lisa said. Rowen stirred with a dissatisfied whimper and she scooped him from Chris's shoulder. "Maybe a night out is what the lady needs to take her mind off her worries."

"I doubt that," Chris grumbled.

Kellan stood and walked to the glass door of his deck, looking at the rolling acres of desert chaparral dotted with cattle. A kick of dust on the nearest slope told him someone had driven the dirt road leading to his property. The doorbell chimed.

Vaughn pushed up and strolled toward the door like he

owned the place. "Expecting someone?" He peered through the peephole.

"Nope."

Vaughn drew a sharp breath and slunk to the far end of the room, swabbing a hand over his face. "You answer, Kellan. It's your house."

Kellan eyed his friend suspiciously and opened the door to Rachel Sorentino. Despite the chilly weather, she wore a short-sleeved T-shirt and her hair was damp, like she'd come straight over after taking a shower. She shared Amy's doe-shaped brown eyes and freckled, pert nose, but though both women were easy on the eyes, the two sisters gave off completely different vibes. Rachel acted and looked every inch the no-nonsense, born-and-raised cowgirl she was, from her athletic build and darkly tanned skin to her work boots and blunt fingernails.

"Rachel, what a surprise. Come on in." He held the door wide open for her to pass.

"Sorry to stop by unannounced like this, but I need a word with you—" She spied Vaughn and ground to a halt. "Sheriff Cooper."

"Miss Sorentino," Vaughn said softly, folding his arms over his chest.

Kellan looked to Chris, a brow raised in question, baffled by Vaughn and Rachel's formality. Chris responded with a shrug of confusion.

With what seemed like tremendous effort, Rachel pulled her gaze from Vaughn and turned to Kellan. "Is there someplace private we can talk?"

"How about the porch?"

"Works for me."

"You want a beer?"

"Sure. Thanks."

Glancing sideways at Vaughn, who still looked shell-shocked by Rachel's sudden appearance, Kellan snagged a beer from the fridge and ushered her out the door. She'd never been to his ranch before, as far as he could recall, and he couldn't imagine a single reason for her to visit unannounced on a Sunday afternoon.

Bottle in hand, she walked the porch like she was checking to ensure every window was closed. Kellan's curiosity mounting, he kept quiet, giving her time to check the windows and collect her thoughts.

Sitting on his porch, watching Rachel's agitated pacing, he realized she was the only member of the Sorentino family who wasn't a Catcher Creek gossip staple. In all the years he'd lived there, he'd never once heard tell of Rachel whooping it up at bars or rodeos, or even church socials. They ran into each other every now and then, at feed stores or livestock auctions, and she was pleasant enough, but aloof. Typical solitary rancher so common in the sprawling, untamed wilderness of Eastern New Mexico.

When Kellan rolled into Catcher Creek fourteen years ago, a scruffy, dirt poor twenty-year-old with a chip on his shoulder the size of a meteor, he'd steered clear of women for a while, particularly the young, jail-baiting set like the Sorentino sisters had been at the time. But still, he'd borne witness to plenty of the youngest sister, Jenna's, raucous partying. That is, until she got pregnant at nineteen and settled down on the family farm. Four years later and folks still whispered their theories about Tommy Sorentino's mystery daddy and why he hadn't stepped up to his responsibility.

Amy had dropped off the radar for years—and, frankly, Kellan had forgotten she existed—until the *Ultimate Chef Showdown* fiasco lit up the gossip circuit like a lightning storm. About the same time, their mother, Bethany, succumbed to a series of very public breakdowns, including one Kellan witnessed at Walmart, followed by a mysterious health crisis many folks believed to be the result of a botched suicide attempt. But not one of them, not Bethany or even Jenna during her wild days, had anything on the stories told of their drunk, gambling, good-timing father.

Rachel stopped moving and hunched over the porch rail, fiddling with her beer bottle.

"Might as well spit it out, Rachel. What's on your mind?"

She sniffed. "My sisters are so smug. They think I'm oblivious, sheltered. Like I couldn't possibly relate to their worldly sensibilities or the drama of their social lives."

Okay.

Angling her face over her shoulder, she shot him a *kids-these-days* grin. "Contrary to their opinion of me, for the most part, I know them far better than they know themselves."

"That doesn't surprise me."

She took a hit of beer and shoved off the railing, dropping to a chair. "You're not good for Amy. I want you to stay away from her. From now on, with regards to Slipping Rock's supply contract, you can deal with me."

Apparently Rachel was aware of Kellan and Amy's date . . . and possibly Saturday's tryst. Seems she'd come to his ranch to assert her role as big sister. The problem was, why would Rachel think Kellan was no good for Amy? He was of a mind it was the other way around.

"Hold on. Is there something being said about me that I'm not aware of—an unflattering rumor or something? Because I don't understand your opinion. I'm a model citizen, a responsible business owner, and a good man with friends who'd vouch for me. What do you find so bad about that?"

"Oh, please. I don't deal in rumors. And I don't have

anything against you as a person. Hell, I don't even know you."

Crisis averted. "Then what gives?"

"The thing about Amy is that she feels too much, too fast. She's spinning in all directions at once and looking for a man who's steady, someone to be the calm center of her tornado life. I'm not sure how the notion got stuck in her head, because our dad was a farmer and she never got on with him, but for some reason, she thinks she can find what she needs in men like you. And maybe she will some-day, but now's not the time."

"Men like me?" Ah. Now he was on to her line of think-ing. "Cowboys, you mean?"

"Exactly. God bless her, she's still optimistic about find-ing that ideal cowboy of her imagination, despite how many times she's been hurt."

"I'm not going to hurt her because we're not having a relationship." That probably sounded harsh, but truthfully, was there any way to tell a woman he was only interested in sleeping with her sister without sounding like an ass?

Someday he'd settle down—he wanted kids too badly not to work toward that end—but his ideal wife would be drama-free. A homemaker and peacemaker. A woman in good standing with the community. He'd built his perfect life from the ground up, brick by brick, carefully choosing his friends and his lovers, and molding his career as a rancher. He had every confidence that, when the time was right, he'd select the perfect woman to be his life-partner. And she wouldn't be a tornado. Even if that tornado was a curvy brunette who set his blood on fire.

"Not having a relationship? You slept with her yes-terday."

Kellan rotated his jaw to ease the tension gathering there. "For the record, Rachel, casual sex between consenting adults is perfectly legal. Hence, the words *consensual* and *adults*."

"You're such a man to believe sex can ever be casual to a woman." Something in her tone spoke of her personal experience in such matters.

"Look, Rachel. There's no hurt to be had. Amy and I have an understanding. Neither of us wants a relationship. We're just having fun."

Her gaze, knifelike in its resolve, finally met his. "All the same, see that you stay away from her in the future so you don't hurt her. Or, more to the point, so you don't encourage her to hurt herself, jumping headfirst into shallow water, as it may be."

Ouch.

Rachel pushed to her feet with a sigh and handed Kellan her empty bottle. "Amy's been damaged enough. If you lead her into more hurt, you'll answer to me. And that's a promise you can take to the bank."

He stood, nodding. "Yes, ma'am."

"I'm glad we understand each other." She offered him her hand to shake, which he took. Her grip was firm, her palm and fingers calloused. Rachel Sorentino was one tough lady.

"I've got something for Amy in the kitchen, if you wouldn't mind passing it along."

She snorted. "What did I tell you?"

"It's produce, Rachel. Relax."

He held the door open, then followed her in and rustled through the fridge for the bag of produce he'd selected from his greenhouse that morning. "I was going to deliver these tomorrow, but since you're here, she might as well use them while they're at their freshest."

Rachel felt the bag. "Vegetables?"

"Cabbage, garlic, and two bunches of celery. In case she

runs low before the stores open tomorrow," he added with a wink.

Rachel nodded solemnly. "Guess you know her better than I gave you credit for."

"You want to stay for dinner? I was fixing to barbecue some Slipping Rock steaks when you showed up. We've got plenty of food to go around." He knew she wouldn't, but found himself interested in gauging her reaction.

She cast a wary look toward the living room, mashing her lips into a straight line. Kellan followed her gaze to the sofa. Chris and Lisa smiled encouragingly. Vaughn stared at the television, his expression blank. "Thanks anyway, but I'm expected home for dinner."

Kellan closed the door behind her. Vaughn wandered to the window, watching Rachel's truck disappear over the hill.

"What was that about?" Lisa asked.

Kellan rubbed his neck. "She wanted to be sure I understood that if I hurt Amy, there'll be a reckoning."

"Gotta admire her," Chris said. "Rachel takes care of her own. Always has. We were in the same grade, kindergarten through high school graduation. All those years, no one bullied Amy or Jenna more than once, I can tell you that."

Kellan walked to Vaughn and slugged him in the arm. "You all right?"

A muscle in Vaughn's jaw twitched; his eyes remained fixed on the horizon. "That woman sucks the air out of a room. I can't believe you invited her to stay for dinner."

Kellan hadn't seen Vaughn so off his game in a while. "Did something happen with you and Rachel? Some kind of bad blood?"

Vaughn wiped his palms on his jeans. "I need a cigarette."

"No, you don't," Kellan said. "You quit smoking in

January. You're almost at your one-year anniversary. How about another beer instead?"

That earned him a wry huff. "Isn't that like fighting one vice with another?"

"I suppose. But beer won't give you lung cancer." He was already headed toward the refrigerator.

Chris wagged a finger in Vaughn's direction. "You said you logged a lot of hours at the Sorentino farm, so you must've spent a fair amount of time around Rachel. Why don't you like her?"

Vaughn ignored the question and motioned to the snack spread on the coffee table, a plastic-looking smile glued to his lips. "What's the deal, Kellan? It's half-time and I'm starving. You want me to fix the steaks myself? A man can't live on cheese alone."

After a split-second consideration, Kellan decided to follow his friend's lead. If Vaughn couldn't give voice to whatever was bothering him, then the least Kellan could do was play along with the topic change. "Nice try, but you know good and well no one touches that beef except me. I hand-picked the steer from my herd to butcher, then dry-aged the T-bones to perfection."

He marched to the kitchen to grab his grilling tools and the steaks resting on the counter. Something on top of the fridge caught his eye. The manila envelope. Chewing the inside of his cheek, he glanced over his shoulder. Everyone's eyes were glued to the half-time report on the television screen.

"A quick peek," he whispered, grabbing it. "Who's the unlucky bastard this time?"

He tipped the contents onto the counter. Several photographs fluttered to the floor. Kellan bent to retrieve them, but stayed doubled over, the wind knocked clean out of him as he looked on the whiskey brown eyes and full lips of the woman who'd been on his mind all weekend.

Amy Sorentino.

* * *

Amy's hands moved unflinchingly as she piped filling over long strips of raw pasta she'd rolled out on the counter. Pumpkin puree seasoned with cloves, coriander, cinnamon, and pancetta tempted her nose and she hummed with delight. After folding the pasta over the filling, she pressed the edges, then rummaged in a drawer for a pasta cutter.

Jenna's fingers paused over the laptop's keyboard. "That smells amazing, sweetie. Which recipe are you working on today?"

"A dish I developed at Terra Bistro. Pumpkin ravioli with a sage cream sauce. Give me about twenty minutes and I'll plate a sample for you."

"Good deal. I'll be ready for a break by then, anyway." She resumed typing. "The oil litigation attorney I'm contacting this week will want copies of our financial statements and the Amarex contract. I haven't found the contract yet, but I've got a few more places to look on the computer and in the attic."

"How's your progress with Dad's financial records going?"

"How do you think?"

"That bad, huh?"

Jenna chortled. "He didn't leave any sort of trail for us to follow to figure out what he did with the money. The money he got from the second mortgage he took out, his and Mom's IRAs, their savings accounts—it's all gone. He leveraged everything he and Mom owned. You'd think if he'd gambled it away or had an addiction, we would've found some evidence. But I haven't found anything."

Amy rolled the pasta cutter between the bumps of filling. "All I know is Dad left Mom high and dry when he died. It's no wonder she had a nervous breakdown."

"I wish she would've opened up to Rachel and me about

the money problems. She didn't need to shoulder that burden alone. We could've helped her."

Amy peeked into the pot on the stove to see how close to boiling the water was, then plunked onto a chair. "If there's one thing we've learned, Jen, with Dad dying and Mom's depression, it's that we can't let the *what ifs* get the best of us. Even when it's the toughest thing in the world, we have to keep moving forward."

"You're right, but it's so hard. Especially with the lawyer requiring us to dig up the past. That was brutal, talking to a complete stranger about Mom's condition. I understand his need to know everything to prove in court she needs a permanent guardian, but sitting there yesterday, describing the morning we found her . . ." She scrubbed a hand over her cheek, her eyes turned glassy with moisture. "That was rough."

A stab of guilt pierced Amy's gut as she hugged Jenna. She hadn't been home when her sisters discovered their mother unconscious in a pasture next to empty bottles of pills and vodka. Rachel had been the one to call 9-1-1 while Jenna administered CPR. Amy had spent the morning peeling and slicing Yukon Golds for a potato challenge on *Chef Showdown*. She'd flown to the hospital in Albuquerque that night, but it made no difference. The damage to her mother's brain and body was irreversible.

Jenna sucked in a slow breath, then seemed to shake off her sadness with a full-body shudder. "Oh, I almost forgot to tell you. I finished designing our Web page last night. The Heritage Farm Web site is ready to launch, pending yours and Rachel's approval."

"I've got a few minutes before the water boils. Let's check it out."

Beneath the splashy title *Heritage Farm* was a description. Amy read it aloud. "'Heritage Farm allows families to participate in the day-to-day running of a working farm.

Guests pick produce grown in the ranch's garden to be prepared for their dinner, assist in the feeding and care of livestock, and ride the fence line on horseback to take in the sweeping views of one of the most picturesque land-scapes in the world.'" Jenna had done a terrific job. Amy had no idea that she was so savvy with computers. "This sounds great. You've got a real knack for marketing and the page design is fantastic."

"Thanks."

Surprised and delighted, Amy read on. "'Guests of the farm stay in luxuriously appointed rooms in the main house, where they begin and end each day with locally grown, gourmet, multicourse meals prepared by—'"

Amy blinked at the screen, her stomach churning.

Jenna finished reading the passage. "'Prepared by na-tionally renowned chef and *Ultimate Chef Showdown* con-testant, Amy Sorentino.'"

Amy pressed a finger to her temple. "I hate that I'll never live down my appearance on that show."

"I know, sweetie, but the sort of publicity we will get from advertising your performance on *Chef Showdown* might be the key to Heritage Farm's success. We have to play that card."

"It was the worst experience of my life."

"Okay, true. But this is our farm I'm talking about. This"—she speared a finger toward the computer screen—"is our last chance to avoid foreclosure, pay for Mom's care, and keep a roof over all our heads. The producers from the Travel Channel will be arriving in January to film a piece that'll air around Valentine's Day. That's huge. Beyond huge. We have to do everything possible to pro-mote the business."

"You're right. I'm still making my peace with what happened on the show, but I'll be okay." She rose and eased the ravioli into the water, then adjusted the heat. *We have to keep moving forward.* Easier said than done.

"Have you gotten any nibbles on the job listing you posted?" Jenna asked.

"Not one." She'd placed ads online and in community newspapers across the state two weeks earlier, looking for a qualified sous-chef. "Hard to believe no one's jumping at the chance to work in a start-up restaurant that's hours away from the nearest big city, working under a failed reality show chef for a pittance."

"Don't be so hard on yourself. It'll work out. You'll see. With the way the economy's been plummeting the past few years, someone's bound to need a job. And once they're here, they'll sense how successful this little start-up restaurant's going to be."

The skeptic in Amy rejected Jenna's optimistic prediction, but even still, in her heart, she hoped Jenna was right—for all of their sakes. "How about, after you sample the ravioli, I'll get you up to speed on the beef supply contract? Maybe you can call Slipping Rock's office tomorrow morning and set up an appointment."

"I believe you have a date on Friday night with Slipping Rock's owner. You can talk to him about a contract yourself."

"No way. You have to handle it, Jenna. I can't be responsible for negotiating a business contract with Kellan. I'm a terrible judge of character—especially when it comes to cowboys. Look at the way he coerced me into going out with him. One kiss and I lost control. If I tried to bargain with him over beef prices, I'd probably bankrupt our business."

"Not all cowboys are bad news, you know."

Tucking a slotted spoon under her arm, Amy opened the fridge. "Wanna make a bet? You watched what happened on *Chef Showdown*, right?"

"I did. It sucked. Brock McKenna was a jerk."

Amy snorted as she rummaged for something to dice, finding a bag of celery, cabbage, and garlic she hadn't remembered buying. "*Jerk* is too nice an insult. That no-good, lying, cheating, rotten bastard tops the list of reasons I hate cowboys. But it's not only him. We can add Dad and every boyfriend I had in high school to that list. And every boyfriend you ever had. And pretty much every other cowboy I've ever had the misfortune of meeting."

"Then why do you keep sleeping with them?"

"Beats the hell out of me." She kicked the fridge door closed and slammed a bunch of celery on the counter. "Look, sis. I get how ridiculous an obsession it is. There's just something about cowboys. I can't explain it."

Grabbing a plate, she fished the tender ravioli out of the water with the slotted spoon, drizzled sage cream sauce over them, and set the plate under Jenna's nose. As Jenna dug in, moaning with bliss, Amy took her MAC knife in hand and got busy dicing, hoping to forget her problems for a while.

Too bad her thoughts kept slipping to Kellan's kiss that morning. Damn him. She couldn't even dice in peace since he had swaggered into her life. She dumped handfuls of diced celery into a bowl, frowning. Friday night, when he arrived to pick her up for the date he insisted on, a date she'd never agreed to, she'd have to find the guts to ask him to leave her alone. How hard could it be?

She grabbed a second bunch of celery from the fridge. Okay, time to be honest with herself. Telling Kellan to go away was bound to be near impossible, especially if he showed up in a truck, wearing that Stetson. She rolled her tongue over her bottom lip at the memory, felt a telltale rush of blood to her inner thighs, and picked the MAC up again, moving the knife over the cutting board with reckless speed.

Maybe she should make an exception to rule number one. Maybe she needed to give herself permission to satisfy her ridiculous desires with one more roll in the hay with the hottest cowboy she'd ever laid eyes on before sending him packing. It was a moral compromise that might work, but only if she kept her emotional boundaries in place. Because Amy's real problem wasn't so much about getting horizontal with cowboys, but her penchant for falling in love with them . . . and her heart had the scars to prove it.

Chapter 5

The clock was nearing midnight as Kellan approached the Texas state line en route to Amarillo. The deteriorating, neon-signed motels and trinket shops of Old Route 66 took on an aura of eerie vacancy in the shadowy darkness, like a ghost town from one of those low-budget horror movies Chris and Lisa were fond of. This was where the pretty young actress's car would break down, or where zombies would strike unsuspecting tourists.

The real-life demon lurking among the shabby buildings was the march of time, which is why Kellan hated this drive, always had. Nothing spelled defeat in his mind more than the route's crumbling businesses, with their desperate bid for survival by evoking nostalgia in an era when no one cared to look back. It was depressing as hell.

His truck was ushered into Texas by a gusty night wind that swirled and whipped the snow over the dull, dark landscape of endless flat plains. He reached across the center console to the passenger seat and ran his hand over the Sorentino file.

Thinking of Amy left him feeling dizzy, detached. Like he'd been dropped headfirst down a well. He'd proclaimed to everyone, from his friends and Rachel to Amy herself, that all he wanted was casual sex. But nothing about his attraction to her was casual. Not remotely.

One look at Amy at church and a ravenous, incendiary hunger replaced his every rational thought. One look and he'd wanted to drag her away and ravish her. He wanted to pleasure her with his tongue and fingers and cock until she was hoarse from screaming his name. Nothing casual about that.

So he'd kissed her after the service. Crushing her against the church office wall, he'd taken her mouth as he'd fantasized about for the previous hour straight.

That kiss scared the shit out of him.

Not because of his loss of control, as disconcerting as that was for a man who prided himself on maintaining careful command of his life, but because the moment their lips met, a deeper knowledge had overwhelmed his lust. Hope. Ridiculous, irrational hope that maybe, despite his aversion to drama and dysfunctional families, he and Amy might have a future together beyond their lust.

What a crock that hope had been. He wasn't at liberty to have a relationship, sexual or otherwise, with a defendant in a lawsuit by the company he was set to inherit. And if that wasn't frustrating enough, the minute Amy learned of Kellan's Amarex connection, she was going to hate him. He might be able to handle the sticky ethical issues, but he didn't have it in him to handle Amy's hatred.

He'd pored over her family's file that night after his friends left, studying the leasing contract between Gerald Sorentino and the oil company, analyzing photographs of expedition drilling sites all over their acreage, and parsing out the data of the expedition results until he'd memorized it. What he discovered chilled him to the bone.

Amarex was preparing to bankrupt Amy's family in order to buy their land. Of course, the legal jargon didn't phrase matters quite so bluntly, but it was all there in the oil leasing contract Gerald Sorentino signed. A clause stating that in the event of a foreclosure, Amarex had the opportunity to purchase every square inch of the Sorentino family's three thousand acres at a fraction of the market value. The fastest way to induce foreclosure was to drain the family's already meager coffers with a costly lawsuit.

What Morton wanted with the Sorentinos' oil-free, seemingly useless plot of land was anyone's guess. Sadistic as he was, perhaps the land itself didn't matter except as a means to provoke Kellan, as he was so fond of doing. No matter the reason, Kellan had two ways out of the situation. Either he could convince Morton to drop the lawsuit and void the oil leasing contract, or he could involve the law.

He fingered the digital recorder in his jacket pocket. Plan B. Involving the law didn't sit well with him because it would thrust him into the public eye along with his family's dirt. He had to try for Plan A, which was why he'd forfeited sleep and driven through a snowstorm to Morton's Amarillo estate.

The driveway of Morton's gated compound began twenty miles west of Amarillo and snaked through miles of desolate desert before ending at a brick wall fitted with a wrought-iron entrance gate. Instead of buzzing the intercom, he dialed Morton's number on his cell phone.

"Kellan, my boy, are you phoning to tell me you've convinced the Sorentino family to sell?" Morton sounded fresh and alert, despite the late hour. The security cameras would've shown him at the gate, so Kellan didn't get why Morton was putting on the ignorant act.

He tightened his grip on the steering wheel. "Buzz me through."

The silence on the other end of the phone was weighted. He could see, in his mind, Morton's smug, sinister smile. "Certainly. What an intriguing surprise."

My ass.

The gate retracted. Kellan ended the call and eased off the brakes. On the winding quarter-mile drive to the main house, Kellan reviewed his strategy. The worst mistake he could make tonight would be to let slip any clue of his personal relationship with Amy. If Morton got a whiff of Kellan's feelings, there was no doubt in his mind he'd redouble his efforts to destroy the Sorentinos, if only because it would torture Kellan.

He crested the final hill to see Morton's southwest-style, sprawling single-story estate shrouded in darkness, save for the faint glow of light from behind a thickly curtained window. The yard's desert landscape seemed to cower beneath a dusting of fresh snow. The moment Kellan's truck hit the cement pavers of the circular drive, four glaring floodlights clicked on.

He reached into his jacket pocket and pressed *RECORD*. The tape would be uploaded to his computer, as had his every conversation with Morton for the past ten years. Regardless of whether he ever made use of them, it felt good—powerful—to have an ace up his sleeve. Hunkering into his jacket, he crunched over the pavers while wind and snow slapped at his body. One of the double doors opened, silhouetting Morton's stocky frame and buzz-cut hair.

Morton squinted at the sky. "Looks like it's going to be a wild one tonight. Helluva storm brewing on the plains." He gave the door a push and backed off so Kellan could pass through. "I've been expecting you."

An approaching rumble of dogs barking—either with excitement or menace, Kellan could never decide—greeted his arrival. With one decisive whistle, Morton commanded three huge, muscular brown dogs to heel a few feet behind him. The dogs sat, but protested with a string of low growls, their beady eyes locked on Kellan.

Morton rubbed a hand over the nearest dog's head. It continued to growl, its gums dripping with saliva. "Has the snow reached Quay County yet?"

Kellan shoved past the dogs, each of whom probably weighed almost as much as he did, and moved farther into a Spanish-tiled entrance hall. The house was cool, cold even, and smelled of cigars, furniture oil, and the residual odor of a long-ago fire in the hearth. "Blew in a couple hours ago. The forecast said the real weather'll pick up around three."

"I heard tell of three or four inches of snow by the time the storm front moves on. We might even have ourselves a white Christmas."

Ironic that Morton would mention Christmas because, although December 25 was less than three weeks away, not a single decoration adorned his sprawling estate. Kellan felt the absence of a woman's touch as much as he'd felt it in his own house before he'd thrown a huge decorating budget at Lisa and granted her free reign to fix the problem. Morton's house hadn't always been so inhospitable. His wife, Eileen, had managed to make the place downright cheery until the day she disappeared.

Kellan followed the clink of Morton's black boots through the hall to his office. The dogs jostled Kellan in their push to catch up with their master. Whereas the rest of the house smelled pleasantly of cigar smoke, Morton's office reeked of it. A collection of stubbed-out stogies crowded a metal ashtray atop a desk the size of a Ping-Pong table. One continued to send a tendril of smoke into the air. Lining the walls were bookshelves weighted with leather-bound volumes of oil and mineral rights laws interspersed with framed photos of Morton's dogs. Not only the three presently sprawled on the carpet, but every dog that had been lucky enough to call him its owner.

"How many of those mutts are you up to now?" Kellan couldn't help but ask.

Morton gestured for him to sit in a stiff-looking chair before sloshing caramel-colored liquor into two lowball glasses. "You ought to take more care with your vocabulary, son. These *mutts* are *Dogue de Bordeaux* purebreds.

They're worth a helluva lot more than your prized steers, that's for damn sure."

Not even a fancy French name could soften the fact that these were mastiffs, bred for bulk and strength, with jaws that could rip a man's arm off in a heartbeat should they be so inclined. He nudged one's hind leg with his boot. It whipped its head up and growled a warning. "Still, what's the count? Fifteen? Twenty? Can you even tell them apart anymore? They all look the same to me."

Morton huffed and offered Kellan a glass before perching on the edge of his desk.

Kellan sniffed the drink. Bourbon. Probably the good stuff, knowing his uncle. Rubbing his nostrils against the fumes of alcohol still tingling there, he set the drink on the nearest table.

With his legs crossed at the ankles, Morton regarded Kellan over the lip of the glass as he sipped his drink. "It's nearly one o'clock in the morning, so let's get right to business. What can I do for you?"

Kellan folded his hands over his chest, faking the same kind of confidence he utilized when negotiating steer prices. "My property, Slipping Rock Ranch, what year did you purchase it?" Kellan knew the answer, but dates and facts seemed like an easy place to start.

Morton scratched his head. "Round about 1985. The spring of that year, I believe."

"Why? What interested you in the land?"

"That's a stupid question from an otherwise smart man. Oil, of course."

"It's not enough for you to pull a salary and bonuses through the company, is it? Any oil-rich land you personally acquire reaps exponentially more cash because the profits land straight in your bank account. Is that right?"

"That's how entrepreneurship works. Doesn't make it criminal, if that's what you're implying. Every property I invest in brings me huge gains when the gamble pays off. It doesn't always, but it's a risk worth taking."

"Then it's fair to assume you've gambled on other properties over the years and achieved better results than the Slipping Rock acreage?"

Morton tossed back the remainder of his drink and walked to the decanter for a refill. "Damn right. A man doesn't become as successful as I have without diversifying."

"At the expense of home owners."

Morton inclined his head, but didn't answer. He sloshed a finger of liquor into his glass.

"Back to Quay County," Kellan said. "After the Amarex exploration crew determined there was no oil to be had under the property that would become Slipping Rock Ranch, you abandoned it. Until I came along."

Morton resumed his perch on the edge of the desk. "Why are we rehashing this?"

"Just making sure I understand everything clearly. So you didn't have any idea before the exploration crew did their thing that my property was dry?"

"Like I said. All the land surrounding it was saturated with pockets of crude oil. It was a fair assumption I'd find oil under that dirt too."

Kellan took a sip and pushed the bourbon around the roof of his mouth with his tongue. "Not all the surrounding land, as it turned out."

Morton chortled. "Well, here we are, then. The real reason for your house call. You want to talk about the Sorentino property. Go ahead and talk."

"Their land is as dry as mine."

"So the exploration crew declared, yes."

"According to the documentation I read, three separate exploration crews have scoured the lot over the last twenty years. Found nothing but dirt and rock every time."

"As we've already covered, the oil business involves a

bit of gambling and a hefty dose of intuition. Sometimes, that intuition is wrong."

Kellan rose. Containing his frustration was becoming more difficult by the minute. Already, his hands quivered and he detected a telltale strain in his voice. Sidestepping the dogs and the desk, he walked with a measured stride to the bookshelves and ran his hands over the smooth, leather bindings of the law books. He was struck by their benign, impotent presence in the room. Struck by the absurd notion that the rules governing people's lives could be harnessed thusly—stripped of humanity, organized, bound, and left on shelves to collect dust.

He picked absentmindedly at a fraying corner of leather. "Why is Amarex fighting so hard to purchase a dry piece of property?"

"It's none of your concern."

"None of my concern?" He turned and looked Morton full in the face. "You made it my concern the night you had a courier deliver the file to my house. Why did you do that, if you didn't want me sticking my nose in your business?"

Morton took a long sip of bourbon, his gaze steady on Kellan. "I have my reasons."

"I'd like to hear them."

Smacking his lips, Morton set the glass on his desk and rose to his full height. "I invited you into Amarex's confidence on this particular problem because you seem to sneak your way into every one of my Quay County business deals whether I want you to or not. Thought I'd save you some trouble by providing the information up front."

Kellan's bullshit meter was sounding the alarm again. "You're being generous, is that all?"

"I'm being generous, yes."

"Not because you're a manipulative bastard?"

"Think what you want about me, son. But that still doesn't explain why you care so much about the Sorentino deal that you'd honor me with a rare visit. Maybe you're hard for one of those cute, young sisters." He shoved off the desk, walked around, and opened a drawer. "Ah, my copy of the file."

He shook the contents onto the desktop and spread the photos out. "Let's see. Three sisters. Brunette, brunette, and a blond. Whose skirt are you chasing?"

Kellan swallowed, watching Morton poke Amy's pretty face with his stubby finger, but he kept his expression steady. "Never mind about them. I want to know what it is about the Sorentino property that's got you falling all over yourself to grab a hold of it."

"You want to know what I'm thinking?"

"That's why I drove through a storm and crossed a state line in the middle of the night."

Morton made a show of placing his lowball glass on a coaster on the desk. "What I think, my dear nephew, is that I've given you too much over the years to deserve this sort of insolence."

Unreal, the nerve of this prick who dared to call himself Kellan's family. "And what, specifically, have you given me, *Uncle Dearest?*"

"I gave you a ranch."

Kellan felt fury uncoiling inside him. He clamped his molars together, fighting his anger and losing the battle. "No. You loaned me a goddamn piece of dirt and I turned it into a ranch with my own sweat and blood."

"With fifty thousand dollars of my money."

Kellan sprang forward, knocking his thigh against the desk. The desk rattled, sloshing bourbon up the side of Morton's glass. "Which I paid back with interest. Along with your ridiculous asking price for the property."

The dogs roused, growling. One positioned itself between the two men. Morton stepped from behind the desk, butting his legs against the animal's side. "You ungrateful son of a bitch. I've given you more than you ever deserved."

Kellan stabbed a finger at the air between them. The growls grew more intense. "You haven't given me jack shit. Everything I have in my life, I've created myself. You had nothing to do with it."

"That's a nice story you've fabricated, but I've got a different recollection. Of an eighteen-year-old homeless punk, nothing but skin and bones, looking for a handout—like your folks did. It got to the point that when I heard a Reed was in town, I hid my wallet."

"When I was eighteen, I didn't come to you for a handout. I came here looking for answers about why, when my brother and I needed a place to live, no one in the family stepped up. About why, with relatives rolling in Texas oil money, Jake and I got sent to fucking foster care."

All three dogs were up now, standing guard over their master, baring their teeth and snarling at Kellan. Their short, brown fur quivered with hostile energy.

Morton's lips curled into a mean grin. "You think you've got it all figured out, don't you? You sit up there on your pedestal of righteousness and point your finger at me like you're God himself."

"Answer my question. Why did you leave us in the system?"

"You already know what I'm going to say. Eileen had a nervous condition, didn't tolerate children well. Two teenage boys would've killed her."

Kellan sneered. "Wouldn't that have saved you the trouble?"

"You better watch what you're implying."

Kellan glanced side to side and spread his arms, his eyes wide with mock-concern. "Where is Eileen? I haven't seen her going on three years. What did you tell me last time I asked—Texas was too hot a climate for her? That she'd run off to Hawaii or something?"

"Yes, Hawaii. And you'd do well to back off that line of questioning."

"One of these days, you're going to get your comeuppance, Morton. Someone, somewhere, is going to kill you."

Rocking onto his heels, Morton laughed. "But it won't be you, Kellan. That conscience of yours will always be a liability."

"My conscience is what keeps me from turning into you, old man."

Morton's eyes twinkled maliciously. "I'm going to ask you one last time. Why the hell did you come to my house tonight?"

Kellan rubbed his upper arms, feeling the pressure of his heart thudding hard and fast against his ribs. The dogs pressed forward, snapping their jaws, pushing him back from Morton. He relented and walked across the room, reaching for the bourbon. They were arguing in circles, like they usually did, but at least they were back to the information Kellan needed. "What do you want with the Sorentino property?"

"I want to own the Sorentino property, you dumb shit. That's why I'm encouraging the sisters to sell it to Amarex and Amarex to sell it to me."

"The property's dry."

"So it's dry. I still want it. If you have it in your mind to stop me, you should know you're going to fail."

Kellan lifted the lowball glass in a gesture of salute. "You're throwing down the gauntlet, Morton? All right, I accept."

Morton relaxed against the desk, folding his arms across his chest. "You and I are playing on the same side. You do know that, right?"

Kellan tossed the bourbon back and relished the rush of heat down his throat. "We might share blood, but that doesn't put us on the same side."

"All these years, I've been waiting for you to come around to my way of thinking. To join my empire. But you're so stuck on past resentments, you can't see the forest for the trees. Damn shame, it is. You and I could've been partners."

Kellan slammed the empty glass onto the desk. "It'll be a cold day in hell before that happens."

"I see that now. Doesn't make it any easier of a pill to swallow."

The dogs preceded the men to the front door as though eager for the unwanted guest to depart.

Morton paused with his hand on the doorknob. "The Sorentinos have a week to sign the property over to Amarex before I unleash the lawyers."

Kellan didn't trust himself to speak. He pushed past Morton and continued to the driveway.

"I forgot to mention," Morton said. Kellan kept walking. "Tina called me."

That stopped Kellan in his tracks. Strange, the way his mother's name set off a clash of emotions within him—revulsion at the idea of receiving a surprise phone call from the woman he'd avoided for nineteen years, and yet anger that she hadn't at least tried to call him instead of her brother.

"You want details, but you're too afraid to ask." Morton's tone had an edge of triumph.

Kellan thought about turning to face Morton. He thought about socking him in the jaw. He thought about the rifle in his car. But rather than play into his uncle's hand by pressing for more information, he set his sights on his truck and kept moving.

Morton's sinister chuckle followed him across the driveway. "Guess what the big news is? Your father's out of prison."

Chapter 6

Kellan squeezed his eyes closed. His father was a free man.

Morton's voice carried across the driveway. "You'll never guess why Tina called—or maybe you will." His voice held a note of amusement. "I'll give you a hint. Nothing's changed."

Nothing's changed. Those two words said it all. She wanted money. She could claim she'd come around to apologize, or that she missed her children, but once she ran out of sweet little lies, the truth came out. Every time.

"She asked me to front her some cash until she can get settled in a new place," Morton hollered at Kellan's back before dissolving into cruel chuckles.

Kellan opened his door and climbed into the cab, willing his expression to blank now that Morton had a side view of his face.

Did she sound sober? he wanted to ask. *Where are she and my dad planning to live? Did you give them money?*

He jammed the key into the ignition and started the engine, drowning out Morton's laughter.

His truck cut through the snow and wind, through endless miles of dark desert and across the state line.

He'd thought he'd breathe deeply once he saw the wooden SLIPPING ROCK RANCH sign waving on the side of the road, but his anxiety only mounted at the sight—the symbol of the life he'd fought to create despite his family's unrelenting efforts to drag him down.

The truck tires crunched onto the snow-drenched half-mile dirt driveway leading to his house. He would not stand for it. He'd worked too hard, for too long, to let the Reeds and Mortons muck up his peaceful existence. The ranch house stood like a beacon in the storm, stalwart and welcoming. This was all he wanted to be—a quiet rancher in a small town, a respected member of the community, unmarred by gossip or family strife. With a beautiful house, a successful cattle business, and great friends he could count on and who counted on him.

Dread ballooned in his chest, threatening to rip him apart from the inside out. He had to get control of the situation before it came to light. He could not let his parents get their greedy claws in him. Six years ago, the last time his father was a free man, they'd honed in on Kellan's weaknesses like the criminals they were and blackmailed him, threatening to appear in Catcher Creek unless he paid up.

He tried to inhale a deep, lung-filling breath, but it caught in his throat.

He pulled into his usual spot next to the barn and sat in the darkness, fingering the digital recorder. His brother needed to know Dad had been released from prison. He deserved a warning. Somewhere in his desk drawer, he probably had Jake's number, but it had been a long time since the two last talked, and to say the conversation had been strained would be a gross understatement.

Kellan needed to get straight in his mind before calling Jake. Tonight, he couldn't cope with any more conflict. After his morning ranch chores, he'd make the call, no matter how difficult it was sure to be. He flipped through the Amarex file on Amy's family and found her photograph. Her beautiful face and trusting eyes stared up at him. Needing his help. With a curse, he flung the truck door open and stomped through the biting wind to his house.

Enough was enough. He was fresh out of good will.

He wouldn't waste another thought, another breath on his parents. Or Morton. Or Amy Sorentino. They were nothing more than headaches that made him doubt who he was and what he wanted from his life. What he needed to do was wash his hands of everything and everyone who took his eyes off the prize. He'd call his brother during the day so he'd be sure to get flipped to voice mail. Then he'd cancel his date with Amy and advise her to contact his lawyer buddy, Matt. If his mom called, he'd tell her she'd have to find a handout somewhere else.

He strode through his darkened kitchen to the living room, tossing the digital recorder on his desk, and turned the Christmas tree lights on. Max regarded him curiously from the kitchen before trotting from the room.

A press of a button and holiday music filled the air. The ambiance always calmed him, the glow of twinkling lights, the soothing melodies of Christmas carols. As a kid, the closest he came to this perfect holiday scene was standing in a department store among the floor models of artificial trees. He would sneak to the toy department, load his arms with everything he'd never get, and place them under the trees. And he'd pretend they were for him. He'd playact the Christmas morning of his fantasy, mimicking the ripping open of wrapping paper. He'd act surprised to receive such glorious toys. He'd pretend to hug and thank his imaginary parents for their generosity.

Pathetic.

Tonight, he lit the gas fireplace and a fire burst into

being. Then it was on to the cinnamon-scented candles on the mantel and coffee table. He didn't need to pretend anymore. He had everything he wanted and only had himself to thank. Life didn't get any better.

He stood in the center of the room, breathing hard through flared nostrils. The tree lights glowed and reflected off the innumerable wrapped presents around its base. "Silent Night" played from the stereo speakers. He inhaled the scents of cinnamon and evergreen and spun a slow circle in the center of the room. It looked like the home in his childhood imagination. It was perfect.

Why didn't it bring him peace tonight?

Amy. Her big, trusting eyes. Her family on the verge of catastrophe at the hands of his uncle's company. He dropped to his favorite chair and focused his gaze on the tree. He sung the lyrics to "Silent Night" under his breath, concentrating on clearing his mind.

It was no use.

He couldn't get Amy out of his head. She'd been so warm and soft crushed between his body and the church office wall. She'd tasted of sugar from the doughnut she'd shoveled into her mouth so she wouldn't have to talk to him. His lips twitched into a smile at the memory of the way she'd broken into a flat-out sprint through the sanctuary to avoid him.

She probably ran because, like him, she knew if the two of them got up close and personal, the pull of attraction was too powerful to deny. She flipped a switch in him, a crackling of electricity. And when he touched her, they'd both felt the surge of hot, unrelenting need. The promise of ecstasy in her arms, in that luscious body that seemed custom made to fit against his.

With a growl, he rolled his neck, annoyed by how tough it was to get past his attraction to her. His desk in the corner of the room caught his eye and he stood. What he needed was a reminder of all the ways she was wrong for him. Not only because of her problems with Amarex, but because she was the opposite of the kind of woman he wanted in his life. She humiliated herself on national television, so everyone had whispered at the time that chef show aired. Like her mother, she'd disgraced her family name, folks had said. Was that the kind of person he wanted in his life? One who couldn't keep her dignity in check while the world was watching?

Hell, no.

The words "Amy Sorentino *Chef Showdown*" entered into a search engine were enough to take him straight to a complete series listing for *Ultimate Chef Showdown*, season five.

He positioned the pointer over *PLAY* for episode one, but stopped. Why did he feel guilty, as though he were violating her privacy? There was nothing private about appearing on a nationwide syndicated prime time reality show. Everyone in Catcher Creek, save for farmers like him who went to bed at nine o'clock and rose at four, knew every intimate detail of her abbreviated stint as a celebrity.

He pressed *PLAY*. It was time to find out what all the fuss was about.

The opening sequence introduced the competing chefs with a cheesy voice-over calling each one's name as if they'd been selected to appear on *The Price Is Right* while flashing an image of them in chef jackets, striking poses while holding various kitchen utensils. Amy was the fifth chef introduced. She'd been glammed up, with fluffy, perfectly coiffed hair and lots of makeup, her white teeth gleaming, her pose awkward. The real Amy still managed to come through in the hint of mischief twinkling in her eyes and the skilled swish of the knife she brandished as her prop.

One of the contestants was done up like a Hollywood

version of a cowboy, with a huge, gold belt buckle, snug Wrangler jeans, and a new black Stetson. Brock the Cowboy Cook, he called himself. He had the look and drawl of the Texas rodeo star he claimed to be, but Kellan wasn't convinced.

Amy was, though. She took to him like a kid to an ice cream truck. It struck a nerve, watching her fall for his lame act, the bald look of desire in her eyes. It was the same look she'd given Kellan at the Quick Stand. A roll of unease coursed through him.

When the first minor challenge began, in which contestants were asked to create a signature omelet, he was irrationally anxious for her. He knew the outcome of the show, but couldn't stop himself from rooting for her to thump her competition.

And she did. Handily.

Throughout the episode, every contestant on the show became known by a stereotypical label of some sort, courtesy of the show's editors. There was a vegan "hippie," a hot-blooded Italian-American, and an older woman who played "grandma" to the younger chefs. Amy was "America's Sweetheart." She was funny and determined, yet never vindictive. Often, the producers edited her remarks to make her sound dim-witted or naive. Kellan had only known her for a couple days, but he couldn't believe what an oversimplification the label was. No one made it as far in the culinary world as she had without being a smart, savvy businessperson. And she'd shown him Saturday morning in his bed exactly how not-naive she was.

Cowboy Brock was positioned as one of the show's villains. In periodic camera confessionals, he expounded on his diabolical plans to win the title by manipulating the other contestants. He came across as such a lowlife that Kellan wanted to reach into the computer monitor and punch him in the face until he remembered that the producers were doing their own Hollywood-style manipulation with the show's editing. He'd played right into their hands.

Despite the show's attempt to degrade Amy's competence, she sliced, diced, and seared her way through the season premiere, grabbing the first major win with her unique spin on Beef Carpaccio, Thai style. She was a culinary genius, plain and simple.

As the episode's ending credits rolled, Kellan's eyes burned with the need to sleep. Yet Amy's magic on screen had mesmerized him. He needed more of her. Before he could think too deeply on why that was, he pressed *PLAY* on episode two and smiled through the opening at the sight of Amy, with her confident smile, her bouncing, curly hair, and her knife swishing through the air.

He settled in his chair, less anxious about how she'd perform. If he'd learned anything from episode one, it was that Amy was remarkable. Not only a top-class chef, but an amazing contestant. Driven by a fierce competitive fire she didn't sacrifice her integrity or kindness.

The second episode, then the third and fourth, drove home her position as the show's early front-runner. No matter how Cowboy Brock and his fellow villains sabotaged her, she overcame every obstacle and created fantastic dishes the judges loved. If Brock turned off her pot of boiling water, she turned it on and persevered. If he coerced her into sharing her limited ingredients, she still schooled him in the eyes of the judges. She was consistently—remarkably—wonderful. Of course, he'd already glimpsed her unflappability. She'd endured setback after setback in her career and her family, but she didn't let anything slow her down.

Near the end of the fourth episode, a funny noise in the distance caught his attention. The blare of his clock radio alarm in his bedroom. He looked at his watch. It was four o'clock in the morning. The interruption irked him. Amy had made it through another Judges Trial and looked poised to continue her reign in episode five. Reluctantly, he rubbed his eyes, stretched the kinks out of his back, and stood. Time for another workday to begin.

He left the computer on, the screen displaying *Ultimate Chef Showdown*'s homepage. Tonight, he'd pick up where he left off.

By midmorning on Monday, Amy was ready for a hot shower and a nap. The alarm had been set to ring at five, but Rachel had shaken her awake at four. A storm had hit during the night and she and Jenna needed all possible manpower to dig the ranch out from the snow and feed the animals. The snowdrifts were a mere three feet, but since they'd let the last of their farmhands go after discovering the empty bank accounts, the storm added hours of work to their day.

Amy was all for helping her sisters, but years of kitchen work had conditioned her body in a particular way that wasn't too useful for manual labor. She could stand at a prep table for ten straight hours, or reach her fingers into boiling water to test pasta, but her calluses and muscles were in all the wrong places for shoveling snow and mucking stalls. After six brutal hours of fighting wind and snow flurries, her hair was snarled, her cheeks felt raw, and her body ached all over. It was a jarring reminder of a fact she'd realized in high school—she was not cut out to be a farmer. *At all*.

She'd worked doubly hard in an effort to keep up with Jenna and Rachel, chipping ice from frozen water troughs, feeding the livestock, mending fence lines. The mini-CAT bulldozer Rachel used for distributing feed and hay wouldn't start, so they delivered breakfast to their stock one wheelbarrow at a time. Not that there were many animals left. Most had been sold, but they'd retained enough horses, cattle, pigs, and chickens to give guests of Heritage Farm a taste, albeit an idyllic one, of life on a farm.

Sometimes, like this morning, Amy couldn't help but think of the venture uneasily, like they were pushing a kind of a scam, exploiting their guests' ignorance of the reality of farm life. Because actual farm work was relentless and tough. It involved mornings like this, working to keep your hands from freezing in the predawn hours of winter, ignoring the rumble of hunger in your stomach until the animals were cared for. Praying for a miracle to pay the bills.

Amy felt guilty packing up her snow shovel at ten, but she had a great excuse. Her eleven o'clock appointment with Lisa from Binderman Dairy. She stood for as long as she could justify in a hot shower, but the nap would remain a fantasy.

Binderman Dairy sat along the historic Old Route 66 section of Highway 40, which demarcated the northern border of Catcher Creek. The dairy hadn't existed when Amy was a kid. The Binderman family had bred dairy goats as far back as anyone could remember, but the dairy had been the brainchild of Chris and Lisa Binderman. Amy had done her homework about all the ranches and producers she hoped to contract with, from wineries to herb farmers, and had been surprised to learn Binderman Dairy was a separate company from Binderman Farm, Chris's parents' property.

Amy pulled into the small, icy parking lot and stared at the roof of the building, at the huge, rotating, white fiberglass round of cheese with a picture of a goat in the middle. The kitschy design had probably been Chris and Lisa's brainchild as well. No doubt, it was eye-catching and fit right in with the rest of the shops along the highway, but it didn't exactly scream *sophisticated organic cheeses inside.*

She watched the cheese spin for one more rotation, then checked her makeup and hair in the rearview mirror, grabbed her briefcase, and reluctantly left the warmth of her car. She'd never met Lisa, but she'd seen her at church the day before and she looked kind. She had that same nurturing aura as Jenna did, like most good moms did. Plus, Amy had known the Binderman family her whole life and kind of figured this supply contract was a sure bet if only as a favor between neighbors.

Lisa stood behind the counter, wearing a pristine chef coat. Her dark blond hair had been pulled into a tight bun and covered by black netting. When the chime of the door sounded, she looked up from the ledger she was studying and offered Amy a wide, genuine smile. Amy returned the smile and closed the door behind her, shutting out the cold and the wind.

What struck her about the shop, besides its clean, simple interior, was the mouthwatering aroma of tangy cheese and baking bread. Amy's culinary imagination stirred to life. A half-dozen recipe ideas sprung into her head between the short walk from the door to the display. Sure enough, behind the counter sat an electronic bread machine. The top edge of a baking loaf was visible through the glass lid, its dough still pale in color. Maybe their meeting would run long enough that she'd get to sample a slice when it was done.

After the two women exchanged introductions and handshakes, Amy couldn't help but ask about the bread maker. "Why bread? Is it for cheese samples?"

Lisa leaned over the counter, like she was going to share a secret. "The truth? I got the idea from a Realtor friend of mine who bakes chocolate-chip cookies inside the houses she's selling right before a walk-through or open house. She says the smell sells the houses. Something about evoking potential buyers' childhood memories. So I thought, people don't eat cheese because of the way it smells, they buy it because of the way it tastes when paired with other foods. I want people to smell the bread and imagine themselves spreading our goat cheese on a slice fresh from the oven."

Amy nodded her approval. "Genius. That's precisely what I thought when I walked in."

"Ha! Good. It works like a charm. I sell more cheese when I've got the bread going than any other time of the week."

Lisa directed Amy to a table for two near a window. "For the record, I loved your pitch over the phone. A restaurant featuring local ingredients is a fantastic idea. Might add a little zest to this sleepy town."

Catcher Creek seemed to have all the zest it needed. Kellan Reed's perfect jean-clad ass popped into her mind. No, Catcher Creek had been anything but sleepy since day one of her return. Heat crept up around her neck and she tugged the collar of her sweater, hoping to cool off before Lisa noticed. "Glad you're on board with the idea because I'd love to feature Binderman cheese."

She took the contract proposal from her briefcase and slid it to Lisa, who rummaged through her chef coat pocket and produced green-rimmed reading glasses. Amy held her breath as Lisa skimmed the first page. With a nod, she glanced up and smiled at Amy. "You know what you need to be doing while I read this? You need to be eating cheese."

"I thought you'd never ask."

In minutes, she had a plate of delectable-looking cheeses and crackers before her. She dug into the most unique one, a round wrapped in a grape leaf. Forgoing the cracker, she sliced off a chunk and popped it into her mouth. It melted on her tongue, a complex yet delicate palate of tang and salty cream with an undertone of herbiness from the leaf. All Amy needed now was for the bread timer to *ding*. She closed her eyes, lost in pleasure, and rolled the cheese over the roof of her mouth, reluctant to swallow.

"This contract looks great," Lisa said after a while, rousing Amy from her euphoria.

"Terrific. Because this cheese is to die for. I'm talking, last-meal greatness here."

"Thank you."

"I have an off-topic question," Amy said.

"Shoot."

"I'm looking to hire a sous-chef for the Local Dish, but I'm coming up short on applicants." Really short. As in none. "Any chance you know of a trained chef looking for work? Maybe someone you've done business with?"

Lisa tapped her chin. Amy slid another bite of cheese from the knife onto her tongue. This one was firmer and crusted with finely chopped pistachios. Heavenly.

"I sure do," Lisa said with a snap of her fingers. "Do you know Jillian Dixon? She and I play Bunco every Thursday night. You should join us, by the way."

It was kind of hard to focus on anything but the cheese. She had the crazy urge to grab the plate and make a break for the door. Dixon. The name sounded familiar. "I remember a Stephen Dixon. He and I were in the same grade growing up."

"Yes. Jillian's his wife. They run Dixon Ranch now that Stephen's uncle died and his father, Douglas, has back problems."

"Whereabouts is Dixon Ranch? I can't picture it."

"Northwest corner of town. Catcher Creek cuts right through their acreage."

"And you think Jillian might be interested in work as a sous-chef?"

"Oh my gosh, no. Have you ever tasted Jillian's ambrosia

salad? She brings it to every church social." Amy shook her head. "Lucky you. Trust me—you don't want Jillian anywhere near your kitchen. I was talking about Douglas Dixon, her father-in-law."

"The retired rancher with back problems?" Lord help her if her professional standards sunk that low.

Lisa chuckled. "That makes him sound old, but he's only sixty-something. Before he worked the family ranch with his brother, he was a Navy cook. Tells the best stories about life on an aircraft carrier, feeding all those sailors day in and day out. Stephen and Jillian are going crazy with him underfoot at the ranch. And Douglas isn't so happy either. He's got a lot of life left in him and I imagine he feels pretty useless these days. You'd be doing them all a big favor if you gave Douglas a chance."

"I'm not in the business of doing favors right now. I'm starting a restaurant."

"Then hiring Douglas is exactly what you need to do. Think of the good karma."

"Karma?" Sheesh. That was a stretch. Still, she had to hand it to Lisa; she was one heck of a saleswoman.

As if she could read Amy's mind, she flashed a bright smile and patted Amy's arm. "I'll make a deal with you. Give Douglas a try as your sous-chef for two weeks and I'll deliver Binderman cheese to your restaurant at cost for the first three months."

Holy cow. Amy thrust her hand out and Lisa shook it with a solid grip. "Lisa, it's not my place to say, but I think you're in the wrong industry. You're a natural-born saleswoman."

Chuckling again, Lisa folded the reading glasses and placed them in her pocket. "That may be true, but I wouldn't give this life up for anything. Making cheese is my passion. And the fact that I work alongside the love of my life is icing on the cake."

Jealousy and admiration battled within Amy. She'd failed at both her career and finding love. Maybe she did need an infusion of good karma. "That's wonderful. Your life is blessed."

Despite Amy's smile, Lisa seemed to sense her turmoil because she stood and pulled Amy into a surprise hug. "You'll be fine, Amy. Your family's tough. You and your sisters—you'll get through this because you have each other to lean on. And family's the biggest blessing of all."

"You got that right. I didn't always see that clearly, but I sure do now."

Lisa scribbled a phone number on the back of her business card and pressed it into Amy's hand. "Here's Douglas's number. Go ahead and draw up a new supply contract for me. You can stop by later this week with it."

"Thank you." Amy took the hint that the meeting had come to a close and said a silent good-bye to the half-eaten cheese plate. Just barely, she resisted the urge to swipe one last taste with her fingertip.

"You're welcome." Amy was at the door when Lisa called, "By the way, have fun on your date with Kellan."

Amy looked over her shoulder. "Word travels fast in Catcher Creek."

"I only know because he's close friends with Chris. We were at his house for dinner last night and I could tell, when your name came up, that he's into you. Really into you."

"Oh." Lisa's words thrilled Amy, even as they terrified her. She didn't want Kellan to be into her . . . did she? "We're not . . . it's not a date. We'll probably spend the whole time talking business. You know, a supply contract for Slipping Rock beef." Lordy, her face was hot. Time to leave. She flung the door open and stuck her head into the gust of cold air that swept through the threshold.

"Of course. How silly of me."

Amy gave a little wave of Lisa's business card, praying she didn't look as jumpy as she felt. "Okay, then. I'll give Mr. Dixon a call. Bye now."

On the road, all thoughts of cheese and Kellan disappeared as Amy's car skidded across a patch of ice. She corrected before plowing into the shoulder, then grinned. Kind of fun, actually. Like a whirly ride at an amusement park.

Yet she missed the zippy sports car she'd driven in L.A. and sold to afford the plane ticket home. The modest-priced sedan from the used car lot in Albuquerque didn't handle ice all that well. Snow either. Or rain. Come to think of it, it didn't handle well in the best of conditions. She pressed on the gas pedal. The engine strained to accommodate her need for speed and the tires slipped and slid along the five miles to Cousins Wine Cellar, the next stop on her errand list. Iffy tire tread was probably to blame, but Rachel would've yammered on about how the tires were fine, and Amy's problem was that she took corners too fast.

Whatever.

Amy loved the way she drove, the unabashed freedom of speed. It was the one reckless vice she allowed herself without guilt.

The errands only took a couple hours and, by early afternoon, she was bouncing along the dirt road to her house. In the backseat, the two cases of New Mexico-produced wine from Cousins rattled in protest of the horrible road conditions, as did Amy's teeth.

That was one aspect of country living she hadn't missed—the dirt roads. Rachel and Jenna had outvoted her when she'd suggested they pave the quarter-mile driveway to ease guests' passage. They'd insisted the dirt road added to Heritage Farm's rustic appeal. It was no use arguing with the two of them when they banded together. Amy figured she'd sock away some cash and eventually add a paved rear entrance to the property. And she wasn't going to ask her sisters' permission, either.

Two people waited on Amy's front porch. Amy gazed with curiosity at her unexpected guests and made short work of gathering her purse and phone and unfolding herself from the car. She recognized Sloane Delgado immediately, though her hair had been released from the severe ponytail of the day before to fall in black curtains around her face. Her cheeks were rosy and her legs bare and pale beneath the hem of her skirt. When she saw Amy, she stood and smiled anxiously. Amy couldn't imagine why the young woman was paying her a visit, but she had the sinking feeling it had to do with whatever she'd agreed to at church while using Sloane and Charlene as a Kellanshield.

An older man sat next to Sloane on the bench rocker, wearing a dark brown cowboy hat that he doffed the moment Amy stepped from her car. He also stood up, but it took him a while and he wore a terrible frown of exertion.

"Hello, Sloane. What a surprise."

The previous night's storm had moved west, and though it was still cold, the sun had pierced the cloud cover enough to melt the snow on the house's roof. Water dripped relentlessly from the eaves, making it impossible for Amy to mount the porch steps without ruining her hair. She leapt through the drips, scrunching her nose at the icky feel of icy water trickling over her scalp, and held out her hand in greeting to the stranger. "I'm Amy Sorentino."

He shook her hand with a deceptively firm grip. "Douglas Dixon."

Lisa must've made some phone calls after Amy left the

dairy. With the trouble he'd had standing and his frail, bony body, Mr. Dixon looked old and tired. Not qualities Amy wanted in a sous-chef. She'd have to figure out a way to break it to him gently.

"Let's get inside. You two must be freezing."

Once they were inside and everyone's coats were off, Amy got a pot of coffee brewing. Mr. Dixon eased into a kitchen chair while Sloane drifted to the shelf of cook-books on the far wall. She wasn't dressed like an Amish bride today, but like a housewife from the 1970s. The huge orange and green floral pattern boggled the mind. Amy wanted to set her in a vase of water.

"You have a unique sense of style, Sloane. Such vivid colors."

"Thank you for noticing." She smoothed a hand over her stomach. "I made this myself from a pattern I found in my grandma's sewing room." That explained a lot. "Sewing is an important skill for my career as a fashion designer."

"I didn't know Clovis Community College had a pro-gram for fashion designers."

"They don't. I'm getting an AA degree in business while I save money to move to New York City someday, like you did."

Oh, brother. Amy was many things, but a career mentor wasn't one of them. "Er . . . good for you. To what do I owe the pleasure of your visit? Are you babysitting Tommy today?"

"You're funny, Amy. I know you didn't forget about my job interview. We set it up yesterday at church. One-thirty on Monday is what we shook on. My grandma told me you might forget. She says pregnant women are forgetful."

What? "Your grandma still thinks I'm pregnant? All because I tried to buy celery at the Quick Stand?"

"That and, well, we saw you running toward the church

office bathrooms yesterday after eating a doughnut. Grandma figured you have morning sickness."

Astonishing, the way some people's minds worked. "Sloane, listen to me. Tell your grandma I'm not pregnant."

"She and Marti Lipshultz think Kellan Reed's the father, but I told them—"

Amy waved her hands in the air, her desperation mounting. "Stop! Oh, God, this is a nightmare. Kellan Reed is *not* the father."

"So you are pregnant. Congratulations. It's not my business to say, but maybe you should think about telling Kellan you're carrying another man's child before your date this Friday."

"What . . . how did you . . . ?" Amy covered her face with her hands. This town was unbelievable. She made a quick revision to her earlier thought. There were two things about Catcher Creek she hadn't missed in her years gone—the dirt roads and the high-speed gossip train, with Charlene Delgado as the conductor. "Never mind. I don't want to know. Can we change the subject?"

"Perfect. Let's get started with my job interview."

"Yes. Okay. Refresh my memory; what position are you interviewing for?"

"Waitress. I've got two years' experience at the Catcher Creek Café."

"Then why are you looking for a new job?"

"The café's only open for breakfast and lunch, which conflicts with my class schedule next semester. I can't start work until noon on weekdays."

That would be fine for the Local Dish. Amy planned to hire a waitress after Christmas, but hadn't given it much thought yet. Hiring Sloane would likely save her hours of work. And two years' waitressing experience was nothing to sneeze at. "I can't pay you more than minimum wage and tips until the business takes off."

"Understood. That's what I made at the café. I don't need much money, only enough for gas and car insurance, and to save for New York City, of course. My grandma pays my college tuition and doesn't charge me rent."

Amy stuck her hand out and Sloane shook it. "You're hired, Sloane. You can start after the new year."

"Thanks. I promise you won't regret it." She fist-pumped her hand into the air.

Amy loved her youthful energy. Now all they needed to work on was her wardrobe. "I'm sure I won't. But can you do me a favor?"

"Name it."

"Tell your grandma and her friends I'm not pregnant."

"I understand you don't want it getting around at such an early date. Lots of women like to wait until the second trimester, my grandma says."

Lordy. Amy knew a lost battle when she saw one and turned to Mr. Dixon. "I'm assuming you're here because Lisa Binderman told you I'm looking for a sous-chef?"

"That's right. Lisa called Jillian, my daughter-in-law. But let me say, right off the bat, I don't need your charity. And I don't need a job. Not for the money, anyway. I've got all the retirement funds I need from my oil leasing contract."

"Okay. Understood. No hard feelings." That was easy.

He waved a hand to quiet her. "Now, now. Hear me out—I'd still like to interview for the job."

"Why?"

He speared the table with his finger and the look he shot Amy was so deadly serious that she gulped. "If I have to choke down one more bite of Jillian's so-called meals, God help me, I'm going to pack up my truck and drive away from this town for good, which is saying something because my family's lived in these parts for sixty-five years. I may not want your money, Amy, but I'll work for my meals if you'll hire me."

"Jillian's cooking is that bad?"

Mr. Dixon scrubbed a hand over his face. "Her spaghetti sauce, I don't know what she does to it, but it's like ketchup by the time she serves it. Hot, pasty ketchup. Have you ever eaten overcooked noodles and ketchup? Looks like bleeding monkey brains." He shuddered. Amy nearly shuddered too, and Sloane's face contorted into a look of disgust. "I play poker with the fellas on Tuesdays at the VFW, which gets me out of spaghetti night, but there's six more nights of the week to contend with. I don't think I can take it much longer. Her meat loaf . . ."

He sipped coffee. Sloane and Amy leaned in expectantly.

"What about her meat loaf?" Sloane whispered in horrified awe.

"She adds shredded radishes and nutmeg. The dogs won't even touch it. I have to sneak it from my plate to a napkin and feed the hogs. They're the only ones who can tolerate it. Them and my son, Stephen. He must have a stomach of steel. Jillian means well and my son loves her so I don't say anything, but I've been praying for a miracle for years."

Amy swallowed back her revulsion. "Lisa told me you were a cook in the Navy."

"Yes, ma'am. Twenty-five years, most of that time in the kitchen of an aircraft carrier. My brother, Lawrence, ran the family farm. I joined him when my stint was up. None of Larry's children wanted in on the family business, but my Stephen did. He's doing a respectable job of managing the place now that Larry's passed on and I retired."

"Can't you help Jillian? Teach her some basics?"

"I've tried, Lord knows. She won't let me through the kitchen door. Shoos me away like I'm a senile old bat. Lisa

Binderman says you need help with your restaurant, chopping and making sauces and such. I'm qualified and I'm fast. All I ask in return is that you allow me to take my meals here. I'm a proud man, but I'll beg if need be."

"Oh, Mr. Dixon, that's not necessary. Of course I'll hire you." She couldn't very well let the man eat Jillian's food any longer. That would be an act of unnecessary cruelty.

He slapped his knee and smiled. "All right, then. I'll show you what I'm made of. You and Sloane talk business, and I'll make lunch."

He opened the refrigerator and stuck his head in.

Amy leapt up. "Don't worry about it, Mr. Dixon. I already hired you. You don't have to prove anything to me."

"You expect me to go home and let Jillian fix me lunch? Do you want me to tell you about her tuna salad sandwiches?"

"Oh, God, no." Already, she knew she'd never eat spaghetti again without thinking about bleeding monkey brains. She couldn't suffer the same fate with tuna salad, one of her lunchtime staples. "Do whatever you want in my kitchen, but please don't say another word about Jillian's cooking."

"Well, get ready, because I'm going to fix you ladies a meal you'll never forget. You like eggs?"

"Yes, yes," squealed Sloane.

He tucked an egg carton under his arm and grabbed a stick of butter from the refrigerator door. "Eggs Benedict it is. Wait'll you taste my hollandaise sauce."

Chapter 7

The Cowboy Cook's horrible manipulations were getting worse.

Once again, Kellan sat in his darkened house, his eyes riveted to the computer monitor where Amy continued her run on *Ultimate Chef Showdown*. He chewed a microwaved frozen burrito and watched, with mounting frustration, as Amy acceded to Brock's every whim.

A crook of his little finger and Amy would scurry to do his bidding, working double time on the show to finish her dishes, then help him with his. Even more disgusting was the way she swooned whenever he paid her the least bit of attention. Surely, the producers had edited the footage to paint the situation in the most character-damaging light, but still, Amy made terrible choice after terrible choice where Cowboy Brock was concerned.

Brock continued to revel in his two-faced intentions in the camera confessional footage, where he'd chuckle about his control over Amy and clue viewers in on his next dastardly plan. What an asshole.

No wonder she'd made up a rule about cowboys.

Remarkably, Amy remained the person to beat. Maybe that was the reason none of the other contestants stepped in to help when they noticed the injustices done to her. Because as far as culinary skills went, she had them all beat by a mile. Not only that, but more than anyone else, she kept her cool and remained optimistic, even with the odds stacked against her.

As the episodes trudged along, though, her energy flagged. The bright wattage of her smile dimmed. She didn't hold her head as high and the bounce left her step. She became careless with her safety, nicking her fingers while shucking oysters and burning her arm during a barbecue challenge. Knowing her story as he did, he could immediately tell which episode filmed the day after her mom's accident. She was distracted, fatigued. She messed up a basic dish, which the Cowboy pounced on with ruthless enthusiasm.

If they were dating off camera, as he suspected they were at that point, then Brock must have known what had happened with her mom. And he took advantage of her anyway. Kellan could barely stand to watch through his fury. At Cowboy Douchebag, but at Amy, too, for allowing herself to get played.

It was the second to last episode of the season. Six contestants remained, including Amy and Brock. Two would be eliminated and the final four would compete for the grand prize of three hundred thousand dollars in the season finale. Amy must have burned with wanting, thinking about how that money could save her family's farm. By then, she and her sisters would've known the financial devastation their father had left them in.

The contestants divided into two groups of three to compete against each other. Their task was to plan a five-course tasting menu for a benefit auction at a museum. Brock's group members, Amy and a lanky younger man named Shawn who'd also been labeled a villain during the competition, designated him the leader. In another confessional-style video clip, Brock stared into the camera and explained that he was going to secure his place in the finale by sabotaging Amy's dishes and setting his group up for the elimination table.

"Y'all watch," he told the camera, "I own this competition and all the players in it. This is my night to shine and ain't nobody gonna stand in my way. Amy thinks we're allies, she thinks we're in love"—he used quote fingers— "but she's got another thing coming to her. Because the Cowboy Cook is a lone ranger, see? I look out for myself and myself only. Just you watch. I've got some tricks for Amy up my sleeve today."

Kellan paused the video stream. Cursing, he rose from the desk chair. He needed some air. Max regarded him curiously from his spot on the sofa, but didn't follow Kellan to the porch.

For the third night in a row, he'd stayed up late, hanging on every minute of *Ultimate Chef Showdown*. He hadn't slept much or eaten right. He'd ignored his friends and had made every excuse not to call his brother. He jumped every time the phone rang, dreading the inevitable call from his mother. Any number he didn't recognize on caller ID, he didn't pick up the phone. Cowardly, sure, but he wasn't ready to deal with her yet. Not that he ever would be.

Instead, his every waking thought was consumed by Amy's performance on *Ultimate Chef Showdown*. What had started as a way to remind himself why Amy was the wrong woman for him had become an obsession that left him with a whole slew of emotions that had nothing to do with why Amy was wrong for him and everything to do with why he was wrong for *her*.

Far from proving she was a screwup as he'd originally pegged her to be, while he watched her performance on the show, his admiration for her bloomed. With tenacity, smarts, unwavering integrity, and positive attitude, she met the problems in her life head-on and braved every obstacle thrown her way. These were qualities Kellan respected, qualities he strived to possess.

And yet, the way he'd treated her hadn't been much better than Cowboy Brock. It sickened him that he'd played on her weakness, same as Brock had. At church, with his belt buckle and bolo tie, Kellan had manipulated her into accepting a dinner date invitation. He'd manipulated her into sleeping with him on Saturday morning too, luring her to his house by preying on her stress. He wasn't a fake cowboy like Brock, but he'd done an ace job of acting like that asshole. As much as Brock didn't deserve Amy, neither did Kellan.

He paced across the porch, shaking off his anger. The episode he was on had to be the one where she melted down. He didn't want to witness it, but he resolved to hang in until the end, if only so he didn't go crazy with curiosity. He strode into the house and clicked *PLAY*, but didn't sit. Standing against the far wall, he watched as Brock did exactly what he'd told the camera he would. With a trusting smile and little touches of affection, he coerced Amy into planning three of the five dishes for the group. Then, while she prepped the vegetables for a quiche, he snuck to the refrigerator and added lemon juice to the cream, curdling it.

He sabotaged her other dishes in similar ways. Kellan's jaw ached from grinding his teeth. It was unbearable, watching Amy's dreams burn to ashes before his eyes. All three of her dishes were disasters. Even worse, with her head held high, she took full responsibility for the failures. When she issued a tearful apology to Brock and Shawn for blowing their chance to win, Kellan stormed into his kitchen and pulled whiskey from the cabinet. He took a long hit from the bottle, listening to Brock's gracious acceptance of her apology, and his subsequent laughter into the confessional camera.

Kellan was certifiably drunk by the time Judges Trial started. He set the bottle aside, lest he throw it against the wall as McKenna faked reluctance in admitting that it was Amy who'd designed the failed dishes. Her tears followed, but she held herself in check until the head judge asked Brock his opinion, as the leader of the group, about who should go home that night.

He pointed to Amy.

She cracked. Screaming and ranting. Throwing things. She kept yelling, "I thought you loved me" at the asshole. That, perhaps, hurt the most. Knowing she threw her love away on a man who didn't deserve to lick the bottoms of her feet.

He turned the computer off, unable to bear seeing the pain in her eyes or hearing the hurt in her voice any longer. Sitting in the darkness, he rolled the now-empty whiskey bottle along his pant leg, thinking about Amy. About the destruction of a vibrant, trusting woman at the hands of one greedy, manipulative man after another.

It was too late to save her from Brock McKenna, but he could save her from Amarex. He would find a way, somehow. And he would save her from himself. No more cowboy act. No more treating her like she wasn't worthy of more than temporarily warming his bed.

He gathered her Amarex file, flicked on a desk lamp, and found the leasing contract Gerald Sorentino had so foolishly agreed to all those years ago. Then he called his lawyer buddy, Matt. It was time to bury his uncle's company.

Mr. Dixon was right. His hollandaise sauce was to die for. Smooth, creamy, and a delectable custard-yellow color. The eggs had been perfectly poached. Here it was days later and Amy couldn't stop daydreaming about his sauce. The next morning, he'd returned to her kitchen and whipped up the most delectable batch of waffles she'd ever eaten. Crispy on the outside, creamy and fluffy on the inside. After one bite, Amy had tacked breakfast duty to his list of job responsibilities at the restaurant.

She'd offered him the option to wait until after Christmas to start work, but he'd looked so forlorn at the idea that she told him he could report for duty as soon as he wanted. He hadn't missed a meal at her house since.

By Wednesday afternoon, Amy had compiled a long enough list of needs from the restaurant supply warehouse in Albuquerque to justify the time away from the restaurant. The following morning, she waved good-bye to Mr. Dixon, who stood on the porch dressed in a white apron and chef coat. His plan was to spend the day perfecting a red wine braising sauce for Slipping Rock short ribs. She'd left a basic recipe on the counter along with a selection of bottles from a winery near Taos.

Sticking to any sort of a budget at the restaurant supply warehouse was impossible, but Amy managed to not completely demolish her bank account. She stuffed her trunk and seats with pots, pans, and gadgets, eager to experiment with them alongside Mr. Dixon.

Her final stop of the day was, by far, the most important. From the parking lot, she stared at the tinted windows of her mom's nursing home and said a quick prayer that she'd find her in good spirits. Most often, she was. In fact, for the first time in her life, Mom seemed happy for extended periods of time. What a cruel twist of irony that it took losing her mind for her to finally find happiness. Only twice since she'd awoken in February from a ten-day coma had Mom plummeted into depression. During those episodes, nothing rescued her from the darkness but sedation. Then again, that had always been the case.

Amy greeted the staff and signed in. Bypassing the elevator, she jogged the three flights of stairs to her mom's level, hoping to work off Mr. Dixon's pecan-glazed French toast from that morning. Her mom resided on the floor where the highest level of care was administered, but where residents were allowed to shuffle around the common room.

She found Mom in her usual spot, her thin, angular body cushioned in a faded chair, staring out the window at the bustling city street outside. Amy perched on the footstool and took her mom's hand. It was cool, skeletal.

Her mom's eyes focused on her. "Amy," she whispered.

A pang of relief shot through her, as it always did when Mom recognized her. Most often, she didn't recognize anyone, but she greeted Amy, Jenna, and Rachel with a polite, distant smile. Invariably, Tommy made her anxious. His little-boy energy was so overwhelming for her fragile nerves that the sisters decided to stop bringing him for visits except on special occasions.

Today, her expression was troubled. Her fingers quivered beneath Amy's grip.

"Amy, I think something bad happened."

"Shhhh, you're okay, Mom. Everything's fine."

She turned her haunted, sunken eyes on Amy. "No, that's not true. Something's wrong, but I can't remember what. Can you?"

Don't cry. Don't cry. "Nothing's wrong, Mom."

"I feel so sad today."

"No, no, no. You're happy here, remember? You have your friends, you do art. You have this window to look out."

Her expression softened. "I like this window."

Amy relaxed the intensity of her grip on her mom's hand. "I know you do. So much to see out the window."

"Yes . . ." Her voice drifted off.

Amy patted her knee. "And hey, you're coming home for Christmas dinner. I made arrangements with Selena and Mary at the front desk. I'm fixing a turkey. You liked the turkey on Thanksgiving, right? Remember Thanksgiving here with Jenna, Rachel, Tommy, and me?"

Mom's eyes shifted, grew distant. Then she was gone, lost in the light from the window. A vague smile turned up the corners of her mouth. What did she see there? What thoughts did she think, if any? Amy liked to imagine she saw colors. Beautiful, rich yellows and greens, violet and royal blue. A swirl of beauty created by her imagination. Maybe she saw the happy days of her life playing like a movie. Or maybe the sky outside was enough. The gray clouds moving across the city buildings along the horizon, the occasional sliver of blue.

"She had a tough night last night," said the voice of her mom's nurse, Selena, behind her.

Amy stood to shake her hand. "Did you have to sedate her?"

"No, but it nearly got to that point. She's been so happy. But lately, the bad days are becoming more frequent. There doesn't seem to be a reason why."

Amy snagged a quilt from a nearby basket and smoothed it over her mom's legs. "The anniversary of my dad's passing is later this month. Maybe on some level she understands."

Selena stroked a hand over Mom's wispy gray-black hairs. "Our minds might forget, but the heart never does."

So true. "Call me if she has another bad spell, okay?" Not that Amy could do anything to ease her mother's troubles, but she hated thinking her mom was alone on those bad nights, without anyone who loved her near enough to hold her hand or whisper words of comfort.

"Will do."

"I'm headed home, but I'll come back as soon as I can."

"Of course, dear."

She bent and kissed Mom's cheek. "Bye, Mom. I love you."

Mom's eyelids blinked but her focus never strayed from the window. Closing her eyes, Amy imagined her mom saying *I love you* back, and said a silent prayer for her to have a restful sleep that night. Then it was time to go.

On her jog down the stairs, she shook off the melancholy of the visit, forcibly turning her mind to the short ribs Mr. Dixon was preparing for dinner. She imagined opening the squeaky front door to the aroma of braised meat and red wine sauce. She wanted to hug Tommy and be henpecked by Rachel. She wanted to run her finger through the nicks on the stair rail from the time she and Jenna pretended to fix it with horse hoof files, and she wanted to read a passage from the crumbling leather Bible that had belonged to her grandmother.

She wanted to go home.

Chapter 8

Friday night, Amy stuffed a condom into her purse and wondered why such a smart choice made her feel so stupid. Then she looked at the condom, its round ridge obvious beneath the cellophane wrapper, and pictured Kellan rolling it on in a display of glorious virility. Sucking in a sharp, lusty breath, she grabbed another condom.

Once Jenna had made it clear she'd be no help in finalizing a deal with Slipping Rock Ranch, Amy had asked around about alternative beef suppliers, and everyone—from produce growers to cheese makers, poultry farmers to the manager at a restaurant supply warehouse—said the same thing. No other beef compared to the cattle raised by Kellan Reed at Slipping Rock Ranch. And how convenient, a few people pointed out, that she and Kellan were neighbors.

Despite her determination that the dinner be purely a business meeting, she'd spent the better part of the day in a state of semi-arousal, fantasizing about his kiss, his hands, and his body. Around lunchtime, her distraction got the better of her and she nicked her finger again while julienning carrots. The man was ruining her ability to wield a blade.

As she stood at the kitchen sink, flushing the cut with water, she made the call. Time to stop fighting what her body wanted. The best way to prevent herself from falling in love with a cowboy again was to control the situation. Keep it about the sex, don't get sucked into personal conversations—don't start to care. It was a bastardized version of rule number one, but if she was powerless to keep her body away from cowboys, which was certainly true where Kellan was concerned, then she needed to work doubly hard to keep her emotions at a safe distance.

Her tiny, black purse barely had enough space for a coin pouch, cell phone, and lipstick, much less condoms. She'd have to be careful not to accidentally flip one out when she paid for her half of dinner. Kellan seemed like the sort of man who didn't allow a woman to pay her own way, but Amy was determined not to let the evening devolve into a date. All she wanted tonight was to settle the Slipping Rock business deal and one last cowboy booty call.

She took one final look at herself in the mirror. Easy-up skirt? Check. Easy-off panties? Check. Not that he needed to remove her thong to get to the action. The bright pink fabric was thin and pliant, easy to pull to the side. Damn, her pulse sped and her skin grew tingly just thinking about him doing that to her in his truck. Maybe they didn't need to waste time going to dinner first. Drawing a flustered breath, she grabbed three more condoms and wedged them into the purse.

In front of the mirror, she smoothed her skirt, made sure the gals were evenly distributed in her bra, and grabbed her purse. The cellophane wrappers crinkled shamelessly.

Mortified, she hustled to the bathroom and stuffed tissues into the crevices of the purse's interior to blunt the noise.

A knock sounded at her bedroom door.

"It's open."

Rachel poked her head in. "Kellan's here. He's waiting downstairs."

"Thanks. I'll be right down."

"Jenna asked me to remind you about drawing up a supply contract with him, but I have a better idea. How about I tell him you need to cancel the date and I'll handle the contract negotiation myself?"

Tempting. Probably, that would be the most prudent course of action. Then again, if she didn't get laid tonight like she'd been banking on all afternoon, there wasn't enough celery in the county she could dice to burn off all that unsatisfied sexual energy.

"Thanks, but no thanks, Rachel. I'll discuss it with him tonight." *After he satisfies my more pressing needs.*

Rachel indulged in a beleaguered sigh. "Fine. But mark my words. You're going to regret this." Amy sent her a look of warning. "Since you're so stubborn, when you talk to him about the contract, would you feel him out about my idea to offer supplier tours to our guests? It would be a great way for him to earn extra publicity and revenue with no risk involved."

"Yeah, I'll feel him out." Amy grabbed the purse and winced at the faint crackle of cellophane. "I mean, about the tours." Thank goodness Jenna wasn't around or this conversation would have turned in a whole different direction, straight toward dirty.

With as much dignity as possible while holding her purse of sin, Amy attempted to squeeze past her sister.

"Amy?" Good Lord, she hated the way Rachel said her name when she was about to start in on a lecture.

"I don't want to hear it, Rach."

Rachel's shoulders slumped. "Look, you need to take care of yourself. Don't fall for this guy. He's a player."

"I know what he is. I'm not looking to start a relationship anyhow, with all that's going on. I just need to blow off some steam."

"Why don't I believe you?"

Amy hitched her purse strap higher on her shoulder. "I don't know. Sounds like a personal problem to me." She started down the stairs. "Do me a favor and don't wait up."

Rachel snorted, but otherwise remained silent as she followed Amy.

Kellan stood in the living room near the Christmas tree, staring at the photograph above the mantel, Rachel's picture of Sidewinder Mesa at dawn. For the first time since she'd met him, he wasn't dressed like a cowboy. He wasn't wearing boots, bolo tie, or a belt buckle. The Stetson she'd looked forward to knocking off his head was absent as well. But even fancified in chinos, black leather dress shoes, and a tailored, button-down shirt, he was still the hottest guy she'd seen in a long, long time.

When he turned to regard her as she descended the stairs, something in his expression made her pause, some feeling he wanted to mask.

Nope. Couldn't think about that. Because then she'd ask what was bothering him and they'd start talking. He might open up to her. She might try to comfort him. And heaven help her heart if she started down that slippery slope.

He walked to meet her at the base of the staircase, his jaw tight, his smile strained. When he took her hand, his was slightly damp, like maybe he was nervous. "You look beautiful."

"Thank you."

He nodded to Rachel. "I won't have her home too late."

Amy narrowed her eyes, studying him. Those weren't the words of a man preparing for a night of seduction. Or maybe he wanted it as hard and fast as she did. If that were the case, this booty call wouldn't take any time at all. Hell, they didn't even need to leave her property.

Rachel handed Amy her coat. "Why should I care what she does so long as she's here to feed the pigs in the morning?"

Amy ignored the vitriol in her sister's tone.

She and Kellan walked in awkward silence to his truck. With a hand on her elbow, he helped her to the passenger seat and closed the door. The truck smelled of him, of work and dust and the kind of manly soap that was liable to burn a hole in a woman's skin if she let it sit too long. She breathed in deeply and considered how little she knew of Kellan's life, how he viewed the world, what made him laugh.

"Idiot," she muttered, smacking herself on the forehead. Instead of wanting to pick Kellan's brain, she should be concentrating on picking his clothes off. Leaving her seat belt undone, she took stock of the truck's potential. It didn't have much of a backseat, so that option was out. She tested the center console and discovered it to be the flip-up kind. Nice. Nodding with satisfaction, she pushed her seat back as far as it would go, tucked her purse at her side, and stretched her boot-clad legs out.

Kellan climbed behind the wheel and turned the truck toward the highway. The hint of tension remained in the lines of his face and the set of his shoulders. He stared straight ahead, and with the death grip he had on the steering wheel, Amy wouldn't be surprised if he were losing feeling in his fingers.

After a couple minutes, she reached across the divide and fingered his sleeve. He flinched and, as if she'd jump-started his voice box, began to chatter. "I know I offered to cook dinner for you at my place, but I think it's a better idea to go out. We have reservations for the restaurant at the Mesa Verde Inn. It's a bit out of the way, but quiet and low-key. Marla Ray does a nice dinner there, seasonal, good enough quality for a chef like you to appreciate. I figured we could use the drive to talk. I don't even know where you lived before this week."

His anxiety was charming. One would think after the righteous nooner they had on Saturday and the blazing kiss they shared on Sunday, he'd be over his nerves. Guess dinner was a different story.

"I lived in Los Angeles. Worked as a line cook at a hot spot named Terra Bistro."

He nodded, but hadn't yet looked her way. "Did you go to culinary school?"

"Yes, straight out of high school. After I graduated, I moved to New York for culinary school, then Paris for a year to continue my studies, then back to New York to apprentice under some big-name chefs in the area." *Until I crashed and burned on a televised chef competition and fled the vicious Big Apple gossip scene.* But she didn't feel like talking about that hiccup right now. Hopefully, he wouldn't ask about it. "And I ended up with the great job I told you about in L.A. Which is where I worked until a week ago."

"You quit a great job to return to Catcher Creek?"

"Quit my job, sold my condo, cashed in all my chips. My mom and sisters needed me, so this is where I had to be. It was a no-brainer."

He peeled a white-knuckled hand from the steering wheel and ran a finger under his collar, like he wasn't getting enough air through his windpipe. A bead of sweat materialized on his temple. "So your family's farm is everything you have now?" His voice cracked and something like sadness blossomed in his eyes. Was it regret? Pity?

She shrugged a shoulder, playing her problems off as though they were nothing to be concerned about—which tonight, at this moment, they weren't. "It's all any of my family members have anymore, and I could tell you more about it, which wouldn't be very interesting. Or . . ." She flipped up the console and stretched her arm into his lap. Lucky for him, she knew the best way to ease a cowboy's troubled mind was through his—

"Hey, now." He removed her hand from his zipper and glanced her way, blinking fast. "Amy, what are you doing? We're not even off your farm."

She hitched a knee up on the seat and angled her body toward his. One by one, she popped the buttons open on his shirt. "All the better. Why don't you turn right at that post? The road leads to our northwest pasture. Our family hasn't used it in years." She eased her hand beneath his shirt and found an undershirt. Undeterred, she grabbed a handful of the cotton fabric and tugged. "The valley's totally secluded."

With her hand on his bare chest, she felt the shallow rise and fall of his lungs, the swift, hard beating of his heart. She glanced at his lap. Oh, he wanted her all right.

"Amy, no," he rasped. The truck coasted to a stop.

Placing a finger over his lips, she straddled him. He squeezed his eyes closed, not as though in preparation for a kiss, but like he was rallying the strength to refuse her advances.

She ran her palm across his freshly shaven cheek, awareness dawning first, followed by mortification. He didn't want her, despite his body's assertion to the contrary. Once again, as if it were her curse in life, she'd humiliated herself in front of a cowboy. "I thought, after Sunday at church, after Saturday . . . but you aren't interested in me like that anymore."

He opened his eyes, his brooding expression telling

her she was correct. Her heart sank and her throat grew tight. She attempted to clear his lap without rubbing against his crotch.

"That's not true." His hands shot up to grasp her hips, holding her atop him. "I want you so bad, it hurts. No man in his right mind could look at you and not want to haul you off to bed." He fingered a lock of her hair. "The problem is me. Something's come up—a responsibility I don't have the luxury to ignore—and it wouldn't be fair for me to lead you on any more than I already have."

She tried to leave his lap again, but he held her firm and she abandoned her efforts. "Why didn't you cancel tonight?"

"I should have, but I couldn't walk away without giving you an explanation. I figured we could talk about it over dinner. More than anything, I need you to understand you haven't done anything wrong. My reasons for backing off our relationship—"

"Hang on. I'm not in the market for a relationship, Kellan. I already told you that." Maybe there was hope for the night after all, if a possible relationship was his only concern.

He afforded her a halfhearted smile. "Let me guess, rule number one?"

"The rule's there for a reason." He looked like maybe he wanted to discuss the details of that reason, so she moved on before he had a chance. "But we're both adults and I want you as badly as you clearly want me." She rotated her hips, stroking him to drive her point home. His lips parted, his eyes darkened.

"What if, just for tonight, I forget about my rules and you forget about your reasons and we give each other what we want? At the end of the evening, we'll part ways, both of us satisfied and with no hard feelings. Like we did last Saturday." He didn't need to know she'd thought about him practically every waking moment since they met. That was beside the point. "After tonight, we'll be neighbors and business associates only."

"I don't want to take advantage of you."

"What if I want you to . . . at least tonight, anyway?"

Amy could tell she'd broken through his defenses. Something still troubled him, but as she watched, he pushed it back, replacing it with a look of pure carnal desire. She'd already made a fool out of herself launching at him the way she had, so making one last brazen move wouldn't matter. Holding his face between her hands, she pressed her lips to his, coaxing his mouth open.

"I can't seem to resist you," he whispered against her lips.

Their eyes met. "You don't have to."

With a growl, he took command of her body with a fierce kiss. She clung to his neck as he bent her back against the wheel and plundered her mouth. Then his hands ducked beneath her skirt and slipped up her bare legs to cup her ass, locking her thighs to his hips. She arched against the steering wheel, grinding into him.

The truck horn blared and they both jumped.

Kellan's hands fell away from her ass. He collapsed onto his seat, his head against the headrest, eyes turned heavenward. "This is wrong."

She fingered his open shirt collar. "I know. Isn't it wonderful?"

His gaze refocused on her. His lips turned up in a charming, lopsided grin. "You knew what you wanted from me tonight before I picked you up."

True, but . . . "What makes you say that?"

He rubbed her backside over her skirt. "You're not wearing panties."

"Yes, I am. They're just teensy. You'll have to look harder for them."

Shaking his head, he laughed, a low, vibrating chuckle. "I agree to your terms, Amy. We'll take this date for what it is, and when it's over, we'll be business associates and neighbors only. No hard feelings. But I've got one condition. I decide what we're doing and when tonight, which means we're keeping the dinner reservation."

Her throat constricted in panic. The only way she could pull off a dinner date with Kellan would be if he took her to some cheap, Route 66 diner or rodeo bar. It would be impossible to engage in a prolonged conversation at a classy restaurant without getting her heart involved. After snuggly, postcoital pillow talk, a romantic dinner with a cowboy was the worst kind of emotional trap. "Are you sure you don't want to skip right to the sex?"

Damn, she sounded like a floozy.

He quirked a brow at her. "Oh, I do. Trust me. But you deserve a nice dinner first, not a quickie in my truck."

"What if a quickie in your truck was my plan all along?"

He chuckled again and tapped his finger to her lips. "Amy Sorentino, get back in your seat and buckle up. We've got a long drive ahead of us."

The Mesa Verde Inn sat two miles from the highway along a pitch-black, one-lane road that cut through a series of low-lying foothills. The inn itself glowed with warm, golden light like a beacon for weary travelers. Until she saw it, she'd held out hope for burgers and beers, one of those Quay County joints with pool tables and a mechanical bull, but it wasn't looking good.

The sprawling parking lot was mostly bare, with only a few cars scattered about. The restaurant, decorated in rich browns and leather to give the feel of a hunting lodge, was equally empty, with only three other couples seated around the edges. The flicker of candle centerpieces, white lights on a tastefully decorated Christmas tree, and a fire in the nearby hearth provided the only light. Amy blinked into the romantic room, aghast.

"Quiet night," she whispered as Kellan supported her elbow and led her along behind the hostess.

He dipped close to her ear, brushing his nose along her hairline. "Word is, another storm's rolling in. Not primo date weather, but the quiet's fine with me."

Amy gulped.

The hostess seated them at a corner table. Kellan held Amy's chair out for her. Once she was settled, he lifted his chair and repositioned it so he was sitting next to her. An intimate gesture, as threatening to Amy as the restaurant's atmosphere.

The hostess adapted without a word, moving Kellan's place setting and filling their water glasses. Kellan ordered a bottle of their nightly wine special and the hostess took her leave.

"Why did you move to this side of the table?"

He tucked a strand of hair behind her ear, his eyes obscured in shadows. "I'd rather we weren't overheard."

"Oh? What secret topic do you wish to discuss?"

His hand found her leg beneath the tablecloth. "I'd like to hear more about your plan."

"The plan for my restaurant?"

He leaned nearer, crawled his hand higher. "No, honey. More about the quickie in my truck you had your heart set on."

That topic, she could handle. In fact, talking dirty was one of her favorite forms of foreplay. Looked like it was Kellan's too.

Uncrossing her legs, she spread them a bit to give him access and took a sip of water. Capturing an ice cube between her teeth, she drew it into her mouth and rolled it over her tongue, but it did nothing to temper the heat ripping through her body. What the heck were they doing in a restaurant, acting like they were hungry for food? "What do you want to know?"

"How were you going to get our quickie started?" He nuzzled her ear. "Were you going to take your clothes off or flip your skirt up so I could search for those panties you claim to be wearing?"

The sting of cold on her tongue was too much. She pushed the ice from her lips into her fingers. "The original plan was to go down on you while you drove us to the northwest pasture. I almost got my way."

"You think so, hmm? You think I'd let a lady go down on me before I'd barely cleared her driveway after picking her up for dinner?"

She popped the ice in her mouth again. "No, maybe not a lady . . . but you should've let me."

His hand crept until his little finger touched the juncture of her thighs. "Nice try. Back to your plan. After you went down on me, once I couldn't take it anymore, what would you've done next?"

"I would've wrapped you in a condom and flipped my skirt up."

"And the panties?"

Her eyes darted around the room. The other diners weren't paying the two of them any notice. "Pulled them to the side."

"Interesting. There's a flaw in your careful plan, though."

"Oh?"

He sipped his water before answering. "In an effort to control myself around you tonight, I didn't bring any protection."

"I did."

He licked his lower lip. "You really did think this through."

"Absolutely."

"Moving on. Your skirt's up, your panties are out of the

way, the condom's on. How did you want it? Did you plan to ride me like last time? Or did you want me to lay you across the seats and drive into your tight, hot body?"

Oh, Doctor. This man knew his dirty talk. She'd be wet and ready even if he wasn't rotating his pinky finger against her panties. "The plan was to ride you, but option number two's sounding pretty great instead."

He grinned, wolfishly. "And would you have been wet enough without any foreplay to take all of me inside you with one thrust?"

"I was wet enough the minute I climbed into your truck."

"What about now? Are you wet for me now?"

A waiter appeared at their table. Amy and Kellan startled, pulled apart. Kellan cleared his throat. Amy took a long, slow drink of water while the waiter poured the wine.

"Do you need another minute to look at the menus?"

Amy's eyes went to the table. Sure enough, two menus lay untouched on their place settings.

Kellan handed the menus to the waiter. "What do you recommend tonight?"

The waiter shifted his weight from one foot to the other, drumming his fingers on his notepad and looking uncomfortable, like maybe he had the right idea about the direction Kellan and Amy's evening was headed. "The roast pork with apples and brandy is our featured entrée of the month. It's served with garlic parmesan potatoes and roasted winter vegetables."

Kellan quirked a brow at Amy, a silent question. She nodded. Then again, she would've agreed to sloppy joes had the waiter suggested it. Food held no interest for her tonight. Everything she wanted to eat was already at the table.

"We'll take two," Kellan said before turning his back to the waiter in a gesture of dismissal.

The waiter left and the world beyond their table fell away

once more. Amy fiddled with the silverware, suppressing her urge to drag Kellan into the restroom and rip his clothes off. Then his breath played across her cheek.

"Answer my question, Amy," he whispered close to her ear. "Are you wet for me now?"

"If you don't know the answer, then you're not as smart as you look."

He smushed his lips together, mischief twinkling in his eyes.

"I think a better question is," Amy continued, "how aroused are you?"

She fluffed the tablecloth over their laps and molded her hand onto his erection. It was hard as steel and smoking hot. She stroked him through his clothes and grinned at his sharp intake of breath. What a waste, to squander such a fine specimen of maleness in favor of roast pork. Following this dinner through to its end might damn well kill her if she didn't make a drastic move.

In her periphery, she saw the waiter and inspiration struck. Releasing her grip on Kellan, she fumbled in her purse and pulled out her cell phone. Two condoms tumbled onto the table. Slick as sin, Kellan pocketed them before anyone seemed to notice.

Smiling her gratitude, Amy waved her phone in the air toward the waiter.

"What are you doing?" Kellan whispered.

The waiter approached. "Yes?"

Amy sighed dramatically and pointed to her phone. "We got an emergency call from home. We'll need those entrées to go. Sorry." She tried to fake sincerity, but was 99 percent sure the waiter wasn't buying it.

Kellan laughed under his breath. "Smooth move. But our agreement was that I'd make the decisions tonight."

Amy repacked the purse. "Yeah, well, I need to get out of here and into your pants before I combust."

The next ten minutes passed in a blur of heated touches and whispered promises. Amy was too flustered to protest when, as the bill came, Kellan stilled her hand over her coin pouch with the threat, "Don't even think about it."

He tossed a stack of bills on the table, grabbed the packaged food from the approaching waiter, and strong-armed Amy toward the door.

They sped to the truck through the now-empty parking lot, holding hands and chuckling conspiratorially. On reaching the passenger side, he spun her around and backed her against the door with a greedy kiss.

He tasted of wine and she could already feel the beginnings of fresh stubble above his upper lip. Wrapped in his hard planes and muscled arms, she felt the stirrings of something other than lust, something wilder and more dangerous. Plunging her hands into his hair, she closed her eyes and concentrated on the physical merging of their bodies, taming the unwanted feeling before it became something she was forced to name.

He tore away from her mouth, panting, and opened the truck's passenger door.

Her whole body thrummed with desire. "It's a dark night. We could drive down the road. Pull onto the shoulder." Dazed and floating, she turned and had one boot inside the cab when Kellan's hand on her back gently but firmly pressed her stomach into the seat.

"Not down the road. Right here, right now."

The sound of a zipper opening, then cellophane ripping, echoed in the still, rural night.

"Someone might see us," she breathed, even though she knew she wouldn't care if they did.

"No one's around. And we're in a shadow, angled away from the windows and road."

Cold air pooled around her legs as her skirt lifted several inches. Aroused beyond measure, she nuzzled her nose into the seat fabric.

Kellan's movements paused. "I'll stop if you want me to. Say the word."

"No, don't stop. Take me like this."

Her skirt lifted. His hands caressed her flesh, kneading and holding. "I found your panties."

She heard a click of something metal, like a pocket knife, then felt a tug on her thong before it fell away. He tossed it onto the truck seat near her head. Guess he didn't care for her plan to pull it aside.

Latex nudged at her opening. Grasping her hips, he surged into her, hard enough that she felt the thrust in her throat. She moaned, lost in sensation. He paused, uttering a blissful curse under his breath. Then, rocking back until only the tip of his cock remained inside her, he lifted a hand from her hip and spanked the flesh of her ass with his open palm, hard enough to provide a delicious little sting.

"Again," she panted.

He let out a deep, throaty chuckle and cracked his hand against her cheek once more. Grabbing a fistful of her skirt at the waist, he slammed his cock into her all the way up to the hilt. This time, they both moaned. He pumped with such force that Amy braced her hands against the seat to keep from sliding forward. With every thrust, zingers of sheer pleasure shot through her flesh, until her mouth locked open in an unending, silent cry of ecstasy.

Reaching around her waist, his fingers swirled against her clit. "Come for me, honey. Let it go."

He drove into her, his movements spiraling to an impossible speed.

Amy's orgasm burst into being with a flare of white-hot

rapture. She smothered her cries in the seat cushion as contractions rippled through her. Kellan's thrusts became erratic. With a final plunge and a breathy grunt, he collapsed over her.

His hand snuck beneath her sweater to stroke her perspiration-dampened back. Gradually, he withdrew. Her skirt dropped and she sat up. She should have felt sated, dreamy even, having gotten what she wanted. But watching Kellan go through the motions of wrapping the condom in a tissue and setting his clothes in order left her feeling hollow.

She wanted more from him than this.

Cringing at the unwanted epiphany, she fingered the cleanly sliced edge of her tattered panties. Of course she did—she never met a cowboy she didn't want to hand her heart over to on a silver platter. Which was why tonight had to be her last no-business contact with Kellan, as she'd originally planned. She tucked the panties in her purse and pressed a hand between her legs, touching her tender flesh until a fresh tremor of sensation shimmered through her belly. This was the prize, the fleeting bliss of an orgasm. Intense, satisfying sex with a hot cowboy was good enough. It had to be.

Kellan climbed behind the wheel and took a long hit off a water bottle, then offered it to her.

She shook her head, forcing a smile. "Thank you for tonight. It was everything I needed."

If only that were true.

He turned to her, a grin dancing on his lips. "Our night together isn't over yet. You've got the drive to my house to recover before I carry you up to my bed, strip your clothes off, and make love to you as slowly and sweetly as I can stand to go." He reached across and grabbed her seatbelt, latching her in. "We did it your way this first time, but for the rest of the night, we're doing it mine."

Chapter 9

Kellan opened Amy's door. She stepped into the bitingly cold air in front of his house. He had been right about the weather. No doubt another storm was liable to hit at any minute. Holding the bag of food and her purse, she followed him up the porch steps. Light filtered to the porch from within the house.

A shaggy dog trotted onto the porch, its tail wagging with desperate hope for attention.

She tucked her purse into the crook of her elbow, knelt, and scratched behind its ears. He whined his gratitude and slapped his tail against the floorboards.

Kellan's legs materialized next to her. "Max, meet Amy. Amy, Max."

He took the food bag and offered her a hand up, then led her into his kitchen. Max followed.

Kellan had forgone the overhead fluorescents, opting instead to turn on the soft lights tucked discreetly under the cabinets. With a turn of a key, a mellow fire sprung to life in the dual-sided fireplace separating the kitchen and living room. The firelight danced on the dark cabinet faces and set the granite countertops aglow, lending an illusion of cozy intimacy to the sprawling room.

"I'll get plates and silverware if you'll open up the food," Kellan said, setting the bag on the counter. "I promised you dinner and I'm nothing if not a man of my word."

Amy rarely missed a meal and after spending the past hour cooped up with the aroma of the pork with apples and brandy sauce in the cab of Kellan's truck, her hunger level nearly matched her need to get Kellan naked again. She worked the knot of the plastic bag and withdrew their half-full bottle of wine while Kellan snagged wineglasses and plates from a cabinet.

With a sigh of disappointment, she stared into the waxed paper carton. The pork had gone gray and sat drowning in congealed oil and mushy apple slices. "The brandy sauce separated." She pushed the roasted vegetables around with her finger. "And the carrots and potatoes are soggy."

Kellan peered over her shoulder. "That looks disgusting."

"I agree. It's okay. I'm not hungry." As though protesting her blatant lie, her stomach growled.

"Your stomach begs to differ. Tell you what. We'll whip up a fresh meal." He opened the fridge. She crowded near him, evaluating their options, and spied an array of vegetables, butcher-paper-wrapped meat, and a package of shitake mushrooms. Several plastic-wrapped bricks with Binderman Dairy labels sat on a middle shelf. "These are cheeses, right?"

"Goat cheese varieties my friends Chris and Lisa make. You had a meeting with Lisa on Monday, right?"

"I did. Their cheeses are phenomenal. But I knew who they were before Monday. Or, rather, I knew of them. Lisa and Chris were a couple years older and ran with a different clique than my sisters and me, but I was in the same grade as Chris's younger brother, Nathan."

He grabbed two packs of meat and nudged the fridge shut with his heel. "How did the meeting go?"

"It was great. Lisa's a shark of a salesperson. She offered me a deal on cheese if I hired Douglas Dixon as my sous-chef."

Kellan shook his head, grinning. "Typical Lisa coercion technique. I thought Douglas retired. A bad back or something."

"He definitely has a bad back. Lisa and Jillian Dixon are convinced he needed something to do to keep him from getting underfoot in the kitchen. They thought he was bored and needed to feel useful."

"I hear a *but* in that statement."

"But I heard a much different story from Mr. Dixon when he came to interview with me." She reopened the fridge and piled ingredients on the counter, including the cheeses.

"Do tell."

"Turns out, he wants to escape Jillian's cooking. He offered to work for meals, rather than a paycheck."

Kellan laughed out loud. "Man, I don't blame him. You ever tasted Jillian's chicken casserole? It's her go-to contribution when people have new babies or funerals. I learned a long time ago not to touch the stuff."

Amy shook her head, then a memory surfaced. "Wait a minute. I remember that casserole from the reception after my dad's memorial service. The dish has the green chilies on top?"

"Those aren't chilies, Amy."

She groaned. "Ew. Good thing I didn't have an appetite that day. We fed it to the hogs."

"Smart move."

She unwrapped the bricks of cheese and popped some crumbs into her mouth. "How long have you and Chris been friends? You two seem close, but you didn't grow up around here with the rest of us."

"No. I grew up in Florida. After high school, I kicked around Texas for a couple years, doing odd jobs for my uncle. One thing led to another and I crash-landed in Catcher Creek when I was twenty. Scrawny and lonely and ready to fight the world."

Amy eyed Kellan's thick, muscled arms and the broad expanse of his shoulders. She tried to picture him as a thin, angry young man, but couldn't get the image to gel in her mind with the strapping cowboy she'd come to know.

"Chris's mom was the first person to look me in the eye," he said. "She saw me hanging around the corner market and brought me home. She introduced me to Chris and his brothers and told me I was staying on at their place until, as she put it, the sallowness disappeared from my cheeks."

Amy had always admired Mrs. Binderman, whose quiet support of Amy's family over the years had been a balm against the judgmental eyes of the rest of the community. She was the only person from town to visit Amy's mom in the hospital. "How many of Mrs. Binderman's meals did that take?"

"About two months' worth. Not long after that, I bought a secondhand single-wide trailer and dropped it right where this house stands. And the rest is history. Ever since that first night sleeping on the Bindermans' couch, they've been family to me."

Amy was about to ask about his parents until Kellan cut the white butcher tape on one package to reveal two thick, marbled cuts of beef. She grabbed his shirt, swooning. "Are those Slipping Rock filet mignons? My God, they're perfect."

"Thank you. I think so, too. How about I sear these

babies up and we'll have your growly stomach satisfied in no time flat?"

She shot him a flirty sideways glance. "Well, you know, filets are my favorite kind of fast food."

"That makes two of us."

"What's in the other package?"

"Mesquite smoked bacon from Salero Farms outside Amarillo. Old man Salero and I trade goods on a regular basis."

With a practiced technique, he peeled a strip of bacon from the mound, wound it like a ribbon around the circumference of a filet, and secured it in place with a toothpick. He repeated the ritual with the second filet. Amy watched, impressed by the skill of this cowboy who didn't just raise cattle, but knew what to do with the beef he produced once it reached the kitchen.

After washing up, he nodded toward a closed door across the sprawling kitchen. "Time to select the perfect seasoning."

Amy suffered a flash of disappointment. "What kind of seasoning do you have in mind? I'm partial to salt and pepper on a premium cut like filet. You'd ruin it with anything else."

He smiled mischievously. "That's what I thought for the longest time. Follow me." Across the room, he opened the door and flipped on an overhead light to reveal a huge walk-in pantry loaded floor to ceiling with cans, boxes, and bins of foodstuffs. "Then a few months ago, Lisa showed up with goat cheese prepared with Celtic sea salt harvested in the south of France."

He pulled a plastic box from a top shelf and backed out of the pantry, setting the box on the hardwood floor near the fireplace and folding himself cross-legged next to it.

Amy slid down the wall and tucked her feet behind her. "And?"

"And the cheese was fantastic. Which gave me an idea. After a little research, I started sending away for exotic salts, experimenting with them on my beef to develop a line of high-end seasoning blends and dry rubs to diversify my business."

He unlatched the lid and opened the box to over a dozen little bottles and jars. Amy lifted a jar and tilted it toward the firelight to read the handwriting on the quaint blue label. GRIGIO DI CERVIA FINISHING SALT. She uncorked the jar and sniffed. It smelled like salt, but richer, more intense. The crystals were gray and larger than run-of-the-mill sea salt. She replaced the jar in the box. "I've used artisanal salts from time to time, some from Hawaii and a few that had been herb-infused."

Kellan sifted through the box, checking labels. He unscrewed the lid of a square glass jar and tipped it in her direction. "This is an interesting variety. Have you ever tasted smoked salt?"

"No." Intrigued, she leaned closer and peeked at the cream-hued crystals. Kellan's breath fanned over her cheek. He shifted his leg to accommodate her nearness.

"Guava wood smoked salt from Kauai. Sweet, smoky, yet mild." The timbre of his voice was low and seductive, thick with implication. Amy turned her face up to his, curious about the expression that accompanied such a voice. The shaft of light from the pantry gilded his hair and the back of his head, casting his eyes in shadow. Wetting the tip of his index finger with his tongue, he pressed it into the jar. "Taste it," he said as his salt-covered fingertip grazed her lower lip.

She ran her tongue over her lip. Kellan watched with rapt attention. The crystals dissolved over her taste buds and she hummed her appreciation as her salivary glands activated. "Braised brisket. That's what I'd use this salt on."

His lips twitched into a grin. "Good call. That's exactly

what I use it for." He screwed the lid on and reached for a second jar. "Let's try another."

This second jar contained gray-green crystals. "Is that salt green or is it the lighting?"

As he did with the smoked salt, he dipped his finger in. "It's actually green. This one is harvested off the coast of Molokai and blended with bamboo extract." He moved his finger toward her lips once more. "Tell me what you think."

This time, Amy drew his finger into her mouth, suckling the salt from his rough, work-worn skin until he removed it with a ragged intake of breath.

"Exotic, slightly pungent. Delicious." She swiped her tongue across her lower lip. The residual salt essence made the underside of her tongue tingle.

Kellan lidded the jar, watching her lips with a heated gaze. "I can't quite remember the flavor of that one." His hand on her jaw coaxed her face up. "Refresh my memory."

He took her lower lip into his mouth. Then his tongue stroked hers, demanding her body's surrender. Amy opened for him, coming up on her knees and winding her hands through his hair. He tugged her onto his lap.

Roving from her mouth, he anointed her collar and neck with kisses. "I think I'll never be able to eat this salt again without thinking of the way it tastes on you."

A jolt of satisfaction coursed through her. "Good," she breathed, fisting her hands in his hair. *Careful, Amy.* She squeezed her eyes closed, steeling herself, damming her emotions before they surged out of control. She tried to move from Kellan's lap, but his embrace was unyielding.

"One more salt to try," he said, reaching into the box. He brought a jar of black, flaky crystals up to the light. "Black diamond finishing salt. Extremely rare and too bold for those with meek palates. But, for a true connoisseur, the flavor is incomparable." With an arm across her lower back, steadying her, he lowered her head and torso to the ground and pushed her sweater up to expose her stomach and ribs. "I want to sample it on your skin."

Amy closed her eyes, lost in the fire of her own undeniable need. Straddling him as her thighs were, she felt his burgeoning arousal and squeezed her legs more tightly around him. The cool tickle of crystals rained over her belly. At the first touch of his tongue, she arched up to him in offering. He kissed and licked and tasted his way up her body, to the underside of her breasts, still covered by her sweater and bra, pressing her to the floor with his heavy frame and angular hip bones.

Then his mouth found hers and stopped her breathing with a hard, deep, wet kiss.

Everything inside and outside Amy's body was heat and flame, earth and salt. As if Kellan were the summer sun in the desert, wrapping himself over her skin like a shroud, setting her body and soul ablaze. His kiss, his touch blunted her capacity for thought beyond a base awareness of the prickle of perspiration on her skin and a low-down burn of desire in her muscles.

She reached between them and unlatched his belt.

With a start, he grabbed her wrists and pinned her arms above her head. He raised his head to gaze at her. On his lips, he wore a smile. "Always in such a rush."

"You go too slowly. Maddening."

"Since this one night is all we have, I plan to wring every last drop of pleasure out of it."

She twisted her wrists from out of his grasp, fighting to ignore the hollow feeling creeping back into her consciousness. This night was all they had. It's what she'd thought she wanted. But, somewhere along the line, everything got jumbled in her head. With increasing clarity, she knew one night was not enough. She wanted more from him than that.

Her instincts told her he felt it, too—the profound

power of their connection. Kellan's kisses didn't feel like expressions of simple, uncomplicated lust. His touches and looks were laced with a desire that ran deep, straight to the core of Amy's being. As if his soul were drawn to hers on an elemental level. Why else would he bring her to his home? Why else would he insist they dine together and talk?

Men who were only looking to get laid didn't behave in such a way, at least not in Amy's experience. Even Brock McKenna, who swore his love for Amy, hadn't shown an interest in talking with her, especially after sex. And yet here, before her, sat Kellan Reed, who kept their evening slow and steady, who refused to be rushed into more sex, though he clearly desired her.

Then again, why did he continue to remind her of their agreement? Nothing made sense except that perhaps he still thought this was all she wanted and he was playing along out of respect for her wishes. That must be it, she reasoned, even though the sinking feeling in her stomach refused to abate.

He rose and offered her a hand up. "Let's cook together, Amy. When we're done eating, I'll take you upstairs and make love to you the right way."

She forced a smile and took his hand. "You mean the slow way."

"Exactly."

She smoothed her skirt and adjusted her sweater, collecting herself. Perhaps if she focused on cooking, she could ignore the nagging uncertainty eating at her. "All right. While you season the filets, I'll work out a simple side dish."

Moving to the pantry, she took stock of her options. A red and white box caught her eye and she chortled. "You have instant mashed potatoes? How is it that a man who owns a dozen varieties of artisan salts also stocks instant mashed potatoes?"

"Call it a sentimental indulgence. I developed a taste for them when I was a kid. Hell, I'd never even prepared a raw potato until my high school home economics class."

She grabbed the box and walked his way. "Home ec? At my high school, no self-respecting teenage boy would deign to take home economics."

He shrugged devilishly. "That's where the girls were."

She laughed. It was easy to picture a younger version of Kellan, with his unruly hair and devilish smile, charming a class full of girls. "Instant mashed potatoes it is. But I get to make a sauce for it."

"You've got yourself a deal."

After setting two wide, heavy-bottomed skillets on the stove to preheat—one for Amy's sauce, the other for the beef—Kellan sprinkled salt, then cracked pepper, over the filets. Amy piled mushrooms, goat cheese, chicken broth, and parsley on the counter, then reached for the knife block.

"Don't use those knives."

Her hand stilled. "Why not?"

"Those are decoys."

"Decoys?"

"Yeah. When I have parties or visitors, my guests use those knives, which work fine for folks who don't know any better."

She smiled, catching on to his train of thought. "But . . ."

"But you're a chef, so I'm assuming you know better. As do I." His grin broadened with unguarded, boyish pride. Amy was charmed. "Check these babies out." He opened a lower cabinet and withdrew a canvas knife bag. She wet her lips in anticipation as he opened it on the counter to expose five gleaming blades.

Her knees went weak and she sucked in a ragged breath. "My God—the entire MAC SPK Ultimate Series."

Just like that, Amy knew why people called it falling. Because even if she'd tried to fight it, even if she'd turned tail and sprinted into the night and never spoke to the man again, the force propelling her straight into love with Kellan Reed was unstoppable, non-negotiable, and completely out of her control.

Kellan knew he was a needy, rotten son of a bitch.

It was a truth he'd been able to ignore for the better part of the evening. Trouble was, reality was catching up with him like a silent predator, stalking closer with each ticking minute that brought the evening nearer to an end.

Amy's captivating presence made it easy to live in the moment and forget everything but his overwhelming desire to bring her pleasure, to entice a smile or a hum of delight from her lips, to make her eyes light up, as they had while her fingers danced over his knife collection. She'd slung an arm around his neck and her body trembled with emotion. In her eyes, he saw affection.

And now, framed by the flickering glow of firelight and his Christmas tree, and set to music by the sound system playing an album of jazz piano holiday songs, Amy looked even more magnificent. As though she belonged in his home in a permanent way.

As though she were the warmth he'd been searching for all his life.

Kellan tore his eyes away, cursing silently. He had no business entertaining thoughts about a relationship with Amy Sorentino. Period.

When he sat her down and told her about his connection to Amarex, she was going to hate him. It hurt, thinking about that affection morphing into hate, yet he couldn't make himself drive her home early like he knew he should. Selfish as he was, he wanted to cling to his final moments with Amy, to relish his time with her before they went their separate ways. Before she hated him.

She slid another bite of filet mignon into her mouth and he said another silent curse as he felt his cock stir to life. How utterly erotic. This lovely creature was savoring beef raised on his ranch, the product of so many years of toil and rising before dawn. Watching her bliss out as she ate made every day of backbreaking labor as a rancher worthwhile.

Burrowing herself even deeper into the cushions of his sofa, she sliced another bite from the steak. Kellan watched her mouth, riveted. Her lips parted in anticipation as she lifted the fork. Her teeth drew the bite onto her tongue. This time, when she closed her eyes, a little moan of ecstasy escaped from her throat. Kellan's hand twitched with the urge to stroke his raging erection. Amy was a carnivore's erotic fantasy. Holy shit.

Once Kellan started breathing again, he asked in a low voice, "How's the filet?"

She grinned and pressed a napkin to her lips. "Heavenly. What salt did you end up choosing?"

"A Japanese sea salt. *Amabito No Moshio*. And I've got to tell you, your mushroom goat cheese sauce has taken these instant mashers to a whole new level of gourmet."

She giggled. "That's not saying much. But I am enjoying the potatoes. I can't remember the last time I ate the instant variety. It's surprisingly yummy."

"Yummy? That must be an official term they taught you in chef school."

"Absolutely." Smiling, she sipped her wine. "Did you go to college?"

He shook off the voice of his conscience pressuring him to cut the evening short and rolled a sip of wine over his tongue. "Sort of, eventually. When I turned eighteen,

I cared more about getting out of Florida than I did about earning a degree. Once I got the ranch up and running, the desire to finish school took root inside of me. Of course, the timing was terrible because the nearest college was in Clovis, which is over an hour drive, and I couldn't manage the time away from the livestock. For whatever reason, though, I couldn't let the idea go, so I signed up with one of those online correspondent universities. It took me six years, but I earned a diploma."

"Is your degree in business or agriculture?"

In petroleum engineering, he longed to admit. But that would lead to questions he wasn't prepared to answer tonight. Man, he was a selfish bastard. "Business." Time to change the subject before he dug himself into a hole. "Christmas is in two and a half weeks. What do you and your sisters have planned to celebrate?"

His favorite worry line appeared between her brows. "Oh, geez, I've barely thought about what I'm going to fix. Definitely a turkey. My mom loves turkey. She'll get to come home for a few hours for Christmas dinner, which will be great. It'll be her first time home since she . . . since she got sick." She blew a strand of hair away from her face. "The best part of Christmas for me is watching Jenna's son, Tommy, open presents. What about you? Do you fly to Florida to see your family? I bet it'd be tough to leave the ranch for more than a day or two."

"You're right, it would be near impossible." No sense in getting into that unpleasant story now. "I stay local, spend Christmas Eve and Christmas Day with the Bindermans. As Daisy's godfather, I work hard to spoil her with lots of gifts."

"Are you an only child?"

Yikes. They were getting into dangerous territory for a whole slew of different reasons. "No, I have a younger brother. Jake. But he's busy with his job in L.A. You know how it goes."

"Hmm." She narrowed her eyes at him in that Superman-vision way women managed, like they were trying to squeeze a drop of water from a rock with their mental muscles. Once again, Kellan was desperate for a topic change as Amy swerved too close to the heart of the matter.

He gestured to her empty plate. "You finished your filet in record time."

"You know me, going too fast, as usual."

Right now, his conscience argued. *Take her home right now before you lose your head over this girl.*

As if he could stop himself from sleeping with her after watching her eat that filet mignon. Transferring his plate to the coffee table, he dropped to his knees and reached for her boot. "Then it's a good thing you've got me to slow you down."

"At least for tonight," she whispered like a question.

Her boot slipped from her leg with a tug. Her sock followed. Cupping her heel in the palm of his hand, he pressed his lips to the inside of her ankle. "Tonight is all that matters," he murmured against her skin.

She slouched on the sofa, spread her knees, and placed her still-booted foot in Kellan's hand. "Carpe diem?"

He tugged her other boot off. "Give me a few more minutes and you won't believe the Latin I'll have you screaming."

"Bet we'll make your cattle blush."

"Don't forget about Max. He's awfully old-fashioned."

She arched, throwing her head into the sofa with a throaty chuckle. A knife of pain and longing wedged in Kellan's heart. *She is the warmth you've been looking for your whole life.*

No, no, no. Just sex with a beautiful woman. Casual. An agreed-upon one-time fling, nothing more. No matter what his heart whispered to the contrary.

He rose, offering Amy his hand. And when she stood, he swept her into his arms and carried her up the stairs, through the darkness, to his bedroom.

Chapter 10

Amy couldn't keep her mouth off Kellan's neck as he carried her, rasping her lips over the thick stubble on skin that had been smooth only a few hours earlier. He carried her like she weighed nothing, his effort showing only in the veins of his neck and the bunch and flex of muscles along the substantial breadth of his shoulders. Never before had she come up against such an embodiment of pure masculinity—broad and hairy and muscled. So capable, so solid a man.

Someone she could depend on—a living, breathing cowboy who weathered storms and hard desert living and the ravages of time. A man who remained, through it all, fighting strong. She splayed her fingers over his firm chest, imagining him fighting for her.

Once in his bedroom, he placed her on her feet and switched on a reading lamp.

She looked around, taking stock of the room. The first time she'd found herself in Kellan's bedroom, she hadn't cared about discovering who the man beneath the Stetson was. All she wanted was a diversion from the stress of the day at the capable hands of a sexy cowboy. Tonight, saturating herself with the details of Kellan's life outweighed her lust. Outweighed everything else.

The room smelled of polished wood and worn leather. A huge, wood-framed bed topped with a blue-plaid quilt dominated the uncluttered space. Amy suppressed the urge to smooth her hand across the quilt and bury her nose in one of the two plump pillows.

A line of boots, some old, some shiny, sat at the base of a looming wardrobe, its doors wide open. Shirts in varying shades of blue and red and black hung in a neat row. Atop a matching dresser sat photographs of the Bindermans' children—their adorable daughter, with a huge smile, sitting on a horse, inside a picture frame that declared *World's Greatest Uncle,* and a birth announcement for Rowen Binderman propped next to a framed picture of Kellan holding the baby boy.

Then Kellan stood before her. "Raise your arms," he commanded softly.

She complied.

With a naughty, lopsided smile playing on his lips, he peeled her sweater off and closed his hands over the cups of her bra. Spellbound, Amy let her fingers dance over his face to trace the beginnings of wrinkles at the edges of his eyes, the corners of his mouth. Laugh lines. How wondrous he was.

Hooking his index fingers under the straps, he tugged her forward, into a kiss.

She melted into him, yielding her mouth to the soft persistence of his lips. His hands grazed her ribs en route to the clasp of her bra. A flick of his wrist and it was loose, the straps falling away from her arms.

Tearing his mouth from hers, he stared down at her body, his eyes dark, his expression reverent. His lips covered her right nipple, drawing it deep into his mouth.

She tangled her hands in the brown curls of his hair, discovering a smattering of gray ones. *The glamorous life of a cowboy.* She grinned, loving the truth she saw in those hairs, of a life lived, of worry and time passing, the flaws that make a person beautiful.

She smoothed a hand along his neck, taking note of his skin's dark tan lines, a reminder of the hours and years he'd spent outdoors, every day sweating under the unrelenting New Mexico sun.

Leaving a hand in place over her right breast, he moved to her left, teasing it with his talented tongue until she was dizzy with pleasure. She arched into his touch, feeding her breast to his mouth as his fingers tugged and caressed her other nipple to a stiff peak.

She squirmed, rotating her hips, knowing she would disintegrate if he didn't quell the aching need gathering between her legs. She would absolutely crumble into pieces if he didn't tend to her clit immediately. With unsteady hands, she unzipped her skirt, pushed it to the ground, and pressed his head lower.

Kellan twisted away from her hold and straightened. "You're getting impatient again."

She scoffed at his gentle reprimand. "Cowboy, you haven't even seen 'impatient' yet."

"Is that a fact?"

Holding his gaze, she slid a hand down her belly and nestled a fingertip into her damp folds with a groan of relief.

His eyes widened a bit, then crinkled as he grinned. "That's how it's gonna be, huh? Either I meet your demands or you move on without me?"

"I'm not moving on without you." She stroked herself with exaggerated movement and made a show of moaning her pleasure. "I'm inviting you to join me, if you think you can keep up."

Kellan raised a brow. "A challenge? I never turn down a challenge as tempting as you." He dropped to his knees and settled her left leg over his shoulder. She wiggled her standing leg more firmly into the hardwood floor and moved her hand out of the way. He took hold of her wrist.

"No. Keep touching yourself. I want to watch."

She replaced her fingertips against her swollen flesh and swirled them over her clit. With any other man, she might've felt self-conscious of him getting so up-close-and-personal with her curves. Like all the women she knew, she'd tried dieting off and on, but she never had a knack for it, choosing instead to indulge in the joy of cheeses and wine and truffles and chocolate, to savor the vivid flavors of the world.

Kellan didn't seem to mind her inability to deprive herself of good food. He bathed her stomach and hips with butterfly kisses, his excitement evident in his shallow, tremulous breaths. Overcome with arousal at his voyeurism, she braced her shoulders and head against the wall. Closing her eyes, she worked her flesh with rhythmic purpose.

Kellan's hand brushed against her thigh. One finger slipped inside her, then a second. Her inner muscles contracted around them as he sunk them deep within her. He scissored the two over her g-spot, a little butterfly of a move that nearly made the knee of her standing leg buckle. She fought to stay upright, fisting a hand in his hair as she inched ever closer to climax.

Encircling her wrist once more, he drew her moistened fingers into his mouth. "You taste so sweet. I want to taste you for myself." His words strained. Wetting his lips, he parted her folds and covered her clit with his mouth. Pleasure rocketed through her and she screamed out, the call of a woman untamed, reckless in her hedonism, teetering nearer to the edge of release with every flick of Kellan's tongue.

Her foot skidded along the floor and she squeaked in surprise, flailing her arms. Kellan's hand clamped around her hip before she tumbled sideways.

"I guess when you make a woman weak in the knees, you go all out."

He lowered her leg from his shoulder and stood. "Then I'd say it's time to lay you down, do this right."

Rocking onto her tiptoes, she guided his face to hers for a kiss. It felt so wonderfully wicked, tasting her own liquor on his lips, rubbing her nude body against his fully clothed one. Like she could abandon every trouble in her life at Kellan's bedroom door and simply exist—a naked, uninhibited, sexual being.

"Oh, no. I don't think so," she said.

He raised a brow in question.

"You're done with me for the moment." She popped open the button of his fly. "It's time to test *your* ability to stay standing."

She knelt before him. After unzipping his slacks, she mouthed the head of his cock through his boxers and he slammed against the wall. His hands wove into her hair.

"Are your knees comfortable? The floor's hard."

A tug and his pants dropped to pool around his ankles. "My knees are fine."

She stretched the elastic waistband of his boxers out and over his erection, then added them to his pants and pulled her face back to admire him. No way around it—Kellan Reed was the finest built man she'd ever seen. Her lips closed over him, sinking until the head bumped on the roof of her mouth. His hot, silken flesh tasted salty, musky, like a man. Her man. She hummed, savoring the knowledge.

He moaned, clutching her hair more firmly.

Exhaling through her nose, she relaxed her jaw and took

him deeper until he groaned and gave a little thrust. Amy's lips twitched as satisfaction flared within her.

Look who the impatient one is now, cowboy . . .

She picked up the pace, cupping his balls, rolling them in her fingers, then lightly scratched his sac with her nails.

"I'm too close. You have to stop."

Not a chance. She was enjoying herself far too much to give up. She loved the give-and-take of pleasuring a man all the way to the end, experiencing his build-up, the tightening of his flesh, the taste and feel of his release in her mouth. She could practically come this way, herself, she thought, as a trickle of moisture seeped onto her thigh.

"Amy, please. Stop." His voice was hoarse, desperate. He pushed at her shoulders, but she was undeterred. "I don't want to come yet."

His hands clamped on either side of her face, forcing her off. She sat on her heels and looked up at him, breathing hard and smiling. His jaw was clenched, his expression fierce.

Tense silence settled over them. Amy swiped her thumb over the wetness at the corner of her mouth, determined to lighten the mood. "Next time we're together, I'm going to have my way with you as long as I want."

As soon as the words were out, she realized her mistake. She saw in the shift of Kellan's expression that meant he, too, heard the expectation—the hope—in her declaration.

He pulled his boxers and pants over his hips. "Amy . . ."

She stood. "Don't say it, Kellan."

Tonight was a one-time event. Hell, this final night together had been her suggestion. A booty call, she'd flippantly labeled it. A means of getting Cowboy Kellan out of her system once and for all. What an idiot she'd been, to believe that was possible. She mashed her eyes closed, hating herself for what she was about to say, knowing how pathetic it would sound. But it needed saying nonetheless. "I need to see you again. Tonight is not enough."

He wrapped his arms around her. "This has to be enough, Amy. We agreed to the terms."

"I know what we agreed, but I've changed my mind."

"There can't be a next time. I wish to God it could be different, and I feel like a total ass for letting things get this far out of control, but I can't seem to help myself when I'm around you. You have to understand, I'm not good for you."

She huffed, fiddling with the buttons of his shirt. "You've been pretty damn good so far."

He slipped sideways apart from her to pace, sighing, his hands on his hips. What did a sigh mean? Did he regret bringing her home? Was he thinking, *Women, what a pain in the ass—they reel you in and always want more?*

Jenna had mentioned more than one remark about Kellan's purported appetite for women. Amy hadn't pressed her for details of his playboy reputation, not wanting anything—not even the truth—to interfere with the fantasy image in her mind. Maybe this was how he usually played the game, worming out of commitments with a tossed-off apology about what a no-good guy he was, putting the onus on himself. No question about it, she felt a deep, powerful bond with him. Maybe he didn't feel it the same way she did.

Or maybe she was as unbalanced as her mom, the way she could conjure the illusion of love out of thin air. She closed her eyes as realization swept through her.

Oh, no. I've done it again.

She'd imagined a love match with the man, the cowboy, she was sleeping with. As she had with Brock McKenna. Or with Bucky Schultz in high school. She could tick off the names on her fingers, all the cowboys she'd thought she loved over the years. What a cruel trick her mind kept playing on her.

Suddenly and uncomfortably aware of her nudity, she ducked to gather her clothes from the floor.

Kellan noticed and strode toward her. "Don't do that, Amy. Don't let this be the way it ends. Please, allow me to make love with you one last time before our night is over."

She jerked her arm away and stepped into her skirt, balking not so much about his suggestion, but his casual use of the phrase *make love*. As though he hadn't just pointed out that all he wanted was a one-night stand. Not that she could blame him for giving her what she had originally asked for. Add to that the fact she'd already set a casual quickie precedent on Saturday morning and it was tough to even feel a sliver of anger at him. She reserved all the disgust for herself.

"I'm sorry I complicated things." She straightened her bra and pulled her sweater over her head. "I told you I wanted a simple night of sex as much as you did and yet I still managed to muddy it with feelings that aren't actually there. Like I always do."

He hauled her up against him. "My God, Amy, stop talking like you've done something wrong. This is my fault." Holding her cheek in his palm, he took her mouth in a demanding kiss. Knowing it would be their last, she opened for him. When lust and love stirred within her once more, she pushed him away, disgusted with herself anew.

He made another move to hold her, but she refused to be lured into his waiting arms and he gave up, instead resting his hands on her shoulders. "This isn't the way I envisioned telling you the truth about me—about my other business connection in Quay County and the conflict of interest—"

"A conflict of interest because I want to sign a contract with Slipping Rock for my restaurant? What a lame excuse."

"It's not an excuse. It's the truth. I'm the heir—"

"Don't say another word, Kellan. I don't want to hear your lies. I'm such an idiot, falling for no-good cowboys all the time." She pushed against his chest. "Stupid, stupid me for thinking you were different."

"I'm so sorry I've hurt you."

She sniffed in a deep, fortifying breath. "Take me home. And don't say another word about how regretful you are or how much you wish it didn't have to be this way. I'm through listening to two-faced, low-down cowboy bullshit. Once and for all."

Raking a hand through his hair, Kellan screwed up his mouth in a look of pain. Then, his expression turned flinty and he nodded. "I was wrong to bring you here tonight. But this conversation is far from over. When we've both had time to cool off, you and I are going to sit down and you're going to hear me out."

He turned on his heel and marched from the room.

Amy's back muscles twinged as her mount, Nutmeg, surged along a steep trail over the rolling hills of Sorentino Farm. Her lips were tender from contact with Kellan's stubbled face the night before, but on her morning horseback ride with Rachel to check the irrigation lines to their southwestern pasture, it was her thighs that commanded all her attention with an ache of awareness. Kellan's mark.

Rachel led the excursion, her body fluid but strong in the saddle, her worn winter coat billowing in the breeze, and her ponytail swishing below the brim of her hat. Despite their frequent bickering and clash of personalities, Amy was proud of the woman Rachel had grown into—an unflappable force, the rock of the family that neither of their parents were.

While Amy had fled New Mexico in pursuit of her dream, Rachel stayed home and held the family and their farm together. If she sometimes felt weak or scared, she never showed it. She never wavered. From Amy's earliest recollection of Rachel, three years her senior, she'd risen before dawn every day of the year, come snow or rain or record-breaking heat, and worked the farm. Taken care of business. Taken care of everyone.

At the crest of the trail, Rachel brought her mount to a stop. Amy pulled alongside her. The wind blew harder here than it had on the trail, whipping up from the valley to bite at her exposed cheeks and neck. Yet the view from this vantage point was awe inspiring, worth battling the raw weather. The New Mexico high desert stretched for miles of rolling hills swathed with deep green shrubbery and patchy snow, craggy rocks and canyons cut by rainwater. A single, red dirt hill rose above the others on the southeast edge of their land. Sidewinder Mesa.

"This is my favorite place to photograph," Rachel said. She held her hands aloft, framing the air between her extended thumbs and index fingers. "At sunset, the mesa turns these unbelievable colors. The red in the dirt glows pink, or sometimes orange. Its shadow stretches into the valley as the sun gets lower." She smiled a faraway smile. "I'll come back tonight. If the snow sticks, it's going to make for a terrific shot."

"Your photographs hang all over the house, and they're all amazing. Hard to believe it's the same pile of rocks and dirt we grew up with. You make it all look so beautiful."

"It *is* beautiful, all on its own." She inhaled, her eyes sweeping the valley. Then her gaze locked on Amy. "I can't lose this land, no matter what. Too much of who I am is in this desert. Scares the hell out of me to think about what we'll have to sacrifice if Heritage Farm doesn't work out."

Amy's heart sank. She nudged Nutmeg closer and squeezed Rachel's shoulder. "We'll do everything we can.

I promise you, Rach, we're not going to give this place up to Amarex or the bank without one heck of a fight."

"Damn right. Been fighting for this place my whole life and I'm not about to give up anytime soon." She tipped her head toward the valley. "Let's get that irrigation canal checked out so we can get on with our work. The roof of the chicken coop has a leak, so I've got to run into town, pick up some supplies. About time I reroofed it anyway."

Their mounts picked their way down the trail.

"How did you learn to do all this stuff?" Amy called up to her. "I grew up here, same as you, and I haven't the first clue how to reroof a chicken coop. Sometimes it seems like you were born with a complete set of knowledge about how to run a farm."

Rachel chuckled. "I wish. Trust me, I've made plenty of mistakes with this place over the years. You just weren't here to see them. But lots of things, like construction, Dad taught me."

"You're kidding. Dad?"

"Jenna and you have it in your heads that Dad never did anything, and a lot of time that was true, but when he was around and he wasn't hung over or napping in front of the television, he was a good teacher."

They reached the valley and picked up the pace to the canal, their conversation paused while they flew over the terrain. With two recent storms, the water in the canal was flowing. They dismounted and set to work, clearing debris and breaking up the ice crusted over the grates.

The physical labor reminded Amy of her body's various aches, which inevitably led to thoughts of Kellan and the disaster that was their final evening together, including the sleepless night that followed. After he drove her home and escorted her—awkwardly, painfully—to her front door, she'd spent the remaining hours of the night flat on her back, staring at the cracked paint on the ceiling of her bedroom, thinking about Kellan Reed, Brock McKenna, and her original example of a no-good cowboy, her father.

How many times did she need to have her illusions shattered before she learned her lesson? She'd sworn to herself, when her father died, leaving her mom broken-hearted and penniless, to never trust that type of man again. She vowed to learn from her mom's mistakes, but despite her best intentions, she continued to perpetuate the cycle begun by her parents.

Brock McKenna rolled onto the set of *Ultimate Chef Showdown* the first day like he was born for the spotlight— his belt buckle shining, a black cowboy hat perched on his head, and a teasing smile playing on his perfect face. Amy was a goner. The first week of filming, she latched on to him like he was her salvation, a champion who would sweep her away from her pain.

A month later, with Amy still in the running to be a *Chef Showdown* finalist, news of her mom's suicide attempt rocked her world off its axis once more. Not long after, Brock showed his true colors, and Amy humiliated herself with a tear-fueled rant in front of a full panel of judges and a camera that didn't miss a second of her tirade.

An *Ultimate Chef Showdown* moment for the ages, the four-minute clip had gone viral in an instant, and in less than a day, she had become an Internet sensation. Late-night talk show hosts included jokes about her in their monologues and nightly celebrity gossip news programs seized on her humiliation. She thought she'd finally been hurt deep enough for the lesson to stick.

Damn Kellan Reed. Damn his trustworthy face and slick moves and MAC knife collection. Damn him for worming his way past her defenses and splaying her spirit open only to trounce on it.

Like mother, like daughter.

No. As tempting as it was to fall into the unhealthy fear

that had consumed her for most of her life, she was learning with each painful experience she endured, the difference between her and her mother. Learning she was stronger than she ever thought possible. Her mother had let her grief over the cowboy who broke her heart destroy her, but Amy was still standing. Time after time, broken heart after broken heart, she was still moving forward, putting one foot in front of the other.

She still felt hope.

She still believed in love.

And that was the difference.

When they were done clearing the grates of the canal, Rachel stood, brushing ice from the sleeve of her jacket. "What gives, Amy? You're too quiet. You haven't said word one about your date. Did something happen with Kellan?"

A rush of warmth pricked Amy's cheeks at hearing his name aloud. She didn't want to talk about him, didn't want to admit to her stupidity. She poked her finger on the rounded tip of her ice pick. "Um . . . I forgot to ask him about setting up tours of his ranch for our guests."

Sighing, Rachel doffed her hat and ran her fingers through her mussed hair. "You slept with him, didn't you?"

Amy stared at Rachel, shocked. As far as she could recall, this was the first time she'd ever heard Rachel mention sex directly. She'd muddled her way through an awkward, brief relationship in her senior year of high school, but according to Jenna, hadn't dated since and certainly didn't act or dress like she was interested in attracting a man. For the longest time, the sisters chalked up Rachel's indifference to the dating scene to her preference for solitude, but in the past couple years, Amy and Jenna had taken to speculating about the possibility that Rachel was gay. Maybe her lack of a love life was due more to a lack of available partners in Eastern New Mexico ranch country.

Yet here Rachel was, asking Amy a pointed question

about her sex life. Not that Amy was ready or willing to discuss it. "What I did or didn't do with Kellan is none of your concern."

Rachel stowed her ice pick in her saddlebag and jerked the strap tight. Probably sensing her owner's agitation, the horse whinnied and sidestepped out of arm's reach. "It didn't go so well, judging by how defensive you're getting." Her voice was quiet, her tone frustrated. "You know, sleeping around with men you barely know is toxic for you in so many ways. Why couldn't you take it slow this time?"

Amy felt her anger winding up. She was feeling bad enough without Rachel adding her two cents. Too often, her conversations with Rachel disintegrated into arguments. They'd always had a terrible time communicating with each other, and probably always would, but that didn't give Rachel the right to lecture her . . . especially on a topic Amy was certain her sister knew nothing about. "You are not the morality police. And you're not my parent, either, so back off."

"No, I'm not going to back off, because you're adding unnecessary complications to our business with your self-destructive behavior."

"That's bullshit," Amy growled through her teeth.

"You think so?" Rachel's breath puffed like smoke in the brisk, morning air. She sipped from her canteen and took her time screwing the lid on. Amy waited, breathing hard through her nose because her jaw refused to unclench. "We're opening a new business—one that relies on local ranchers' support—and we can't afford to burn bridges, especially with a rancher as influential and connected as Kellan Reed. When are you going to learn to be less careless about who you give yourself to?"

Amy wrenched her molars apart as her anger unleashed. "I don't care how naturally bossy you are, you don't get to talk to me like that."

"Someone's got to. Do you have any idea how hard it is to watch you and Jenna turn into idiots around men, and then, when things go south, watch you both cope with the repercussions of your bad decisions? I'm entitled to an opinion because I love you both, and I'm sick and tired of you allowing yourself to be treated like crap. You're twenty-eight. You have to stop acting like some insecure teenager looking for validation through sex."

"Are you calling me a slut?"

Rachel stomped closer. "Don't twist my words. All I'm saying is you deserve better than a one-night stand."

"Maybe so, but it doesn't matter. I thought Kellan was different from the others and I was wrong." Amy heard the shrillness of her voice and swallowed, reining in her anger. "I should've stuck to my rules and steered clear of him the minute he came on to me at the Quick Stand. But I didn't, so here we are. Why don't you lay off, okay? I'm beating myself up enough for the both of us." She kicked a rock and watched it tumble into a cholla cactus, then kicked another. "Besides, I can't think of anyone less capable of giving me relationship advice than you."

*Tsk*ing loudly, Rachel stalked to the canal and stared at the water. "You and Jenna think I'm this . . . this *prude*. Like I couldn't possibly fathom how difficult it is for you two to keep your legs together every time some good-looking man waltzes across your paths."

Amy raised a hand in a gesture for Rachel to stop. "Save it, Rach. It won't happen again. Kellan and I agreed last night to go our separate ways." Her voice hitched. "But even so, just because you've never had a moment of weakness over a man doesn't give you the right to lecture me about the choices I make."

Rachel stomped to her horse and swung into the saddle. She fiddled with the reins and said quietly, "That's not completely true."

Because she was a few inches shorter than Rachel, it took Amy a couple bouncing tries to remount. "Excuse me?"

Rachel squinted into the distance. "Look, I've been where you are, I've had moments of weakness I regret, which is why I can see the path you're headed down with Kellan. It doesn't lead anywhere good, I can tell you that. Not for you and not for our new business either."

She turned her horse and started up the path they'd come.

"Rachel," Amy ventured. "What kind of moments of weakness are we talking about?"

"Not worth rehashing. Look, there's a time for romance and now's not it. We have too much on the line."

Amy gaped at Rachel's back, then decided to make a subtle play for more information. "Hearing you talk about romance is weird. You've never seemed to want a man in your life like Jenna and I do."

"That's because I don't want someone in my life. I can barely keep up with the demands of the farm. When I'm done working for the day, I don't want to worry about what outfit I'm going to wear for a date or what my hair looks like, or some baloney like that. I want to shovel food in my mouth, take a shower, and collapse into bed."

"Yes, but if you were in the market for a romantic relationship, what sort of person would you be interested in? A big ole man like Jenna and I like, or someone a little softer around the edges?" Amy cringed, thinking the implication about Rachel's sexuality was too obvious.

Rachel twisted in the saddle and flashed Amy a look that said, *Are you insane?*

Amy smiled. "Humor me."

"Okay. If I were in the market for a relationship—which I'm not—I'd want someone as passionate about being a farmer as I am to help me out. I've been running this place by myself for a long time and it would be nice to have a partner."

"A partner? You mean, like a life partner?"

"Yeah, a life partner who would run the farm with me. What are you getting at?"

Their conversation was going nowhere, fast. Amy pinched the bridge of her nose between her fingers and thought, *What the hell? Here goes nothing.* "Well . . . I don't know how to ask this, but . . ."

"Spit it out, Aim. What's pinging around in your head?"

"Jenna and I have been wondering for a while now. . . . Um . . . are you gay? Like, a lesbian or something. Because when I was in New York, I met—"

Far from acting offended, Rachel busted out with a belly laugh. "Woo-wee, I bet you and Jenna have thought long and hard about that one, huh? You two can invent gossip like nobody else. You think I'm gay because I'd rather eat and sleep than waste time primping and pining over a man? Trust me, I work so hard every day I wouldn't waste time primping and pining over a woman either."

Amy's brow furled at Rachel's ambiguous response. "So . . . does that mean you *are* gay?"

Rachel looked over her shoulder, an amused grin playing on her lips. "Nah, I'm not gay, but you and Jenna are free to think whatever you want. Doesn't matter to me. I know who I am."

Amy remained unconvinced. "Jenna and I would love you the same if you were, you know. It's no big deal."

"Sounds like you and Jenna already made it a big deal."

The trail opened up and Amy urged Nutmeg alongside Rachel's mount with the decision to give prying one last try. "So . . . who was the guy you had a moment of weakness over?"

"I plead the Fifth."

"But you're not gay?"

"I'm not gay."

"Then why won't you talk about him? Wait, you're blushing—are you a virgin?"

Rachel's eyes widened. "Geez! You're terrible. Number one, I'm not talking about it because I don't want to. And number two, I'm definitely not a blushing virgin. My cheeks are red because it's so damn cold."

"Mmm-hmm."

"Give it a rest."

Amy punched her playfully on the arm. "Someday you'll tell me about him."

"Not likely. But then, you always were the dreamer of the family."

They rode toward home in companionable silence through muddy fields and stopped on a ridge overlooking Jenna's cottage, with the roof of the big house peeking over the top of the barn a quarter mile down a dirt road. Jenna's car sat out front and a metal-framed swing set took up space on the side. Melting snow dripped off the sides of the roofs.

"I'm sorry it's not going to work out with you and Kellan."

Amy sighed. "Me, too. He told me he doesn't have room in his life for a relationship right now, and I don't either, truth be told. It still stings, not to be wanted."

Rachel shrugged. "He wanted you, just not in the same way you wanted him."

Amy winced. "That he did. But it was my fault. We seemed to have so much in common. I felt a powerful connection to him. I honestly thought he felt it too. I was wrong. Again."

"How do you end up picking such good-for-nothing men all the time? I mean, you can't possibly be that bad a judge of character, can you?"

Amy chuckled. Rachel never had been one to mince

words. "It's not as though I had great role models for a healthy relationship. Dad barely seemed to tolerate Mom. I don't think I ever saw him hold her hand or kiss her. He never took her out to dinner or made time for her."

"I always figured they were private about their affection. I mean, they created three kids, so they were obviously connecting on some level."

"Ew. I don't want to think about that."

Rachel shrugged a shoulder. "All I'm saying is there had to be some kind of love between them."

Amy watched a cloud slide across the midday sky, suddenly sad for them all. For the lack of romance and the loss of their parents. "Yet here we are, we three sisters, and not one of us has found success in love. What are the odds? Me, picking every rotten apple in the bunch, Jenna getting pregnant out of high school and won't even name the father, not that any man's come around wanting to claim Tommy. And you've got some secret romantic regret you won't talk about." She poked Rachel in the arm. "And plus, you're maybe a little gay."

"I'm not—oh, you're teasing. Ha, ha."

At that moment, Jenna ran out of her house, holding Tommy. She stopped in the driveway, her phone to her ear.

Rachel's phone chimed and she fished it from her pocket. "Hey, Jenna. Amy and I are up on the hill. Can you see us waving?" Her expression grew pensive. "Wait, slow down. What do you mean we have to get to the hospital? What happened?" Amy put her hand on Rachel's arm. Her gaze flickered to Amy, her eyes wide. "We're on our way. Strap Tommy into the car and pick us up at the main house."

Chapter 11

Kellan had been waiting on Amy's front porch for a long time. Long enough to play a dozen different games on his cell phone and watch a group of wild turkeys scramble across the road and back again. He had to take a leak but no way did he want Amy to show up while he was relieving himself in the grass. Or even worse, for either of her sisters to catch him in the act.

Out of nervous habit, he adjusted the knot of his tie. He was in his business duds today, ready to come clean with Amy about his connection to Amarex, her family's dire situation and limited choices, and how he planned to help as much as he could. In the briefcase near his feet, he'd packed a financial calculator, contracts, maps, and anything else he could think of that might help his cause. As a peace offering, he'd brought several pounds of beef loaded in a cooler. It wasn't as poetic as flowers would've been, but if anyone could appreciate the gesture, it would be Amy.

Over and over, her words from the previous night bounced around his head like a cruel taunt. *I need to see you again. Tonight is not enough.*

That made two of them.

The hurt in her eyes damn near killed him as much as the knowledge that he might never have the chance to hold her again. He shouldn't have brought her to his house. He dialed her cell phone number for the fourth time, but once again, it flipped to voice mail. Letting out a belabored exhale, he scrolled down the touch screen to the game mode.

Probably, he should think about his parents. About his father's release from prison and his mother's call to Morton. He needed to prepare himself for the possibility that one of the two of them would be calling to hit him up for money sometime soon. He should formulate a ready response so he wouldn't be caught off guard. And he still needed to call his brother.

The more he thought about his family, the more that old, familiar hollowness crept into his consciousness. And with the hollowness came the caustic memories he wished he could forget. Dredging up the past led to nowhere but hurt. He was a move-forward kind of man who had risen from the muck of his youth to build himself a better life, a better family than the one he'd first been born into.

His brother, Jake, had done the same. And maybe it was for that reason the two men had such trouble connecting as adults. They reminded each other of a shared history neither of them wanted to remember. Jake was a Los Angeles cop, and a damn good one from what Kellan had gleaned from their handful of phone calls over the years and the articles Kellan sometimes found on the Internet about Jake's law enforcement heroics. The LAPD had become Jake's new family, as much as Chris, Lisa, Daisy, Rowen, and Vaughn were Kellan's.

In the distance came the thunder of horse hooves approaching. Kellan pocketed his cell phone, listening. Maybe Amy had been riding the range that morning with Rachel, which would explain the empty house. The thought of seeing her move in the saddle got him feeling a bit tight in the groin, which was the last way he should be feeling at the moment. He stood, stretching out his legs. The horses were coming from the south, at the rear of the house, so he hopped over the rail to the ground, bypassing the porch steps, and followed the noise.

Sure enough, Amy and Rachel were galloping down a hill toward the house like a flood was chasing them. Kellan admired the sexy way the wind whipped through Amy's hair before registering both women's wide, panicky eyes, tense shoulders, and pursed lips. Fear. The minute Rachel reached the corral fence, she swung off her mount and hustled to open the gate. Her hands shook, rattling the chains keeping the gate locked but not making any progress. Amy leapt down to help her.

One of their horses was skittish, stomping and swishing its tail nervously. It seemed on the verge of rearing up, so Kellan walked to it and took command of its reins. "Amy, Rachel, is something wrong?"

Their heads swung around to regard him. Clearly they hadn't noticed his presence until he spoke.

"It's our mom," Amy said, her voice cracking. She looked like she was barely hanging on to her composure. "Doctors think she had a stroke. She's not conscious. We've got to get to the hospital."

Shit. Life for the Sorentino family was getting worse by the day. "Give me those," he said, grabbing the reins of the other horse too. He led them into the corral and checked the water supply. "Where's Jenna?"

As if his question conjured her, a small, white sedan stopped hard a few paces away, its brakes screeching. Jenna burst out from the driver's side. "The nurse called again. Mom's going in for emergency surgery, but there's a chance she might not pull through. They think the stroke was caused by a bleed. Oh, God, we have to get there."

Amy's hand flew to her mouth as a strangled sob broke free. Rachel ran for the car, snagging Amy's arm on the way. "Keep it together until we're on the road, Amy. Then you can freak out all you need to."

Kellan latched the gate and ran to intercept Jenna before she reached the car. "I'm driving," he said. "None of you are in any condition to be at the wheel."

Jenna wrung her hands and nodded, but didn't move toward the car.

Kellan draped an arm across her shoulders, led her to the backseat, and tucked her into the car next to Rachel and Tommy. Amy sat, trembling from head to toe, in the front passenger seat. He made a quick call to his ranch foreman to send workers to tend the Sorentino horses, then folded himself as best he could into the driver's seat and managed to get both legs in, though his knees hit the steering wheel.

The women were silent as Kellan negotiated the road to the highway. Once they thumped onto blacktop, he put a hand on Amy's knee. "Take a deep breath," he whispered. "Nothing you could've done differently."

She hugged herself. "I thought I'd be prepared to handle her passing. But I'm not ready."

"I'm going to get you there as fast and safely as I can. The nurse who called Jenna, she'd call again if there are any developments. I'm sure of it."

She looked bleakly out the side window, tears streaming over her face.

With a glance into the rearview mirror at Rachel and Jenna's own forlorn, distant expressions, Kellan wrenched Amy's quaking hand from around her ribs and took it firmly in his. Albuquerque was a three-hour drive, slightly less if conditions were ideal and the traffic light. Thank goodness the storm had passed before dawn and the roads were clear and dry.

The more miles they ate up, the more the tension in the car eased, due in large part to Tommy, who babbled on about road signs and asked nonstop questions to anyone willing to answer. Which pretty much meant Tommy and Kellan were having a two-way conversation about everything from tractors and pizza to cows. Kellan told him about his dog, Max, and Pickle, the horse he'd bought for Daisy the week she was born. For his part, Tommy expounded to great lengths on cartoon characters Kellan had never heard of.

An hour into the drive, Amy flipped her palm over and squeezed Kellan's hand. She looked his way, a sad smile on her lips. "Thank you for doing this."

Kellan nodded. "You're welcome." He chewed his lower lip, wondering how to approach such a delicate topic as their mom's downward spiral. "Any chance you feel up to telling me more about what happened to your mom?"

She wiggled her hand away from his grip and he thought, *Oh, man, I had to go flapping my lips, causing her more pain.* In the ensuing silence, he tugged his tie, loosening it enough to pop the top button of his shirt.

But then, she started fidgeting with her fingernails and talking. "Mom never was very stable, mentally. Superdepressive, but like on a roller coaster, you know? One day, she'd be the happiest woman in Catcher Creek and the next, she couldn't even get out of bed. Too proud to take medicine for it, she was this wild card in our lives."

Jenna leaned forward. "I remember getting ready for school and I'd listen at my bedroom door to figure out what kind of mood she was in that day. We never knew what to expect."

"Why do you guys think I worked such long hours on the farm?" Rachel added. "It wasn't because I was a glutton for hard labor, that's for sure. But it got me out of the house before anyone else was awake and kept me away until dark. I didn't have to deal with all her mood swings like the two of you chose to."

"We didn't choose to," Amy said. "Not consciously, anyway. Since you weren't around, you didn't only miss out on her bad days, but the good ones, too. I lived for her good days. She could be so much fun."

"She'd let us eat pie à la mode for breakfast," Jenna said.

"I love pie!" Tommy squealed.

Amy twisted in her seat to smile at Jenna. "Remember the morning she started a pie fight in the kitchen?"

Jenna laughed. "Our clothes were toast. And we were late for school because we had to shower to get the berries out of our hair. Mom lied to the school secretary that she had car trouble."

"That was a great day," Amy said quietly, her gaze drifting to the window. "But the bad days . . ." She shook her head.

Kellan squeezed her hand. He knew about bad days, about never knowing what you'd find when you woke up that morning. The not-knowing created a constant ache in your belly, burning a hole right through the middle of you. He knew about the desperate clinging to the good days, to the flashes of happiness and harmony. "Your dad died in a car accident, right?"

"Last New Year's Eve. He drove off Hoja Pass when the steering mechanism of his truck malfunctioned," Amy said.

Rachel leaned forward. "And before you ask—no, he hadn't been drinking and, no, he wasn't depressed. That day, he was stone-cold sober. He worked the morning milking and fed the livestock, like most days."

"I'm a little surprised you don't know the whole story already," Amy said, her tone wary.

"At the time, I heard talk in town, but never got a feel for what happened."

Jenna huffed. "You mean, your bestie, Sheriff Cooper, didn't fill you in on all the sordid details of our private lives?"

Jenna's hostility threw him off, though he shouldn't have been surprised. No one wanted to be the subject of rampant gossip, which was why Kellan had worked so rigorously to keep his parents and his past a secret. "Believe it or not, Vaughn takes his job seriously. He's tight-lipped on cases he's involved in."

Thinking about Vaughn got him wondering again about what happened between him and Rachel, how their bad blood got started. Both Vaughn and Rachel were strong, stubborn personalities. Maybe they'd disagreed over his handling of Gerald's accident or the conclusions he'd reached. He filed the questions away to ask Vaughn about later.

"He died around the time you were filming *Ultimate Chef Showdown,* right?" He didn't want to pile the unpleasant memories on Amy, but since watching the show, he'd wondered why she hadn't quit and gone home, given how close she and her sisters were.

"Three days before filming started, actually."

"Was going on the show a difficult choice to make after that?"

Amy shrugged a shoulder. "Yes, and no. I wanted to support Mom, Rachel, and Jenna more than anything, but Dad was always one to follow his dreams no matter what, even if others didn't understand or agree with him, so I knew he'd be proud of the choice I made not to quit when the going got tough. And when we discovered the debt he left us, the three-hundred-thousand-dollar grand prize on the show sounded awfully good."

"Was your mom overcome with grief when your dad died?"

"I'm not sure *grief* is the right word. My folks had a

rocky relationship. Dad was a good-timer, a gambler. And Mom, with her shaky mental health, was too fragile to stand up to him or tell him what she needed."

"And when your father died?" he prompted.

Rachel answered. "When Dad died, Mom was . . ."

"Stricken," Jenna added. "There's no other word for it. Since she was already so emotionally fragile, after Dad died, she needed to be watched over all the time, but that was easier said than done. She'd wander off in the middle of the night and we'd get a call from the police to come pick her up at some random bar or gas station. We tried to get her on medication, but she wouldn't take it. Looking back, we should have put her in a facility immediately."

He witnessed one of her less lucid episodes in the Clovis Walmart. She'd wandered the aisles in the gardening section, muttering nonsense about buying dirt to fill in holes so people wouldn't steal from her, working herself into a fit before security whisked her away. No need to bring that incident up now.

"You two did all you could," Amy said. "Don't beat yourselves up. You can't help someone who doesn't want it. Besides, we were all grieving for Dad. We had so much stuff to deal with, it's amazing we didn't need to check ourselves into a facility."

"If it hadn't been for Tommy, I would have considered it after Mom's overdose," Jenna added.

"How long after your dad passed did that happen?"

"Four weeks."

He had a lot of questions, but how did one ask for details of such a painful memory? Maybe he should've kept his trap shut, but he found himself asking, "Who found her?"

"Jenna and I did," Rachel said. "It was an hour or so after daybreak, I went to her room to wake her up and she was gone. By then, we'd taken away her car keys, so we knew she couldn't have gone too far. We found her on the northern edge of our property, unconscious. There was blood everywhere because she'd hit her head on a rock, but she had a pulse and she was breathing. Thank God we had cell phones."

Kellan navigated around a trailer hauling oil drilling equipment and kept his speed steady. Only an hour or so until they reached the outskirts of the city. The nurse hadn't called again, which he took as a good sign. "She was so lucky you found her."

"Maybe, maybe not," Amy said quietly.

Kellan glanced sideways at her. "What do you mean?"

"Rachel and I found vodka and an empty bottle of painkillers next to her," Jenna said. "With the pills and the alcohol and hitting her head on the rock, the damage to her brain was devastating. She regained consciousness after a ten-day coma, but her mind is gone for the most part. She can't even take care of her own basic bodily functions."

No wonder Amy hedged her answer. How lucky was it to stay alive, but never really be able to live again? "Do you think she meant to kill herself?"

"We weren't sure at first," Jenna said. "Amy jumped on a plane and met us at the hospital. We all stayed in Albuquerque together, so we didn't know about her note until Sheriff Cooper found it in her bathroom during his investigation. That was the toughest part for me, knowing it wasn't an accident, that she'd made a choice."

"Me too," Amy said.

"You returned to *Chef Showdown* after that. I'm honestly surprised."

She folded her hands in her lap and stared down at them. "In hindsight, I shouldn't have. But at the time, I was only thinking about winning the money so we could keep the farm. I didn't want our family to lose that on top of everything else. I told myself that Mom was my biggest supporter, so she wouldn't mind. She was the one who suggested I audition. I never felt closer to my mom than the day I called to tell her I'd been accepted onto the show. If anything, I thought it would upset her if I quit, that giving up would be like letting go of her dream for me. But after I returned to film the semifinals, I had a complete breakdown while the cameras were rolling."

"I know." He admitted quietly. But it felt like a lie of omission not to confess. "I watched it online this week. I'm sorry."

She nodded. "It's okay. I'm still making my peace with what happened, but the truth is, I knew what I was signing up for when I joined the show. It was a career gamble that would've paid off if I hadn't—"

"If you hadn't been victimized by that conniving asshole, Brock," he finished.

"*Victimized* makes it sound like I wasn't part of the problem. But what happened to me on *Chef Showdown* was my fault alone. I allowed Brock to take advantage of me because I fabricated an emotional intimacy that wasn't real." She regarded him with sad eyes. "If you haven't figured it out yet, that's my M.O."

Kellan swallowed and tightened his grip on the steering wheel. He wanted so badly to tell her their electricity had been real. He not only felt it, but it knocked him on his ass. He wanted to confess to everything—his unwanted, exhilarating feelings for her, his link to Amarex, the truth about his parents. Now was hardly an appropriate time, though. Not with her mother's life hanging in the balance and her two sisters in the car, analyzing his every word.

"You're being too hard on yourself, Amy," he croaked. "The other contestants on the show, they were scared of you. Scared of your skill and your heart. The way you light up a room by walking in it. They were quaking in their boots because they knew you were the best contestant on the show. You outshone everybody."

Including him.

"Kellan's right," Jenna said, laying a hand on Amy's shoulder. "Brock and the others sabotaged you because they knew there wasn't any other way to beat you at the game."

"Stop it," Amy said, sounding tired. "You don't need to massage my ego. What's done is done."

Rachel squeezed Amy's other shoulder. "They're right, Aims. You owned that show until Mom . . . until she . . ." Her voice trailed off.

Amy reached up and took both her sisters' hands. "I feel like we've been saying good-bye to Mom for almost a year, but I'm still not ready to let her go."

"None of us are."

Jenna set her other hand on Rachel's shoulder. "We'll get through this together, as a family, no matter what. Like we do with everything else."

Amy rested her ear against Rachel's hand.

A thick silence descended over the car. Kellan's thoughts turned to Jake, and how differently Amy and her siblings handled tragedy from him and his brother. The Sorentino sisters banded together. They held hands and stuck it out. They didn't run. They didn't give up on each other. They had a mess of a family—a verifiable disaster of a legacy—but their closeness called to Kellan in an unfamiliar way.

He was jealous.

In the months following his parents' arrests, he and Jake hopscotched through foster homes, awaiting word about whether any of their extended family would take them in. At first, they'd spent every possible moment together before and after school and on the weekends. After a while, they morphed from joined-at-the-hip brothers to roommates. They never could seem to articulate their individual pain, never could figure out how to work together. They ended up in a group home for teenage boys. The food was plentiful, and the couple who ran the house was nice enough.

Kellan's eighteen-year-old logic didn't see the problem in leaving his fifteen-year-old brother behind when the system kicked him out. On his own, he could think of nothing but getting as far away from Florida as possible. He wanted answers from his family as to why they hadn't opened their arms and their houses to two neglected kids who needed a place to stay.

Once Jake aged out of the system, he followed Kellan's lead by hitting the road west. They'd met briefly at a diner in West Texas. The resentment in Jake's voice toward Kellan was palpable, shocking. Until that night, it had never occurred to Kellan that Jake felt like he'd abandoned him. Kellan was only twenty at the time of the meeting, and still angry at the world. Instead of apologizing to Jake, he'd gotten defensive and stormed out again.

Thinking back to that meeting made him ache with regret. But he never could figure out a way to make things right between them.

The parade of ranches scattered over the plains of the high desert gave way to rocky slopes and pinion trees. The white-topped mountain ridges that signified the outskirts of Albuquerque grew nearer with each passing mile. Kellan rested his forearm along the closed window, concentrating on the bite of cold glass and the dashed lines of the highway, anything to keep from taking Amy's small hands in his, or thinking about how different his own fractured family was from the damaged, yet united, Sorentino clan.

They crept down the final descent through the mountains behind a convoy of semitrucks and after two and a half hours on the road, finally spotted the WELCOME TO ALBUQUERQUE sign nestled between two audacious billboards. The four-lane route stretched into a broad freeway as Albuquerque passed by them in a blur of concrete suburbia.

"Can we talk more about pie?" Tommy asked, breaking the silence.

"Maybe when we get to the hospital, you and I can go in search of some pie," Kellan said. "If it's okay with your mom."

"She says yes," Tommy squealed, clapping his hands.

"Hold on, there, buddy. Let's get there first," Jenna said. "I can't think about anything else until we do."

They reached Presbyterian Hospital around two o'clock. The sprawling campus buzzed with activity, but Rachel, Amy, and Jenna negotiated the crowds at a breakneck pace, pushing through the sliding glass doors and across the reception area, to the elevators leading to the ICU. Clearly, they knew their way around the place.

Inside the elevator, Kellan snagged Jenna's attention long enough for her to transfer Tommy to his arms and rattle off her cell phone number. When the elevator doors opened on the ICU floor, Kellan and Tommy remained inside, with Tommy waving merrily at the backs of his mom and aunts as they disappeared down a hallway. As soon as they were alone and the elevator had begun its descent to the basement that housed the cafeteria, Kellan stood Tommy up and squatted so they were at eye level.

"If the cafeteria doesn't have pie, are you going to fuss?"

Tommy shook his head, his eyes wide and serious. "Oh, no. I'll eat any kind of sugar. That's why I have a sweet tooth."

Kellan ruffled his hair. "Fair enough, let's see what we find."

Hand in hand, they strolled from the elevator into a quiet hallway, following the signs and smell of coffee to the cafeteria.

* * *

Three hours, four cups of coffee, and two slices of apple pie later, Kellan stared at a muted television set in the waiting room adjacent to the ICU, with Tommy passed out on his chest, his face burrowed into Kellan's neck.

Jenna had popped out once, an hour or so earlier, to check on them. Tommy was already deep in slumber. Jenna smoothed the hair around his ear and kissed his cheek. Her eyes were red and puffy, but she sounded strong as she explained that their mom had survived surgery. They didn't know any more details and were awaiting the arrival of their mom's primary doctor, who was on the way from her office across town. Meanwhile, all three daughters felt the need to keep vigil at their mom's bedside.

After assuring her that he was fine taking care of Tommy for as long as was necessary, she kissed the tip of her finger and pressed it to Tommy's lips, then slipped through the doors to the ICU.

Kellan turned his face into Tommy's hair, smelling his little-boy smells, measuring the rhythm of his breaths. It felt good having a child sleep in his lap. As it felt with Daisy or Rowen—good and peaceful and life affirming. Holding him got Kellan thinking about what a lucky little guy Tommy was, growing up in a household of smart, vibrant women who loved him. It got Kellan thinking about the things he wanted for his own children one day, and about innocence and forgiveness. Hope. Holding Tommy made him sad for himself and Jake, and the years they wasted with hurt feelings and purposeful negligence.

Carefully, carefully, he threaded his fingers through his pocket, past the tie he'd stuffed inside after Tommy had used it as a napkin, and wrangled his cell phone out. He scrolled through the contact list, searching for his brother's name.

He didn't remember inputting it into his phone, but his need to hear Jake's voice hit him with a fresh urgency.

Jake's phone number wasn't there. And with him being a cop, Kellan knew he wouldn't find any personal information in an Internet directory. He considered leaving a message at the LAPD, but had no idea what location he worked out of. Frustrated by his own pathetic ignorance of the details of his only brother's life, he navigated to an Internet search engine and typed "Jake Reed." A six-month-old article on Jake's latest heroics popped up. Kellan had read it before, more than once, but he read it again. This time without so much of a sense of brotherly pride, but a sense of longing.

The door to the ICU opened. Rachel stepped out and flopped into the seat next to Kellan, puffing her cheeks with a belabored exhale.

Bracing a hand on Tommy's back, he shifted in his chair so he could look at her. "Any news?"

"Yeah, but none of it good. The surgeons weren't able to do more than patch the bleed. And every single doctor in the room is hedging their bets about whether or not she'll wake up or breathe again without a respirator. It's *wait and see* about this and *only time will tell* about that. Hundreds of thousands of dollars in education in that room and all they have to say is that we need to wait and see." She huffed. "No shit, Sherlock."

No one Kellan loved had experienced a medical emergency like this. The closest he got was the two times Lisa had gone into labor. He thought about how he'd feel if Vaughn got hurt on the job. The horrible waiting, trusting doctors to know their stuff and make the best choices. It would be brutal, the helplessness.

"Is there anything more I can do? Get you all something to eat or drink? Call anyone?" he asked.

Rachel's gaze settled on Tommy. Her expression softened. "No. This is good, what you've done. Jenna would've crashed the car if she'd driven us here. I appreciate you stepping up."

"Not a problem. Glad I was there."

"Why were you at our house, anyway?"

"I needed to talk to Amy. Still do, but it can wait until a better time."

Rachel's mouth screwed up. "You hurt her last night. Pretty badly. She didn't give me the details, but she never was good at hiding her feelings. Did you come over this morning to apologize?"

His heart sank at the confirmation that he'd caused her pain. Almost seemed inevitable after the chain of boneheaded decisions he'd made the night before, starting with the way he'd ignored his conscience and kept their date in the first place. He needed to apologize and explain as best he could, but he certainly wasn't going to bring Rachel into the loop before he squared things with Amy.

"Think I'll wait and talk to Amy first."

"When you and I talked on Sunday, you promised me you wouldn't hurt her. And that's the first thing you did."

"The circumstances changed, okay? And really, it's none of your business."

"When someone hurts my sister, I make it my business."

Kellan crinkled his eyebrows in an *oh, please* look. He felt his hackles stir, his defenses gearing up for battle. "You know what? I don't care what you say, you're as nosy and gossipy as everyone else in this town. This is the second time you've tried to put yourself in the middle of our relationship. If Amy wants you to know what's going on, she'll tell you."

They glared at each other until Kellan broke away, a

little ashamed for snapping at someone whose mom was suffering a life-threatening health scare a few rooms over.

"You think I'm being pushy." She picked at a splash of mud on her jeans. "But Jenna and Tommy and Amy are my only family. I'm going to protect them no matter what."

"I respect that about you. I do. All I can tell you right now is that I'm going to do the best I can for Amy. You'll have to trust me."

"Why would I trust you?"

He squinted up at the florescent lights. "That's a good question. One I hope time will answer."

She snorted. "Wait and see—my least favorite phrase in the English language."

He smiled, a peace offering. "You want me to say it in Spanish?"

"Nice try."

"Is Amy okay?" he asked. "I mean, with your mom. Is she coping? I haven't seen her since we got to the hospital."

"She's hanging in there, but she can't hardly tear her eyes away from Mom, like she might disappear or something. One thing about Amy is she's tougher than she looks. And she's definitely tougher than she thinks she is."

"You're right about that." He'd only known her for a week, but in that time, she'd proven herself to be one of the strongest, most resilient people he'd ever known. Rachel got up to leave, but Kellan stopped her with a hand on her arm. "Listen, you're going to think this is the pot calling the kettle black, but I have to ask you something."

She settled into the chair. "Shoot."

"What's going on with you and Vaughn?"

Her spine stiffened and her expression grew defensive. "And you accused me of inserting myself into other people's business?"

"Like I said, pot and kettle. So . . . what happened between you two?"

She found a splash of mud on her forearm to pick at, and took to bouncing her leg. "What did Vaughn tell you?"

"He didn't tell me anything." Not true, but he was a smart enough man not to tell her that Vaughn didn't seem to care for her. "It's just that, the other day, after you left, he was agitated. He had the urge to take up smoking again."

Her bouncing leg stilled. "He'd stopped?"

Interesting. "Eleven months ago."

She swallowed, her stare growing more vacant. Then she seemed to shake herself awake. "Good for him. For his health, I mean."

With an observant eye on her, he fleshed out the details. "He never said what prompted him to quit. The decision seemed to come out of the blue. But once he made the choice, he was all in. He stopped cold-turkey and was impossible to be around for a month or so. He yelled a lot and moped around. Lisa Binderman swore he was going through the classic symptoms of heartbreak."

"Heartbreak?"

Kellan didn't miss the catch in her whispered word. "You know, because he ended his relationship with nicotine. Anyway, after a time, he started smiling again, cracking jokes. Got back to his old self. But it took a while. Smoking really had a hold on him." Narrowing his eyes at her, he decided to take a calculated risk. "But when he saw you on Sunday, something inside him seemed to snap. He got that same damaged look in his eyes as he had after he quit smoking. Why do you suppose that is, Rachel?"

"How should I know what's going through his head?"

"Something tells me you do."

She turned her eyes to the ceiling and sighed. "And if I told you it was none of your business?"

"Then I'd say, when someone hurts my family, I make it my business."

"Touché."

"Look, I've known Vaughn for twelve years and other than the month he quit smoking, he's never gone to such a dark place in his head as he did when he saw you. I don't like having one of my best friends upset."

Sniffing, Rachel stood. Discomfort rippled over her features. "I'm sorry I upset him. I'll have to work harder to avoid him in the future."

Whoa, there. What in the hell happened between them? Something major, that much was clear. Because now Rachel was looking like Vaughn had the other day— restless and bitter and full of private pain. He snagged her hand. "Hey, did Vaughn hurt you?"

She wrenched away from his grip. "Yes, he did. But I hurt him too. And that's all you need to know."

She strode away, the ICU doors flapping closed behind her.

Chapter 12

Amy must have drifted to sleep while Kellan drove to Catcher Creek because she roused when the car paused at the base of the highway off-ramp to find her cheek pressed against the cold window. Then a picture of her mom, frail and unconscious, buffeted by tubes and wires and machines, pierced her haze of drowsiness. Sorrow, colder than the window, seeped into her system.

Then guilt arrived, trotting out to sit on her heart, threatening to crush her. She'd wished for her mom to die. Sitting vigil at her mom's bedside, she'd prayed—spoken directly to God—about allowing her mom to leave this world for the next, for Him to have mercy on her and let her die. What a horrible daughter she must be to think such thoughts.

She resisted further movement, feigning sleep. She needed this quiet time to sift through her memories of the day. A blanket draped over her midsection and legs kept her warm enough to stave off shivering. She fingered the material. Kellan's suit jacket. A sweet gesture, kind and chivalrous. As he always was. Except when he admitted his mistake in bringing her to his house. Except when she laid her heart on the line and he reminded her that all he wanted was a one-night stand.

She moved her partially closed eyes to the left. The clock read eleven-fifteen. They'd remained at the hospital until Mom was stable enough to move to the stroke unit on the seventh floor. The whole time, Amy longed for Kellan's reassuring presence, the strength of his embrace . . . and hated herself for wanting him despite everything. Jenna brought reports of his goodness to Mom's room, gushing about how sweet he looked holding Tommy as he slept, and how much of a lifesaver he was to care for her son so she could focus on Mom.

She angled her head to watch him. He drove left-handed, with his right elbow resting on the center console. Though his face was little more than a silhouette in the darkness, she could make out the chiseled plane of his cheeks, the dark dusting of stubble over his square jaw, his expression of concentration.

Allowing her heavy eyelids to flutter shut before he felt her staring, she smoothed a hand over the silky fabric lining the interior of Kellan's suit jacket. Why had he been standing outside her house that morning? Dressed in a suit like a door-to-door salesman. No, the suit reminded her more of the clothing the *Chef Showdown* producers wore—crafted of high-end fabric, beautifully tailored. Was her mind playing tricks on her or had she actually caught a glimpse of a black leather briefcase on the porch?

He'd seemed so straightforward at first glance last weekend at the Quick Stand. A local good ol' boy, with the wardrobe and the physique of one too. He owned and operated a ranch, and kept the schedule to prove it. Early to rise, early to bed, with lots of hard labor in between. But every time she'd seen him since church on Sunday, he appeared less like a cowboy. More city-dwelling and so-phisticated. More complex.

She cracked her eyelids open again and studied him, her instincts on alert. Where was his tie? Doffed for comfort? The sleeves of his white dress shirt were rolled up to expose his forearms. His face gave nothing away except a hint of his fatigue, but Amy's instincts wouldn't shut up. She had no evidence to support her theory, and could easily blame her fatigue for her paranoia, but she couldn't shake the feeling that Kellan was more than he seemed. That he was concealing a crucial piece of himself. Like Brock McKenna.

What had he said to her the night before, in his bedroom as Amy scrounged on the floor for her discarded clothes? *This isn't the way I envisioned telling you the truth about me—about my other business connection in Quay County and the conflict of interest.*

What other business?

At the time, she was too humiliated by her wanton behavior to listen. But now, she wanted to know. Had her manipulations at the hands of Brock McKenna left her looking for betrayal where none existed . . . or was Kellan hiding something?

The car slowed, then turned. The road grew bumpy. They'd arrived at Sorentino Farm. The sound of movement from the backseat told her Jenna and Rachel were stirring, probably jostled awake by the change in terrain. Amy stretched and straightened. In her periphery, she saw Kellan's gaze dart to her, his brows pinched in concern.

She didn't acknowledge him, knowing her eyes would give away her tumult of emotions. Her body felt electric, alive. Angry. She wanted answers. And so help her, Kellan wasn't leaving her property until she got some.

He pulled to a stop in front of the big house, angling it so the headlights illuminated the porch, and shifted into park with the engine running. He opened Rachel's door and offered her his hand. Amy twisted in her seat and squeezed Jenna's hand. "Get some rest, sis. I'll call you in the morning."

Jenna yawned. "Not too early. Maybe Tommy'll let me sleep until seven or so."

"That would be awfully considerate of him."

Amy's door opened. Cold night air whooshed over her. She stared up at Kellan, who regarded her solemnly and offered his hand. She hung his jacket over his fingers as though it were a coat hook and stood. "You're going to drive Jenna and Tommy home?"

"Yeah. I'll walk back for my truck."

"I'll be waiting. We need to talk."

A flash of surprise crossed his features before disappearing, replaced by resolve. "Not tonight. You need to rest. And I do too. It's been a long, draining day for all of us."

Nice try. She brushed past him toward the house.

"Good night, Amy," he said quietly.

She paused, one foot on the stairs, her gaze settling on the elegant black leather briefcase tucked on the floor near the porch swing. "Take Jenna and Tommy home. I'll be waiting."

The screen door banged shut behind Rachel. The porch light flickered on. The shadows on the porch shifted as Kellan swung Jenna's car around and drove away. Amy propped the screen door open with her shoulder. Rachel had left a trail of lights on for her, leading to the second floor.

"I'm going to watch the stars for a bit, see if I can screw my head on straight before I try to sleep," she hollered at the staircase.

Rachel's head poked over the railing. "Don't push Kellan tonight. He did us a big favor, driving us to the hospital and keeping an eye on Tommy."

With a plastic smile, Amy shut the front door on Little Miss Bossypants. She settled onto the porch's bench swing and hauled the heavy briefcase onto her lap. Her palms slid over the cold, smooth leather.

This isn't the way I envisioned telling you the truth about me.

Her thumbs settled on the latches. Time to open it and discover Kellan's secrets. Then again, perhaps he'd come to her farm that morning with a Slipping Rock beef supply contract. If so, then violating his privacy would be a huge mistake. But she didn't think today's surprise visit had been about beef, not with the designer suit and tie. And yet, he'd driven his beater truck. The pricey briefcase and truck didn't line up. A flick of her thumbs pushed the latches open. The sound cracked in the silent night. A fist through the darkness.

Rancher Kellan or Businessman Kellan. Worn-out Cowboy Boots verses Polished Loafers. Who was he?

She sounded as paranoid as her mom on one of her bend-ers. Another flick of her thumbs resealed the case. She hugged it to her chest. Papers inside shifted, along with the clink of pens sliding and resettling. Rocking the swing with the heel of her boot, she waited, staring at the outlines of distant mountain ridges framed against the moonlit sky. The winter air numbed her fingers and ears.

The crunch of boots on gravel preceded Kellan's arrival. Amy's heart rate picked up. Locking her fingers together to steady them, she blanked her expression and watched Kellan approach.

He stopped at the base of the stairs, his dark eyes intense on her, toggling from her face to the briefcase, then back. The line of his lips straightened and thinned. His cheek rippled, like he'd clamped his teeth together. "Did you look inside?"

"No." But now she wished she had.

He nodded and took the stairs two at a time. Perching on the far edge of the bench, he eased the case from her lap and set it on the floor, out of her reach.

Amy gnawed her bottom lip, working up the nerve to begin the interrogation. "Why did you come to my house this morning?"

"You've been through enough today. Can't we save this for tomorrow? Get some sleep?"

"I'm going to the hospital tomorrow. So we'll talk about

this now. Why did you come to my house, when last night you didn't want anything more to do with me?"

He shifted his weight more fully onto the swing and propped his elbows on his knees, head in hands. Amy counted stars, giving him time to work up to an explanation. Clearly, it was going to be a doozy.

"I grew up in Henderson Mill, Florida, Calhoun County," he said, leaning back. "Me, my mom and dad, and my brother, Jake."

Okay. "What are you getting at? I want to know about this morning."

"This is part of it—how I grew up, my family. You need to understand."

He seemed tormented, as though he were confessing to dark secrets or sins. She had no idea how stories of his childhood related to their discussion, but she'd indulge him to a point. "All right. Is your family still in Florida?"

"No . . . I don't know . . . I'll get to that. My mom worked the evening shift at the local grocery store. She was like a ghost. We felt her presence in the house, found evidence, but didn't see much of her. Most of the time it was only Jake and me, and my dad in the evenings. He was the one who made us dinner, tucked us in bed most nights. We did all right for three guys until he decided it was more fun to be high than deal with his real life."

"Sounds like my dad, more or less. Did your dad have a job?"

"He worked at a silkscreen factory. By high school, I looked for any excuse not to be at home. It was so depressing, seeing my dad half baked. My mom, too, on her days off."

Amy shoved her hands in her pockets, lest she reach out to comfort him like she wanted to. "So what did you do to fill the time? Wander the streets? Stay with friends?"

"Football."

She visualized a younger version of Kellan, beefed up

in football gear, looking tough. "Bet you were the star quarterback. Girls probably threw themselves at you on a regular basis."

He cracked a halfhearted smile. "They might've, if I'd stuck with it. I only played my freshman and sophomore years. Never got a chance to be the star quarterback, though I dreamed about it every night."

"Were you injured?"

"No. We moved school districts, Jake and me. After that, there wasn't any money for football." He paused, his eyes distant and sorrowful. With a slow exhalation, he raked his fingers through his hair. "When I was sixteen, the summer before my junior year, my parents were arrested."

That was not at all the direction of the story Amy had anticipated. "Arrested?"

"For embezzling money from the grocery store Mom worked at. They were convicted on multiple counts, with a fifteen-year sentence each."

"Oh my God."

He leapt to his feet and walked to the rail. "Don't say it like that."

"Like what? Like I care?"

He whirled to face her. "No, like it's so shocking. Like it's the first time in the history of the world people got arrested for being greedy and stupid. Stuff like that happens all the time. Greed's not a new sin."

Amy nodded. He didn't want pity. She collected herself before asking, "What about the instant mashed potatoes you love because they remind you of growing up? When you told me that, I assumed you had a great childhood."

"I like remembering that part. When I was young and sometimes my dad would let me cook. I was so proud to help. The potatoes were one of the few foods I knew how to fix. Besides opening a can. And I felt like a man, like Dad trusted me to be safe around the boiling water, even though I was only six or seven. I think about it now and he was probably high. Or drunk."

That's how Amy learned to cook. When her mom was too depressed to leave her room, and her dad was nowhere to be found, Amy took charge of the meals. The kitchen was the one place where she had control of the outcome. "What happened to you and your brother after they went to jail?"

"Jake and I entered the foster care system, but there weren't many placement options for teenage brothers. We ended up in a boy's home the next county over."

"And when you were eighteen, you left."

He turned to the rail, hunching into his arms. "When I was eighteen, I left."

"And Jake?"

"When he was eighteen, he left, too. He's a cop in L.A. A damned good one, as far as I can tell. We aren't close." His tone was laced with regret.

"Why not?"

Kellan shook his head. "He hated me for leaving. He took it personally, like I was abandoning him. And you know what? He was right. It was a shitty thing for me to do."

She joined him at the rail, not so close that she brushed his sleeve with her arm, but near enough to feel his heat and wish she were at liberty to lean into it. "You were only eighteen. It wasn't fair for him to put that burden on you."

"I should've stayed in Florida. I was way too immature to become his guardian or anything, but I should've stuck around. We could've celebrated Christmas together, and our birthdays. I could've helped him when he aged out of the system. But I was an angry, selfish punk. We had family in Texas—my mother's brother and his wife. All I could think about was hitchhiking to their doorstep to demand answers about why they didn't take Jake and me in when we needed a place to stay. I didn't give any consideration to what Jake needed from me. I'll regret that choice for the rest of my life."

"Have you told him that?"

"No. Tried once, but he was too angry to hear me out."

"What about your parents?" She did some quick mental math. "They must be out of prison by now."

"Yes. My mom served eight years of her sentence. My dad, ten. Didn't take him long to violate his probation, though. Not only did he fail a drug test within the first year, but he was caught with possession and stolen property. Dumb bastard served five more years."

"Did you stay in contact with them while they were imprisoned?"

"No." He spit the word out so vehemently, Amy didn't dare push for details.

"What about since their release? Your mom—"

"Yeah, my mom called after she got out, even managed a *Honey, I missed you* before hitting me up for bus money and a place to crash."

"And?"

His broad shoulders grew even stiffer, sliding up toward his ears. He watched his hands close into fists and release, over and over. "I don't have any use for my parents, or my uncle. My friends in Catcher Creek, the Bindermans and Vaughn, they're all the family I need."

Liar, she thought. No one who spoke with such pain could convince her of his indifference—especially to family. She'd learned the hard way that blood ties weren't a coat to shed when they became inconvenient or painful. Family was forever, no matter how often or how desperately one wished otherwise.

Kellan's tone, the tension in his body, told Amy he knew it too.

"Did you actually hitchhike to Texas and confront your uncle?"

"I did. Took four months of working odd jobs along the way, but I made it."

"What did you say to him?"

A bemused smile flashed on his lips. "At first, I didn't say anything. I socked him in the jaw."

"Seriously?"

"Like I said, I was an angry punk. But half-starved and weak. My uncle, Bruce, wrestled me into a headlock and dragged me into his house."

"Did he hurt you?"

"No. He gave me a shot of whiskey and a job. Never did like his answer about why he didn't take me and my brother in—his wife, Eileen, couldn't have handled teenage boys, he said—but I took the job he offered."

"Why?"

He met her eyes. "I wanted to take his money. I wanted to make him pay."

"And did you make him pay?"

"No. Revenge never actually works, does it? He gave me the property that I turned into Slipping Rock Ranch and a fifty-thousand-dollar loan when I turned twenty."

Amy's brows raised. "That's a lot of money. Not too many folks have cash like that sitting around, much less available to loan."

He shook his hands out and braced them against the railing. Looking up at the sky, his next words were strained. "Here's where we get to answering your questions about what I was doing at your place this morning. Why you and I can't see each other again on a personal level."

Oh, how she wanted to cover his hand with hers, the pain on his face was so deep. One glance at the briefcase on the floor, though, and she remembered how he'd hurt her, remembered that he'd withheld secrets. "This is about what you mentioned last night, your other business connection in Quay County."

He walked to the northern edge of the porch and

looked in the direction of his property. "My uncle originally bought the Slipping Rock property to look for oil. He thought it would be a great investment, but it turned out dry. So he gave it to me, daring me to make something of it. Which I did."

Amy wasn't getting how the story pertained to Kellan's visit that morning. "Your uncle, how did he make his money? Oil investments?"

"Yes."

"And he gave you a slice of his oil riches, didn't he?"

Kellan nodded. "Yes. The year I paid him back for the property."

A niggling feeling started in Amy's gut. She knew where he was headed with this windy tale he'd told her. He was secretly rich. The cattle ranch was only a front. Oh, God, he was a fake cowboy. *Like Brock McKenna.*

Rule number four: no tears in public. Rule number five: don't say anything stupid. She took a deep breath. She could handle this turbulent day; she wasn't her mom. She had the rules to prove it. "What is your secret business connection?"

He turned and looked her square in the eye from across the porch. "Amy, I'm the sole heir of Amarex Petroleum."

He held his breath. It felt odd, coming clean to Amy. Saying the truth aloud. He expected to feel relieved, not ready to pass out. Or throw up. He found himself hoping for any reaction, silently urging her to explode with the anger he so rightly deserved, but her face was blank.

A moth swooped near her head. She flinched and swatted at it.

"Your uncle is Bruce Morton?" She stared at the dirt near Kellan's feet as she spoke. "CEO and founder of Amarex Petroleum?"

"Yes."

Her cheek twitched. "And he made you his . . ."

"His heir, in his will. Yes."

She blinked at him. Not really at him, because she wouldn't meet his eyes. The blinking turned to nodding. Man, was she nodding like a crazy person. Her eyes flickered to his face, then she lunged and snatched up his briefcase.

She marched down the porch stairs and into the darkness, nodding and muttering, "Stupid, stupid, stupid."

Kellan jogged behind her. "Amy, listen to me, I'm not like him. My uncle. I don't want you—"

"Shhhhh!" she scolded, flinging a wild arm back toward him.

Pursing his lips, he stayed a few paces behind her, staring at her ponytail and the pale, smooth skin of her neck. Her stride was purposeful, determined. She turned onto a dirt road that led deeper into the property.

Desperate for her to know the whole truth, he tried again to explain. "I never asked my uncle to do that, and he won't change his mind. You have to understand, I don't want anything to do with Amarex. I'm not that guy. I'm a rancher."

She stopped walking at the edge of a pond, the sort of man-made watering hole for livestock to use as drinking water. She wound back and chucked the briefcase into the air like a Frisbee. With a splash, it landed in the middle of the pond.

There wasn't much in there that Kellan didn't have extra copies of or couldn't easily replace. He watched the briefcase bob, hoping the act had helped to alleviate her fury.

He touched her shoulder. "Amy . . ."

Quick as a whip, she whirled on him. Her hands were fists. Her eyes, fire. "I let you in to my life," she hissed. "I told you family secrets. Things Amarex can hold against us."

"I would never . . ."

Her hand sliced through the air. "I don't want to hear your excuses."

Nodding, he shut up. She wasn't going to listen to him tonight anyway. Anger was too great a barrier to hear through. He'd been in that place himself and knew it was a hell of a haul back to normal from an emotion that powerful.

She kicked a rock into the water, then another. "Do you know why I had a breakdown on *Ultimate Chef Showdown?*"

It was his turn to blink. Where was she going with that kind of question? "Yes."

She nodded, still scowling at him. "Brock McKenna sauntered onto the set a bona fide cowboy, complete with a championship rodeo belt buckle and a new black Stetson. Called himself a cowboy cook from Texas, like he was really something special. He certainly had me going, that's for sure."

Kellan knew all that. He'd seen it for himself, but no way was he going to interrupt her.

"But it was a lie," she continued. "He used me. I didn't realize how deep his manipulations went until the show aired and I watched it happen, episode by episode. And you want to hear the real kicker? He wasn't even a cowboy. He grew up in Portland. The rodeo thing was a shtick. And everybody knew it but me. Viewers laughed at me. Brock McKenna laughed at me. And the show's producers laughed at me all the way to the bank. They milked my stupidity for everything it was worth."

She paused, as though expecting him to respond. But what could he say? What she went through must have been hell on earth. "I'm so sorry."

She seemed not to hear him. "I thought I'd learned my lesson. But I didn't learn shit. Because, come to find out, you and your uncle and all his Amarex cronies have been laughing at me as you screwed me over too."

"Amy, no."

"When you drive onto my property, are you sizing it up for the day it belongs to you?"

"No. Never."

"Are you going to raze the house and barn, give your cattle more acres to roam?"

"No."

"Bullshit." She huffed and flapped her arms out, shouting her words up to the stars. "All my rules, they haven't done me a lick of good. I'm so stupid. I'm not even disciplined enough to follow my number one rule—stay away from cowboys. Why can't I do that one thing right?"

Kellan squared his chest and took it like a man. He deserved whatever cruelty Amy needed to dish out, now that she'd finally gotten around to yelling. Maybe it would help her heal.

She turned to him again. "I thought it was bad enough that you didn't feel the spark between us like I did. And, boy, I felt it with you. But no, you really did just want a casual screw. Hey, I told myself, at least he's being honest. I've never had a cowboy be so honest with me before." She swabbed a hand over her face, then burst forward, charging him, smacking him square on the chest with her fists. "You used me. You lied to me."

Kellan braced his feet on the ground and let her pummel him. The pain felt good. Necessary. Because he had used her, only not in the way she'd assumed. He'd used her because he loved the way he felt about himself when he was with her. He held himself within the circle of her warmth even though he knew it was wrong to get close to her.

Stumbling, she wiped the tears from her cheek and seemed to run out of steam. "You let me believe you were different from all the other no-good, two-faced cowboys I've shared myself with. But you're as rotten as the rest of them."

She was right. He was.

"Get the hell off my land before I call the police."

It was the hardest thing he'd ever done, walking away without defending himself. He didn't realize his hands were shaking until he tried to put the truck key in the ignition. With a quiet curse, he took a deep breath and tried again. This time, the key slid into place and he brought the truck to life. Then he drove away, his eyes on the rearview mirror, but Amy never walked into view.

Chapter 13

Kellan handed Vaughn a hammer from the tool kit balancing on the top of the stall. Vaughn secured Remington's front foot on his thigh over his worn leather farrier apron and got to work. The horse complied, but snorted in annoyance. He always had been an ornery beast, by far the most opinionated of Kellan's horses, but also his favorite to ride.

He'd skipped church that morning. If Amy was there, he wanted her to be able to worship in peace, without his unwanted presence mucking up her day. After chores, he saddled Remington and spent the early afternoon riding his property line. On their journey home to prep for his friends' arrival for football and barbecue, they'd crossed a pasture made muddy by melting snow and Remy's front shoe came loose. Perfect timing because Kellan had something to discuss with Vaughn in private.

After a heartbreaking loss by the Denver Broncos, Chris, Lisa, and their clan left, and he and Vaughn headed to the stable. Replacing a horseshoe was one of the few ranching skills Vaughn possessed. Inevitable, in his case, considering he grew up the son of farriers.

Vaughn had worked his way through high school and

college at his folks' farrier and blacksmith shop, one of the few mom-and-pop operations of its type left in the area. With a self-deprecating twinkle in her eye, his mom loved to tell stories of how Vaughn broke their hearts when he confessed to them his dream of going into law enforcement instead of taking over the family business.

Back when Kellan bought his first horses for Slipping Rock, it had been Vaughn's folks who shoed them. One afternoon, Vaughn burst in with the news he'd been hired as a Quay County deputy sheriff. His father, Greg, took everyone in the vicinity out for a celebratory beer. And the rest, Vaughn might say, was history.

As he had innumerable times before, Kellan acted as an assistant while Vaughn worked his horseshoe magic by the light of the fluorescent bulbs strung along the stable ceiling.

When Vaughn had straightened the clinch of another shoe nail enough to clip it off, Kellan traded the hammer for a clinch cutter. "I need to talk to you about something."

He snipped the tip and took the hammer from Kellan to start on the next one. "Let me guess. Amy Sorentino?"

"Sort of."

He glanced up, an eyebrow cocked in question, as he hammered. "All right. Talk away."

"My uncle contacted me last weekend."

"Lucky you, right? What a prick that guy is."

Kellan snickered. "Got that right. He sent a courier over with an Amarex file."

"One of those wayward youths he employs under the table?" Vaughn finished with the last nail and exchanged the clinch cutter for a nail-puller.

Like I used to be. "Yep."

Vaughn repositioned the hoof between his legs. "Do the world a favor and call me next time. I'll come by and arrest the punk for trespassing, maybe scare some sense into him about his chosen career path. Call it a community service."

"I took care of that with my .45. I don't think the kid'll make the same mistake again."

Remington gave another snort of protest as Vaughn tugged the first nail out. He made it look easy, but Kellan had tried it a few times and knew how much muscle was involved in getting the nail to budge. "Nice. Why did Morton send you stuff from the company? He's got to know you don't want anything to do with Amarex."

Kellan had never shared with his friends that he slipped cases to his lawyer buddy, nor that Morton regularly forwarded files to him. "He does it when the contract involves Catcher Creek property, just to get under my skin. My guess is that he enjoys my reaction to finding out that his company's screwing my neighbors."

"Like I said, a real prick. Which neighbor is the file on this time?"

"Amarex is preparing to sue Amy's family for breach of contract."

Vaughn paused midpull. "Breach of contract? Sorentino Farm is dry."

"That's just it. The lines in the contract that the lawsuit cites are all about exploration privileges. Totally bogus. Amarex hasn't explored this sector of Quay County in nearly a decade. There's no new oil to find. So I paid Morton a visit to press for answers."

Vaughn went back to pulling nails. "He give you any?"

Kellan shrugged. "He said he knows the property's dry but he wants to buy it anyway."

"How would suing them accomplish that?"

"There's a clause written into the oil leasing rights contract Gerald Sorentino signed giving Amarex first right of purchase should the property be foreclosed on."

Vaughn shook his head. "That man never did one right thing by his women."

"I'm with you there."

With the final nail out, Vaughn took a puller from Kellan, adjusted his grip on the hoof, and put his back into a push that levered the shoe free. Remington tossed his head, impatient to be done. "Easy, big boy. You know I have a treat in my pocket for you when we're done." He released the hoof, handed the puller and shoe to Kellan, and rubbed the horse's flank to settle him. "I know the sisters have had their share of financial trouble, but is their farm in imminent danger of foreclosure?"

"Not imminent yet. Morton admitted he's suing to push the Sorentinos into bankruptcy and force the sale."

"Whoa. He told you that? That's so illegal I want to arrest you for talking about it." After wiping his hands on a rag, he took up a rasp and claimed Remington's foot again.

"That's why you and I are having this conversation."

The rasp moved rhythmically over the foot, smoothing out the jagged edges in preparation for a new shoe. "Does Amy know of your involvement with Amarex?"

"She does as of last night."

"How'd that go?"

"Not good. Didn't help that her mom had a health scare yesterday. Bethany might not make it through this one."

"Aw, no. Are Amy and her sisters taking it hard?"

"Hard enough. But I think they knew it was coming." Kellan collected the pile of nails from the ground, glancing sideways at Vaughn. "Rachel seems to be handling it best. Nothing seems to get under her skin." *Except you.*

The rasp stopped. Vaughn's lips were a thin line. He stared at the hoof for a few beats, then resumed his task, never meeting Kellan's eyes. "If Amarex is suing the Sorentinos, you can't have anything to do with Amy on a personal level.

Honestly, I can't believe you took her on a date Friday night. That's wrong on so many levels—ethically, morally."

"I know, but—"

Finally, Vaughn looked at him square, pointing the rasp at him. "But nothing. You've got to quit seeing her immediately and keep your distance until the Amarex business is sorted out. No more dates, no more looks at church. And whatever you do, don't sleep with her again."

Kellan poked a shoe nail with the pad of his thumb, not hard enough to break the skin, but enough to sting. "You're right. I shouldn't have. She hates me now, so there's no danger of repeating the mistake."

"I don't mean to be harsh, man, but you've got to understand. There's a line you can't cross."

"Yeah, I know. You can get off my back now."

Vaughn released Remington's foot, tossed the rasp into the tool bin, and straightened. "I don't think you get it, but okay. About this lawsuit. Morton's confession would be enough to open a criminal investigation. FBI would need to be involved, since the situation crosses state lines, but I've got a contact there I could reach out to. Too bad you didn't get it on tape."

"Actually, I did."

The car's clock flipped to ten-thirty as Amy pulled in beside Rachel's truck. Her day at the hospital had been draining, to say the least. Hours spent filling out paperwork and deliberating with doctors about Mom's care options. The doctors and nurses were kind. They spoke in low, grave tones and gave Amy sympathetic looks. A few patted her arm and offered words of comfort.

Mom was still unconscious, but stable. The surgery stopped the bleed in her brain, but how much damage had been done was a mystery. Amy sat at her bedside for as long as she could, holding her hand and babbling on about safe, happy topics. She outlined the Local Dish's grand opening menu, recounted Tommy's latest escapades, and read Psalms from the Bible she'd brought. Though she'd never needed its calming effect more, she'd missed church to be with her mom. A Sunday worship took place in the hospital's chapel, and she'd planned to slip away from the stroke ward to attend, but Mom's physician breezed into the room in time to dash her plan.

Frustrating, that in the past two days she'd broken four out of her top five personal rules. From public crying to spewing a whole load of idiotic, verbal diarrhea. And, of course, the megarule failure—falling for Kellan Reed's act. As for her other rule, saying sorry when she needed to, she'd avoid breaking it tomorrow when she sat her sisters down and apologized for bringing an Amarex spy into their private lives.

She dragged her weary legs up the porch steps.

"Hey."

Amy squeaked in surprise and slipped down a step. She grabbed the handrail and scanned the darkened porch. Rachel was sitting on the swing, holding a beer bottle. "Oh, my heart. I didn't see you there."

"Sorry. I couldn't sleep."

Amy crested the stairs. "Okay, but what are you doing outside? It's freezing."

"House is too small."

It was an old saying of their dad's. No house, not even a grand mansion, had enough breathing room for either him or Rachel. Only expansive vistas and endless desert valleys gave comfort to their restless spirits.

With her hands on her chest, measuring her still-quickened heart rate, she flopped onto the bench next to Rachel. Her feet inadvertently sent two empty beer bottles rolling across the floor.

She could count on one hand the times Rachel had taken to drinking. None of the situations had been in celebration, or even *just because*. "What's wrong, Rach?"

"Hmph." She took a pull on the bottle in her hand. "How's Mom?"

Amy *tsk*ed, annoyed. Typical Rachel to avoid emotional exposure, even when asked a direct question. And how totally opposite from Amy. With a stoic foil like Rachel, no wonder Amy felt like a crazed lunatic since coming home. Blowing a strand of hair away from her eyes, she tossed her purse onto the side table. "She's no better or worse than the last time I updated you over the phone. Not conscious, but not in pain, either. Which is a blessing."

"Doctors have any idea when she might wake up?"

She snagged Rachel's beer and took a long gulp. She wasn't much of a beer drinker, but the stuff hit the spot tonight. "They're not sure if she'll ever wake up. Honestly? I don't know if I want her to. She looks so peaceful, lying there in bed. It's hard to pray for her to wake up when she might not want to. Her mind and body have been through a lot this year."

Rachel nodded. "We'll pray for her to be in peace, then. Whatever that entails."

"That, I can manage." She took another swig of Rachel's beer. Maybe she could get her sister to open up about her troubles by approaching the subject from another angle. "Did you eat dinner?"

"Yes. Mr. Dixon made enchiladas. Pretty good, too."

Amy stretched her arms up and her legs out. Damn, she was tired. "Anything new around the farm?"

Rachel kicked one of the toppled bottles and watched it roll to the edge of the porch. "We were served the Amarex lawsuit this morning."

"Oh, no."

Rachel leaned forward, hunching into the elbows

she'd propped on her knees, the beer cradled between her hands. "Some muscle-headed moron came right up to me while I was reroofing the chicken coop. Asked if I was Rachel Sorentino and when I said I was, he handed me a manila envelope. He said, *You've been served*." She huffed. "And here I thought they only said that on TV."

"No wonder you're drinking."

She puffed her cheeks with air and let it out in a slow stream. "After this moron left, I was pissed. Couldn't concentrate on the roofing project, so I took a walk to let off some steam. Know what I found?"

"What?"

"A briefcase floating in the pond."

Amy's stomach lurched. So much for waiting until tomorrow to apologize.

"I fished it out, laid the papers on the kitchen table to dry. They were Amarex documents. Our family name on every page. Including a duplicate of the papers I got served today. You know anything about how that briefcase came to rest in our pond?"

Amy snatched the beer and downed the rest. "Yes, I do."

Headlights and a noisy diesel engine announced someone's arrival.

Vaughn was at Kellan's kitchen sink, scrubbing his hands after finishing with Remington. At the table, Kellan was elbow deep in a bag of potato chips. They exchanged questioning looks.

The clock on the oven read eleven-fifteen. Way past the good folks of Catcher Creek's bedtime. Kellan shrugged. He had no idea who could be calling at his house so late at night. Abandoning the chips, he slunk to the window and looked through the slats of the closed blinds. Nothing. "Whoever's here parked around the corner, out of view."

Vaughn's expression turned grave, alert. Pure cop. He drew his firearm and positioned himself at the door. With the barrel aimed at the ground, he peered through the peephole and waited. A minute later, he cursed under his breath and holstered the gun.

"Who is it?" Kellan whispered.

Throwing him a grim look, Vaughn opened the door.

Rachel Sorentino stumbled in, her fist raised like she'd been about to knock, her other hand gripping Kellan's briefcase. The one Amy had winged into the pond. His heart stopped.

Rachel's disheveled hair flopped over her face. She swiped it away and took in the room, her eyes flitting to Vaughn before honing in on Kellan. Her whole body quivered, but Kellan didn't think it was from the cold, despite that she wore only a long-sleeved T-shirt and the night air hovered near freezing. The expression on her face was murderous.

She wound back and hurled the briefcase across the room. It smacked into the kitchen island and landed on the floor with a clatter, flopping open. Empty. She and her sisters had kept the papers that had been inside. Kellan would have too.

Panic twisted his gut into a knot. Amy knew about the lawsuit.

Vaughn inched toward her. "Rachel, what are you doing driving around in the middle of the night? It's pitch black and freezing out there. Too dangerous."

She speared a finger in his direction. "I'll deal with you next." She whirled to face Kellan. He held his ground. "You son of a bitch. Taking advantage of my sister's good will. Taking advantage of all of us."

"I can explain."

Her expression flared in challenge. She stretched her arms out. "Go ahead, then." She wasn't yelling. If anything, she'd lowered her voice. Fury, harnessed but potent, poured from her every word. "Explain to me how you looked me in the eye and promised not to hurt Amy, when all the while you and Amarex were planning to crush our livelihood."

"I know what it looks like from your perspective, but I didn't know anything about Amarex's legal claims against your family until after I asked Amy out at church last Sunday."

"Didn't stop you from seducing her, did it? Or from squeezing us for all our family secrets."

He glanced at Vaughn, who stood statue-still with a somber expression, his eyes locked on Rachel, his hands clenched at his sides. No help there. "You're right, Rachel. In the end, it didn't stop me. But I didn't start out thinking along those lines. I kept the date with Amy because I wanted to explain the situation. You have no reason to trust me on this, but I had the best of intentions. The night got away from me. Amy's so . . ." *Intoxicating, amazing, everything I didn't know I needed.* "She's better than I deserve and I guess I lost my mind a little bit."

She laughed, a thick, angry laugh. "You lost your mind? You mean, like my mom lost her mind? Because I don't think you know what that's like. Pick a different excuse."

Oh, man. How could he make her see? "Yesterday, when you and Amy rode up on your horses, after Jenna got the call from the hospital, I was there to talk to you all about the Amarex situation." He gestured to the ground. "That's why I had my briefcase and all that paperwork. I swear to you."

She nodded, but her eyes glinted with sarcasm. "Uh-huh. Have you filled Morton in on our family secrets yet? The weaknesses in our case against Amarex?"

"The opposite, actually. If you looked in the briefcase, you probably saw the business card of my friend, Matt Roenick. He's an—"

"Save it, Kellan. Because you know what? This is a blessing in disguise, you helping Amarex destroy us. It certainly opened Amy's eyes to the truth about you and your intentions."

She glanced sideways at Vaughn. He shifted his weight, but his expression remained unflinching. His only tell was in the subtle ripple of his cheek as he clenched his jaw.

"It's opened my eyes too," she continued, swinging her gaze back to Kellan. "I'm done breaking my back to hold on to the farm. Every day, my entire life, working myself to the bone. The whole time, worrying about money and my family's future. You better believe I've got the ulcers to prove it. So this lawsuit I got served today got me thinking—what's stopping me from taking my sisters and my nephew and starting over somewhere else? Far away from this loose-lipped, judgmental hole of a town. There's nothing here worth fighting for anymore."

"Rachel . . ." It was Vaughn. He took a step toward her, his hand outstretched like he was aiming for her shoulders.

She pivoted to face him. "Don't *Rachel* me. You allowed this to happen. You let my sister get taken advantage of by your best friend, knowing his family's company wants to ruin us." She took a deep breath. "Or is that what you want? Amarex takes my land and forces me to leave. Then you don't have to deal with me anymore. Do you hate me that much?"

"Rachel, no . . ." He tried to reach for her again.

"Not another step closer, Vaughn."

He stopped, his hands out like a buffer between them. "I don't hate you. Not even close."

Kellan wasn't in a position to see the expression on Rachel's face, but her shoulders slumped. "I wish you did," she whispered.

Vaughn's lips screwed up. "Sometimes I wish that too."

She nodded and lurched away. "Kellan, go ahead and

tell your uncle I'm not going to put up a fight. All that matters to me is my family, and Amarex can't take them away. No matter what power they think they have over us."

Without looking at Vaughn, she opened the door and walked out, into the night. Vaughn followed. Knowing him, he wanted to make sure she made it to her truck safely. As if evil strangers were waiting in the shadows to ambush her.

Kellan stood next to Vaughn and watched her leave in silence. The minute her taillights disappeared, Vaughn put the full force of his strength into a kick that launched a potted plant off the porch. It sailed into the driveway and smashed to bits. Max must've been sleeping under a porch chair because he army-crawled down the steps and slunk out of view.

Cursing loudly, Vaughn stomped to his truck and flipped open the glove compartment.

He emerged with a pack of cigarettes in his hand and hung one from his lips.

"Vaughn, don't."

"Shut up, Kellan. You have no idea how bad I want to punch you right now." Cupping his hands over his mouth to block the wind, he lit up and took a long drag, holding the smoke in his lungs for a few beats before releasing it in a slow stream. "Damn, that's good."

Leaning against the truck, he looked up at the stars as he took another slow drag.

Kellan was as rattled by Vaughn's reaction as he was by his exchange with Rachel. Mechanically, he walked to the barbecue deck for lighter fluid and matches. Back out front, he snatched the cigarette pack from the roof of Vaughn's truck and a metal bucket from the side of the house. He couldn't stand the idea of Vaughn having to quit his addiction a second time. Once had been hard enough on them all. The pack went into the bucket, followed by the fluid, then a match. The bucket exploded in flames.

"They sell more at the Quick Stand, you know," Vaughn said evenly.

"Don't do this to yourself again. I know something happened between you and Rachel, but don't use cigarettes to cope. Damn near killed you to quit last time."

He took another drag. "It wasn't the quitting smoking that nearly killed me."

"I was there. You suffered like a dog for weeks of nicotine withdrawal."

"I'm telling you, it wasn't the cigarettes."

"Then what?"

For the first time since Rachel drove away, Vaughn looked Kellan in the eye. "What I did to Rachel, the shame I have to live with every day. It's worse than nicotine withdrawal. Worse than anything I've ever experienced."

Vaughn Cooper was one of the best men Kellan had ever known, with a sense of honor set in stone. He would never purposefully hurt anyone, especially a woman. "What, exactly, did you do to Rachel?"

Chapter 14

Vaughn kicked off the truck and walked toward the house, crunching right over the shards of the terra-cotta pot he'd destroyed and the corpse of the plant. At the base of the porch stairs, he flicked the cigarette into the dirt and ground it out with his boot. It was a nostalgic move, one that took Kellan back. He'd seen Vaughn snuff out a cigarette butt the same exact way a million times over the years they'd been friends.

A sneaking disquiet oozed into the spaces of Kellan's mind. He thought he knew Vaughn so well—better than anyone else on earth. He had his mannerisms down, knew all his jokes. They'd tackled their twenties and early thirties together, fended off mothers eager to marry their daughters to one of them, squeaked out of more than one hairy situation, and over time became as close as brothers. Closer, he amended, thinking of how he'd dragged his feet over calling Jake. Yet, clearly, something big had happened between him and Rachel, and he'd chosen to leave Kellan in the dark.

Vaughn settled into a chair with a tired sigh and scrubbed his face with his hands.

Kellan joined him, his curiosity and concern mounting.

He folded his arms against the puffs of cold breeze coming off the hills. "Were you and Rachel romantically involved?"

"Something like that."

"Why did you two keep it a secret?"

Vaughn brought out the disposable lighter from his shirt pocket and flicked a little flame into life with a satisfying sound of friction. "Because I screwed up. Bad."

Click. His thumb lifted from the lighter and the flame vanished.

"Can't be as bad as you think. Nothing's unfixable." He pulled his face back, surprised by his own words. He didn't believe that . . . did he?

The rasp of friction and a flame appeared again. Vaughn gave an incredulous snort. "Never took you for an optimist, K. For the record, this thing with Rachel is not fixable."

Desperation, that strange, heavy yearning, dropped like a lead weight in his stomach. He felt like begging, the need to connect with his closest friend was so powerful. *Don't shut me out. After everything else that's gone on with Amy and my brother, I can't lose you too.* "Why don't you start at the beginning? Tell me what happened."

With a flick of his thumb, the flame disappeared. He tapped the lighter against his knee and seemed to draw into himself as he spoke, staring at the floor beyond his feet. "I knew who Rachel was because when I was a deputy, I had to return Jenna to her family more than once after I found her partying in bars with a fake ID, drunk, and up to no good. I'd haul her home in my patrol car, ring the doorbell, and her older sister would be the one to answer. Rachel. She was pretty, but I kept telling myself she wasn't my type, you know?"

Kellan agreed—he couldn't think of a less likely couple, with Vaughn thriving in the public spotlight and Rachel as classic an introvert as he'd ever met. But he kept his mouth shut, offering a noncommittal nod instead.

"Once Jenna got pregnant and settled down, the only place I'd see Rachel was at the Catcher Creek Café for lunch every now and then. We'd wave and I'd ask after Jenna and her boy. It went on like that until Gerald Sorentino died last New Year's Eve."

"He ran his jeep off of Hoja Pass, the sisters told me."

"That's exactly what he did. He grew up on that land and probably traversed that stretch of road a thousand times in his life. Tox report was clean, inconclusive evidence of possible tampering. No seat belt on, but that was about it. Forensics ruled it an accident. The steering mechanism failed. I could never prove otherwise, but it's always nagged at me that maybe I missed something." He shrugged. "Anyhow, the accident put me at Sorentino Farm a lot. Rachel was as pretty as ever, and strong. If she was grieving, she didn't show it. She took care of the people around her and ran the farm, her spine straight, her chin high. Pure steel running through that woman's veins.

"I got to thinking about peeling that armor away, finding the softness underneath. I couldn't stop thinking about it, about her. Wondering what it would be like to be the man she let down her guard around." With a huff, he looked at Kellan. "Stupid reason, right? But there it is."

"Doesn't sound stupid to me." He'd been way worse gone with Amy. All she had to do for Kellan to throw his integrity out the window was take a bite of filet mignon.

"So one night, about a few days after Gerald's death, I went out to her place. I had questions about the investigation, and she was alone. She'd been drinking, not too much, but enough that I could see it in her eyes."

Vaughn dug through his jeans pocket and produced a business card. Holding it by one corner, he set it on fire. Kellan watched it burn, afraid to speak or move lest Vaughn think better of sharing the rest of his story. When the flames licked too close to his fingertips, he dropped the burning card to the ground and stomped it with the toe of his boot.

He shot Kellan a pointed look. "I took advantage of her vulnerability." His voice was raw, pained. "I seduced a grieving witness in an open investigation I was the lead on."

Kellan had formulated a general idea of the direction Vaughn's story was headed, but still, he couldn't wrap his mind around the possibility that his best friend, the greatest sheriff Quay County ever elected, would've made such a terrible, unethical choice. "When you had a clear head the next day, did you end things with her?"

Vaughn smeared the charred paper across the floor, leaving a black gash in its wake. "The next day, I didn't have a clear head. I was even more fucked up. Because all I could think about was how soon I could get back with her. The minute I got off work that night, I drove to her house. And every night after that it was either my place or hers."

Kellan winced. "When did you end it?"

"That's the thing. I didn't have the willpower to drag myself out of the situation. Talk about addiction, man—I was crazy. I couldn't eat, couldn't sleep, couldn't concentrate. For four weeks, my world spun around Rachel. The worst days of my life, but also the best. When we were together, we burned the fucking walls down around us."

Kellan thought about last January. He hadn't seen Vaughn much that month, but he'd written it off as a surge of crime and crazies following the holidays, as sometimes happened. The more he thought about the risk Vaughn had taken by being with Rachel, the more he couldn't believe in its possibility. "You could've destroyed your career."

"I didn't care."

"You must've cared a little because you kept it a secret from all of us."

"Yeah, you're right. But I didn't care enough to stop."

A frightening new possibility came to Kellan. "Rachel could throw you under the bus if she got it in her head to. She could get you tossed off the force. She was pretty angry tonight."

"If she did, I wouldn't blame her one bit. But she won't. She's too private a person to expose herself to the kind of scrutiny that would come along with filing such a claim." He wrung his hands and looked at his truck. "Wish you hadn't incinerated my stash. I could use another smoke right now."

"Then I'm doubly glad I torched them."

Vaughn scowled and leapt to his feet. He prowled to the end of the porch.

"You said the affair lasted four weeks. How did it end?" Kellan asked.

"I would've kept going back to her until it destroyed us both. But the night of her mom's suicide attempt, Rachel was with me. It's why she didn't know her mom left the house. That brought her to her senses, all right. After I finished the preliminary investigation, I drove to the hospital, worried about how she was dealing with everything.

"We were standing next to my car in the parking lot because we didn't want her sisters to know I was there. She told me she couldn't take it anymore—the sleepless nights, the sneaking around like criminals, the guilt over what happened with her mom. Her family needed her too much for her to be selfish, she said. She was in charge of the farm, all by herself, and she had to concentrate on that. She didn't have time for an affair that would never amount to anything real."

"Ouch. No wonder she thought you hated her."

He paused midstride. "I don't. I can't believe she

thought that." He resumed his agitated pacing. "Anyhow, her words were like a slap to my face. Woke me up from the fog I was in. I took a good look at her, really looked. She had dark circles under her eyes, and she'd lost too much weight. Our affair was destroying her as much as it was me. That's when it hit me—nothing as wrong as what we did, what I did to her, can lead to anything but pain and regret. I sacrificed my professional and personal integrity for nothing, because it didn't matter how perfect we were together, we were doomed from the start."

Kellan did the math in his head. Bethany Sorentino's suicide attempt was four weeks after New Year's Eve. The end of January. "That's around the time you quit smoking."

He shuffled dirt off the edge of the porch with his foot. "I needed to suffer. I needed the physical pain to distract me from the shame. I didn't quit smoking for my health, but for survival."

Kellan joined him at the porch rail. "You're not over her."

Vaughn's face turned heavenward and he chewed the inside of his cheek. "How do you get over someone like that? Who makes you feel more alive than you've ever felt in your life? I can't stop the *what ifs*. If I'd only waited, kept my wits about me and my pants zipped, I could've asked her out properly once her family issues settled down, treated her like she deserved, instead of some shameful secret. I would've been proud to have her on my arm. What we had could've been beautiful, and I poisoned it."

"You can't think like that, man. You could still fix it with her."

"Gimme a break. This is why I'm telling you. Because you can't let the same thing happen with you and Amy. If you care anything about her, and I'm guessing you do, you have to leave her alone. Bide your time. Don't do something that goes against your personal and professional ethics. It'll poison everything you touch."

Frustration tore at him at the sight of his friend in pain. He wanted to solve the problem, to fix things for Vaughn. What a useless desire, considering his own life was screwed six ways to Sunday. Vaughn was right about Kellan's choices, but knowing logically what he needed to do and hearing firsthand how the same situation had torn his friend's relationship apart were different animals entirely. Mostly, though, it hurt that Vaughn hadn't confided in him sooner.

"When you were going through all that, you should have let me know. I would've been there for you."

He propped an arm on the rail and raised an eyebrow at Kellan. "Would you have been? I'm not so sure. You're like a brother to me, K, but I'm sorry, I don't think you would've handled it well."

"What do you mean?"

"Look, a big part of my job is reading people—their motivations, their emotions. All that criminal psychology bullshit really works. Best weapon I have for solving a case, so I know what I'm talking about. I know you better than anyone and I can tell you that you judge other people and yourself by this impossible standard of perfection."

Kellan opened his mouth to protest, but Vaughn cut him off.

"No, listen—you know it's true. And I didn't want you judging me. I was going through too much already. You would've pulled the *I told you so* card."

Kellan reeled, too angry and surprised to speak. Vaughn's comment cut him to the bone. Any way he looked at it, the people he cared about held themselves apart from him. His best friend hadn't trusted him with his biggest secret. His brother thought he'd abandoned him. And Amy . . . It was too upsetting to consider how she felt about him now. He wondered about Chris and Lisa, if they'd agree with Vaughn's assessment. "Am I really so bad?"

"Not bad. I think, with the way you grew up, you can't help it. You're protecting yourself. I get it."

"I'm sorry . . . I don't know what else to say."

He slugged Kellan's shoulder, flashing his characteristic Vaughn smile. "Don't sweat it. You and I are cool. I'm here, aren't I? Fixing Remington's shoe, solving your Amarex problems, and giving you advice about your love life. I gotta say, I wish you hadn't blown up my smokes."

"I'm not sorry about that."

"Nah, me neither. I don't want to get started again." Gradually, the pain that had gripped Vaughn's features melted away. Kellan was relieved to see his old friend again. "I'm going to grab my tools and hit the road." He waggled his finger at Kellan and pulled a face. "Some of us need our beauty sleep more than others."

Kellan gave him a playful shove as he walked inside. "You talking to me, ugly?"

"Aw, now, that hurts. You better watch it or I'll send you a bill for my farrier services."

"That would be a first. How about I pay you in steaks?" He stuck his hand out.

Vaughn shook it with an exaggerated up and down. "Man, you're getting the short end of the stick with that deal."

He grabbed his tool bag and the CD Kellan had burned for him of his conversations with Morton. "I'll be in touch about the Amarex plan once I've lined all the pieces up with the FBI. Do me a favor and sit tight until then. Don't contact Morton until I give you the green light. And for the love of God, don't tell Amy what you're up to."

"Thanks for your help on this."

They shook again, more genuinely this time, and thumped shoulders. "You and I are family, K. And I don't take that lightly. Someone messes with my family, they mess with me."

He watched as Vaughn let himself out, marveling at how he'd inadvertently echoed Rachel's words from the night before at the hospital. He tried to visualize the two of them together, on Kellan's sofa, drinking beer and eating steak, but he couldn't see it. For his friend's peace of mind, he hoped the two of them found a path through their heartache, back to each other.

He caught sight of his desk in his periphery and moved toward it. After more than a week of mostly sleepless nights, he should've been ready to collapse from exhaustion, but too many dark thoughts left him restless. Tired, yes, but not the least bit sleepy. Time to bite the bullet and make the phone call he'd put off for too long.

It took him the better part of an hour to locate Jake's number, scribbled on the back of a Slipping Rock business card. As he dialed, he prayed the number was current. His brother could've easily moved or gotten a new phone in the two years since they'd last spoken.

That call had been brutal. Jake had phoned to let him know he'd gotten married the week before to his girlfriend of three years. Kellan vividly recalled his initial shock, and the indignation that replaced it. His only sibling had gotten married and he hadn't been invited. He hadn't even known Jake had a live-in girlfriend.

When Chris and Lisa got engaged, Chris sat Kellan down and explained that he was obliged to make his younger brother, Nathan, the best man at his wedding to Lisa. It was a family thing, he said. And Kellan understood, no problem. He accepted Chris's invitation to be a groomsman along with Vaughn and Chris's older brother, Tom, and a couple cousins. Kellan felt honored to be included even that much, given Chris's expansive family ties.

He'd sent his brother a gift, a deluxe espresso machine from their Internet registry, but four months later, the machine arrived on Kellan's doorstep with a brief note.

Apparently, Jake and his new bride had already divorced. Looking back, Kellan should have called Jake to offer support and condolences, but he was sore about being excluded from the wedding. And anyhow, what would he have said? The rift separating them was too vast to bridge.

The ringing of the phone stopped. Then, "Kellan?" Jake's deep baritone was groggy. He cleared his throat. "Something wrong?"

"Jake, sorry to bug you in the middle of the night. Nothing's wrong." He couldn't bring himself to update Jake about their parents. Not yet. That part of the conversation would be tense, loaded with the weight of their shared nightmare. For the moment, he just wanted to talk with his brother. "How are you?"

"Uh . . . fine." Jake's unspoken question radiated through the phone. *What do you want?* "And you?"

"Things are good. Business-wise, I mean. Beef prices rose 2 percent this last quarter. Er . . . you know, that's always good. Weather's been cold. Two separate storms rolled through this week. Looks like it might be a white Christmas if the storm track stays put." Kellan cringed. Why was it so awkward to talk to his own flesh and blood? "So, where are you living now?"

Another long pause, then a sigh. Disapproving. Kellan shook his head and stood. He wanted to shove something. Like maybe his fist through the nearest wall. Instead he prowled through his dark house and onto the porch. Max trailed behind. The cold soothed his nerves and gave him something to focus on besides impotent frustration.

"It's two A.M., Kellan. I've got to be at work in four hours. What do you say we get to the real reason for your call?"

Didn't that say it all? "Mom contacted Bruce. Told him Dad was out of jail. She hasn't called me yet, but it's only a matter of time. I thought you should know, in case they call you too."

"Thanks, but I already knew from a contact of mine in Florida."

And you couldn't extend me the same courtesy of a heads-up call? "Okay, good." What else could he say? He wracked his brain, his anxiety mounting. He didn't want the call to end. If he hung up the phone, what reason would they ever have to speak again? "Tell you what, I'm going to send you some beef, all right? I've got a surplus of the good stuff. You'll like it. Grills up tender."

"Nice. Thanks." At least Jake didn't hesitate to accept his offer. Kellan took a measure of solace in that.

"Are you still at the same address?"

"No. I moved into a condo in Burbank last year. You have a pen and paper handy?"

"Just a sec." Kellan strode inside and dug around his desk for scrap paper and pen. "Yep, ready." He scribbled the address. Now what did he say? "Guess I'll let you get to sleep."

"Thanks for the call. And the beef."

"Wait, Jake. One more thing. Have you ever heard of Terra Bistro? It's in L.A."

"What? Uh . . . I think so, if it's the one I'm thinking of, near the Strip. Driven by it a few times. Never been in. Too fancy for my taste. Why?"

"I know a chef who used to work there. My neighbor. Just curious, is all."

"Good night, Kellan."

Okay, I give up. "'Night, Jake."

Wandering back outside to settle in a porch chair, he fingered the paper with Jake's address. Birthing a calf with his bare hands would've been more enjoyable than that phone call. Then again, what had he expected—a surprise declaration of brotherly love?

This time, as opposed to after all their other failed attempts at communication, Kellan didn't vow to punish Jake with silence. He was still angry, but he knew he'd reach out to his brother again soon. He'd mail Jake a nice pack of steaks, along with a Christmas card. Maybe he'd sign him up for a regular monthly delivery, free of charge. The idea of sharing that part of himself with Jake, the part he was most proud of, felt right.

It was easy to pinpoint what tipped the scales in his head and heart, and made him want to try harder with Jake. He'd spent years amidst Chris's perfect, functional family, and made numerous trips with Vaughn to his parents' house. But neither clan had flipped the switch like Amy and her sisters had with their messy, dysfunctional love and loyalty to each other, with their willingness to fight for their family's survival despite the odds stacked against them.

And then there was Tommy, sleeping and drooling on Kellan's chest for hours in the hospital, dripping pie and juice on his shirt, cuddling his sweet moon face under Kellan's chin. He'd never been loved as fiercely as this little boy had been since the moment of his conception and would continue to be for the whole of his life. Amy gave up a big-city career to help salvage Tommy's future, and Rachel, with unmitigated fury in her eyes, stormed into his house that night, ready to protect her clan at all costs.

Sitting on his porch, holding Jake's address and stewing over his envy of the hand Tommy had been dealt in life, the truth hit Kellan like a sucker punch. He'd been wrong about so many things, but mostly this—he'd thought he could build a better family than the one he'd been given. He thought he could choose the elements that created a perfect life like he might choose a bull for breeding. He thought an ideal family involved tranquillity and constancy, not drama and strife and pain.

But his parameters had been too rigid. Love involved constancy, yes, but so much more. Love was not so much about harmony, but about the fight to hold on to it, no matter what. Even when it hurt. Amy and her sisters had taught him that what mattered most about love was its ferocity.

Brisk knocking sounded at the front door.

Amy looked up from the papers spread before her on the dining room table. The clock read eleven A.M. If Kellan was at her doorstep, she wasn't sure what she'd do. Two hours ago, she would have sent him packing. After tossing a bowl of diced celery at him along with a slew of obscenities and insults.

Now, though, she wasn't so sure. Because she'd spent the morning studying the dried papers from his briefcase, all of which painted a startlingly complicated, albeit confusing, picture of Kellan's motives with his family business.

In a desperate bid to make sense of it all, she'd snagged Jenna's laptop and entered Kellan's name into an online database. Before long, she'd found information on his parents' crimes and jail sentences. A search on Amarex's CEO, Bruce Morton, revealed his family tie to Kellan. She kicked herself for not taking this simple step before their date last Friday.

If she'd bothered to research Brock McKenna at any point during *Ultimate Chef*'s filming, she would have spared herself from heartbreak and public ridicule, and probably stayed in the running to be crowned the winner of *Ultimate Chef*. From now on, rule number six was to research her prospective dates.

The knock sounded at the door again.

Mr. Dixon poked his head into the dining room, drying his hands on a dish towel. "Would you like me to get that, Amy?"

Sigh. "I don't know. I'm thinking."

He slung the towel over his shoulder. "You're afraid it's Kellan Reed?"

"You bet."

"I've got a pot of dirty water soaking from last night's enchilada sauce. If you want, I can toss it on him."

They shared an impish grin. "No, no. Whoever's here, you can show them in."

He crossed through the room and disappeared.

Amy strained to listen, praying it wasn't Kellan despite the fact her pulse quickened in anticipation. The door opened and a female voice echoed through the house. Heels clip-clopped over the floor behind Mr. Dixon's rubber-soled gait. Amy couldn't decide if she were disappointed or relieved.

Sloane Delgado materialized in the doorway, dressed in what could only be described as a two-piece sailor skirt suit, with a backpack dangling from her hand. "Hi, Amy."

"Hey there. Don't you have school this week?"

With a weary roll of her head, she clomped across the room and hefted her backpack onto the table. "It's finals week, so the schedule's different. I studied all weekend at home, but Grandma's off work this week and she's babysitting my sister's brats."

"Brats, huh? You're not a fan of your nieces and nephews?"

"I love them. I just don't *like* them. All that shouting and running. Biting." Shuddering, she unzipped her bag and emptied the contents on the table. "I couldn't take it anymore. So I thought, it's quiet here and you have a lot of extra space. Can I study here this week?"

Amy eyed the stack of books. Her first instinct was to send the girl to the library. She and her sisters had planned a meeting about the lawsuit in an hour, then she'd drive to the hospital that afternoon. With her family's future in limbo, she didn't have time to run a charity home for the town's misfits and stragglers. She could barely manage her own life, for Pete's sake.

Mr. Dixon patted the top book on the stack, a huge statistics tome. "Of course you can stay, honey. I'm making biscuits and gravy for lunch. There's more than enough for everyone."

Sloane's shoulders relaxed and she flopped onto the bench. "Thank you."

Well, that settled it.

She gathered the dried Amarex papers to make room for Sloane. Something small fluttered to the ground. A blue and white business card. She retrieved it. Scrawled on the back in sloppy, male writing were the words: *He works pro bono and is expecting your call.*

She flipped it to the front. MATT ROENICK, ATTORNEY AT LAW. SPECIALIZING IN OIL AND MINERAL RIGHTS LEASING LAW. Beneath his title was a Santa Fe address. Why would Kellan, the Amarex heir, offer her an attorney recommendation? That was the thing about all these papers. They didn't add up to an easy conclusion. Kellan had a copy of Amarex's lawsuit, but he'd also brought a spreadsheet detailing past suits that Amarex lost to other New Mexico home owners.

She glanced at Sloane, whose nose was already deep into a book, and nearly gasped. The sailor blouse was backless. Go figure. It looked as if a piece of fabric had accidentally dropped off. Beneath the wide, white polyester collar, her bared spine curved over the table, her muscles working as she scribbled notes on index cards.

Clattering pots and running water sounded from the kitchen as Mr. Dixon puttered through his day. It was an unexpected comfort, hearing those familiar noises from her childhood kitchen. If her mom had the energy to work in the kitchen, it meant she was having a good day and Amy and her sisters could breathe easy. Closing her eyes, she could see her mom at the sink, washing dishes and staring at the fields through the window. Her expression distant, much like it had been this year.

Maybe instead of seeing vivid colors through her nursing home window, Mom saw their farm in its glory days, back when high school junior Bethany Davis was courted by Gerald Sorentino, one of the most popular boys in town. In pictures taken of the family land around that time, the fields surrounding the big house teemed with life. Amy's grandparents bred cattle and hogs, and supported a long list of employees and farmhands. With her eyes still closed, she said a prayer that her mom was at peace.

With Mr. Dixon's soothing kitchen noises as her background music, Amy dove into the papers again, looking for anything that might allow her family to keep their farm. When she looked up again, it was because Jenna's, Tommy's, and Rachel's voices had broken the silence. She glanced at her watch. Time for their lunch meeting. Sloane raised her head and frowned, looking thoroughly put off by the interruption.

"Sorry, Sloane. Jenna, Rachel, and I have to talk business. You're welcome to move to the desk in the front room."

"Thanks," she muttered around the pen she was holding in her lips. Scooping her book and stack of index cards into her arms, she sidestepped Tommy, who was running at turbo speed into the room, making airplane noises.

"Tommy, watch where you're going," Jenna hollered, trotting after him. "Oh, hey, Sloane."

"Mmm," Sloane answered, and kept moving.

Jenna did a double take at the back of Sloane's blouse and looked to Amy for an explanation.

"Future fashion designer," Amy whispered.

Jenna shot her an okay sign with her fingers. "How did the Internet research go?" she asked, taking a seat on the bench across from Amy. Rachel took the seat next to her.

"Bruce Morton, Amarex's CEO, is definitely Kellan's uncle. I couldn't find anything naming Kellan as Morton's heir, but it makes sense because Morton has no children of his own and only one sibling, Kellan's mom, Tina."

Rachel picked through a bowl of oranges on the table before selecting one. "I didn't think modern companies worked like that, naming an heir and whatnot. Seems pretty archaic."

"It's probably not so much about inheriting the company as inheriting stock interest, would be my guess," Jenna said.

"The *hows* and *whats* of Kellan's inheritance don't matter," Amy said, "because nothing changes the fact that we're being sued for breach of a contract that doesn't make any sense. I can't believe Dad signed something so outrageous."

Jenna picked an orange from the bowl. "Let's save the Dad grumbling for later. It'll make Rachel even crankier than she already is. She doesn't like it when we get critical of Daddy dearest." She and Rachel scowled at each other, then she handed Tommy the orange and took his other hand. "Come on, buddy. Let's see if Mr. Dixon would mind if you ate lunch in the kitchen with him today."

With a chirp of agreement, Tommy did a happy skip and pulled his mom through the swinging kitchen door.

Amy met Rachel's gaze. She looked weary, with pallid skin and tired eyes. And no wonder. The night before, after Amy told her the truth about Kellan, she'd lit off like a rocket, shouting curses and stomping from the porch to her truck. Amy tried to stop her, but she was beyond reason, hell-bent on driving to Kellan's ranch and cutting him down to size.

Amy waited up for her, and when she returned, she looked much the worse for wear. She refused to discuss what happened at Kellan's ranch, and tried to shoulder past Amy through the front door, announcing, "I'm done with this place. If Amarex wants it, they can have it."

"Like hell they can," Amy had shot back.

The argument grew more heated from there. They fought fervently, debating in circles for a solid hour before finally reaching an agreement on one crucial point—Jenna had the right to be in on the fight as well. Grudgingly, they decided to wait until after the morning chores to hold a family meeting.

"Have you changed your mind about giving up?" Amy asked in her most civil tone.

"No. You?"

"No. If anything, I'm not so sure Kellan's the enemy anymore."

Rachel gave an incredulous head shake. "Oh, please. Spare me your bleeding heart mentality."

"I do not have a bleeding heart."

Jenna pushed through the swinging door. "Who has a bleeding heart?"

"No one," Amy said.

"Amy does," Rachel amended.

Jenna snickered.

"I'll prove it to you," Rachel went on. "When I went out back this morning, I found a stray cow by the pigpen. Looks like a heifer. Slipping Rock branding. How about I butcher it up and we have ourselves a nice, steak dinner tonight?"

Amy wrinkled her nose. She'd grown up on a farm and understood with perfect clarity the process of killing livestock for food. Heck, she was a chef—and not remotely a vegetarian one, either. But the thought of looking an animal in the eye and then ending its life still turned her stomach. She liked her meat to come wrapped in butcher paper, thank you very much. "Not fair, Rach. You know I'm squeamish about that."

With an acerbic laugh, Rachel got busy peeling her orange.

"See what I mean, Jen? Bleeding heart. She probably wants to do the right thing and return the cow to Reed's ranch."

"It'd be good karma," Amy countered, fully aware she'd scoffed at Lisa Binderman for using that same argument. Rachel didn't need to know that, though.

"That's not karma. It's called being a doormat."

Amy balked and shot to her feet, too riled to stay in her seat. "I'm a doormat? You're the one who wants to give up and hand our land over to Amarex without a fight."

"Time out, you two," Jenna said. "You've obviously talked about the Amarex situation without me—which I hate, for the record—"

"We know you do, that's why we saved the discussion for today."

Jenna rolled her eyes. "How kind of you. Why don't we sit and talk about this rationally?"

"Rationally? That'll be impossible for Amy," Rachel said. "The closest she'd ever come to rationality is if she had the word tattooed on her arm."

Jenna shot her a chastising glare, but Amy took another tack. If Rachel thought she was so irrational, then she might as well act the part. She grabbed Rachel's half-peeled orange and threw a segment at her face. It hit her cheek with a satisfying splat and fell in her lap.

"Are you insane?" Rachel hollered, wiping her face.

"Just living up to expectations." She pelted her with another segment that hit her on the nose.

"Oh, it's on, little sister. It's on."

Chapter 15

Jenna snagged an orange and dove under the table.

Rachel got to peeling her orange at warp speed. Amy lobbed a segment at the vee of her T-shirt and squealed when she made a bull's-eye, right into Rachel's cleavage.

Rachel gave up peeling and chucked the whole orange Amy's way.

Amy countered with rapid-fire throws of her remaining orange pieces. Two landed in Rachel's hair.

"I need backup," Rachel called to Jenna.

"I'm on it," she answered. A hand appeared and deposited a pile of orange on the tabletop.

"No fair. You can't team up on me." Amy grabbed a fresh orange and used a chair as a shield, peeling it as fast as her fingers would work. Rachel managed to hit her in the forehead. Juice dripped down her nose. She swiped at it and finished prepping her ammunition. This time, she began her assault with bits of rind. With a yelp, Rachel ducked behind the table.

In her periphery, Amy saw Jenna worming her way out the far end of the table. "Oh, no, you don't." Grabbing a chair cushion as a shield, she stood and hammered Jenna with her remaining orange pieces.

Jenna squealed and returned fire.

Hearing a great roar, Amy turned in time to see Rachel flying at her. The next minute, she was flat on her back, with Rachel straddling her. Rachel lifted a whole peeled orange over her head and squeezed. Juice and pulp rained on her face, hair, and neck. Amy was laughing too hard to care.

"Uncle! Uncle! I give up," Amy said between giggles.

Rachel was laughing too. Jenna dropped to her knees next to them. Both looked terrible, with bits of pulp and juice everywhere. Their hair and clothes were a mess. Amy could only assume she looked equally ridiculous. She blinked some juice away from her eyes and licked the corners of her lips. The juice was sweet. She picked a segment from Rachel's shirt pocket and ate it. Both her sisters wrinkled their noses at the move, then dissolved into a fresh round of chuckles.

Jenna lay on the floor next to Amy and took her hand. "Mom would've loved this."

Amy squeezed Jenna's hand and patted Rachel's knee. "Yes, she would have."

A throat clearing got their attention. Mr. Dixon stood near the kitchen door, a bread basket in one hand and a covered pot in the other. His shoulders shook with silent laughter. "I see you ladies found a way to work through your differences."

Rachel stood and helped Amy and Jenna up.

The juice that had pooled on Amy's chest trickled into her bra. Gross. "You missed the fun, Mr. Dixon. You could've been on my side, since Jenna and Rachel double-teamed me."

He set the dish and basket on the table. "You'll forgive me for leaving you to fight on your own once you taste this gravy. And the biscuits are the same as my mother made. The recipe hasn't changed in sixty years."

Jenna hummed. "Smells divine. Let me wash up, then maybe we can get to that rational conversation over lunch?"

"Sounds like a plan," Rachel said.

The sausage gravy made concentrating on any kind of conversation nigh impossible for Amy. She shoveled another huge bite into her mouth and stifled a groan. If someone had been standing outside the window, they would've thought something naughty was happening in the room, the moaning from Amy and Jenna was so enthusiastic. Rachel didn't make a peep, but was the first to pile a second helping on her plate.

After taking a bite of biscuit number two, Rachel tossed her napkin on the table and got the conversation rolling. "I know you two don't want to admit it, but Amarex has backed us into a corner. We don't have a good choice, only bad or worse. Either we cut our losses and leave now, with a little money left in our pockets, or we leave bankrupt after giving all our money to a lawyer to fight Amarex's suit."

"I hate that idea," Jenna grumbled.

The idea of giving up made Amy sick. "This land has been in our family for three generations. Our dad was raised here. It's worth saving."

Rachel raised her arms in an impassioned gesture. "Do you think I don't know that? This farm is my life. Do you think I want to live in some crappy apartment in the city?"

"What would you do for work if we moved?" Amy asked Rachel. "All you know is farm life. You'd hate a desk job." More than hate, Amy knew if Rachel left the countryside, she'd languish. Her inner light would extinguish, Amy was sure of it. If nothing else, she'd fight to keep the farm for her sister's health and sanity.

"I'm not qualified for a desk job, even if I wanted one. But I could hire on as a ranch foreman somewhere. And you could find work at a restaurant, easy. We were lucky to have our dream jobs for as long as we did. Not many folks get that opportunity, even temporarily."

She was right. They'd lived a charmed life compared to most people in the world. Even Jenna, who'd had the luxury to stay at home with Tommy, despite being a single mom.

Rachel continued, "There's nothing tying us to Catcher Creek. We don't have any family left here anymore, and our true friends would understand."

Amy wondered if Tommy's father, whoever he was, would care if he and Jenna left town. Or if he even knew he was a father in the first place. She thought about Mr. Dixon and Sloane. It would be so painful to turn them out, when they were beginning to feel like a part of the family.

"I hate to pick sides," Jenna said, "but Rachel's right— something's got to give. I know our bank accounts inside and out. We can't afford a lawyer to defend us against a suit of this magnitude. We poured everything we had into funding the restaurant and inn, and Mom's nursing home and doctor bills. There's a good chance that if we fought the lawsuit and won, Amarex would be on the hook for our lawyer fees. But that's a pretty huge risk to take."

Rachel crumbled her napkin and threw it on her now-empty plate. "The suit was filed in Texas so it would go to court there, right? How are we going to run a farm, restaurant, and inn while we're holed up in a Texas courthouse?"

Despite Rachel and Jenna's readiness to give up, Amy wasn't convinced. Maybe it would be the most dignified course of action, but no one had ever made the mistake of calling Amy dignified. She was no doormat, as Rachel surmised, but a fighter—a scrapper. The cutthroat culinary world had toughened her hide and steeled her spine. And she knew, without a doubt, that she and her sisters would never find lasting happiness if they gave up without fighting for their way of life.

She may be an irrational bleeding heart, but even more importantly, she was resilient.

Rummaging through the pile of paperwork, she found the oil rights lawyer's card. Matt Roenick. Kellan's note said he did pro bono work. It was time to set aside her pride and accept the help Kellan seemed to be offering.

She dropped the business card on the table between Jenna and Rachel. "This was in Kellan's briefcase. It's the business card of an oil rights lawyer who does pro bono work."

Rachel shoved the card away from her. "I wouldn't take Kellan Reed's legal advice if he were the last man on Earth."

Amy flipped the card to the back. "There's more to Kellan's involvement than I originally assumed. Does this note look like the move of an Amarex spy?"

Jenna lifted the card and examined it. "No, it doesn't."

Rachel scoffed in protest.

Amy rested her hand on Jenna's shoulder. "Will you call this lawyer? Talk to him about our situation?"

"Yes, absolutely."

"We're going to fight this. True, we might lose everything, but at least we won't have any regrets because we'll have done everything we could. No *what ifs*. Are you with me?"

Jenna patted Amy's hand. "I'm with you."

They looked to Rachel.

She cradled her head in her hands. "I don't know if I have it in me. Honestly, you guys, this last year has been hell on me. I'm worn to the bone."

Amy walked around the table and draped an arm across Rachel's shoulder. Jenna did the same. Together, they pulled Rachel into a hug.

"We know you are, Rach. We'll hold you up," Amy said.

"We'll hold each other up," Jenna added.

Rachel squeezed her eyes closed and when she opened them again, she seemed stronger, if only a little. "Okay. I'm in."

Sloane's finals were going great, which was about the only bright spot in Amy's week. With two exams down and two to go by Wednesday morning, Sloane's face was starting to reflect her fatigue, but she powered through it valiantly. She'd set up camp in Amy's front room, with books and papers scattered over every flat surface and the sofa turned into a makeshift bed. To maximize her study time, she'd taken to rising when Rachel and Amy did before dawn.

Amy was impressed. She'd written Sloane off early as an immature, dingy young woman, but she'd proven herself the opposite. There was probably a lesson in there about not making assumptions about people, but Amy was too busy with lawyer meetings and hospital visits to think hard on the matter.

All she knew was that Mom wasn't waking up. The doctors continued to run tests, but had begun to hint that there was little likelihood she'd have any quality of life if she emerged from the coma. Amy, Jenna, and Rachel, each in their own way, were coming to terms with the choice they knew they'd need to make soon, to say good-bye to their mom and allow her to go to a better place.

Amy found it difficult to concentrate for long stretches of time. After multiple failed attempts at planning the Local Dish's dinner menu, she gave up. She sharpened her MAC blade to a deadly point and took to dicing every vegetable in the house. Mr. Dixon, who had quietly taken over all meal duties after Mom's stroke, worked alongside her in comfortable silence.

After a solid hour of dicing, Amy ran out of vegetable

options and hauled the bowls full of celery, onions, carrots, and potatoes to the hog trough. A nudge from a cold nose reminded her to save enough celery to share with Tulip, the heifer waiting not-so-patiently for her fair share. Amy emptied the remains of the bowl into the cow's makeshift trough and massaged its silky ear in her fingertips. It grunted in pleasure as it snarfed its meal.

She should've called Kellan about his runaway cow already, but she couldn't bring herself to speak to him yet, even though she no longer thought of him as the enemy. She'd found too much evidence to the contrary in the waterlogged papers from his briefcase. He'd created a spreadsheet template for the farm's finances, along with ideas on how to pay the bank while her family contended the Amarex lawsuit. She'd found oil maps of the area that clearly illustrated her family's property was dry, along with reports by Amarex engineers that stated the same thing. It was as though Kellan was helping her build a case against his uncle's company for some unfathomable reason.

What she needed to do was hear him out about his role in the Amarex mess. But as emotionally drained as she was over her mom, she wasn't ready to talk to anyone, much less apologize. So instead, she named his cow Tulip and took to feeding her.

Rachel thought the idea of assigning livestock anything other than an identifying number preposterous, which is why Amy had not only named the cow, but strung flowers through its ear tag and around its neck. Daisies, not tulips, but still, she was a cute thing. And Rachel was annoyed beyond measure. Amy found Rachel's reaction so amusing, she was considering hanging a photograph of Tulip in all her floral splendor in the bathroom.

"I see she likes celery."

She turned to see Mr. Dixon, walking her way with a bowl of kitchen scraps in his arms. He divided the goodies between the troughs, then propped a foot on the pigsty fence.

"You're probably wondering why I haven't returned this cow to Kellan."

He shook his head. "Not at all, honey. She won't be missed at his ranch for a while longer. And she's awful purty with these flowers. My kids used to do that with goats around our farm when they were little."

"Plus it aggravates Rachel."

He let out a whoop of laughter. "'Course it does. Which is as good a reason as any not to return the cow." He patted the cow's haunches. "I've been meaning to talk with you, but I could tell you needed some time to yourself. How about now?"

Amy quirked a brow at him. "You're not after me for a raise already, are you?"

He caught on to her joke and grinned before getting serious again. "Naw, I want to talk to you about the Amarex lawsuit."

"I don't want to talk about it, if it's all the same to you."

He was quiet for a minute and Amy grew hopeful that she'd staved off an awkward conversation. "I knew your parents from way back. They were good people. Had their faults, sure as I do, but good people. Raised three fine daughters."

She couldn't see what rehashing the past had to do with their Amarex troubles. "I suppose they did."

"Kept a roof over your heads and food on your plates. Not many people in the world can say that, when you think about it. I've traveled all over this godforsaken planet with the Navy and I'm telling you, by world standards, your parents were saints."

Saints? Amy wouldn't go that far, but Mr. Dixon had a point. "I know they loved us the best they could."

"They did. I'm glad you can see that."

"What are you getting at, Mr. Dixon?"

He sighed. "One thing I will say about your folks is that they didn't care about keeping this farm up. Farming wasn't in their blood. Back in the day, Dixon Farm and Sorentino Farm were competitors in the alfalfa industry. I'm sure you knew that. My brother and your grandfather were rivals, through and through. Our families played fair, but we played to win."

"But when my dad took over . . ." Amy prompted, when he paused.

"When your daddy took over, everything changed. Good for Dixon Farm, bad for the legacy he left you girls. But neither of your folks cared enough to change their ways. Rachel's done the best she could with the place, bless her heart, but it's not enough to erase the damage done by years of mismanagement and neglect, I'm afraid."

"Maybe not, but we've got to try."

"I know you've got it in your head to, and I'll support you best I can, but I want to make sure you're fighting for the right reasons. Don't do it because you think your parents would've wanted it that way. Do it for yourselves and yourselves only. You don't have nothing to prove to anyone. You do what your heart tells you to and not a thing else."

"This is what we want. For Tommy. For Rachel. She'd be miserable without the farm."

"Seems she's miserable now, with it."

"I know, but we'll see what we can do to change that for her. Get her some help. If we can beat Amarex—"

"Which brings me to the other issue I wanted to discuss."

"Okay . . ."

"This old man doesn't know the first thing about matchmaking or whatnot, but I have some advice for you about Kellan Reed."

Oh, heck no. She was not going to discuss her love life with Mr. Dixon. She backed up, waving the bowl. "We don't have to talk about this. Please . . ."

"Now, now, hear me out."

She blew an errant hair away from her eye and tried not to cringe outwardly. "Okay."

"All these things you kids think are important, they don't actually matter in the long run. I know because I was the same way. Took me retiring and my wife of thirty-two years dying to figure that out. Who cares who his family is and your family is? This isn't *Romeo and Juliet*. If you want to be with him, be with him. Have fun while you're young."

Amy blinked at him. "That's really bad advice."

"Why? What's he going to do, break your heart?"

"Well, yes."

"So what?"

"What do you mean, so what? So I don't like having my heart broken. It feels terrible and reminds me that I'm a total loser in the love department."

"Mark my words, honey. There will come a time when you look back on your life and miss the heartbreak."

She almost bought into his crazy advice, he spoke with such conviction. He and Lisa Binderman should get together and form a company. Sales sharks like those two could make a fortune selling sand in the desert. "I don't think so."

He straightened indignantly. "You didn't let me finish. You'll miss the heartbreak because it meant you'd fallen in love. And there's no other feeling in all the world that compares. I haven't fallen in love in forty years. Before my wife, I'd fallen in love and gotten my heart crushed three times by three wonderful women. I wouldn't trade those feelings for anything—not the joy of being in love or the heartbreak of losing it. That's the stuff life's made of."

She adjusted a flower on Tulip's neck. "I'm all for the falling in love part. It's the feeling like an idiot afterward that's so hard to bear."

"No one can make you feel foolish unless you let them."

Maybe that was her problem. Not a weakness for cowboys, but the way her behavior made her doubt her sensibility. Seems she spent half her adult life acting impulsively and the other half feeling like a fool because of it. She couldn't help but wonder how her life would change if she didn't allow her slipups to weigh her down. What if happiness was actually a product of attitude, not how stridently she adhered to her rules or hid in the kitchen?

Mr. Dixon patted her shoulder. "You're not your mom, Amy. You look like her, you laugh like her, but you're not her."

Turning to the pigsty, she squeezed her eyes closed, emotion welling within her. How was it that a retired Navy cook could manage to cut to the heart of her issues when she barely understood them? Her fear of turning into her mother had crippled her since she was old enough to recognize their physical similarities.

"My whole life, people have told me how much like my mom I am." Her voice cracked and she cleared her throat. "I hated the idea, but it stuck with me. Every morning, I wake up wondering when I'll snap for good like she did. It happened to her in her twenties. And I'm twenty-eight already, so I can't help but wonder if it's coming." She'd never voiced her deepest fear aloud before, and it made her insides ache. Tears fell over her cheek and pooled in the corner of her lips. She licked at them.

"Your mom's depression is a disease, one you don't have."

She scoffed. "Are you sure? Because I'm not. I had a screaming, crying meltdown on national television that ground my career to a halt, and I make terrible choices with men. Sounds like my mom in a nutshell. Maybe someday I'll be so depressed that I'll want to kill myself too."

"You won't."

"You can't know that, and neither can I. Who's to say it's not genetic?" She swallowed and lowered her voice, fighting to remain calm. "I work so hard to keep my emotions level, but it's a constant battle. Sometimes I think if it weren't for all the rules I hold myself to, I'd be out of control in a bad way. Like one tip of the scale too many and I'd fall into her same craziness."

She turned from him so he wouldn't see her crying, but he walked around to face her and set his hands firmly on her shoulders. "None of that is true. At all. Want to know how I'm so sure?"

"How?" she ground out.

"Because suicide is selfish. It's selfish and irresponsible and cowardly. And you, my dear, are none of those things."

Amy wrinkled her nose and smushed her lips together. She refused to openly sob.

He took her hand. "Time to let go of your fear. You don't need a list of rules to keep yourself in check. What a horrible drain on your energy that must be." He was right; it was draining and rather pointless, since she constantly broke them. "Repeat after me: no more rules."

"No more rules," she whispered.

"I am not my parents."

"I am not my parents," she echoed.

He grinned and pulled her into a hug. "Thank goodness, because I'd be out of a job and back to eating Jillian's so-called food."

Amy drew in a tremulous, but fortifying, breath. She wiped her runny nose and shook her head. "I'll never look at spaghetti the same again. I can't stop picturing bleeding monkey brains."

He nodded gravely. "You don't know the half of it. She sent a chicken casserole over here with me after she heard about your mom's stroke. I walked it straight out here to the pigs."

The absurdity brought a laugh up from her throat. "That was sweet of her."

Mr. Dixon rubbed her shoulder. "She's got a good heart, even if she doesn't have the cooking skills to match. I've put on five pounds since I started working at your house. My pants are fitting better already."

"Glad to hear it."

He took her bowl and nested it with his. "I'll take care of the dishes and clean up. You should talk to Kellan, clear things up with him."

"Okay, I will soon."

With a smile of gratification, he wrapped an arm around her back and guided her toward the house. With every step she felt stronger, healed.

He opened the door. "You need to stop holding yourself back and start discovering the real Amy Sorentino."

Amy cocked her head at him, contemplating his nugget of wisdom. "What does that mean, really?"

An impish grin lit his face. "I have no idea, but I hear it all the time on those daytime talk shows Jillian watches. Seems to be the advice women give each other when they're sharing their feelings."

Amy chuckled. "Oh, Mr. Dixon. You had me thinking you were some closet self-help guru for a minute."

He raised an eyebrow. "I could be. You might never know." When she chuckled again, he gave her shoulders an affectionate shake. "Don't count Kellan out yet. Things might turn out fine. Miracles do happen, you know."

She nodded and looked over her shoulder, drinking in the sights around her, the back porch of the white and gray house she grew up in, the rolling hills and deep valleys that had sustained her family for generations. She smelled the fragrance of dried winter grasses wafting through the breeze and the pungent scent of snow melting into the dirt. Boy, she hoped Mr. Dixon was right. They could all use a miracle right about now.

A miracle was not what the following morning brought, however. The phone rang while Amy was pouring her second cup of coffee at six-fifteen. It was Mom's doctor, who opened the conversation by explaining that she usually didn't discuss this sort of thing over the phone, but she knew how far away Amy and her sisters lived so she decided to make an exception.

Taking a hint from the doctor's sad tone, Amy had a feeling she knew what *this sort of thing* was. She dropped into the nearest seat, and covered her mouth with her hand, too numb to cry.

Mom's vitals were weakening rapidly and her latest MRI came back with bad news. Six days after the stroke, her brain showed no significant activity. It was time for Amy and her sisters to make some hard decisions about continuing life support, the doctor gently prompted. Amy managed a thank you, but couldn't think of anything else to say except, "We'll talk over the options and be there as soon as we can."

After the call, she gathered Rachel and Jenna in the kitchen. They huddled over untouched cups of coffee, already knowing what needed to be done.

Not that knowing made it hurt any less.

Jenna arranged for Sloane to take Tommy to her grandma's house to spend the night. Mr. Dixon usually didn't arrive until ten-ish, so Amy called him at eight to ask if he'd drive them to Albuquerque. She debated calling Kellan instead, longing to lean on his strength. But with so much unresolved between them, she didn't want to make a mistake by complicating their relationship even further.

Jenna put Tommy in Sloane's car along with his over-night bag. Amy and Rachel waited their turn to kiss him good-bye while Mr. Dixon pulled his car around to pick them up. The drive passed in a blur. Amy's only vivid thought came as she crossed the threshold of the main entrance, when she realized she was walking into the lobby for the last time. She took her sisters' hands, gritted her teeth, and braced herself to face the most difficult, painful thing she'd ever have to do.

Kellan stepped out from his walk-in freezer with a box of beef to send Jake. His two office employees were busy at desks, monitoring holiday online and phone orders.

It had been a great month, businesswise. The last orders of roasts and prime ribs for Christmas dinner were shipping that Friday. Once that was accomplished, he'd shut the business down until after the holidays, as he always did, to give his employees a week paid vacation. Out of necessity, a few ranch hands stayed on, but he paid them double to make it worth their time.

When the office phone rang, his heart rate sped up. Could be his mother. She always called the office number because it was published on the Slipping Rock Ranch Web site. Since Morton dropped the bomb that she'd been sniffing around, every ring of the phone had him jumping out of his skin. He'd begun to consider that it might be healthier to answer the call and get the confrontation over with.

His employees were tied up with other calls, so Kellan peeked at the caller ID and answered the phone with a sigh of relief.

"Hey, Chris."

"Kellan, did Amy call you today?"

"No, why?"

"My mom heard from Charlene Delgado that Bethany's at her end. Amy and her sisters left for the hospital to say good-bye. They're taking her off life support."

Kellan's heart sank. "Did they drive themselves?"

"Not sure, man. But I thought you should know."

"Thanks. I'll see if I can figure out what's going on."

He tried Amy's cell phone but she didn't answer. He called her house, but the answering machine picked up. He had to do something. He couldn't continue on with his workday knowing what Amy was going through.

The hospital phone number was easy to find online. The front desk receptionist who answered knew Amy and her sisters by name and confirmed that they hadn't arrived yet. He thanked her and stood holding the phone, considering his next move.

The truth was, Amy hadn't called him. She hadn't asked for his support. The last time they spoke, she threatened to call the police if he showed his face on her property again. The most obvious course of action would be to leave her alone. That idea didn't sit well with him, though. Not well at all.

Staring at his land through the window, he got to thinking about what he'd learned from Amy's family about love and ferocity. About fighting to hold on to the people he cared about despite the obstacles. He fished his truck keys from his pocket. She might not want to see him, but he needed her to know he was there, fighting for her.

From the road, he called Vaughn. It was a long shot, but worth a try.

He picked up on the second ring. "Hey, K. What's up?"

"Chris called. He found out through the grapevine that Amy and her sisters are taking their mom off life support today. I'm on my way to the hospital in Albuquerque."

Vaughn sighed. "Those poor women. It's like it never ends for them."

"Tell me about it. I thought you might want to know, in case you want me to pick you up on my way."

Silence. Then, "Why would you do that?"

There was a time that Kellan would've let Vaughn get away with playing dumb, but he was beginning to realize the value in boldly speaking his mind instead of hiding from the truth. "So you can be there for Rachel. She's going to need someone, like they all will."

Another bout of silence was followed by a curse. "I can't believe you'd suggest that. Didn't you listen to anything I told you? Me showing up where I'm not wanted will only cause Rachel more pain than she's already got. And she's got plenty, from the sound of it."

"Things could still be fixed between you two."

"No, K, they can't. Stop pushing."

"Fine." He turned onto the highway, headed west. "I'll update you as soon as I know something."

But Vaughn's rant wasn't done. "You know what? You shouldn't be going to the hospital either. You're going to make a mess out of the Amarex investigation. Don't forget you're the whistle-blower in the billion-dollar corporate corruption case the Sorentinos are involved in. This is not ethical."

"So be it. I'm not letting Amy go through this alone."

He ended the call, pressed the accelerator, and sped toward the rising sun.

In the hospital, he stopped in the hall outside Bethany's room. The door was closed. Through the slit of a window, he saw Amy and Jenna on the far side of the bed, and Rachel on the near. Their arms were around each other, their heads bowed.

When a nurse passed by, he snagged her with a gesture.

"Excuse me. I'm a friend of Bethany's family." He motioned to her room. "Have they removed life support yet?"

The nurse looked into the room, worrying her lip as though debating the ethics of sharing the information. "No. They arrived not too long ago and asked for a few minutes alone with her first. We have a waiting room down the hall if you'd like to sit."

"No, thanks. I'd rather stay here, in case they need me."

She nodded and hurried on with her duties. Kellan settled against the far wall, keeping them in view through the window. After a while, the sisters raised their heads and spoke. Jenna blew her nose. Amy skirted the bed and walked to the door.

When it opened, Kellan straightened, prepared to stoically accept whatever reaction Amy had to his presence. She didn't startle when she noticed him, but held his gaze with her wet, red-rimmed eyes. Her expression was so sad, Kellan had a tough time staying still and not reaching for her.

"You heard," she croaked.

My God, it was torture, not pulling her into his arms. "Amy, I know you hate me right now, but—"

With a hand over her mouth, she shook her head. A sob bubbled violently up, wracking her body with tremors. She squeezed her eyes closed, struggling against it.

Kellan snapped. She could tell him to go to hell later, but he couldn't bear to stand there any longer. He crossed the hall and embraced her. Burying her head in his chest, her cry tore free. He backed into the wall, out of the way of the bustling corridor, and held on to her like his life depended on it. Which, in some important ways, it did.

The minute Amy's tornado had touched down in his life, he started to see the world differently. She challenged his perception of family and love, pushing him to be a better friend, a better brother, and a better man. Because of her, he was finally going to stand up to his uncle in a real, public way. Because of her, he would try harder to make amends with Jake. It was extraordinary, really, the changes she'd wrought without even trying.

And it had all started with some celery.

Pressing his cheek to her temple, he allowed himself a small, melancholy smile. Thank goodness he'd followed his instincts to go to the hospital. He'd continue to be there for her family throughout their grief, for as long as she let him. And no matter what he had to do to make it happen, he vowed to save their farm. Even if Amy never stopped resenting him for hiding his Amarex ties, he owed her that much for helping him discover the man he wanted to be.

When her tears subsided, he asked, "What's the next step?"

She sniffed, but remained in his arms with her forehead resting on his chest. "I have to tell the nurse that we're ready."

"Ready?"

"To turn the machines off and let her go."

"You stay with your family. I'll take care of that."

He shuffled her toward the door, but she didn't release him. "Kellan?"

"Hmm?"

"I'm glad you're here."

Oh, man. That alone was worth the drive. "Me too."

She kissed his cheek and reentered the room.

At the nurses' main desk, he leaned against the counter, waiting for the nurse to finish her phone call. Vaughn, dressed in his work uniform, walked down the hall from the direction of the elevators, his expression solemn.

Kellan worked hard to mask his surprise. "Hey."

"How are they?"

"I'm waiting to tell the nurse they're ready to turn off the machines."

"Shit."

"Tell me about it."

Vaughn motioned to Kellan's chest. "Your shirt's all wet."

Kellan looked down at the splotches. "Amy," he offered as explanation.

Vaughn nodded and leaned on the counter next to Kellan. "You're not going to stay away from her, are you?"

"I have feelings for her, Vaughn."

"All the more reason to cool things off until your job as a witness against Amarex is over."

"Relationships don't work that way." That much he'd figured out, thanks to Amy. "You can support me or not, I don't care. I'm going to do what I have to do."

"All right, all right. I get it."

The nurse turned to him and he relayed Amy's message. She nodded and walked toward Bethany's room. Vaughn and Kellan trailed behind.

They stopped in the hall outside the room. "I know you get it," Kellan said. "Because you're in the same boat."

Vaughn's expression was blade sharp. "Don't start with me. I don't know what the hell I'm doing here."

"Sure you do." He nodded toward the door. "Those Sorentino sisters, they really are extraordinary."

Vaughn fiddled with the knobs on his walkie-talkie. "Yes, they are."

A single, muffled cry filtered out from the room. Both men's heads shot up. Kellan looked through the window and saw Amy, Rachel, and Jenna embracing. The nurse flitted around, removing tubes, powering down the equipment. Vaughn and Kellan stood in heavy silence, watching.

After a few minutes, Douglas Dixon appeared at Kellan's elbow, a cup of coffee in hand.

"Douglas, what are you doing here?"

"I drove the sisters in. None of them felt up to driving, bless their hearts."

Kellan offered him a hand to shake. "Thank you for taking care of them."

Douglas shook his hand. "Glad to help, after everything they've done for me. Hard workers with hearts of gold, those girls are." He shook Vaughn's hand. "Sheriff Cooper, sorry to see you under such unfortunate circumstances. I didn't realize you were a friend of the family."

Kellan held his breath for Vaughn's response, but he simply said, "Yes, sir."

"Since you're here, how about you drive them home?" he asked Kellan. "I'll get back to their place and open it up, put some food in the oven, and tend to the livestock so they don't have anything to worry about tonight."

The old man's eyes twinkled with awareness, like maybe he had some idea of Kellan and Amy's relationship. With the Catcher Creek gossip circuit, there was no telling what Douglas knew. "Thank you. I'll give you a hand with the livestock as soon as we get there."

A good long while after Douglas left, the door opened. Jenna filed out first. She walked straight to Kellan and threw her arms around him, which caught him off guard. He hugged her back. Then she moved on down the hall, as though she might need some time alone.

Amy was next out of the door. Kellan gathered her in his arms and tucked her head under his chin. "I'm so sorry," he soothed. She melted into him. Kellan stroked the side of her face, collecting fallen tears.

Rachel was the last person from the room.

Vaughn stepped forward. "Rachel."

She regarded him with weary eyes that were dry without any trace of red or puffiness. Vaughn reached out. She stared, blinking, at their joined hands. Seconds passed.

Kellan tensed, waiting. For the first time, he could sort of picture the two as a couple.

Rachel's eyes closed. Her thumb stroked the back of Vaughn's hand. He took a step nearer and she opened her eyes. Shaking out of his grasp, she walked away.

"Rachel, please," he called.

She swatted the air with her open hand as she walked. "Go away, Vaughn. Just . . . don't."

His hands fisted at his sides, Vaughn watched her until she disappeared around a corner. With a scathing look at Kellan, he strode in the opposite direction, toward the elevators.

"Why was Sheriff Cooper here?" Amy said.

"Same as me. He wanted to make sure you and your sisters were all right."

She sniffled. "I don't even know what *all right* means anymore."

He tightened his embrace. "We'll figure it out together."

Chapter 16

Amy slipped into the church sanctuary through a side door and took a seat in the second pew from the front, successfully avoiding eye contact with anyone. Which was saying something because, with Christmas three days away, the sanctuary was packed with visiting relatives and grown children who'd flown in to spend the holidays with their families. She felt their prying eyes on her, almost wishing she'd cause a scene and give them something to talk about at their Sunday dinners. Maybe she would, but she no longer cared.

She busied herself flipping through her grandmother's Bible in search of the passages referenced in the worship program as she waited for the service to begin. Neither of her sisters had been interested in attending that morning, but Amy could think of no better place to lay her troubles down than at church. They'd agreed not to hold a public memorial for their mom, knowing how few people would attend, but Amy still wanted to pray for Mom's soul within the hallowed walls of the church her family had belonged to for three generations.

Nearby movement caught her eye and she glanced up. Kellan. With a grim smile, he dropped onto the pew next to her. Lisa Binderman scooted around Amy, squeezing her knee as she went, and sat on her other side, followed by her daughter, Daisy, and her husband, Chris, who held their baby boy. Sheriff Cooper took a seat next to Kellan.

"Good morning," Kellan said, brushing a kiss on her cheek.

She still hadn't decided how she felt about him, other than gratitude that he'd provided her a solid shoulder to lean on. They hadn't discussed their argument, or the Amarex lawsuit. Mostly, he'd been a quiet, strong presence around her house, arriving daily with bundles of celery and little gifts for Tommy, then taking over Sorentino Farm's chores, along with two ranch hands he pulled from their duties at Slipping Rock.

He'd asked the day before if she was planning to attend church and offered to pick her up, but she declined as politely as she could. With her own set of wheels, she had the option to bolt at any time if her sadness became overwhelming. All things considered, though, she was doing okay and didn't expect her emotions to suddenly run amok in the middle of the service, much to the disappointment of her fellow parishioners. After grieving the loss of her mom for nearly a year before her death, Amy was all cried out.

Lisa patted her shoulder. "How ya doin'?"

Amy nodded. Lisa had stopped by over the weekend to deliver a cheesy tuna casserole and had stayed to help with the laundry. Amy could easily see the two of them becoming fast friends over time. "I'm better every day."

"Good."

Kellan took her hand as Pastor Schueller assumed his place at the front of the room. She didn't mind, even though so many of their issues were unsettled. He was still the heir to the company suing her family. He was still the man who lied to her about who he was. But she liked the feel of his hand over hers. Maybe Mr. Dixon was right.

Maybe it didn't matter who his family was. Maybe nothing mattered but the joy of *feeling*. Vivid, immediate feeling—good or bad, complicated or simple. Right now, she wanted to hold his hand. They could hash out the details another day.

The organist paused and the service began. Amy settled into that old, comfortable routine, singing, praying, and listening to the pastor's soothing cadence. She barely processed the sermon, a Christmas-themed lesson of re-birth and growth, but she relished the peace that settled in her bones as she sang from the same hymnal she'd used as a child, songs her grandmothers probably sang during their lives. She loved the sound of Kellan's deep, slightly off-tune voice singing those same songs at her side.

Toward the end of the service, Pastor Schueller announced the prayer requests. Amy was prepared for this part, for she'd contacted him the day before, asking him to include her mom. When he said "Bethany Sorentino," she cried anyway. Quiet, healing tears as she prayed along with the rest of the congregation for her mom's soul. Kellan released her hand and slung his arm across her shoulders, holding her steady and offering her a tissue from his pocket.

"Are there any other prayer requests this morning?" Pastor Schueller asked the parishioners.

Kate Parrish, who'd been one of Amy's closest friends in high school, stood. "I have one."

Amy and Kate had lost touch almost immediately after graduation, not due to animosity, but because both had left town in pursuit of their dreams. Rejecting the idea of working at her parents' feed and grain store, Kate had gone to some Ivy League school on an academic scholarship to prepare for her career in politics. Amy considered snagging her after church to set up a coffee date so they could catch up.

"I'd like to ask everyone to pray for my brother Carson. He was deployed to the Middle East last week."

Kate's younger brother Carson had been a friend of Jenna's. Not a boyfriend, though plenty of people had speculated. Whatever their relationship, they'd gotten into a lot of trouble during high school together. So much so that both his parents and hers had forbidden them from hanging around together. Amy's parents had breathed a sigh of relief when he enlisted in the Marines.

"We will definitely pray for Carson. Thank you, Kate," the pastor said. "Any other prayers?"

In the rear of the sanctuary, a woman with bright orange, thinning hair and sallow cheeks stood. Kellan's arm went stiff. Amy thought she heard him curse under his breath.

The woman gripped the jacket folded over her arm like a lifeline as she spoke in a thin, tremulous voice. "Could you pray for me? I've come to ask my son's forgiveness. We haven't spoken in five years and I could use the Lord's guiding hand when we talk."

Kellan let go of Amy. He scooted to the edge of his seat like he might stand. Or run. "No," he whispered. Amy massaged his shoulder blade in an effort to soothe his agitation.

Pastor Schueller offered the woman a benevolent smile. "Of course we'll pray for you. Tell me your name, dear?"

"Tina. And my son is Kellan. Kellan Reed. He's sitting in the second row."

Kellan's head spun. His mouth went dry. His mother had interrupted church to call him out. She announced their private struggle to half the Catcher Creek population. Holy shit.

He didn't remember standing, but suddenly Vaughn was in front of him, his hand on Kellan's chest. "Keep it cool, K."

"I have to get her out of here."

Someone tugged on his arm. Amy. My God, Amy was watching this. Everyone was watching. He saw them whispering, but heard only the roar of air in his ears.

"Is this your son?" the preacher asked his mother, gesturing to Kellan.

"Yes, sir."

"I can't . . . I have to get her out of here," Kellan muttered.

"Okay," Vaughn said under his breath, "but keep it cool, calm."

He couldn't breathe. "Yeah."

"What's happening, Kellan?" Amy asked.

He glanced her way. No time to explain. He had to get his mother out of the building before the scene she caused exploded out of his control. He pushed Vaughn's hand from his chest. "Out of my way."

Vaughn moved to let him pass.

He walked, floating. The edges of his vision turned black, the walls of a tunnel through which he passed to reach his mother, standing across the aisle in the back row of the sanctuary, her arms open, beckoning, waiting to embrace him. Like he'd ever let that happen.

"My son, oh my son!" Her shrill voice echoed in the silence.

His ears burned. He took her wrist in his hand, gently but resolutely. "Come with me."

She planted her feet on the floor. "No, Kellan. Don't you see? The preacher is going to pray for us. We need all the help we can get to heal our bond."

Their bond? What a load of crap. "We'll discuss this privately. Let's go." He tugged her wrist.

She stomped her foot and jerked her wrist out of his hand. A child having a tantrum. "You can't throw me out. I won't let you."

He tried to speak again but his tongue stuck to the roof

of his mouth, it was so dry. He couldn't move, he couldn't think. The situation had spiraled out of control too fast. All he knew was that he had to get them both out of the congregation's judging eyes.

"Sit with me. We can pray together." She reached for his hand, but he refused to relinquish the fist it had formed.

He stood, frozen, staring at the wall beyond her. The stained glass depicted Mary holding a crucified Jesus across her lap. The grieving, devoted mother, helpless to prevent her son's suffering. It was a desecration that Tina Reed shared the title of *mother* with Mary.

"Son," the preacher said. "Have a seat and we'll pray for you and your mother." His patronizing tone set Kellan's teeth on edge. The preacher sounded like Morton, calling him *son,* like they had the right to tell him what to do. Rage sizzled through his chest like tendrils of fire.

An arm came to rest across his mother's shoulders. Amy. Her posture was serene, as though she were impervious to the prying eyes of the witnesses. He blinked at her.

"There's a prayer room off the fellowship hall," Amy said in a low, firm voice. "Let's pray in private. Pastor Schueller will understand. Tina, as a mother yourself, would you help me pray for my mom?"

"I would be honored," she answered.

Amy turned her gaze on Kellan, and the strength radiating from her poured into him, dousing his anger, unsticking his feet from the floor. "Kellan, you can help us." She cupped his fist with her hand and worked her thumb into his palm.

He nodded. "Good, let's walk together."

With her arm around his mother's shoulders and her hand holding Kellan's fist, she guided them out of the pew and through the swinging doors into the vestibule, commanding them with the sheer strength of her will through the sunny courtyard and into the fellowship hall.

The prayer room door shut with a click that shook Kellan from his trance. How dare his mother show up unannounced and create a public spectacle in his place of worship? He watched, sneering from against the closed door, his anger building again as Amy guided her to a seat. She looked much older than her fifty-eight years, with her hair thin enough to reveal her scalp and her skin hanging loose over her bones like an ill-fitting slipcover.

He waited for her to arrange herself in the chair before starting in on her. "How did you find me?"

"Kellan," Amy warned from her seat next to his mother, like she expected him to be on his best behavior, even after the stunt his mother pulled. Yeah, he'd get right on that.

His mother crossed her legs at the knees and hugged herself. "This is a small town. I asked the cashier at the Quick Stand where you might be. Nice woman. Char Something. She said if you weren't at your ranch, you'd be at First Methodist." She shrugged. "This was closer. Figured I could get a ride from someone out to your place after the service."

"You had no right to burst into my place of worship and make a public announcement about our private business. A phone call would've worked fine."

"So you could've left town before I got here?"

She was right. He would've avoided her at all costs, in person or over the phone. Embarrassing, that Amy was finding out what a coward he was. "Did you drive?"

"No. Can't afford a car and insurance and all that junk. I took a bus from Florida."

"Is Dad with you?"

She raised her chin a notch. "I left him. For good this time. Two weeks ago."

Kellan dropped into the chair. "You . . . what? Bruce told me he was released from prison."

"My brother, always with the half truths." Her tone was

exasperated. "He told you Declan got out of jail, but left out the part about me and him separating?"

"He didn't mention it." That son of a bitch. "Did you see Bruce when you passed through Texas?"

"Tried to. The bus doesn't swing near his house, so we made arrangements to meet at a diner in Amarillo." Her cheek twitched. "I guess he forgot because he never showed. I hopped on the next bus to New Mexico. And here I am."

"Where's your final destination?" Amy asked.

"Los Angeles."

Kellan huffed. "Does Jake know? Or are you going to blindside him too?"

"He doesn't know because I don't have his phone number. Or an address. But I have to try to see him. It's too important for me not to."

The truth at last. "You're going through the AA steps again, aren't you?"

"Yes, I am. And this time, it's going to stick."

Sure it was. "So you're here to apologize to me. Again."

Her eyes turned glassy with moisture. "For the hurt I've caused you, yes."

Amy tutted and took his mother's hand. "That sounds like a good first step toward healing your relationship." She sounded like one of those therapists on talk radio that his office employees listened to while they worked, expounding bullshit generic truisms to down-on-their-luck callers, despite not having a complete picture of the callers' troubles.

"It sounds that way, doesn't it?" Kellan said, his tone harsher toward Amy than he would've liked. He couldn't help it. "But you're missing some information. This is Mom's third time going through the steps. Her third apology. So it's not like she's making amends because of some deep-seated desire to repair our relationship. She's only doing this because she's reached that step in the AA program and she's required to. Pardon me if I don't put much stock in its significance."

Amy stared at him. Her cheeks flushed and the way her lips had gone white and thin, he knew her anger was whipping up to a frenzy inside her. He braced himself for her retort.

"You've gotten *two* apologies from your mom before today? Two of them?" Her voice was soft, but harsh. Like a pressure cooker letting off a wisp of steam right before it exploded.

"Yeah, two. Which is why I have so much trouble believing her sincerity this third time."

Amy stood and stalked toward him. "Do you have any idea what I'd have given for my mom to apologize *once* for what she put my sisters and me through? For what she put herself through? Do you have any idea what that would've meant to me?" Her voice was raw with pain.

How could he make her understand when her grief over losing her mom was so fresh? "Amy, your situation and mine are totally different."

"Are they?"

Before he could respond, his mother spoke. "Amy, let me answer my son's concerns. After everything I've done wrong, I don't blame him for being skeptical."

Amy narrowed her eyes at Kellan. "Sorry, Tina, but I can't stand seeing someone squander the chance to make things right with the people they love, as if they have all the time in the world to waste. I learned the hard way that you never know when an opportunity will be your last."

Kellan reached for her, but she pulled her hand away and stomped to her seat. His mom patted her knee—a soothing, motherly gesture that stoked Kellan's disgust. Scowling, he averted his eyes and said, "Give me one good reason why I should believe you this time."

"Because I'm finally free of your father's influence."

He looked at her, confused about what one had to do with the other. "His influence?"

"Declan and I brought out the worst in each other from the start. Never could be around each other sober. This time when he was in jail, I got straight with myself. Clear eyed. That was the last time I apologized to you."

He remembered all too well the burgeoning hope he'd felt that perhaps the sobriety would stick that time. What a fool he'd felt like when she proved him wrong again.

She turned to Amy. "I had a job for two years cleaning houses. First week Declan was out of jail, I started lighting up again—meth. Second week, I lost my job. Third week, I realized it was him, all this time, bringing me down. Now, that's not to say I didn't have any part in it, because I take full responsibility for what I did to myself."

"And what you did to me and Jake?"

Her lips pursed and her head shook, like she couldn't decide to nod or shake it. "I know what I did to you two. And it's a vicious cycle, let me tell you, to have that understanding of the lives you've screwed up. Drove me back to the drugs to dull the pain of my regrets. That's why the program requires us to apologize. We can't heal unless we own our mistakes, and stop trying to forget what we've done wrong. Maybe someday you'll forgive me, but either way, I can't stay clean without acknowledging to myself what a mess I made of all our lives."

Amy took her hand. The sight turned Kellan's vision red. He tried to breathe deeply, but the room's stuffy, heated air closed in on him. He dragged a finger between his shirt collar and his neck, but it didn't help. His watch read eleven-forty. Five minutes until the service concluded. He needed to get out of there, off the church property before he had to confront the gossip-greedy stares of the parishioners again.

He stood, swaying with lightheadedness. Once the

dizziness passed, he opened the door and gestured for the women to precede him out. "Okay, you apologized. I'll drive you to the bus terminal in Albuquerque. Let's go."

His mother rose, her spine straight as a rod, and she met Kellan's eyes with a hard, prideful expression. "Thank you for the offer, but I have a ticket on a bus out of Tucumcari tomorrow morning. I'll find somewhere in town to stay tonight."

"The Highway Flyer Motel is a good choice, close to the bus terminal. I'll drive you there. But we have to get out of here. Now!" He opened the door more widely and glanced at the doughnut table. In a couple minutes, it would be swarming with people.

His mother took a step toward the door, but Amy stood and blocked her. "Nonsense. Tina, you'll stay at my house tonight. We have plenty of room."

Panic flared inside him. "Amy, no. She can stay at the Highway Flyer. You have enough to deal with."

She wagged her finger at him. "You don't treat family like that—shoving them off in some motel for the night. I'm going to give your mom a place to stay and there's nothing you can do about it unless you're inviting her to stay with you."

Damn it. He gnashed his teeth. Didn't matter how hard he wished it were otherwise, he couldn't stop looking like an uncaring coward in front of Amy. But neither of his parents were welcome in his home, even if Amy thought him the Devil for it.

Amy sniffed. "That's what I thought." She took his mom's hand. "Tina, did I understand correctly that your son, Jake, is not expecting you in Los Angeles?"

Shifting her weight, his mother fussed with a button on her jacket. "No."

"Can we talk about this by our cars?" Kellan asked. "We've got to get out of here before the service ends."

Amy kept her focus to his mother. "Christmas is in three days. Do you have someone to celebrate with?"

Kellan sucked in a pained breath. He was dizzy again, and sweaty. He gripped the arm of the nearest chair. This couldn't be happening. *Don't say it, don't say it,* he silently pleaded with Amy.

"No one should be alone this time of year. Would you like to stay with my family for Christmas? We can get you a new bus ticket to Los Angeles after the holiday."

Oh, God. She said it.

Then the sound of doors rattling open gave way to a din of a hundred people filling the courtyard, chatting and laughing. Someone noted the excellent doughnut selection, while another whined about the powdered coffee creamer. A group of men discussed the slate of football games that afternoon.

Kellan closed his eyes. They were too late to escape.

He drove home on autopilot. He didn't know what to think or how to feel about Amy or his mother. He could only imagine what the people of Catcher Creek were discussing over their Sunday suppers.

He didn't see Bruce Morton's truck until he was in the driveway. Morton leaned against the shiny red exterior, waiting. Dread uncoiled in Kellan's chest, making it tough to breathe. He parked at an angle, blocking Morton's truck in, and reached for the rifle under his seat. Holding his phone where Morton couldn't see it, he speed-dialed Vaughn and tucked the phone in his pocket. If Vaughn answered, he might be able to listen in on the conversation and send backup, if need be.

He stepped from the cab, his eyes on Morton, the rifle pointed at the dirt between them. His finger on the trigger.

Morton laughed. "You look like a pussy swinging around

that ancient .22 like you're scared of an old man like me."
The potential for violence radiated from his being and
twinkled in his eyes. "How about I even the playing field,
just for shits and giggles?"

He reached beneath his shirt and withdrew a black
Berretta from the small of his back. "She's a beaut, ain't
she?" He flicked the safety off and aimed it at Kellan's
front truck tire.

Kellan lifted his rifle in his uncle's direction. It felt like
a child's toy in his hands compared to the Berretta.

Morton swung the pistol skyward and fired. The boom
echoed through the nearby canyons and mesas. Kellan
clamped his molars together and did his best not to flinch.

"Fuckin-a, I love that sound," Morton said with a
chuckle.

"What do you want?"

"You'll never guess what happened to me last night."

Kellan had a pretty good idea. He held the rifle's aim
steady. "Do tell."

"FBI showed up at my door, hauled me to Dallas for
questioning. Seems they've opened an investigation
against Amarex."

"Guess you should've played by the rules."

"Here's my question for you, son. Are you recording our
conversation right now? Because, let me tell you, I was un-
prepared to learn that my own flesh and blood set me up."
He trained the pistol on Kellan's chest.

Run or stand my ground? Run or stand? It was tough to
formulate a thought, standing at the business end of a nine
millimeter as he was. Staying put seemed like a stupid
choice, but then, if he ran, Morton might shoot him in the
back. He raised his rifle and looked down the barrel with
one eye to make sure Morton was lined up in his sights.
Then he locked his eyes on Morton's trigger finger. One
twitch of that finger and he'd shoot his uncle in the gut.

"I'm not recording this, to answer your question. Now I've got one for you. You had to know I wouldn't put up with your bullying of my neighbors indefinitely, so why give me the Amarex file in the first place?"

"You want an honest answer?"

"Might as well give it to me at this point."

Morton widened his stance and checked the sights on his pistol. "All right. I hoped you'd join me. I hoped somewhere inside you, the Reed and Morton blood still flowed through your veins. I wanted you to be my partner, not some hillbilly rancher."

"Your partner?"

"Why do you think I wrote you into my will?"

"I figured you did that because it was a way for you to keep your claws in me."

Morton huffed. "You think I'm a monster, don't you?"

"You want an honest answer?" Kellan said, echoing Morton's words.

Shaking his head, Morton dropped his gun to his side. "I never had kids. Eileen saw to that. When you came around, I thought I had a second chance to pass my legacy to a new generation. I tried over and over to bring you into my company, but you never could get on board."

Taking Morton's cue, Kellan lowered his rifle and took his first deep breath since arriving. "What happened to Eileen? Did you kill her?"

Morton huffed. "No, I didn't kill her, damn it. She left me. Took half my money and moved to Hawaii. Told me I didn't talk to her enough or some such female bullshit. You always thought the worst about me, so I didn't see any reason to share the truth with you."

Was that hurt in Morton's voice? He wasn't aware that Morton felt any emotions other than greed or menace. "Since we're on a truth-telling kick, why don't you illuminate me about why you want the Sorentino property, even though it's dry and useless."

"No, it ain't."

"Come again?"

"The property's not dry. Our exploration crews missed a deep pocket of petroleum in the farm's southwest pasture. Gerald Sorentino found it."

Surprise rocketed through him. "Gerald Sorentino was in on a scam?"

"He came to me. The scam was his idea. He proposed the two of us go into business on the sly, split the profits fifty-fifty. He had the oil and I had the equipment and know-how. Of course, I talked his percentage down and his investment price up."

A 50 percent profit was a solid 20 percent higher than the usual home owner rate, and 30 percent over the pathetic contract Gerald originally signed way back when. The thought infuriated him all over again. The whole mess, the ruined finances, the burden he put on Amy and her sisters, all came down to Gerald's greed. Like Kellan's parents. And his uncle. He scowled, the taste of disgust like acid in his mouth. "Let me guess, you upped his investment price because you were aware, all along, of the foreclosure clause in the Sorentino contract."

"I'm no fool. All I had to do was bankrupt him and the oil would be mine. Then, he died."

"Did you kill him?"

"Hell, no. My life's been exponentially more difficult since the bastard ran his car off a cliff. I had him exactly where I wanted him. Maybe he knew. Maybe he was stupid enough to think his death would render the contract void. Like I'd leave his wife and kids alone, and ignore the glut of oil sitting beneath their dirt."

Morton's gaze shifted to the horizon. He tucked the Berretta beneath his shirt and cursed.

Kellan chanced a look over his shoulder. Dust billowed along his dirt road. A few seconds later, three patrol cars barreled into the driveway. The officers ducked behind their open doors, guns drawn and trained on Morton. Kellan placed his rifle on the ground.

Vaughn's voice bellowed into the silence from behind one of the cop car doors. "Put your hands in the air. Now!"

Morton took in the scene around him before sneering at Kellan. "You pussy, calling the cops instead of handling your own business. You would've made a god-awful business partner. No stones at all." He raised his arms.

Vaughn rushed forward, his firearm at the ready, motioning for the other officers to follow.

"He's armed," Kellan said. "In his waistband. A nine millimeter Berretta."

One of the deputy sheriffs flipped Morton's shirt up and seized his weapon. Another was ready with handcuffs.

"What am I being charged with?" Morton sneered.

"Possession of an unregistered firearm within the state of New Mexico, for starters," Vaughn said. "But threatening a witness in an investigation will probably be what sends you to prison for a good long time, Morton. Then, when you're convicted of your Amarex crimes, they're going to throw the key away to your cell, you greedy son of a bitch."

Two deputies led him to the backseat of their car.

Holstering his weapon, Vaughn nodded at Kellan. "You called."

Kellan removed his cell phone from his pocket and hit END on the call to Vaughn. "You came. Thanks. I don't know if Morton would've shot me, but I'm glad I didn't have to find out."

"You and me both." They shook hands. "Now for the not-so-fun part. You get to ride with me to the stationhouse to answer questions and make a statement."

"Any chance you recorded the phone call?" Kellan asked.

"Every word. Makes me wish Gerald Sorentino was alive so I could arrest his ass too."

Kellan rubbed his arms. "Are you going to tell Amy, Rachel, and Jenna the truth about their father?"

Squinting into the sun, Vaughn sighed. "Not before Christmas, that's for sure. But they'll need to hear it from one of us before it comes up at Morton's trial."

Good call. "After Christmas, I'll tell them. Hopefully, it will be the sisters' last piece of bad news for a good long while." He and Vaughn started for his patrol car. Kellan made a detour for his rifle. He nearly put it in his truck, until he realized that concealing a weapon without a permit in front of six police officers was maybe not the best move. "I'll be right back," he told Vaughn before jogging into his house.

All the officers but Vaughn had driven away by the time he returned.

"There is a silver lining to this story, you know," Vaughn said.

Kellan climbed into the passenger seat of the patrol car. "What's that?"

Vaughn started the ignition and pulled out of the driveway. "If Morton was telling the truth, then Sorentino Farm has enough oil underneath it to sustain them indefinitely. No bankruptcy, no foreclosure. That ought to bring the sisters some piece of mind."

"And, with any luck, a shitload of money to go along with that piece of mind."

"Amen to that, brother. Amen to that."

The next morning, the day before Christmas Eve, Amy battled the pull of grief by working through kitchen prep on an elaborate Christmas meal. She held out hope that Kellan would join them, but doubt had taken root in her mind. He hadn't come to visit that morning, but sent his Slipping Rock workers to manage the farm chores for Rachel. By midmorning, he still hadn't called.

Could he possibly be that upset with her for taking in his mother? Well, she was mad at him, too. His behavior toward Tina at church had been appalling. After they'd maneuvered their way through the post-service masses, he hadn't said a word to her or Tina before speeding out of the parking lot. She understood that his actions stemmed from a place of profound hurt, but still, giving her and Tina the cold shoulder was inexcusable and uncharacteristically immature.

For her part, Tina had been a quiet, unassuming guest at Amy's home. After a low-key Sunday supper, she'd taken a several-hour walk over the dirt roads of the farm and had generally stayed out of everyone's way.

This morning, she'd meekly asked if Catcher Creek hosted any AA meetings. Amy and her sisters shrugged, but Mr. Dixon knew all about the daily meetings at the VFW. He was twenty years sober and happy to escort her, he announced, which is where they'd disappeared to a few minutes before Matt Roenick pulled his dusty, red SUV to a stop in front of the house. Amy, Jenna, and Rachel watched from the porch. Sloane and Tommy had retired to the kitchen to bake cookies for an afternoon snack.

Of the three sisters, only Jenna had spoken to the lawyer, so Amy had no idea what to expect before his door opened. He was as tall as Kellan, but slim beneath his white dress shirt and charcoal slacks in a marathon runner sort of way. He offered the sisters an immediate, genuine smile, which earned him tons of bonus points in Amy's book.

"Well, Jenna," Amy said under her breath. "Does he look like he sounded over the phone?"

Jenna tilted her head. "Cuter. Way cuter."

"Oh brother," Rachel added.

Rachel led the procession into the dining room. While Matt shuffled through papers in his briefcase, Jenna took his drink order.

"I was surprised you were willing to make a house call this close to Christmas," Amy said, sliding onto the bench across the table from him.

He shrugged. "House calls are my style. I primarily work with home owners who are experiencing problems with oil companies. Not only are people more comfortable talking to me at their homes than driving to my stuffy little office in Santa Fe, but then we can actually go outside and look at the land involved in the home owner's legal issues."

Made sense. Still a pretty cool philosophy. None of the other lawyers they'd dealt with had given a rat's ass about comfort or common sense.

"As far as it being Christmas week," he continued, "if I'd had bad news to give you, I would've held off until after the holiday. But we've got nothing but good things to discuss today. Plus I'm Jewish. Chanukah was last week."

Jenna bent over the table to set a glass of soda near his elbow. Maybe it was an optical illusion, but it looked like she'd pulled her shirt lower so her cleavage could say hello to their guest. Rachel was right—oh brother.

"So here's a question for you," Jenna said, straddling the bench next to him. "What do Jewish people do on Christmas Day? I've always wondered."

"Jenna," Amy warned. No need to start their first meeting with the lawyer by asking insensitive questions about his religion.

Matt chuckled, not seeming at all offended. "Christmas is one of my favorite days of the year. Santa Fe is like a big empty playground. My family raises and trains therapy horses, and on Christmas, they take our latest 'graduates' on a multi-day trail ride and I usually join them if I'm not working. It's a blast."

"Therapy horses?" Rachel asked.

He scooted to the edge of his seat, his eyes sparkling with enthusiasm. "For disabled kids and adults. My family's ranch sells horses to special needs camps and mainstream tourism outfits who want to make sure their services are accessible to all their guests. Blows me away, what a difference these specially trained horses make in people's lives. Balances my lawyer karma out, you know?" He swatted the air. "Aw, I'm only kidding. I'm the good kind of lawyer."

Amy and Rachel exchanged a look of disbelief. Who the heck was this guy?

He slapped a stack of papers on the table. "Enough about me. Let's talk about this lawsuit."

"You said you have good news," Jenna said. "Are you planning to fight the suit on the grounds that the contract is null due to our father's death and the property transfer, like you mentioned over the phone as a possibility?"

"We can still fall back on that if we need to, but there've been a couple developments I didn't anticipate when we last spoke. On Friday, the FBI opened a criminal investigation against Amarex in conjunction with the Quay County and Potter County, Texas Sheriffs' Departments. It's huge. Unprecedented. In light of the charges the company's facing if convicted, there's an excellent chance their lawyers will drop the lawsuit against you."

My God. Amy couldn't stop blinking. Rachel grabbed her arm. They shared a wide-eyed look filled with shock and hope. Amy tried to temper her excitement because news that wonderful was usually too good to be true.

"What are the charges?" Rachel asked.

"Corruption, coercion, fraud—a laundry list of corporate abuse that leads straight to Amarex's CEO, Bruce Morton.

He was arrested yesterday in Quay County. I'm headed to the sheriff's station after this to find out the details."

Did Kellan know? If he did, he sure hadn't brought it up all the times he'd come over to her house that weekend. Maybe he thought it would be inappropriate to bring up the lawsuit in light of her mom's passing. If he didn't know, then how would he react? Bruce Morton was his family. Not to mention that he was set to inherit Morton's company.

"How . . . what?" Jenna stammered.

Matt turned his bright smile on her. "An insider witness has come forward with damaging information about Amarex. Handed multiple recordings to the FBI of private conversations between himself and the CEO. I haven't heard them myself, but I'm hoping my meeting with the Quay County sheriff clears up my questions."

Amy swabbed a hand over her forehead. "A witness? Like a whistle-blower?"

Matt flipped a pen around his fingers like a baton. Though Amy hadn't thought it possible, the wattage in his smile cranked up another notch, revealing rows of straight, white teeth and a dimple on his right cheek. "I believe you all know Kellan Reed."

Chapter 17

Amy drove at an uncharacteristically slow speed to Slipping Rock Ranch, giving herself time to get her thoughts in order. Did she start with an apology for assuming he was an Amarex spy and flying off the handle? A large part of her was too stubborn to apologize, feeling that he'd probably deserved her wrath for lying to her. Besides, she was done with her rules, done with apologizing for every little misstep.

She wanted an explanation about why he'd ignored his mother and her for the past twenty-four hours, but she was still irritated about that, which wasn't the tone she wanted to set with this conversation. Not after what Matt Roenick told them. Maybe, instead, she'd skip straight to a thank you that he'd stepped forward to help her family fight Amarex. No matter what happened between them in the future, or how angry she was at him for lying or ignoring her, she'd always be indebted to him for that.

As she climbed his porch steps, she realized that she didn't want to do the talking during this conversation—either to apologize or thank him. What she wanted most was to listen to what he had to say so she could understand why he couldn't forgive his mother, but longed for forgiveness from his brother. And why he'd lied to her about who he was and still slept with her the second time, knowing about the Amarex lawsuit. And she definitely wanted to try to understand why the heir to a billion-dollar empire would elect to bring the company down on criminal charges, likely at the forfeit of his inheritance, to protect her piddly little farm.

She rang the doorbell and waited.

No answer.

After a minute, she knocked. Then rang again.

Max sidled up next to her, thumping his tail on the floor and whining for attention. She scratched behind his ears. "Hey, cutie. You know where your boss is?"

He whined again and scooted himself closer, until he was sitting on her feet. Sighing, she lowered to the porch stairs to wait. Max stayed right with her and laid his head in her lap. She petted him absentmindedly, watching the gray clouds roll through the sky and the sun dip west toward Sidewinder Mesa.

A horse with a rider crested a rolling hill in the distance. She squinted until she could make out the identity of the rider. Kellan.

He rode with the abandon of a man who was born in the saddle. His chocolate brown horse was tall and lean and tore up the ground beneath it as they dropped from the hill into a canyon. The closer he got, the more detail Amy could make out—his worn, brown cowboy hat, his jean-clad thighs, his strong back emanating strength and control as he moved in rhythm with his steed.

He was magnificent. Amy's every fantasy come to life. But so much more than that.

He was Kellan Reed, a real cowboy who'd single-handedly created a renowned cattle ranch from the dust of New Mexico's high desert, not some chef from Portland playing dress-up. It didn't matter that he grew up in a lower-class Florida suburb. There was no faking his skills on a horse or the scuffs on his boots. There was no faking those muscles, carved from years of hard labor, or the deep tan of his skin from working every day under the unforgiving sun.

But he was also a man of sharp intelligence, with a passion for fine food and unwavering loyalty to his friends. He loved Christmas, but was haunted by the scars of his childhood. He held Tommy in his arms for hours in the hospital without complaining, then brought her endless bunches of celery after her mother's passing. This was the man who hated public spectacles, but elected to expose his private life and give up millions of dollars in inheritance so Amy's family home would survive.

She'd thought she'd fallen in love with him that night at his house, when he revealed his MAC knife collection. How wrong she'd been. Love wasn't about a Stetson hat or the right knife, or any of life's superficial details. That had been infatuation, along with a heaping scoop of lust.

What she'd learned from her roller-coaster relationship with Kellan was that a person did not fall into real love, but built it. Slowly over time. With painstaking care and patience. Real love was the fusion of two people's flaws and strengths, sitting atop the rubble of their past, cemented by the hopes for their future. It was humor and steadfastness and a little bit of magic. It was a creation stronger and more durable than either person had been alone.

What she'd felt for Brock McKenna, or even Kellan on their first date, paled in comparison to the potential for love she felt in her heart as she watched him fly over the terrain on his horse. Hell, yes, she felt loads of hot cowboy lust, watching him ride. Everything about him called to her—his hands on the reins, his thighs rubbing against the saddle, the curls of brown hair beneath his hat. And those lips . . .

Thinking about his skill with those lips made her body

heavy and achy, and demanding of attention. She shifted her weight and her jeans rubbed just the right way, making her aware of her panties clinging to her wet center. She nearly touched herself, her yearning for contact was so potent. This time, though, her cowboy lust was only for Kellan, and had as much to do with the man he was as it did with his command in the saddle.

When he entered the yard, he tugged on the reins and brought the horse to a stop, then dismounted in one powerful, lithe move. Amy's reaction was swift and visceral. A zing of sensation shot through the juncture of her thighs. She sucked air in through her teeth and gripped the porch rail.

Leaving the horse untethered in the middle of the yard, he walked toward Amy. She wondered if he recognized the desire burning hot on her cheeks, in her eyes. She certainly felt its flame.

He stopped a solid ten feet away from her, breathing hard, studying her with a dark, inscrutable gaze. Even with a chasm of space between them, tension, wicked and hot, stretched like a band around them both, binding them to their basest needs.

She wanted his hands and mouth on her flesh. She wanted to explore the infinite possibilities of their joined bodies. To make love to him so slowly and tenderly that time stopped. But also for him to control her as he had in his truck outside the restaurant, with his raw masculine power that made her limbs weak. She wanted him to fuck her until they collapsed, sweaty and sated, knowing they could do it again, as often as they wanted for the rest of their lives.

He was dressed in worn work jeans and a loose, long-sleeved T-shirt. Her gaze zeroed in on his pants. A button fly design. She could work with that. And, as luck would have it, there wasn't another soul in sight. He could take her right on these steps with his clothes on and no one would be the wiser.

"Amy."

Her name on his lips in that deep, rumbling voice snapped her focus to his face. Could he tell she'd imagined him screwing her brains out on his porch steps? She swallowed, not quite knowing what to say now that she'd decided she'd rather stick her hands into his pants than listen to him explain his side of the Amarex debacle.

His scowl took her aback. He looked past her, to his house, then at his horse. Then he sighed, deeply, wearily. Apparently, Amy was alone in her lust. Why, oh why, couldn't she stop making a fool out of herself in front of this man? Mr. Dixon told her she needed to find her true self, but the *me* she'd found was an idiot.

"Sorry I didn't call first." Oh brother. An apology? Precisely what she swore she wasn't going to do. And her voice, husky with desire, was definitely not cool and collected. In fact, nothing about her was cool and collected at the moment. "I take that back," she amended with a toss of her hair. "I'm not here to apologize."

His lips didn't smile, but the edges of his eyes wrinkled with amusement. "You don't owe me an apology, for not calling or anything else. I'd say it's the other way around."

Oh. "Maybe not an apology, but an explanation would be good."

"I owe you that too." He hooked his thumb over his shoulder. "I need to get Remington settled in for the night. We can talk in the stable while I work. I'll tell you anything you want to know."

After putting in a twelve-hour day on the ranch and in the office, Kellan smelled terrible. Probably looked even worse. When he got close enough to see Amy clearly, he was baffled about why she was staring at him like she was debating about the most efficient way to rip his clothes off. Why would a classy woman like her get all hot and bothered over a stinky, sweaty cowboy?

Then it hit him. Amy's cowboy fantasy. Hell.

Since watching *Ultimate Chef Showdown,* he'd worked diligently to sidestep the John Wayne image she'd formed of him, but he'd walked right into it today. Or rather, cantered into it.

He was glad she was finding her way out of the fog of grief that had settled over everyone in her house that weekend. No one got a look *that* hungry in their eyes while in the throes of sadness. Then again, a little sorrow might help him keep his clothes on and his hands to himself, because he refused to settle for the role of *cowboy-of-the-moment* in her life any longer. If Amy couldn't lust after him because of who he was, then thanks, but no thanks.

Even if she looked sexy as hell in those tight jeans and black sweater, which were snug enough to frame her curves and offer a hint of the softness beneath. He could have her top off in a half second flat.

Nope. The best course of action was to keep busy tending to Remington. He led the horse into the open stable, feeling Amy's eyes on his ass as he walked. She always seemed to be staring at his ass. Funny, he was always angling for a look at her ass too. He pictured it now, juicy and round, turned up on his truck seat while he gave it to her good on their date.

His pants grew snug at the memory. Lord Almighty, he and Amy were quite a pair. Like two hormonal teenagers without a lick of self-control. Thirty-four years old and he was a hairsbreadth away from pinning her to the stable wall and having his way with her, personal ethics be damned.

Cursing under his breath, he snagged the bucket of grooming supplies, then set to unfastening the saddle strap, working on the opposite side of the horse from Amy so she wouldn't see his hard-on. She settled against the far wall, watching him through half-closed lids, breathing through parted lips.

"You can't look at me like that, Amy."

"Like what?"

"Like you're picturing me naked."

"What's wrong with that? I know firsthand how good you look naked."

He jerked the strap clear and lifted the saddle. "What's wrong is that if you keep it up, I'm not going to have the strength to do the right thing."

"What's the right thing?"

He met her gaze. "Keeping my hands off you."

"How honorable."

If she only knew how dishonorable—how downright filthy—his thoughts about her were at the moment, she'd amend that conclusion. He worked Remy's bit away from his mouth, selected a brush from the bucket, and got busy brushing his flank in large circles, grateful for the distraction.

"Watching you groom your horse is not helping."

He didn't look at her, for fear it would unravel the last shreds of his control to see the expression that accompanied such a breathy, sexy tone of voice, and instead bent to brush lower on Remy's leg. "Why's that?"

She let out a long, slow exhale that answered his question better than words could. Apparently, horse grooming fell under the purview of her cowboy fantasy.

Frustration knifed through him. He didn't want to be some interchangeable guy in her fantasy. When she looked at him with those lusty brown eyes, he wanted her to see him and him alone—not some stereotypical image she'd conjured up.

He tried to ignore how much he wanted her, despite all

that. But the rustle of material as she shifted her legs and the shallow rhythm of her breathing made it tough to focus on anything except her arousal and how desperately he wished to transform her shallow breathing into whimpers of pleasure.

He couldn't see her lower body, but she seemed so turned on that he half expected to find her touching herself as she had in his bedroom that Friday night of their date. The image of her leaning against the wall, her fingers working in the slick folds of her flesh, took root in his mind.

Holy hell, she was right. Grooming his horse wasn't helping. Mashing his eyelids closed, he shook his head, clearing it. Maybe if he could keep a conversation going, he could overcome his lust. Maybe his common sense would prevail after all.

So he plunged into the least sexy topic he could come up with. "You asked for an explanation, so how about we try that?" His voice was thin, strained.

"Okay."

Clearing his throat, he kept his eyes glued to the task at hand. "I started working for Amarex when I was eighteen. I told you I went looking for my uncle to confront him, right?"

"I remember."

"Well, he offered me work and I was too broke and angry to turn him down. Didn't take long for me to realize Morton didn't offer anything without strings attached, especially a paycheck."

His uncle had been manipulative even then, calling on Kellan to scare home owners into signing papers, much like the courier who'd visited him a couple weeks earlier. Kellan refused and the two clashed heads more often than not. After two years of that, Kellan was ready to move on and find work somewhere else because what Morton was asking him to do was reprehensible in every way.

"So, then, it was a good thing he didn't take you and your brother in when you were kids?"

Kellan froze mid brushstroke. He'd never thought about it that way. All the resentment he'd built up over the wrongs committed by his family and their neglect had weighed on him like a dragging anchor for the past fourteen years. He couldn't see through his resentment to the truth Amy had parsed in seconds, that he and his brother had been better off in foster care than living with Bruce and Eileen Morton. "You're right. That would've been terrible. I . . . huh."

The more he thought about it, the worse he realized it would've been.

"What did you do when you found out about Morton's strings-attached policy?" Amy prompted.

Kellan resumed grooming. "I quit. We had a huge fight. Physical. We beat each other to a bloody mess." His aunt, Eileen, broke them apart and put them in separate rooms. Kellan vividly recalled the drops of blood he left along the tile floor like a trail. Morton sought him out as Eileen was cleaning Kellan's cuts, a stack of papers in his hand, including a property deed. "And that's when Morton offered me the land I turned into Slipping Rock Ranch."

"What? That doesn't make sense. Why would he do that? And why did you accept, if you knew he never offered anything without strings attached?"

Kellan moved to Remington's other side. From this new angle, he had a full view of Amy leaning against the far wall. But he had himself in check now. Something inside him blazed with the need to share himself with her like he'd never done with anyone before. He wanted her to know the parts of himself he was proudest of, like the thriving business he crafted, and even the ugly, twisted parts that made him look bad, too—the greedy punk he was at eighteen, the vindictive twenty-year-old.

"Even back then, I hated everything Morton stood for.

At the time, I accepted his land and his money because I thought he owed me for abandoning Jake and me to the system. And not only because we didn't have a loving home. That man, with his money, could've put us both through college, but he didn't lift a finger to give us a better life."

"You thought you deserved whatever he gave you."

"Damn right I did. Then I saw the land and what a worthless piece of crap it was—dry of oil, dry of irrigation. Nothing there but dirt and scrub brush." He pointed toward the stable door. "I stood where my driveway is now and cursed him to hell. I wanted to drive to his place and throw the deed at him, but I was out of gas money. After a night spent in my truck, I changed my mind. I decided to prove to him I could make something out of nothing, to show him I could amount to more than he ever thought possible. And, not to toot my own horn, but I made a damn fine business out of this worthless land."

"Yes, you did."

He knew he was smirking, but that was the part of the story he loved, the making something out of nothing, with only his sweat and blood and the need to prove himself. "Paid him back seven years later with interest for the property and the loan. I thought he couldn't touch me after that."

Amy pushed away from the wall. She took a comb and started in on Remington's mane. "When did that change for you—your motivation to run the ranch? At some point, it must've stopped being about proving yourself and turned into a passion for raising cattle, because I can tell you love this life."

"That happened pretty quickly. I realized I'd found my place in this world and a career to go with it. Plus I had this new family here with the Bindermans and Vaughn, which made it all the sweeter."

"When did your uncle make you his heir?"

"Six years ago." Morton had phoned him at work, insisting on an after-dark meeting in the shadow of an Amarex oil derrick outside Glenrio, Texas, under the guise of passing on information about his parents that he didn't want to discuss over the phone. The flimsy excuse had Kellan's bullshit radar on high alert from the get-go. But there they were, meeting in Glenrio at eleven o'clock at night.

The week before, Kellan had pulled a brash, if necessary, stunt—discreetly hiring Matt Roenick to negotiate a better contract for a home owner in Tucumcari who had no idea of the particularly high value of the crude oil sitting beneath his house. No one but Matt knew Kellan had arranged the deal, nor that he'd paid for the supposedly pro bono work out of his own ranch savings. Kellan had been confident that his secret was sound until Morton's out-of-the-blue phone call requesting the Glenrio rendezvous.

Morton had beaten him to the meeting place. He kept his eyes on Kellan's truck as it slowed to a stop, his face a sinister web of shifting light and shadow as the derrick's rhythmic up-and-down crossed in front of his truck's high beams. Kellan recalled with perfect clarity the tingle of foreboding that washed through him.

"I've got some news to discuss. A turn of affairs with my estate involving your inheritance," Morton had said, moving a wad of chew around in his cheek, his usual volatility simmering in his eyes.

"My inheritance?" Kellan had prowled nearer. He could still hear in his memory the hiss and whir of the derrick's pistons working at their eternal task. "Are you talking about Slipping Rock Ranch? Because I paid you up free and clear on that property a year ago."

Morton had sniggered at that. "I don't have any interest in a worthless piece of dry acreage like Slipping Rock turned out to be. What I'm saying is that I've rewritten my will."

"Taking me out or putting me in?"

"Making you the legal heir of my oil empire."

The shock of Morton's announcement had left Kellan speechless. He waited for the catch.

Morton turned on his heel and snatched a legal-size envelope from the hood of his massive red truck. He held it out to Kellan.

Kellan had shaken his head, refusing to touch the envelope. "I might've welcomed that once upon a time, but things have changed and you know it."

"And yet, you're still living in the heart of Amarex country." Morton shoved the envelope at him. "I should've known you'd act like an ungrateful SOB in the face of such a gift as I'm offering you."

"I don't want anything to do with your company."

"You don't have a choice, son. What I put in my will is my business alone."

True enough, but why would Morton appoint an unwilling man as his successor? "On what terms am I receiving your so-called gift?"

That had earned Kellan another snigger. "All you have to do is wait for me to die and my world will be yours. Think you can handle that?"

"Kellan?" It was Amy, rousing him from his memories. "What did he do, write you into his will?"

"Exactly. He's leaving me everything he owns—his stake in the company, his ranch, the properties he's amassed over the years. Everything." Well, at least he *was* until Kellan handed the recorded conversations over to the FBI. He knew he needed to tell Amy what happened, but he didn't want to veer anywhere near the unsavory truth about her father's role in the Amarex scam just yet.

She moved the comb through the ends of a snarl in Remy's mane. "How does that make you feel?"

"You sound like one of those mandatory therapists Jake and I were forced to see when we were in the system. You want me to lie on the sofa so you can analyze me?"

She pursed her lips, fighting a smile. "Probably not the best idea if you're trying to be honorable. If you lie on the sofa, I'll want to join you there."

Kellan smiled. "You're right, that would be terrible," he deadpanned.

Returning his smile, she moved with her comb to Remy's tail. "I know what you did, stepping forward to the police as a whistle-blower against Amarex. Matt Roenick told us."

Ah.

"That probably means you won't receive his inheritance anymore. I'm so sorry."

"Don't be. Really. I never wanted anything to do with Amarex in the first place. All I want to be is a rancher. Wearing a business suit and working in an Amarillo high-rise isn't in my blood. I belong here."

"What would you have done with the inheritance?"

"Sell. The company stock, the house, everything. I would've split the money with Jake and given my half to Matt Roenick to set up the low-cost legal clinic he's been itching to start."

Amy was silent. He snuck a glance at her. With furrowed brows, she finessed the comb through Remington's hair. He changed out the brush for a wet sponge and kept working, an ache of vulnerability sitting on his chest, squeezing his insides. He'd expected to experience a rush of relief at coming clean to Amy, but hands down, this soul-baring stuff felt like shit. No wonder they called it *spilling your guts*. "You're too quiet."

In his periphery, he saw that she'd stopped combing to stare at him. "Would you like to know what I'm thinking?"

Sounded like a trick question, but he took the bait anyway. "Okay."

"I'm thinking about how alike we are. We both figured out our life's passions when we were young. Not everyone is that lucky. My sister, Jenna, for example. She still doesn't know what she wants to do, besides be a mom. But you and I know our true places in the world. That's a gift."

"You consider this town your true place in the world?"

She grinned. "No. See, in that regard, I'm even luckier than you, because I'm at home in any kitchen, anywhere in the world."

"That is lucky. If that's what you were thinking, why were you frowning?"

She puffed her cheeks full of air and let it out with a slow hiss. "I'd rather not say."

"Aw, come on now. I told you all sorts of personal things about myself. You should even the playing field by doing the same."

"You want me to tell you my secrets?"

The way she said the words had him picturing her naked again. Naked beneath him. He wanted to discover her secrets with his tongue and his fingers and his—

Whoa, boy. He wiped his hand across his forehead. "I like that idea."

"All right." She dropped the comb into the grooming bucket and fluffed Remington's now-shiny tail. "Here's a secret. I'm afraid, all the time, that I'm going to end up like my mom. Depressed and alone. Like all those things are lurking inside me, dormant. Waiting."

"Are you depressed, in general?"

"No." She separated Remy's tail into three sections and braided them together. "But I'm pretty high-strung most of the time. I've thought about going on antianxiety meds. My doctor doesn't think I need them, but I wonder sometimes if it would help me stay even keeled."

"What stops you from trying them?"

"It feels like a slippery slope, starting medication. Meds didn't help my mom one bit. Sometimes it seemed like they made her problems worse. In fact, I'm sure of it."

He already knew she landed on the high-strung side of the emotional spectrum, so that wasn't actually a secret. "That's not why you were frowning."

She was quiet, braiding. Kellan nearly told her that a manly specimen of horseflesh like Remington shouldn't have braided hair, but stopped himself. He could take it out after she left and no one would be the wiser.

"I feel like an idiot around you," she blurted out. "Like an out-of-control, slutty idiot."

Kellan finished grooming and added his brush to the bucket. "You're not any of those things, not even close."

"I beg to differ." She wandered away and fiddled with a length of rope hanging on a nail. "Think about it—you and I have this vicious cycle going. I throw myself at you and you give me commonsense reasons why I shouldn't. But it's like my body won't take the hint and I throw myself at you again, shamelessly." She whirled to face him, the rope in her hand, spewing words faster than Kellan could process them. "After one date, I honestly thought I was in love with you. Isn't that crazy? Who thinks like that after one date? A crazy idiot like me, that's who. Just because a cowboy shows you his knife collection and it's the same knife collection you have doesn't mean it's love. I know that now."

She banged the rope against a beam, then jumped out of her skin when Remington snorted and reared back. Kellan guided the horse into his stall before the animal's reaction to Amy's agitation grew unmanageable. When he turned to look at her again, she'd collected herself. The rope was back on its nail.

"What I'm trying to say," she said in a calm, slow voice, "is that I'm annoyed at my lack of self-control where you're concerned." She avoided looking at him and teased the fibers of the rope apart. Her spine was rigid, her chin defensively high. "Is that enough of a soul-splaying to even the field?"

Kellan blinked at her. She'd thought she was in love with him? Did that mean she wasn't now? He hated that being around him made her feel bad about herself. That was the opposite of how he felt about himself when he was around her. All he knew was that she wasn't a crazy idiot or a slut. He'd felt something surge between them that night too. Something electric and full of infinite possibility. Maybe it had been love and he was the idiot for not recognizing it at the time.

He sure recognized it now. He loved the way she threw herself into the things she was passionate about, including him. Truth was, since the morning he met her, he'd spent most of his time every day wishing he was with her. Not just naked, but talking like this, grooming horses or cooking. Sleeping. He wanted to kiss her good morning and come home to her at lunch. Damn it, he wanted to *provide* for her.

He sure hoped she didn't need him to say pretty words to express what he felt, because he couldn't think of any right now.

He walked behind her and brushed her body with his. Her nervous fingers stopped picking at the rope, but she didn't turn. So he wrapped his arms across her chest and pulled her securely against him. Resting her head against his collarbone, she closed her eyes. Her hands came up over his arms, embracing him.

"I'm so sorry I made you feel that way about yourself. Please don't ever change who you are. Not for me, not for anybody."

A tear landed on his forearm. "That's what Mr. Dixon said."

"Smart man. Did he give you any other advice?"

She snorted and maybe laughed a little. Another tear landed on his skin. "He told me if I wanted to be with you,

I should be with you, Amarex lawsuit or not." Turning in his arms, she snaked her hands around his waist and pressed her cheek to his chest. "Thank you for helping my family by stepping forward as a witness. I knew when I saw Matt Roenick's card in the paperwork from your brief-case that you weren't out to get us along with Amarex. Then Matt told us that the lawsuit would probably be re-scinded in light of the criminal investigation and Morton's arrest." A fresh round of tears pooled in her big, brown eyes. "And all because of you."

He squeezed his arms. She felt so perfect there, warm and soft and smelling of flowers like she always did. He didn't even mind her curly brown hair tickling the under-side of his chin. "I know whose side I'm on. I'm not going to let Amarex bankrupt you or kick you off your land. Not without waging war against them in return." Another fat tear made its way toward her mouth. He flicked it away with his finger. "I owe you a thank you too . . . for everything. For touching your tornado down in my corner of the world and opening my eyes to so many things I was missing before."

She was quiet and still. He held fast to her and kissed her temple. She lifted her face to look at him. A tear trick-led over her cheek, landing on her lip. Her tongue darted out to taste it.

Kellan's self-control cracked wide open. He threaded his fingers through her hair and slanted his mouth over hers, teasing her lips until she opened for him with a breathy little sigh. He delved deeper, stroking her tongue with his. Relishing the taste and feel of this wonderment in his arms. Amy Sorentino, in all her beautiful, passion-ate, nutty complexity. His Amy.

Her hands slid under his shirt, spanning his back, send-ing ripples of sensation straight to his groin. He was a dis-aster from the long workday, sweaty and dusty, but she didn't seem to care and he wasn't about to stop and shower.

He'd get to that eventually, but he couldn't get the idea of taking her against the stable wall out of his head. He wanted her there, then in his shower, then again on the sofa under the twinkling lights of the Christmas tree.

He felt wild, out of control in a way he'd never experienced. His blood pounded through his body, throbbing in his cock, urging him to tear her clothes off, sink into her, and claim her as his own. He wanted *Kellan Reed* written all over her body, in the flush of her skin, the tightening pebbles of her nipples, the moisture he could picture gathering between her thighs as her body prepared to take him. No man but him. He wanted to brand her being with his love.

Frightened, he tore his lips from hers and held her at arm's length. "Amy, walk away now, or so help me, I'm going to take you right here in this stable and it won't be gentle. I don't have the strength to go slow."

She stepped back, bumping into the post that held the rope. He fisted his hands at his sides, breathing hard. He'd never wanted anything as desperately, as uncontrollably, as he wanted her. And she'd backed away. He would respect that. He would let her go. For now.

She melted against the post, gripping the rope above her head with one hand. Her other hand went to the waist of her jeans and popped the button open. "I never did like it slow."

Amy did her best, but she couldn't get her pants off fast enough.

Kellan must've agreed because the moment she touched her zipper, he knelt before her and yanked the jeans to the ground. Her panties followed, his rough hands snagging on the silk. A rush of cool air tingled against her skin. His fingertip found her clit, then slipped lower. Two fingers pushed inside her.

"You're so wet for me." His voice was thick with desire,

his fingers deft in their movement. "So wet and tight and ready to take me inside you."

"I want you, Kellan. Badly."

He added a third finger deep inside her and curled to stroke her g-spot. "You want to get fucked by a cowboy in his stable, is that it?"

Pleasure swept through her, swift and brutal. Damn, she loved that he talked dirty. Turned her on big-time, even though he had the wrong idea about what she wanted. She fisted a hand in his hair and forced his gaze to meet hers. "No. I want to get fucked by you—doesn't matter where, as long as it's you."

She must've given the right answer because he stood and took her mouth ravenously, crushing her against the post, swallowing her moans. She gripped the rope hard, its coarse fibers cutting into her skin. She couldn't move, pinned by the weight of his torso and impaled as she was on his fingers.

When his hands and mouth left her body, she groaned and opened her eyes. His missing fingers left an aching vacuum in her body. His gaze, blazing with intent, locked with hers as he released his straining erection from his jeans. She let go of the rope and reached for it. She stroked, milking a drop of moisture out.

Kellan groaned and thrust into her hand. From his pocket, he brought out his wallet, then a condom. As he rolled it on, she grabbed the rope again in anticipation of their bodies joining. The post wasn't going to be comfortable against her back, but she wanted him too much to care. Then his hands locked around her wrists, pulling her from where she stood.

He led her to a saddle sitting on the floor and straddled it. Through his open jeans, his erection curved up to his belly button, dark red beneath the clear latex and hard as steel—waiting for her. "Is this cowboy enough for you?"

His words were harsh, verging on angry. But she sensed the vulnerability behind them.

It was his second mention of her fantasy, like he thought that was the only reason she wanted him. Time to prove him wrong once and for all. She tossed his hat across the room and swung a leg over the saddle. Hovering over him, she took his face in her hands and locked her eyes on his.

"I don't want you to make love to me because you want to satisfy some fantasy of mine. I'm over that. When you're with me, you better bring your whole self, not just the cowboy part."

He pulled his face back, clearly caught off guard. She smoothed her hands over his hair. Not that it mattered. Unruly as it was, it sprung into wild curls almost immediately. She tucked a strand behind his ear.

"I thought that was the part you wanted."

"Of course I think of you as a cowboy. It's who you are." He made a noise of protest that she stopped with a finger over his lips. "But it's only a piece of you. You're also a boy from Florida with instant mashed potatoes in his cupboard and cinnamon-scented candles on his mantel. You're the man who stands up for what he believes in and takes care of the people in his life. You're the man I love." She cupped her palm over his cheek. "I want you—all of you."

He looked at her with a terribly serious expression, so she smiled teasingly. "Although I must say, you do have an impressive knife collection."

That earned her a grin. "It wasn't my knife collection I was hoping to impress you with tonight." Reaching between them, he palmed his erection and stroked it, hardening it even further. Amy watched the erotic display, her inner muscles contracting in anticipation.

"What did you have in mind, cowboy?"

"I want you to ride me, of course."

Chapter 18

With one hand around the base of his shaft and another spanning her hip, Kellan guided Amy's body down around him, sheathing him to the hilt. The stable was silent but for their labored breathing and the scrape of Kellan's boots along the floor as he adjusted his position to support Amy's weight.

The horn of the saddle cut into the middle of his back, but it was a pain he'd gladly bear because nothing had ever felt as good, as perfect as holding Amy above him, his erection locked within her. She lowered her lips over his and their tongues slid into the other's mouth. Their bodies breathed into each other, bound in an intimacy more powerful than Kellan had thought possible with another human being. Eye to eye, belly to belly, heart to heart.

Amy stirred first, rotating her hips, squeezing her inner muscles with each deliberate circle. Torturously slow. Kellan fought against his body's urge to speed up, to drive into her with animalistic force until her rapturous screams echoed off the stable walls. He distracted himself with the feel of Amy's lips and body, focusing on the obvious pleasure she felt with each rotation.

But a man could only take so much.

With his hands on her hips, he lifted her weight off him so he could move. He thrust up, impaling her, while at the same time pulling her down again. Over and over, until the sound of flesh colliding superseded even Amy's whimpers of pleasure. Taking his lead, she bounced in rhythm with his hips, faster and faster, until they'd reached a frenetic pace.

It was almost too much. Her breasts moving against his chest, her velvet, wet body gripping him, the tangle of her hair falling over them both.

He watched her reach inside herself, digging for her orgasm, her head thrown back and eyes closed. He delved into the skin of her neck with his teeth and tongue, savoring her sweet, singular taste, wonderful in its familiarity, still as intoxicating as it was the first time they were together.

"Come for me, honey," he rasped against her neck.

She reached a hand between them, manipulating her flesh, pulling the trigger of her release. She came with a piercing cry, her body bucking wildly, her inner muscles pulsing around him, pushing him over the edge with her. With a final, hard thrust, his world exploded in a shock of pleasure so intense, it hurt.

He pulled her against his chest and held her there. She clung to his shoulders, pressing her cheek to his. Resting his palm against her neck, he felt the life within Amy. Her heartbeat, the expansion and contraction of her lungs, her breath on his shoulder. The quiver of energy inside her, all around his cock.

Something shifted inside him, opening his heart to the idea of a life with Amy Sorentino at its center. The joy, the craziness, the passion. The quiet moments like this, holding her in his arms.

Emotion surged through him, making him light-headed. His heart ached, it was so full. In all his thirty-four years, he'd never experienced anything like it. He tightened his hold on her and brushed his lips across her cheek. She sighed contentedly and burrowed her nose against his neck behind his ear. He felt like crying, the feeling was so magnificent, so eternal. So . . .

Fierce.

He pressed his cheek to hers.

"I love you too, Amy."

Amy tapped the melody of "I'll be Home for Christmas" on Kellan's bare chest as it played on his living room stereo. The soft, multicolored lights of the Christmas tree danced on his skin. The lights probably danced on her bare back, too, but all she felt was Kellan's hand stroking a pattern up and down her spine.

After a steamy, soap-slick loving on the floor of his shower, Amy had figured they'd crawl into his bed together, but Kellan had other plans. As the night marched ever closer to Christmas Eve, he led her, buck naked, to the living room. From the sofa, wrapped in a quilt, she watched his methodical setting of the mood. First a fire in the fireplace, then music, candles, and Christmas tree lights.

He'd stood over her and peeled the quilt from her body. "I've fantasized about taking you on my sofa like this since the day we met."

Then he'd laid her down, settled on his knees between her legs, and done exactly that. Hours later, she still couldn't muster the motivation to move upstairs to bed. She was too comfortable snuggled into the heat of his body, with the quilt now covering them both.

She breathed deeply. "You're on to something with those cinnamon candles."

"It's tempting to leave them up year-round, but Vaughn would never let me live it down."

Grinning, she snuggled closer. "From now on, you can tell them you're leaving them out for me."

His hand stopped stroking and hugged her tight. "Amy, when I think about the life we're going to have together, cinnamon candles don't even break the top thousand of all the things I'm looking forward to."

"Maybe not the cinnamon candles, but sex on your saddle definitely makes the list for me."

She listened to the rumble of his chuckle with her ear pressed to his chest, loving the sound. Loving that she was lying in the arms of the first and only cowboy who'd deserved her love, and who loved her back.

He wound a strand of her hair around his index finger. "Can I ask you something?"

"Sure."

"I don't care about the wrecked briefcase, but what did you do with the cooler of beef I brought? The steaks were probably still frozen after we got home from the hospital, the weather was so cold."

"Don't worry. I put them in the fridge. I was spitting mad at you at the time, but I couldn't take it out on those beautiful steaks. We ate them for dinner last night. Your mom loved it. She kept muttering, *Who would've guessed? My son, a cattle rancher*, over and over while she ate."

He unwound her hair from his finger and started again. "Good. I'm glad she enjoyed it. How is she doing?"

"She's fine. Quiet. Mr. Dixon drives her to the local AA meeting every morning, then she spends most of her time after that going on long walks and playing with Tommy. She seems happy at my house. You need to talk to her, allow her to apologize so she can keep going with her fight to stay sober."

His body went rigid, but the truth needed to be said. "I know. You're right. I don't want to, but I will. After Christmas Eve church service tomorrow night."

"Good. You won't regret it." She paused, chewing the

inside of her cheek while she contemplated the wisdom of bringing up another sore subject. With a here-goes-nothing breath, she added, "Have you told your brother about your mom's plan to go to L.A.?"

"Not yet."

She didn't want to push him too hard, but it would be one more tragedy in a family burdened by them to allow this opportunity for reconciliation to slip through their fingers. "Tonight would be a great night to call him."

He gave a noncommittal grunt.

"You don't want your mom wandering around L.A. looking for Jake."

"No, I don't. But Jake's not exactly easy to talk to."

She stroked his hair. "Family seldom is. But you have to try anyway." She started her hands moving over his chest. Her finger flicked over his nipple and he inhaled through gritted teeth. "Tell you what, cowboy. After you call, I'll reward you for good behavior."

He pushed them both to sitting and grabbed his cell phone from the coffee table. "That's an incentive if I've ever heard one."

For the first time, Kellan wasn't nervous about calling Jake. He figured there was zero chance Jake would answer. After three rings, Kellan started planning the message he'd leave on voice mail.

Halfway through the fourth ring, Jake answered with a cranky "Hey. What now?"

"Hi. Sorry to call again so late . . ."

"Mmm-hmm." Jake's tone oozed skepticism.

"The thing is, Mom came to see me this weekend. I wanted you to know because she's going to L.A. next."

"Is she staying at your house?"

"No. She's staying with my . . ." What was Amy—his

girlfriend? The term sounded trite and juvenile. And it didn't even offer a hint of how deeply in love he was with her.

"Girlfriend?" Amy whispered in suggestion with a shrug.

"My significant other." Shit. That sounded as awful as *girlfriend*. He needed to get a ring on Amy's finger, STAT.

"What's Mom's angle this time?"

In his peripheral vision, he noticed Amy's bare breasts and reached for one, cupping the underside, enjoying the heavy weight of it in his hand. Geez, he loved her rack. "Maybe not an angle. She wants to apologize to each of us."

"The AA thing again?"

He closed his thumb over Amy's nipple and gave a little tug. She scooted closer and sent him a smile of wicked promise that made the painful conversation with Jake semitolerable. "Yeah. Look, Jake, I'm calling because she says she's going to search L.A. until she finds you."

"Christ. I don't want her out here."

"You could . . ." Why was this offer so hard to make? Did he fear the rejection he'd most likely get? What a coward. "You could come out here and talk to her on neutral ground. That would keep her from going to L.A."

"The three of us? Like one big happy family?"

The venom in Jake's voice mirrored Kellan's feelings not so long ago. Had he sounded that harsh to other people's ears? "It's a start."

"Thanks, but no thanks."

Kellan's mouth screwed up. He dropped his hand from Amy's breast. Her arms went around his ribs in a fortifying hug. "I understand." *Take a breath, man.* "Is it okay if I give her your name and address so she won't wander aimlessly around the city asking people where to find you?"

"Tell you what—give me the number where she's staying. She can apologize to me over the phone like she did the last two times."

He relayed Amy's phone number to him. "One more thing, Jake."

"Yeah?" He heard the impatience in Jake's voice to end the call. Kellan scrunched up his nose. There was so much he wanted to tell his brother, so much he needed from him. The feeling of vulnerability was horrible. He felt like his insides had been cut open, his guts spilling everywhere. "Merry Christmas."

"Back at you. Have a good one."

With a click, the line went dead. He cradled the phone in his hands, staring at his feet. Then he remembered Amy's arms were around him. He hauled her onto his lap and clung to her, comforted by the knowledge that even if he couldn't make things right with his brother or mom, it was worth the try because, no matter what, he'd have her love to sustain him.

The afternoon of Christmas Eve, Amy waited impatiently in the kitchen for Kellan to arrive, dicing her second bunch of celery to pass the time.

She'd kissed him good-bye at six that morning, ten long hours ago. Despite her wistful desire to laze the day away in his bed, he had work to do and so did Amy. The early-morning work was the only part of Kellan's being a rancher that she didn't particularly care for, but she was more than willing to put up with it for the rest of her life if it meant she got to enjoy the millions of other things she loved about him.

She heard the creak of the front door opening, followed by his deep-voiced "Hello?"

"In the kitchen," she called.

He walked up behind her and kissed her neck. "You've got a new member of the welcome committee out front, a real friendly lady."

"I do?"

He grabbed a stalk of celery and straddled a chair backward. "About yay big, brown eyes, brown hair. Flower behind her ear."

Amy glanced sideways at him, smiling, and set her knife aside. "That's Tulip."

Kellan took a bite of celery. "Never seen one of my cows look so fancy before."

"She wandered over last week and I was too mad at you to call you about it."

"And the flowers?"

She scooped the celery into a mixing bowl. "Those are to annoy Rachel."

"Did they do the trick?"

"You betcha. Check out the picture in the downstairs bathroom."

He wandered from the room. A minute later, his hoot of laughter shook the walls. Guess he approved of the framed photo hanging over the toilet of Tulip in all her flowery glory.

He took his seat again. "That's a photograph for the ages. I bet Rachel blew her top when she saw it."

"She's taken it down and destroyed it four times. Little does she know that Walmart had a special on picture frames, so I picked up a dozen. She takes one picture down, I put a new one up."

"That's right sisterly of you."

Amy sat next to him. "It is, isn't it?"

Kellan pulled a string from the celery rib and fiddled with it, nervous like. "Where's my mom?"

"Upstairs getting primped for church." She squeezed his forearm. "Are you ready for tonight?"

"Ready as I'll ever be."

On the drive to church, everyone was unusually quiet, except for Tommy, who sat between Jenna and Kellan in the backseat, and was delighted to have the attention of his favorite grown-up. By the time they'd reached the church parking lot, he'd secured a promise from Kellan to sit next to him during the service and share a hymnal. Tina, in the front passenger seat, stole glances at her son like she couldn't quite believe he was real.

Amy knew the service must've been hard on Kellan, as he wasn't used to suffering the stares and whispers of the Catcher Creek parishioners the way Amy and Jenna were. After Sunday's drama with Tina's surprise arrival, the town gossips had enough fodder to last them for weeks, but returning three days later with said mother and Catcher Creek's resident family of crazies in tow was an event for the gossip train's record books. He handled it like a champ, with his head held high and a firm grip on both Amy's and Tommy's hands.

The Bindermans supported them by sharing a pew. Vaughn Cooper wasn't in attendance. When Amy asked about him, Kellan said he was already at his folks' house for the holiday.

After church, they gathered around Amy and Rachel's dining room table for a dinner of tacos and tamales and ice-cold Mexican beer. Jenna took Tommy home early. Being four, this was the first year it all made sense to his little mind—Santa and presents and Christmas sweets. He was determined to get to bed early to hasten the coming of Christmas morning.

Amy cut a thick wedge of cheesecake for Jenna to take home while everyone else transferred to the living room for dessert. Rachel flipped on the television to *Miracle on 34th Street* and they dug into the plates of cheesecake Amy passed around. Even though the loss of her mom still felt raw, Amy had settled into a place of peace, surrounded as she was by so many people she loved.

Halfway through her massive slice of cake, she noticed Tina slip out the front door, a pack of smokes and a lighter in her hand. She nudged Kellan and motioned with her eyes toward the closing door.

Kellan noticed his mother heading outside for a cigarette before Amy elbowed him. He already knew it was time to get the conversation over with. After a quick mental debate on whether he could get away with bringing his cheesecake with him, he begrudgingly set the plate on the side table. Amy hooked an arm around his neck and pulled him into a kiss.

"You can do this," she whispered. "Forgive her so you can both move on."

He kissed her back and stood. Forgiveness was a prickly bitch he'd never had much luck with, but Amy was right—he needed to move on from the pain of his past with a clear conscience and an open heart. The bitterness in Jake's voice the last time they talked had been a shock to his system; he didn't want to be like that for a single day more. He'd wasted too many years in that dark place already.

His mom sat folded on the bench swing, her legs tucked under her, a lit cigarette balanced between her fingers as she stared into the dark night. Loose, pale skin hung from her bones. She looked one gust of wind away from coming down with pneumonia.

"Cold night," he said. "Can I get you a blanket?"

"Nah, the smoke's nasty enough without stinking up one of Amy's blankets."

He sat next to her. The bench joints creaked. "I talked to Jake last night."

She took a slow drag on the cigarette and blew it out in a thin stream. "Told him to run for the hills 'cause I'm headed his way?"

"No. I asked his permission to give you his phone number and address to save you from wandering the streets of L.A. searching for him."

"What'd he say to that?"

"He asked for Amy's phone number so he could call you himself." It was a kinder version of the truth, but Kellan still felt the stirrings of guilt. The woman next to him was fragile, with dull, paper-thin skin and sunken cheeks. A wisp of how he remembered her. Time hadn't shown her mercy. How did someone hate such a pathetic creature? For the first time, Kellan felt sorry for this woman who had wasted her life and her health and her family and had nothing but a decrepit body to show for it.

"He doesn't want me coming out there, is all."

Maybe the drugs hadn't dulled her mind as much as Kellan thought. "I didn't say that."

"But it's true. I don't blame either of you boys in the least for hating me. I never did put you first in my life."

What could he say to that? She was right, but he didn't feel like piling on his resentment tonight. He strained to think of something she'd done right as a mother. "I remember you bringing groceries home from your job."

She looked at him for a long time, her unattended cigarette turning into a tube of ashes between her fingers. After a while, she said, "S'pose that's true. That's something, ain't it?"

"It is. I still love instant mashed potatoes."

She laughed, a thick, phlegm-laced chuckle. "I remember the first time you saw a real potato. It was at our neighbor's house, Mrs. Castillo. You must've been ten or eleven. You thought that potato was the ugliest thing God created. You said, '*That's* what I've been eating? It looks like a dirt ball.'" She laughed again and took another hit off the cigarette. "Never thought I'd miss those days until I was locked up, with no one coming around to visit and no drugs to help me forget how alone I was."

He started the swing in a slow back-and-forth. "I

never thought I'd miss those days, either, but sometimes I do. I wish I didn't. Would be easier if I didn't have any fond memories of growing up. But there are parts I can't let go of."

"Like the potatoes."

"Like the potatoes, yes."

She set her hand on his knee. Since her release from prison, he hadn't allowed her to touch him, thinking she did so not out of motherly love, but as a manipulation. Tonight, her touch still didn't feel like motherly love, but he didn't recoil from it either. And he didn't think she was buttering him up to ask for money, as she had in the past.

"I'm sorry for what I put you through. You and your brother. Not just while you were growing up, but every time I came around since, drugged out and expecting you to help me. You did the right thing, turning me away."

"You think you have a shot at staying sober this time?"

"I do. Now that I've left your father behind, and am attending meetings every day, I know I can do it."

Hope, like a small flame, flickered to life inside Kellan. "How do you like it here in Catcher Creek?"

"From what I've seen, it's a good place. A good match for you. And the people have been so nice to me. Especially Amy's family and Douglas. They're good folk, all of them."

"Yes, they are." He patted her hand. It was ice-cold, so he gathered it between his two palms to warm it. Realization hit him hard. He didn't want her to leave. This new sober, repentant mother was someone he needed to have more of these kinds of talks with. He wanted to hear more stories of his childhood and listen to her laugh. She'd never achieve Mother-of-the-Year status, but now, he had the capacity to help her, not only monetarily, but within his heart. Thanks to Amy.

"Mom, what would you say about sticking around here

a while, going to meetings with Douglas, and getting your feet under you? I bet you could find work easily enough."

"That's sweet of you to say, but I don't want any handouts. I'm going to take care of myself this time. Besides, I need to see Jake."

"If you find yourself wondering what to do after you get straight with Jake, call me. You can come back here."

"That would be okay with you?"

"It would, as long as you stay sober."

"I will. I promise you that. No—I promise myself that."

Headlights topped the rise leading to Amy's house. Kellan stood.

"Mom, do you know if Amy or her sisters are expecting anyone tonight?"

"Not that they mentioned."

As the headlights neared, he made out a black SUV. His first thought was of Morton. Maybe this was one of his goons, there to claim retribution. "You should go inside, Mom. Until I figure out who's come visiting so late."

Standing, she took a last puff of the cigarette before dropping it in a plastic water bottle on the floor. As he debated whether he had time to make a break for the rifle in his truck, the SUV rolled to a stop alongside Kellan's truck. He leapt over the porch rail to the ground. Two strides into his jog, the SUV door opened. Gasping, Kellan skidded to a stop as his brother stepped out.

Chapter 19

"Jake!" their mom shrieked, tearing from the porch, her arms outstretched.

Jake backed up, his expression flinty, his hands up to stop her from getting any closer than arm's length. Mom ground to a halt, breathing hard, and hugged herself as she drank in Jake's face as though searing his image in her mind.

Jake stuffed his hands in his pants pockets and allowed her to gawk. "Hello, Mother."

Clean-shaven, with short brown hair, he was an inch or so shorter than Kellan, but they shared the same dark eyes and broad chin. He'd filled out in the eight years since they'd last seen each other. He wasn't as brawny as Kellan, whose workouts included digging fence posts and hauling hay bales, but defined with the kind of deliberate muscle one built in a gym. He imagined it was as much a function of Jake's job as Kellan's physique was of his.

Kellan stood still, even though he wanted to rush at him like Mom had and hook him into a bear hug. He wasn't sure they'd ever hugged. Teenage boys didn't, that was for sure. Shaking hands would be a good start, but Kellan was afraid to approach him. Like Jake was a wild animal who might flee at the first sudden move.

He'd seen Jake twice since leaving their foster home
sixteen years ago. Not for Jake's high school graduation—
Kellan hadn't even considered attending, a truth that he'd
go to the grave regretting—but first at the ill-fated diner
meeting in Texas during Jake's journey west the summer
after his graduation, and again eight years ago, when Jake
graduated from the police academy.

Kellan found out about that one from the foster group
home dad, Allen, who'd been invited while Kellan had not.
After a lot of debating with himself, he made the trip to
L.A. anyway. A bit of pestering of the officers guarding the
door got him into the graduation ceremony. Afterward,
Jake invited him out with friends to celebrate, only to
spend the rest of the night pointedly ignoring him. The
experience had been awkward and painful, and Kellan
had returned to New Mexico in a huff.

He didn't want to bust Jake's balls for arriving unannounced at nine o'clock on Christmas Eve. He didn't even
want to act surprised to see him. He planned to play it
cool and somehow coax Jake from where he stood frozen
next to his car into the house. "It's good to see you, Jake."

Jake gave his head a frustrated shake and waved dismis-
sively at the car. "I used the phone number you gave me to
look up the address, but the GPS didn't have this area on
the map. That's why I'm here so late at night." His voice
was as deep and resonant as it was on the phone.

"We would've helped you navigate."

He scowled, raking his fingers through his hair. "I took
a red-eye. But I don't know what I'm doing here." Then the
hands went back in his pockets, and his shoulders hiked up
near his ears. "I didn't call because . . ."

Kellan knew exactly why he didn't call. Same reason
Kellan hadn't called ahead from the road before Jake's
police academy graduation. "Because you wanted the
option to change your mind at the last minute."

He snorted. "I'm that transparent, huh? When that

piece-of-shit GPS choked up, my stubborn streak won out. I was going to find this place or die trying."

"I'm glad you did," Kellan added. And he meant it, too, despite the shock.

"I am, too." Mom's voice hitched. A silent tear traveled along her cheek.

They all turned at the sound of the front door creaking open. Rachel and Amy. Only Kellan was close enough to hear Rachel's whisper to Amy. "Who is that?"

Amy must've recognized Jake's resemblance to Kellan, because she said, "I think it's Kellan's brother." She sounded as amazed as he was.

Rachel's whispered tone turned harsh. "You can't take in any more strays. We don't have the space and we can't afford the food to feed them all. You have to learn how to say no."

Kellan smiled at that. Amy did seem to collect lost and drifting souls in her orbit, him included, along with his run-away cow, his mother, Douglas Dixon, and Sloane Delgado. Sorentino Farm was turning into a veritable misfit refugee camp. Spending the rest of his life with Amy would mean accepting that tendency of hers. Not a problem.

"It's Christmas, Rach. Don't be such a Scrooge," Amy countered in a voice that left no room for argument.

His attention turned to his mother. She was trembling, whether from the cold or the shock of Jake's sudden appearance, he wasn't sure. "Mom, let's get you inside before you freeze to death." He approached and took her hand in his. Her touch felt less foreign now, more ordinary.

"But, Jake . . ." she protested.

"He's coming inside too." He looked at his brother.

Jake gave a terse nod of assent.

Kellan led Mom up the porch stairs and shared a wide-eyed look of surprise with Amy, a kind of nonverbal *Oh my God*.

"Can you take Mom inside?" he asked her. "Jake and I'll be along in a minute."

"Sure."

Once Rachel shut the door, Jake and Kellan stood on the porch, looking in through the window at Amy settling their mom on a chair with a quilt and a fresh slice of cheesecake.

"Which one is yours?" Jake asked.

It felt amazing, having an answer to that question and knowing inside-and-out that she was his forever. "Curly hair, green sweater." Which didn't even begin to describe the woman he'd fallen in love with.

"What's her name?"

"Amy." Kellan laughed, watching her dab a piece of cheesecake on Rachel's nose. Rachel's counterattack nearly upended the sofa and both sisters squealed. "Do you have anyone back home?"

"Not for a while now. Job makes it tough. Women are all about this hot cop fantasy until they get their nails in you, then they're bitter about how much time the job sucks up. They don't want you putting yourself in danger or any shit like that. After the divorce, it happened again and I thought, forget it. I'm done. It's not worth it."

It was the most Kellan had heard Jake talk since they were kids. He tried not to gape. *Play it cool, keep him talking.*

"What's your division and rank now? Last I heard you were SWAT."

"Still SWAT. I'm a lieutenant. I don't see myself changing divisions anytime soon."

"You love it?"

"Yeah, I do."

"I feel the same way about ranching."

"No fooling, huh? I would've never guessed that for you."

"I'd like you to see my ranch sometime. I've got plenty of room." He hoped he didn't sound desperate, but like he was making a casual, brotherly suggestion.

Jake's cheek twitched. "Yeah, maybe someday."

The way he said it, with those arms crossed tightly across his chest and his eyes glued to Amy and her sisters, meant that conversation topic was closed. No harm in breaching the elephant in the room at that point, Kellan figured. "This is the first Christmas we've seen each other in sixteen years. I'm glad you're here."

There, he'd said it. Another round of gut-spilling out of the way. Maybe Jake would finally man up and have this long-overdue talk with him.

"That's not why I came."

Ouch. Jake wasn't conceding an inch in this conversation. Cue another round of gut-spilling. "All those Christmases you and I missed when you were a teenager, that was my fault. I shouldn't have left you alone in the system."

"No big deal."

Kellan ripped his gaze from the window to stare at his brother's blank face. Like hell it wasn't. "It's the biggest regret of my life."

But Jake wouldn't look at him. He shrugged. *Shrugged.* "The past is the past."

Kellan ground his molars together and took a long, slow breath through his nose. There would be no breaching Jake's walls tonight, but Kellan could take a hint from their mom and AA to apologize anyway, if only to settle it in his own mind and heart. "Maybe so, but all I know is, when I look at those sisters"—he nodded toward the room— "I'm jealous as hell of what they've got with each other. I'm sorry I wasn't there for you when you needed me."

Jake's eyes got shifty, like he was looking to bolt. "No need for that."

"I'd like to come visit you sometime soon. I could leave my foreman in charge of the ranch, take a few days off. I haven't ever taken a vacation before."

"L.A.'s a shithole. Don't take your first vacation there. Go to Aruba. Somewhere tropical."

You're not getting out of it that easily. "I'd like to come visit you," Kellan pressed. Maybe the female gender was on to something, because the more gut-spilling he did, the easier it got and the better he felt. Especially now that he understood he couldn't control Jake's reaction, only his own.

"Cool, whatever. There are lots of motels I could recommend."

It was the same suggestion Kellan had given their mother when she surprised him at church, so he could hardly fault Jake for thinking along those lines. He clapped a hand on Jake's shoulder. He flinched, then stiffened. "I'm not going to give up on you. Like I'm not going to give up on Mom. I've asked her to stay in New Mexico, to get her legs under her. She's got a friend in town who takes her to meetings, and I know firsthand that Catcher Creek is a solid place to land when a person decides to stop falling. Could be good for her. You should go talk to her right now. Let her apologize to you so she can move on with her steps. It won't kill you, and it might help her stay sober."

He scowled. "Aw, hell . . ."

"No, now. That's why you flew out here, isn't it?"

Jake went on scowling, but at least he didn't argue. "What are you going to do if Dad comes around?"

He hadn't had time to think about that yet and shrugged. "I don't know. Talk to him, see what he wants, and do my damnedest to keep him from screwing up Mom's sobriety."

Jake nodded.

"Would you like to stay at my house tonight?" Kellan asked.

"Nah. There's a motel I passed in town, the Highway Flyer. I'll stay there."

"But you'll come back here tomorrow for Christmas dinner?"

"I don't know."

Kellan had pushed hard enough for one night. "Well, if you decide to join us, Amy and her sisters have plenty of room at their table. Amy's a chef; she's fixing a prime rib from a steer on my ranch. Beats spending the day in the airport, in my opinion."

Jake turned and walked to the porch rail to look at the sky, dismissive like.

"One more thing, Jake."

Jake interrupted him with a dry laugh and a sardonic grin.

"What?" Kellan asked.

"You always say that. *One more thing.* What is it this time?"

Kellan returned his smile and joined him at the rail. Maybe they were getting somewhere. Finally. "I'm going to marry Amy. Not next month or anything, because we're not even engaged yet, but someday soon, I hope. I want you to be my best man. Would you do that for me?"

Jake looked at the stars, squinting. Then his shoulders relaxed. He turned to Kellan and stuck out his hand. "Okay. I can do that."

Kellan shook his brother's hand and tried not to cry. "Thank you."

Around eleven, Kellan had reluctantly gone home to tend to his livestock that night and again in the morning. It wasn't fair to ask his ranch hands to work on Christmas while he took the morning off, he'd explained. He'd touched base with Amy on her cell phone as soon as the sun rose while she was at Jenna's house, watching Tommy open gifts. She broke it to him as gently as she could that Jake had come and gone, but that he and Tina had taken a walk together and even hugged before Jake took off for the airport.

Kellan took it well. He was due to arrive that afternoon for Christmas dinner after a brief stop at the Bindermans' house to deliver Daisy's and Rowen's presents. Amy could hardly wait to see him again.

An hour after he arrived, he and Amy gathered around the longest table in the dining room along with Rachel, Jenna, Tommy, and Tina. Jenna had set out an extra place setting and a candle in memory of their mom, which seemed fitting because Amy knew she was looking down on them from on high, finally happy. Finally at peace.

While Amy brought the prime rib to the table, Jenna lit the candle for their mom.

Amy's sadness was there at the dinner table with her, and she felt it in her sisters too. But with the grief came a celebration of all the great moments they'd shared with their mom. Amy knew that whenever she saw the striking oranges and pinks of sunset playing on the mesas, or the bountiful hues of vegetables on a dish she'd created, she'd think of her mom's love of all things bright and colorful.

Looking around the table at her sisters and her nephew, the man she loved and his mother, Amy knew for certain that she wouldn't trade her crazy life or her crazy past for all the money in the world. The memories of her parents and her life choices, even *Ultimate Chef Showdown,* she'd hold fast to forever, like the precious treasures they were.

When everyone at the table joined hands, Amy said the prayer. She prayed for peace, and for her mother and father. She glanced at Kellan and his mother's joined hands and added a wish for all the people in the world who were lost to find their rightful place in the world. She'd certainly found such a place in her childhood home.

"Amen," everyone at the table said as one when she finished.

Kellan stood at the head of the table and picked up a MAC knife to carve the prime rib. Amy's heart spilled over with love at the sight of him. All those rules she couldn't help but break, all that heartache she experienced at the hands of other cowboys, it was all worth it because those experiences led her down the bumpy, windy road to Kellan Reed's door. She had a lot of work ahead of her to make her restaurant and inn a success, but she was home, with her family around her, and the cowboy of her dreams by her side.

Life didn't get any sweeter than that.